Pernille Hughes has had many words printed in the *Sunday Times*, most proudly the word "boobs". Seduced by the promise of freebies she took her first job in advertising, but left when Status Quo tickets was as good as it got. After a brief spell marketing Natural History films, she switched to working in Children's television which for a time meant living in actual Teletubbyland, sharing a photocopier with Laa-Laa. Now, she lives in actual Buckinghamshire, sharing a photocopier with her husband and their four spawn. While the kids are at school she scoffs cake and writes in order to maintain a shred of sanity.

 @pernillehughes

 www.facebook.com/pernillehughesauthor

Also by Pernille Hughes

Sweatpants at Tiffanie's

Probably
the Best Kiss in
the World

Pernille Hughes

A division of HarperCollins Publishers
www.harpercollins.co.uk

HarperImpulse an imprint of
HarperCollinsPublishers
The News Building
1 London Bridge Street
London SE1 9GF

www.harpercollins.co.uk

This paperback edition 2019

First published in Great Britain in ebook format by
HarperCollinsPublishers 2019

A catalogue record for this book
is available from the British Library

ISBN: 9780008307721

Typeset by Palimpsest Book Production Ltd,
Falkirk, Stirlingshire

MIX
Paper from
responsible sources
FSC C007454

Printed by CPI Group (UK) Ltd, Croydon CR0 4YY

To the naysayers.
In
Your
Face!

Chapter 1

This was decidedly crap.

Regardless of what the photographer insisted, Jen's nose was very precise and if it smelt like cow crap, she'd gamble plenty on it being cow crap. He'd said the photo-shoot location wouldn't be too muddy, hence her now crap-covered and immobile trainers. She evil-eyed his wellies. *Git*. So much for client-care. Any uncontrolled movement and she'd risk face-planting into the boggy mire he'd insisted was the only position from which to get the angle he needed. *Pretentious inflexible git*. Ankle-deep in the stink, she was fairly stuck and now Ava, one of her bosses, had turned up, wanting a word. Jen took a quick look at the *List*IT app on her beloved iPhone: there were so many shots left to get and the light wouldn't last much longer. Not that Ava would think or care about that.

Eight white-haired walking-booted men and women stood on the drier ground with their walking poles, looking thoughtfully into the middle-distance as if they were intrepid explorers, not in fact the Westhampton Rambling Society who were being paid with M&S vouchers for a

1

marketing shoot. Ava coughed loudly in an unsubtle chivvy and Jen resigned herself to risking the journey.

It was hard work; a trial of strength, balance and swear words, as more than once she nearly toppled in her expedition to the shiny white Porsche Cayenne. Door open but sitting safely in the car, Ava was keen not to get her white jeans or pristine Hunters besmirched, her huge sunglasses pushed back to harness her long blonde-to-scarlet ombré locks. Ava and her sister-slash-business partner Zara rather fancied themselves as the Olsen twins of the organic sanitary-supplies world.

"Darling, far be it from us to question your choices," *Here we go* thought Jen; questioning choices was their modus operandi, "but shouldn't we be using more ... *aspirational* models."

"Aspirational? They're ramblers, Ava, and we're using them to promote incontinence pads."

"Yes darling, of course, but they could still be a little more, well, let's be blunt about it, *attractive*. Our customers won't aspire to be them." Oh Lord. Jen did not have time for this.

"Ava, *nobody* aspires to wear inco pads, organic or otherwise. The point here is to show *ordinary* people, so our customers can see incontinence affects normal people, and equally, normal people – not just the posh ones – can wear organic pads. That was the brief you approved, remember? I don't think people believe celebrities experience incontinence, and we want people to believe our ads. We're all about the honesty, aren't we?" Jen ignored the grimace on

Ava's face. She'd seen it so many times she considered it a tic and best not acknowledged. Being marketing manager at *Well, Honestly!* for seven years had taught her plenty about tact and restraint.

A splat of something hit the inside of the rear passenger window and slid down the glass. A small chubby hand tried to wipe it away, spreading possibly yogurt, further across the pane. Ava's head ducked towards the interior of the car.

"Are you behaving, Ferdinand? Remember what Mummy said; bad behaviour equals no iPad, no iPhone and no laptop."

Turning back to Jen, Ava pursed her lips. "We'd best be off. These three are getting excited and Keane needs picking up from his Junior Krav Maga. Then it's two hours to Glasto. Thank goodness Rupes has gone ahead to sort the yurt." Jen knew Ava's husband Rupert always went a day early under the guise of "prep" time, involving several of his mates and various herbal substances. Jen's sister Lydia had seen it first-hand. Or else he was simply hiding from his four demon spawn. "So, if you're really sure about the models?"

"I am," Jen insisted, keen to get back to the shoot and hopefully home to dry socks this side of darkness. Ava still wasn't looking convinced, but a wail from inside the car distracted her.

"Leave Ferdinand alone, Beckham. He doesn't want you filming down his pants. Rooney, sweetie, no Lego up nosey." Turning back to Jen, she started to sit back down in the driving seat. "I've left some things on your desk, darling. Just a few bits I didn't get to finish up. Perhaps you'll handle

3

them on Monday?" Ava always took the Monday after Glasto off to "reflect". "Think of the quiet you'll have, just you and Aiden, with me out and Zara still in the Seychelles. Heaven." Jen chose not to flag Aiden the Intern's mouth-breathing was plenty loud enough to be disturbing. She was more dreading what the "few bits" might be. Ava's ability to deflect work was tantamount to a Teflon coating, and past experience said there'd be far more than a day's work there. Moreover, Jen had never once been able to pass anything back to Ava on her return. The only upside was she'd know it was done properly and wouldn't come back to bite her on the bum. It might take longer, but at least she was in control, and as far as Jen was concerned control was the only way to dodge life's curveballs.

"We'll be off then, darling," Ava said, giving the ramblers a last look and slight shake of her head. "Enjoy your weekend." Slamming the door, she wheel-spun away, leaving Jen mud-sprayed from head to toe and wondering if this was really what she'd studied all those years for.

Having smeared the slurry from her eyes Jen trudged over to the photographer and updated her shot-list with a sigh. She'd be a while yet, but it was almost the weekend and that meant time away from the inco pads and time with her real passion. She could tuck herself away in the safe confines of her outbuilding and concentrate on the thing that brought her joy.

Some women loved to bake, some to knit, Jen Attison loved to brew.

*

The opening expletive caused Jen to spill beer all over her hand. She mumbled one of her own under her breath. The following litany of filth carried across the small courtyard from the open kitchen door to the outbuilding. It wasn't quite the sound of summer as she imagined it. Being a Friday night, the town was bouncing, the pubs and wine bars full with locals and the weekend tourists, all making the most of the balmy evening; sitting out where possible, or moving down onto the beach. The seasonal warmth brought the joy out in them, their chatter and laughter filling the air, the distant echo of fun snaking down the warren-like alleyways and over the garden walls of the houses in the old town. Jen could clearly hear it from the comfortable seclusion of her small stone outbuilding; the singing, the *Oi, Oi's* and the banter.

Jen looked at her phone. Eleven. She'd been expecting to pick Lydia up at midnight from the station. She had an alarm set. Yet here she was, spouting loud angry vocabulary that would make a fishwife blush and no doubt there would be more, so Jen braced herself.

"For fuck sake. Come out, you shitpin!" There was a silence from outside, as Jen waited, calmly finishing tapping the beer from the conditioning tank into the brown bottle she was holding. "Jen? Can you help me? Please?"

Jen sighed as she capped the bottle and placed it in line with the others she'd already filled since getting home. Slipping down from her stool, she looked out into the courtyard to see her sister, still swearing while crossly attempting to extract her ankle-strapped high heel from between two cobbles.

"*Easy*, tiger. The kids next door don't need to know those words," Jen said, crossing the distance.

"Where do you think I learnt them?" They both knew this wasn't true. Lydia had merrily collected a ripe vocabulary as a child when visiting Jen at uni, sponging up the vernacular of the rugby team who Jen had bizarrely acquired as a fan club. A secret home-brew kit in your fresher dorm room and indiscreet dorm mates will do that for a girl. Proud of the words they were teaching Lydia, the rugby lads had virtually made the thirteen-year-old their mascot. Nine years on, her word choices reminded Jen daily of that lost circle of friends.

A firm yank released the heel, allowing Lydia to teeter the rest of the way to the outbuilding where the comforting scent of malt, hops, yeast and beer enveloped them. The outbuilding wasn't tiny, spanning the breadth of the rear-yard wall, but given all of Jen's paraphernalia, it felt cosy and snug nonetheless. With the help of an old kitchen she'd salvaged off Freegle, and the addition of a small mash tun and two fermentation tanks which she'd bought from eBay and struggled to fetch home because large metal vats did not fit in a vintage Ford Capri, Jen had transformed the space into her own mini-micro-brewery.

"Why are you back so early? You said the midnight train. And why didn't you call me to collect you?" As usual, Lydia's refusal to stick to agreements irked her. But that was little sisters for you, a law unto themselves. Sometimes – *most* times – Jen suspected Lydia did it just to wind her up. Leaving the door open for some fresh air and pulling the hair-elastic off her wrist, Jen dragged her unruly hair up in a ponytail. Given the warmth out, the outbuilding could get pretty toasty and her hair was due a cut – as her *Book*IT app would remind her any day now; Jen always made her next appointment as she finished the last. Same with the dentist, waxer, window cleaner, optician, chimney sweep, boiler servicer and financial adviser. She was organised like that.

"I'm twenty-two Jen, I can get home by myself. You don't need to collect me." Lydia perched herself up on the worktop opposite Jen's bottling. The two of them were clearly sisters; same heart-shaped face, brown eyes and chestnut hair, though Lydia wore hers shorter and had far fewer frown lines, while Jen was hoping their freckles disguised hers.

A battalion of capped bottles sat neatly on the counter top, products of a one-woman production line of Jen tapping the new IPA from the conditioner into the brown glass bottles and sealing the caps on with the new capper Lydia had bought her for Christmas. She'd worn out the one her dad had first taught her to use, in the days when she had to stand on a kitchen chair to help him with his home-brew. It now sat on her shelf next to his photo. She owed all of this to him. Her fine sense of smell had come from him, along with her taste for beer – she'd been sneaking sips since primary school. His hobby had grown to become hers, even after she'd left home for uni. By then the hobby had become a passion, as she experimented with recipes and flavours. Gradually, it had formed her career plan. The brewing industry was a siren's call to her.

"We agreed I'd collect you," Jen said, sitting down to start her labels. This batch was destined for the County Show. She generally sold her beers at a few farmers' markets, the money coming in handy for restocking supplies and raw ingredients for the next brew, but the County Show was a bigger deal. She'd reserved a stall and was hoping to shift the mass of boxes currently stockpiled in their lounge, but more importantly there was the brewing competition to be won. The last two years' first prize rosettes hung above her head on the shelf. Jen wasn't a particularly competitive person, but admittedly she loved the validation the rosette gave her. She could brew, and brew well. She had an excellent understanding of flavours – this wasn't vainglory, the judges had said so – and in lieu of not having the career she'd dreamed of, it was wildly pleasing to have her skills recognised.

Jen pulled out several sheets of adhesive labels. Her friend Alice had designed them, simply stating *Attison's* in beautiful cursive. The remaining space allowed Jen to neatly handwrite in the beer's name and tapping date. Handwriting them rather than printing them added to the beer's handmade touch, extending Jen's notion of artistic creativity. Neat handwriting when annoyed however, was a bitch.

"No, we didn't," sighed Lydia, hoiking her skirt up her left thigh, undoing the Velcro above her knee before grabbing both sides and pushing her lower leg off. Placing the prosthetic beside her, damaged shoe still in situ, she began to massage the stump through its polyurethane sock. "You agreed with yourself. I didn't get a say. As always. Can I have a beer?"

"On the shelf behind you," Jen said, not looking up from her labels. This was a regular argument. Jen liked to collect Lydia when she got home from London, whether it was from work or from a date. She liked knowing she was safe. She didn't want Lydia being jostled on the street or her leg getting avoidably chaffed. She didn't see why Lydia couldn't have trained at a local firm, but instead she'd insisted on applying to the graduate schemes at the accountancy globals in London. She'd stormed the interview process, which hadn't surprised Jen one bit, because Lydia, swearing aside, was both quick and engaging. So while the location wasn't Jen's preference, it made her ridiculously proud of what her sister had achieved, when at one point it had looked as if there would be no future at all, and Jen allowed herself the commendation of not having made a total hash of bringing teen-Lydia up by herself.

"Need a hand?" Lydia asked, selecting a Golden Ale from the odds and ends shelf by her shoulder and uncapping it on the wall-mounted opener. "I've got two of those."

Jen hated it when Lydia made those jokes, but didn't say. Lydia got to deal with it however she wanted.

"It's fine. But thanks." The many rows of bottles in front of her said she had a couple of hours' writing and sticking. Still, she'd been spared the trip to the station. She took a second to strike it off *List*IT and cancel the alarm.

"Come on, Jen. I can write the labels."

"Really, it's all good," Jen said, keeping a firm grip on

the pen and sheets. "I've got everything under control."

Having been through this before too, Lydia gave up, mouthed "Control Freak" at Jen's back then leaned back to take a slug of the beer while her sister worked on.

"Got anything planned for the weekend?" Jen asked, finishing another sticker, peeling it off and sticking it neatly on the bottle. Each label would be perfectly aligned. *Meticulous* was technically correct, *anal* would have been Lydia's word of choice.

"Hmm," Lydia murmured, as she swallowed her mouthful. "Just popping out somewhere." Jen bit her tongue to stop herself from pursuing it. She knew when Lydia was being deliberately vague.

"How was tonight's date?" She moved swiftly down the labels. She might be a perfectionist, but she was an efficient one.

"Shite."

Jen paused briefly then carried on, knowing it was better to let Lydia vent at her own pace. Lydia spun the bottle cap on the counter like a spinning top, before successfully lobbing and landing it in the corner bin.

"Are all bankers wankers, do you think? This one was so far up his own arse I'm surprised he could walk."

"How'd you find him?" Jen hoped Lydia was laying off *Tinder*. Lydia's dating calendar was busy enough as it was, but if not being used simply for casual hook-ups, *Tinder* seemed to Jen like people were fighting a "marriage mate-rial" tick-list from the off. Not that she'd say so to Lydia, but she worried that a missing limb might not count favourably in such a judgemental framework.

"Bloody Callie from work set me up with him. Said they went to sixth form together and he was a hoot. Uni obviously nixed that. He kept talking about his ex and even sent her a text at one point. And Callie had clearly told him about the leg as he was trying not to study it. Epic fail."

"Drink choice?" Jen asked. Both sisters believed you could tell a lot from what men chose to drink. They'd worked out a fairly efficient shorthand over the span of Lydia's many *many* dates.

"Lager. Kronegaard. *Unimaginative* wanker." Jen hmm'ed in agreement. Danish brewing giant Kronegaard wasn't the worst of the global beers out there, in Jen's book, but his failure to recognise there was more to beer than mass-produced lager would forever be a black-mark against the guy. Their dad and his love of craft beer had seen to that.

"Ah well, better to know now," Jen soothed. The thought of Lydia being hurt pained her.

"Definitely," Lydia agreed. "He was rubbish in bed too. Hence the earlier train."

So, *that* label wouldn't be going on a bottle, the jog in the writing being enormous.

"You slept with him?" Jen asked, trying for calm, but getting more of a squeak.

"Well, I hoped to salvage something from the evening, but no. Crap all round. Not that we slept, but considering it was a speed shag, it was fairly catatonic."

Jen took a long breath through her nose, reminding

11

herself Lydia was an adult and entitled to place her body where she pleased, with whom she pleased. But it was hard. She felt somewhere along the parenting process she might have slipped.

"Speaking of dullards," Lydia went on, "where's the Bobster? Didn't feel like helping you out here?"

"*Robert's* on a golf weekend. I'm seeing him Sunday night. *As always,*" she said pointedly. This too was a broken record conversation. Lydia was having a dig. Jen and Robert had a long-standing but simple arrangement of dating on Sundays and Wednesdays. It suited them both, it fitted with his sporting commitments and she could work late or brew undisturbed. The fixed nature of the date-nights gave clear structure to their week. Perfect.

There was a long pause before Lydia gave flight to her thoughts. "Jen? Have you ever thought you might not be living life to the full? That you might be missing out?"

Jen paused, looking around her, at her bottles, the tanks, the sacks of hops and malt. She saw her tightly-run micro-empire, tucked secretly away in the back streets of the bustling town, safely away from randomness, and she initially couldn't think what Lydia might mean. Then her Parenting mode kicked in and it dawned on her Lydia must be referring to herself.

"Lyds, lovely," she said, putting her fountain pen down and giving her sister her full attention as she always tried to do when it came to "growing up" conversations, "is this a FOMO thing?" Lydia looked confused for a second, then opened her mouth to speak, but Jen beat her to it. "Honestly

Lyds, as you get older you'll see most events are overrated and actually happiness is easily reached if you keep your expectations simple and realistic. Just look at me." Jen gave her a big smile and a pat on the leg for good measure, hoping her sister was reassured. Lydia exhaled abruptly, shook her head and roughly reattached the prosthetic before alighting from the worktop. Maybe not so reassured. She'd have to give Lydia's fear of missing out issues more attention.

Still holding her beer Lydia muttered something that might have been *Sleep well*, but could also have been *Bloody hell* and stormed back to the house. With a sigh, Jen went back to her labels, enjoying the return of serenity. She'd deal with Lydia tomorrow. For now she'd savour the peace and simplicity of the life she'd constructed for herself. *FOMO* indeed. Sure, she'd made some sacrifices – a career in incontinence pads instead of brewing, for example- but needs must and there was no point crying over that. All things considered, Jen had everything *Just So* now and exactly where she needed them to be for a straightforward, no-surprises, quite-happy-thank-you-very-much life. Lydia couldn't possibly be thinking of *her* – Jen's life was solid. Where should she be missing out?

Chapter 2

Being a lawyer, Robert was fairly straight-laced (or "uptight" as Lydia would say), but now and again he did something quirky. Jen had first noticed this years ago in his office, as he sombrely went over the details of her parents' wills, formally assigning Lydia's guardianship to her. Still shell-shocked and grieving, her eyes had wandered to his pink and orange striped socks. They were a marked contrast to the sobriety of his tailored dark suit and the uber-traditional (Lydia would say "cliché") polished leather and wood of his office decor. Jen regularly wheeled the socks out as a positive example when Lydia was on one of her "Robert is boring" attacks.

That Sunday evening, as Jen walked towards the beach, she suspected there might be a spot of quirk in the air. They normally met around seven at a local bar or at the golf club if he'd just played, but tonight he'd texted her to meet him at the family beach hut. Westhampton's beach wasn't one of those wild windswept moody backdrops with sand and marram grass, nor a bouncing surfers' paradise a la Cornwall. This was a proper town beach with large uncomfortable shingle, candy-coloured beach huts and ice cream stands, but thankfully no pier chocked full with arcade machines. There were no features of particular natural beauty, and nothing really to write home about, which was why Westhampton had never quite made it onto the list of popular Victorian bathing resorts. But it was *home* – so Jen loved it, and as the flashier neighbouring towns were getting expensive, more and more tourists seemed to be coming. She smiled to see them this evening, as she walked briskly along the promenade, hands in the pockets of her khaki shirt dress. The lure of quirk had pushed her to make a change from her usual blouse and tailored trousers, but the pockets were non-negotiable.

"Anyone home?" Jen asked, stepping onto the small deck area. The small port-holed door was open, but she couldn't see Robert. The Thwaites beach hut was bang in the middle of the single row, the paintwork pristine in its pale blue nautical palette. Robert's mother insisted on it being repainted every spring. Jen suspected this was more to keep up appearances and one-upmanship over the neighbours than down to any weathering necessity.

"Hello Gorgeous." Robert appeared holding a blanket which he unfurled with a flourish onto the wooden boards at her feet, before giving her a brisk kiss on the cheek. "Exactly on time, as always." That was one of the many reasons they got on: mutual appreciation of punctuality. He disappeared back into the hut, and reappeared with an ice bucket complete with champagne bottle and flutes, along with a picnic basket. A picnic was definitely not what she'd been expecting. It seemed rather, well, *rustic*, for Robert – he was more of a croque-monsieur chap than a sandwich guy. Not that it was a problem, Jen certainly wasn't above sitting on the floor, it just wasn't what she was used to with Robert. He was definitely making a particular effort this evening, only *at what* she wasn't quite sure.

"Take a seat," he said and laughed at his joke, then popped the cork on the bottle. The cork ricocheted off the peak of the roof to clock Jen on the head. Unaware, he reached for the flutes and poured them each a glass. There followed a moment of awkwardness as he attempted to fold himself down onto the deck without use of his hands, in spite of Jen reaching up to help. "To us," he said in toast, brushing the worst of the spillage from his striped shirt.

"To us," she agreed, discretely giving her head a soothing rub, and taking a sip. The champagne was delicious. She couldn't see the label, but he wouldn't have skimped. Robert took a week off every year for wine tasting in France, so he had his standards. As he delved about in the basket, laying out a fine spread for them, Jen looked about her. The sun was low but it was still comfortably warm and there were plenty of people about on the shingle. The air was rich with scents: the salt of the sea, the smoke aroma from a distant barbecue and the fragrant notes from the champagne. Her thoughts started to meander as to how she could emulate it all in a beer. It was all rather lovely and dare she say it, *romantic*. Overt romance wasn't normally their thing. They were both far too practical and realistic for that – another of the things that had them well

16

suited by Jen's estimation – but for all of that, he'd put together a sweet little scene for them. She was glad she'd worn a dress now.

She asked him about his golf and he talked her through the first eighteen holes while she ate her Quiche Lorraine, Scotch egg and numerous other picnic standards. The napkins told her the local deli had catered, which was fine by her as Robert wasn't known for his cooking. In fact, both Ava and Zara teased their brother mercilessly on his ineptness in the kitchen. Jen pushed the thought of Ava and Zara aside. It was still the weekend, and for now she would concentrate on Robert and staunchly overlook the fact she dated her bosses' brother. There were days when she wished he'd never pushed her CV their way, but then she'd been desperate for a job and Westhampton was hardly the marketing capital of the world.

"What did you get up to then?" he asked, brushing a crumb off her chin and sliding his hand into hers. They'd both relaxed back against the wall of the beach hut. Having known each other for many years, sitting together peacefully was something they did quite well.

"Tapping. And labelling. The boxes are ready for the County Show. And I brewed two new beers, which are now safely in the tanks."

"Right oh," he murmured, pulling the picnic basket towards him with his spare hand and perusing the contents, "Lydia help you out?"

"No, she was gone most of the weekend. Not sure where, just said she was popping out with mates. She offered though." She didn't mean it as a hint, but he didn't take it as one either, as he was busy setting up the desserts.

Two ramekins of something with a brown sugar topping sat on the blanket and he fished out a small kitchen blowtorch. He looked quite excited to be holding it. "I saw them do this on *Saturday Breakfast*." He must have seen Jen's look of concern as he released her hand and stroked her cheek. "Don't worry, Jen. Fire-handling comes with the Y chromosome."

Minutes later, the flames were quickly doused with a bottle of Evian, but the blanket was a goner.

"Never mind," he insisted, unfazed and more intent on pressing the alleged Crème Brùlée into her hands, "Mumsie will be pleased with the shopping excuse."

Jen looked at her dessert. It wasn't fully burnt, there was still a small patch she could breach to access the custard. The intense way that he was nodding her on, eager for her to tuck in, suggested perhaps he'd made this part himself. She swallowed her gulp quite admirably.

Credit where credit was due, the patch she stabbed made exactly the right cracking sound, much to his delight. Robert didn't seem overly concerned with trying his own dessert though, which was worrying, but he'd made such an effort and appeared so keen, that she couldn't do anything else but delve out a substantial spoonful and put it in her mouth.

She knew instantly she'd made a mistake. There was something big and hard in there, definitely not smooth and creamy. She looked about, not sure what to do; spitting was not a seemly option. Finally, she looked at him distressed and what was that in his eyes? Mischief? It certainly looked like it. Slowly, carefully, trying to appear as ladylike as possible while desperate to gob it out, she extracted the object from her mouth.

In her hand lay a ring.

Even without the half-saliva half-custard coating it was easily the ugliest ring she'd ever laid eyes on. Large and bulky, the square cut stone was held in an oblong setting. Beyond the murky gem, the filigree ivy detailing was the only thing to set the ring apart from a knuckle-duster. Staring at it, it took Jen a moment to realise Robert was on one knee in front of her, grinning proudly at his dessert wheeze.

"Jennifer Attison, will you be my wife?" His eyes and smile widened even further at her shock. "Surprised?"

"Well, yes," she stammered. It *was* a surprise. A great big astounding surprise given they'd never talked about the future and in Jen's head their two dates a week routine had worked perfectly for the last six years, so why would he be looking to change it?

Jen's brain couldn't keep up, as his expression now changed from amused to ecstatic. He jumped to his feet, raised his hands in the air and channelling Tom Cruise on Oprah's sofa, shouted to everyone on the beach "She said Yes!!"

Wait, what? Jen looked around, panicked. That wasn't what she'd meant. He grabbed her hands and dragged her to her feet, before clamping his hands to her face and kissing her. She could hear onlookers clapping, and the noise made a disturbing duet with the alarm bells in her head.

"This ring was my great-grandmother's, on Mumsie's side," he explained, plucking it off her palm as she stared shell-shocked at him, "apparently, it hasn't seen daylight since the undertakers took it off her finger and handed it to my granny." Jen fought the urge to paw her tongue clean, as he slipped it easily onto her ring finger. Very easily. "Oh. It's too big."

Great-granny must have had salamis for fingers, the ring would have fallen freely off Jen's thumb.

"Oh dear," she said, the relief nearly felling her, "what a shame."

"Don't be upset, Jen, I'll have it resized."

Jen's feigned joy was Oscar-worthy.

"I'm glad you love it though. Mumsie will be too."

"It ... It's remarkable."

"Certainly is," he said wistfully gazing at it. "I'm the first boy in the family for generations, hence it's mine to give."

He kissed her again and Jen began to realise how happy this was making him, how overjoyed he was she'd accepted his proposal. She couldn't help but be deeply flattered. Robert was a catch by anyone's standards; sensible, solvent and career savvy. His height and broad golf-toned shoulders gave him gravitas in a room; other women looked his way when they were out together. And he had a kind face. She'd always thought that.

They'd first met when she was thirteen and her mother had dragged her along to a dress fitting for Robert's mother.

Marooned in the hallway, listening to Mrs Thwaites' loud voice through the walls, Jen had at first been shy when the eighteen-year-old Robert had stopped to greet her, dressed in muddy rugby kit. He was on route to the shower, but he'd taken the time to chat and ease her awkwardness. After that she'd seen him at various times in her dad's mechanic's workshop when his father had brought the Jag in for tyres or tinkering and she'd been there doing homework after school. The private school boys of Westhampton didn't normally mix with the state school girls, but that didn't seem to be the case with Robert. He'd always made a point of saying hello and her dad had remarked he was a "decent lad". It hadn't surprised her at all that her parents had chosen him as their lawyer when he qualified.

So when he'd first asked her out, a respectable time after her parents' affairs had been settled, it had been easy to accept because it was like going out with a friend. What you saw was what you got with Robert and that was important to Jen.

And he *knew* her. He knew all she'd been through. Taking his lawyerly duties seriously, he'd pitched up at the hospital as soon as he'd heard. He'd seen her at her worst, grieving for her parents, devastated over Lydia's injuries, wracked with guilt as she'd agreed to the amputation. He'd borne the brunt of her anguish when Lydia was screaming from waking up to a missing leg. He'd taken Jen's guilt-ridden tongue-lashing head on, never once holding it against her. He'd been there for all of it and he'd *still* been attracted to her. It amazed her.

Jen looked up at him properly and the panic began to subside. She'd been surprised, that was all. No wonder she panicked – heaven knew she'd had enough surprises for a lifetime. Why should this *not* be a good idea? He knew her, *really* knew her and he wanted her. They worked well as a couple, their routine was testament to that. They were clearly compatible, she reasoned; they'd never argued over anything. How could this be anything but the most sensible, comfortable and right marriage ever? What more could a marriage need than what they already had? And she had as close as she could ever get to having her dad's approval.

"And I'm delighted to accept it," she finally said with a genuine smile, careful to keep her eyes on his face and off the god-awful ring.

"I knew you would be," he said, wrapping her in his arms and pulling them both back down onto the bare deck, the smouldering blanket having been flung onto the shingle. Once they'd rearranged themselves from their unbalanced heap, they returned to sitting against the beach hut wall, hands entwined, the setting sun casting a warm glow on their faces – it almost felt like a blessing, only slightly marred by the skinny-dipping stag party and the smell of burnt wool.

"I've got more exciting news," Robert blurted, his exuberance now at unprecedented levels, "I made partner!"

Was it her, or did he look even more thrilled than before? She decided excitement must be cumulative. Partnership on top of an accepted proposal would make anyone ecstatic.

"That's wonderful, Robert!" She was over the moon for

him, he'd worked so hard for it, played all that golf for it too. It was madly pleasing to see someone's drive come to fruition. That was more they had in common; drive, ambition and a sound work ethic.

"Old Solesworth's decided to cut back his hours at last, and losing all those matches has finally payed off." Jen leaned across to kiss him on the cheek. It reminded her to buy him a new aftershave, the bergamot notes in this one were too strong, not just for him, but any sentient being.

"I couldn't be happier for you. You completely deserve it. Solesworth & Thwaites. Sounds good."

"And this is just the beginning, Jen. Now with the extra cash our plans can become reality." He let his head drop back onto the woodwork, relieved.

"Plans?" she asked. She wasn't aware they had any. He'd once mentioned the Highlands for a long weekend, but that had gone by the wayside when a friend had scored tickets to the Rugby World Cup. Perhaps he meant they should make some plans now. Her fingers twitched towards her phone in her pocket, instinctively wanting to start a new list. This was going to be a major project. And somewhere in her head, the idea of a wedding beer had started to germinate, a one-time brew only their guests would ever try, and maybe she'd give them each a bottle home instead of those sugared almond favour things. Perhaps she would base it on the scents from this evening and tell its story on the rear label ...

"Jen? Jen, you're miles away."

"Sorry." She shook her head, primarily to clear her head,

but also in befuddlement at herself. Thirty minutes ago a wedding was the furthest thing on her mind, now she was concocting favours. "Plans. Yes. You had a plan."

"I'm sure it's *our* plan, Jen," he smiled, pulling the back of her hand to his lips. "You and me. Me and you. Our life together." He said it like some wistful song. The champagne had gone to his head.

"Okay," she said hesitantly. "Tell me the plan."

"Surely you know all this? It's obvious; I make partner, we get married, set up home, have a family and live together happily ever after." His face was beaming. Jen hadn't seen him so chuffed since England had last won the cricket. Curiously though, she could feel the edges of her mouth cranking up towards her ears, because he was nodding as he spoke and her reflex was to nod along, reluctant to spoil his moment.

"Wow," she said, "you've got it all planned out." Considering she was a planning fiend, Jen couldn't work out why it didn't sit better with her. It was hardly a revolutionary plan – he wasn't suggesting they should run away and become freedom fighters. Only, she hadn't had any part in this, and she felt firmly on the back foot.

Robert cocked his head at her, at last sensing her discomfit.

"I surprised you good and proper, didn't I?" he acknowledged with a grin. "I'm not sure why though, Jen, we've been together for years."

"But you haven't even suggested living together."

"I'm rather thinking that'll be part of the engagement

deal." He gave her a wink and waggled his eyebrows, which looked so funny she almost snorted champagne out of her nose. Well, if that was the plan, he'd have to move in at hers, given the ties the house had to her parents. And there was Lydia to keep an eye on. Not to mention his apartment was in a weird area of town and the shared hallway always smelled dubious. "Which bit is bothering you, Jen? Is it the family bit?" He turned to properly face her. "Look, you've pretty much been Lydia's parent these last years, so I know you'll be a great mother, but I appreciate you might feel you've-been-there-done-that already. So I wasn't thinking of a team – to be honest they can be bloody expensive little buggers by the looks of it. Two would do me. A boy and a girl. After school fees that should still leave money for decent holidays and a weekend pad somewhere." Finally he drew a breath. "Sounds perfect, right?"

It did. Or rather, it would, to many. And Jen felt it should to her, (though she didn't see the need for school fees) – after all, what was not to like? It had comfort and dependable written all over it. But something was niggling.

"Am I working in this scenario?" she asked.

"Oh, is *that* the issue?" he said with a relieved laugh. "No, of course not. The pay rise should cover you looking after the kids. And remember, when you sell your house, and I sell the flat, that's going to cover a vast proportion of the new place. If we buy something dated, you can spend the next few years doing it up as the pups come along. The rent on the Arches won't hurt either." He'd factored in the two commercial units under the railway bridge her parents had ploughed all their savings into. One had been her dad's workshop, now rented out to his then partner, the other was leased to a business run by two of Jen's friends. But that money was what had funded Lydia through uni, and Jen wanted it safe-guarded to cover the future prosthetic legs Lydia would need.

"But what if I want to keep on working?"

"Really? I thought all girls want to be ladies-who-lunch?"

"No. I like working," Jen said, calming a little. He'd just been mistaken or programmed by his parents. Of course he wouldn't mind her carrying on with her job.

"Inco pads? Really?"

"No," she winced, "not inco pads per se, but I like going to work, doing things with my day, making my own money."

"But Jen, when you have the kids, you'll still be *working*. God, Jen, give me some credit. I'm not some dinosaur who thinks looking after kids is the easy option. You'll still be *working*: it'll just be from home, and for our family. As for the money, I'm sure we can work something out, so you feel you're getting a wage, even if it does just go into the family pot. We can do that. And don't worry about projects, Mumsie already has a list of charity events she wants your help with." She could see from the furrow in his brow he was bemused by her questions. "Jen, you shouldn't worry about this. This is where we've always been heading."

"And ... and what about my beer?" Jen, asked quietly.

Robert now looked totally confused. "What about your beer?"

"I ... well, I had thought ... What I really wanted to do

is, maybe someday, try to build it up to be a business." There. She'd said it. Jen had the oddest conflicting sensation; relief from having mentioned her plan to him, but also something tantamount to having a public wardrobe malfunction.

"The beer?" He thought he had misunderstood her. She nodded. "But Jen, that's just your hobby. Your *childhood* hobby. I rather assumed you'd grow out of that. And honestly, you wouldn't want our family home constantly smelling of beer." She took a surreptitious sniff of her hair. She was pretty sure her shower had eradicated any beer smell.

"You like beer," she said, unable to conceal the hurt. Back in the day, when he'd played rugby rather than just watching it, he'd consumed plenty.

"True. But in a pub, darling. Not in a home. Not around kids."

With that he planted a kiss on her forehead, stood up and toed all the paraphernalia from their picnic inside the door. "I'll sort all that tomorrow. Come on Nearly-Mrs Thwaites, let's tell Lydia our good news." He stopped, looked at her and barked a laugh. "You still look stunned, darling – imagine how she's going to take it."

Jen already had an inkling.

Chapter 3

"What the actual fuck??" Lydia had waited a full ten seconds for Robert to reach the end of their path before she slammed the front door and let rip at Jen. "You've agreed to *what*?"

"To ... um ... be his wife?" Jen didn't know why she sounded so wobbly. She was the adult here. Well okay, Lydia did technically qualify as an adult, but Jen held seniority and wouldn't be cowed by a junior. She drew herself up. "You know Lydia, *Congratulations* is the more customary response."

Lydia stopped and stared at her sister goggle-eyed. She was looking a bit peaky, Jen thought, even before Robert had dropped the marriage bomb on her which was approximately four minutes after they got in the door. He hadn't been able to contain it longer than that. Really, the more Jen thought about it, his excitement about the whole thing was utterly endearing.

Lydia stormed into the lounge, fully expecting Jen to follow her, which she did, as much to check Lydia's crutches didn't snag on the rug. Whenever she'd roll the rug away to avoid exactly that scenario, Lydia always found it and brought it back out again. While she preferred being prosthetic free around the house to give her stump a break from the sweat and any chafing, Lydia was adamant she didn't want things changed to accommodate the crutches. Jen considered this to be asking for trouble.

Normally Lydia would take up residence on the larger of the two worn blue sofas, spreading out and massaging her scar as she watched TV. Tonight though, she nodded brusquely for Jen to take a seat, while she propped herself against the wall, crutches hanging from her forearms as she crossed them angrily in front of her. With the sticks angled askew, the overall effect was a pretty hostile.

Lydia took a deep huffy breath and composed herself. "Jen, I love you and I want you to be happy, honestly I do, but this is an epic mistake. I'm sure Robert's a good enough guy, but Jen, really? He's SO dull. You deserve someone who can bring excitement to your life. God, you deserve someone who can just bring you back to life full stop."

Jen was instantly offended. "My life is just fine, thank you." She had everything she needed. Plus Robert had just offered her a whole lot more. "And Robert's not dull, for your information. Aside from all the legal stories he has, he has a healthy, busy social life. He's sporty, he runs every day. He plays his golf, he's on the club committee. There's cricket too. He takes me out. How is that dull? Just because those things aren't your cup of tea, Lydia, doesn't mean you can condemn them as boring and somehow beneath me." Lydia made a face. Ha! Jen knew she'd scored a point.

But Lydia wasn't stopped so easily. "But apart from your regimented date nights, none of Robert's activities include you."

"Why should they? It's good if couples have their own interests. Mum wasn't interested in Dad's motorbike meets, was she?" Lydia faltered for a second, but rallied quickly.

"They did lots of other things together. Raising us, obviously, but they also enjoyed each other's company; they went walking, they sat for hours on the sofa together just chatting. Remember that time he lost a bet to her and had to see a film of her choice every fortnight for a year? He saw every chick-flick going. They did fun stuff just to be together. They went *dancing*, Jen. Can you remember how unconvinced he was, but he tried it and they had a hoot." Tears were forming in Lydia's eyes. Jen's own eyes were beginning to sting at the memories. Their parents had been eccentric, in Jen's opinion. Lydia took another breath and went on, "When did you and Robert last have a hoot? Ever have a hoot? I've never seen it. I don't think you're compatible, Jen. I honestly don't. Not the real you."

Well, Jen had no idea what *that* was supposed to mean. She was the real her. Who else would she be? This was feeling like an attack now and she wasn't going to take it. "Robert and I are totally compatible. We have the same values and outlook on things. We want the same kind of life. It might not be as adventurous as some, but adventure isn't for everyone. Some people, like he and I, enjoy simplicity, creature comforts and a straightforward life. And there is nothing wrong with that Lydia. You should stop judging things by your standards."

Lydia banged the heel of her palm against her forehead with a frustrated *Aargh*. Closing her eyes she took a moment to recompose herself and regroup her argument.

"Mum once said to me that 'sex and laughter are the heart and lungs of a marriage', Jen. Did she ever say that to you? I'd overhead the two of them going at it and had complained about it being gross for old people. She'd pilfered it out of one of her novels I think, but it meant something to her. 'Communication', she said too, 'is the air a marriage breathes'." As Lydia spoke their mother's words, Jen couldn't help but think how much she looked like her, with the same big eyes and light freckles. Granted, they both took after her, but Lydia's expressions were closer to their mother's where Jen was more a daddy's girl in manner- isms. It made her ache. "And I look at you and Robert," Lydia continued, "and I can't see the laughter and I wonder about your communication, because it always sounds like small talk or business conversation to me. God knows about the sex."

"There is nothing wrong with my sex life, thank you Lydia," Jen growled, getting het up now. "I've stayed at Robert's most Wednesday and Sunday nights since you were eighteen, so you can back right off there." Just because Lydia was busier with her body, it didn't lessen what she and Robert had.

"Let me ask you this then, Jen. Where is he now?" Lydia's expression was rather smug. Jen felt she was walking into some trap.

31

"He went home, Lydia." There was no mystery there. He'd said *I'll be off then; early one tomorrow. Goodnight ladies.* And then he'd kissed her and whispered *Sleep well Nearly-Mrs Thwaites.*

"Precisely!" Lydia was triumphant, but Jen was mystified. "He got engaged tonight, Jen. To *you*. Why aren't you upstairs ravishing each other, swinging off the rafters in celebration?"

"He has an early start tomorrow!" Jen's voice had raised now in exasperation. Lydia clearly had little concept of professional behaviour. And besides, on date nights they always stayed at his out of consideration to Lydia and the fact that Jen's bed had been her parents' bed.

"He shouldn't care!" Lydia shouted right back. There was a sudden banging on the wall from the adjacent house. Considering how deaf the oldies next door insisted they were, they had no problem complaining when the sisters' bickering interrupted their telly viewing. "I'm not talking about your shared values and mutual respect, Jen, I'm talking about the fact he shouldn't be able to keep his hands off you. There's no spark between you, Jen."

Jen didn't know what to say to that, not without over-sharing; her and Robert's nights together could be frisky enough. They had a selection of positions. She tried to curb the conversation.

"You're wrong about that. We are compatible outdoors and in. We aren't boring. You make it sound like the two are one-in-the-same and they're not. The whole 'sparks' thing is a nonsense, like relationships are somehow lesser if people aren't pawing all over each other in public. Ever considered that sparks and fire are generally – actually *universally* – considered dangerous?" *There*, thought Jen, bet she hadn't thought of *that*.

Lydia shook her head.

"You're right Jen, compatible doesn't need to mean boring, but you're wrong about relationships not needing sparks. Something has to ignite it. And here's the thing you've lost sight of; not all fires are bad. Fire's been used for some pretty good stuff through the ages. Warmth for a start. I don't see a lot of that with you and Robert." Lydia was shaking her head now, sad. "You used to be fun, Jen. I get why you lost it, but I thought if you met the right person you'd get it back. Robert doesn't do that for you."

Enough! Jen's temper was piqued. She was not being pitied by her little sister. She'd just been proposed to. She was supposed to be revelling blissfully in it like a pig in poo, but here was Lydia peeing all over it, instead. Suddenly Jen worked out why.

"This is about you, isn't it? You think you'll be left all alone."

"What?" Jen was sure she was right, but had to admit Lydia was good at looking shocked at the suggestion. It didn't stop her though.

"You might think I'm not fun, but this is what growing up looks like, Lydia. You'll see that over the next few years. There's work and responsibilities and all the frivolous stuff falls away and that's natural. And all the silly dreams we have need to be shelved in the cool light of day. That's reality. Life moves on. It's called being an adult." She knew it would wind Lydia up, but it was true, so she ignored the way her sister's eyes suddenly hardened and her face grew puce. "Mum and Dad knew Robert and they liked him. Dad said he was a 'decent guy', Lydia, and that speaks volumes in *my* opinion. Robert is an open book; no hidden shockers there and that does it for me. *That* is the spark for me, if you really need one. And the rest of the family isn't totally mad, they are just effusive," Lydia had taken a pop at the sisters, hadn't she? Jen was sure she had. "Me marrying into it won't cut you out. You'll be part of it. Robert knows that." Jen took a softer tone, understanding this must be a big deal and a shock for Lydia. "My home will always be your home, Lyds. I'm not leaving you alone."

Lydia's jaw flapped up and down a couple of times, but she couldn't verbalise her feelings. Instead she gripped her crutches back in place and stormed out of the lounge door. Jen had never heard her negotiate the stairs so fast, but the slamming of the bedroom door on the other hand was an all too familiar sound. Lydia hadn't believed her. She'd have to spend some more time convincing her, but for now she knew it was best to let her calm the hell down.

Flopping exhausted back on the sofa, Jen dug out her phone from her dress pocket and started to browse Appstore for a useful tool. A wedding was going to need its own app. She found one she thought best suited to her needs, ChAPPel, and installed it. She loved watching the little dial completing as another tool was uploaded onto the device that kept her life organised and controllable. Each was a little cog of orderliness slotting into place in her life, shoring up her defences.

Opening it, she found herself staring at the screen in front of her. Normally her fingers would race across the keys to spill all her ideas for a project immediately. Jen definitely considered herself an ideas person. That she got them actioned was purely down to her being conscientious and no one else being around to do the jobs. But right now, she couldn't think of anything she wanted to list.

The low TV buzz from next door went silent. It was late and she'd been up early. Of course she couldn't think of anything to list, she was knackered. She closed the app. She could look at this in the morning. Who knew what gems of inspiration would come to her in her sleep? That happened all the time. Several of *Well, Honestly!*'s marketing campaigns had evolved during the night. They were always the best ones.

Jen locked up and scaled the stairs. Lydia's door was firmly shut. She hesitated for a moment, but turned for her own bedroom, the room her parents had slept in. It had taken her ages to move in there. Sleeping in a bunk again after her uni room hadn't been ideal, but she'd wanted to be around Lydia, for when the phantom limb pains came during the night. But now, lying spread-eagled across the double bed, Jen considered the space between them a blessing. She gazed at the ceiling, as her parents must once have done, and reminded herself they too must have found parenting and adulting hard at times. Lydia might not always like her decisions, but then Jen probably hadn't always liked theirs either when she'd been growing up. And she'd turned out all right, hadn't she?

Pulling her mother's green patchwork quilt to her chin, she reassured herself Lydia would come round eventually. But perhaps her argument with Lydia had been a good thing on another level. It had focused her thoughts. Life did move on, people did grow up, they adapted their dreams. The more she thought about it, looked at things in the context of their life, of Lydia's care and her own future, Robert's proposal was a gift. Being his wife and making a home for them all would fill her time she was sure, because she'd give it everything. So of course, something had to give – that was the way change worked. And the beer she made, which as Robert said, was a hobby, would fall by the wayside. But that was okay, Jen told herself as her eyes lolled shut; not everything in life was forever. She'd experienced enough to know that. She could adapt and adjust. Surely her happiness didn't depend on beer ...?

Plucky amputee Lydia Attison (22), raised £2,000 for children's prosthetics last Sunday morning, when throwing herself out of a plane. Poor Lydia lost both her parents and her left leg at the age of 14, in a horrific crash on Westhampton High Street when a run-away lorry smashed into them. Now, back on her feet and raring to go, Lydia was on the first plane up and first to jump out. Camera-shy Lydia said it had been "a rush". Her skydiving instructor, Glen Harris (26), to whom she was strapped for the tandem jump, was happy to tell the

Echo, "She's a natural; fearless and a fast learner. I'm hoping we can hook up for another jump sometime," he said, giving her a cheeky wink.

–Neil Finch, Staff Reporter,
Westhampton Echo, Page 6

Chapter 4

"OH MY GOD, OH MY GOD, OH MY GOD!! Sister!" Jen wanted to crawl under the desk and disappear as Ava scuttled across the office in her skinny jeans and wedges.

"Robert's told you then?" Jen asked, turning around in her office chair to face her future sister-in-law, who might have been grinning from ear to ear, had Botox allowed. Oh good grief, she'd also had one side of her head done in cornrows.

"Darling, we *knew*," Ava said with a giggle. "Mumsie rang Sunday morning to say he'd asked for the ring. Took her a while to find the thing. It was hidden in the depths of her knicker drawer. Anyhoo, we're all delighted." Ava pulled Jen up from her seat and crammed her into a hug. Over Ava's shoulder, she saw Aiden the intern watching them with a rather heated expression. Jesus God, it was just two women hugging, not lesbian office porn. She had her reservations about Rupert's eighteen-year-old godson, which was why she generally set him tasks that kept him away from her. Today she'd given him a stack of the local newspapers she'd been ignoring, to scrapbook the ads *Well, Honestly!* had placed in recent months.

"How was the festival?" Jen asked, wanting to move the conversation, and Ava, off her. She still hadn't quite got her head around her newly-fiancéed status. Monday had flown by as she'd been immersed in Ava's mountainous workload. Robert had sent a goodnight text, but that was it and not out of the ordinary. All in all, Jen wasn't experiencing much difference, with the exception of Lydia giving her the cold shoulder, but they'd been through that enough times. So really, Jen suspected her initial panic and Lydia's concern was a gross overreaction.

"Glasto was fabulous. Aiden darling, two teas pronto per favore." Ava sat on the edge of Jen's desk, but didn't give her ex-workload a glance. Jen had most of it sorted and piled neatly for filing. "The bands were amaaazing as always, and the kids just loved it. It's so good to see how they thrive when we sleep under canvas and get back to nature." Jen wasn't sure glampy yurts counted as camping. Nor did she think hot showers, porter services and spa facilities constituted getting back to nature.

A thought suddenly hit Ava and Jen worried she was having a seizure, but no. "Oh. My. God. I nearly forgot. Something mind-blowing happened at the festival. I was coming out of a laughter workshop in the Healing field and there was this woman making these things. Actually making them with her own hands. They're the next Best Thing. For the company I mean. I'm soooo excited."

39

"Really?" Whatever it was, it had to be astounding, as Ava was flapping her hands like little birds' wings.

"Yah, totally. I FaceTimed Zara immedo. She sends her love and congratulations by the way. Says not to bother with the Seychelles for your honeymoon, the hotels still let children in. Which made me laugh as Zaz adores having my babies over. Isn't that funny? Must be other people's children she despises. Anyhoo, the *thing*."

"The *thing*," Jen encouraged. She wanted to know what it was that had Ava so excited, but also she wanted her off her desk as she had tonnes to do. There was an advertorial deadline for *Saga* magazine to hit and she wanted to get a call in to the National Trust for a flyer in their next mailing.

"So, you know Zaz and I have been talking about expanding the company? Growing the range?"

Jen bit her tongue. *She* was the one always pointing out the entire business plan was based on one product type. Pads and pants counted as one. It seemed like an all-eggs-in-one-basket approach to business. And okay, on a purely selfish note, more products would give her options when it came to telling people what she did for a living. People always asked what *specifically* she marketed.

"Well obviously, given our niche strategy and our dedication to the ethical values of the products, it's been a bit tricky, but this thing just nails it. And once I'd spoken to Zaz, who was totes on board, like 'duh, no brainer,' I marched right back to the Healing field and signed the woman up as a supplier on the spot. I had to send Rupes off to all the cash machines with all our cards to get a decent wad for exclusivity too. I don't mind her selling them at festivals once she's fulfilled our orders, but there's no way I'm having any of our competitors getting hold of them."

Bloody hell. If she'd managed to get Rupert to haul his bum from the yurt and his mates then Ava must have been on a mission. Plus this almost deranged excitement Jen was witnessing was the tail-end of the hurricane. Aiden appeared with the teas, dodging Ava's flinging arms.

"Well come on then, what is it?" Jen prompted. Hating surprises as she did, the build-up was not fully appreciated, but she had to admit she was intrigued as to what this thing was that had blown Ava's already blown mind, and Jen was about to be landed with.

Ava looked behind them, lest anyone should be eavesdropping. The office had only the one door and any spies would have been noticed. She then swept a look between Jen and Aiden who was still hovering.

"Crocheted tampons," she whispered dramatically.

The ensuing silence was deafening; exactly the affect Ava had been wanting as she nodded them through it. "Precisely," she said, acknowledging their stunned state. "That's what I thought." She closed her eyes and shook her head at the momentous memory. "One hundred per cent organic cotton, filled with bamboo, hand-made and machine washable. Available in non-bleached ecru for the die-hards, but otherwise in pristine white. We'll have to research how the bleaches are disposed of. But they tick all the boxes; organic, a national product and what's more they're even artisan.

She doesn't make her children help her either. I checked."
Ava's beaming face could have kept ships from rocks.

Jen had no idea what to say. Crocheted tampons. Her
brain didn't know where to start. She opened her mouth
a couple of times but had to keep shutting it as the right
words, office-appropriate words, wouldn't form.

"I know, right?" Ava was still nodding. "Rupes said I was
a business wizard, a *Biz Wiz*, and Zara opened a bottle of
Bolly right there on screen."

"Do you think there's a big market, Ava?" Jen managed
tentatively.

"Well not *yet*, silly, nobody knows about them, unless
they've been hoiking around Glasto, but once you start
getting the word out there Jen, you betcha. All those women
who use the mooncups but find it uncomfy having a rubber
thingy up their ninny? They'll love it and they'll still avoid
the years of expense, waste and eco-destruction of disposable tampons. All they need is a small stock, a waterproof
pouch with two compartments – you know, one in one out
– and they're good to go until the menopause. Like I said,
Jen, *No Brainer*."

Jen wanted to call Lydia and howl. She'd feel better
hearing Lydia mercilessly take the piss. But Lydia still wasn't
talking to her. This though, this might just be the thing to
thaw Lydia out. This would tickle her no end. She already
thought Ava and Zara were bonkers, this would send her
over the edge. Well, if there was silver lining to be had from
the crocheted tampon issue, then that might be it.

"How about, Ava," Jen started carefully, "how about I

run a few focus groups first? Say three for example, across various age groups and see how women feel about it."

"Not just women, Jen," Ava raised an eyebrow at her, "men can use tampons too. Gay men use them all the time. You need to widen your reading. Organic is important to men too."

"Right," Jen said, ignoring Aiden's look of confusion. He could Google it. "I'd do a group for them too." She couldn't wait to do a focus group covering anal sex after-care. That might just be the highlight of her career to date. Her eyes flitted to the clock and calculated how soon until home-time. She needed a drink. She needed to cocoon herself away in the non-bonkers safety of her brewery, la-la-la-ing to herself and casting all of this out of her mind.

"No need, darling. I appreciate your conscientiousness – one of the many, many things we love about you – but the extra work's not needed given the response the things got at the festival. I saw it with my own eyes and both Zaz and I know in our hearts this is the right thing."

Jen had been here before. Once the sisters "knew something in their hearts", it was effectively an executive order. The vital-but-unused flotation tank in the meeting-slash-inspiration room was testament to that.

"And that's not all, Jen" Ava said, suddenly looking terribly serious and moving to sit opposite Jen in the nearest chair. "I said I'd wait until Zaz got back for this conversation, but given the engagement thing and our need to act fast on the tampons, I can't see the benefit of waiting." This sounded ominous. *Even more ominous*, Jen adjusted, the great tampon reveal had set a new bar.

"This is a big step for the company and we're going to require everyone's efforts. Particularly yours, Jen and we'd like to show you we value you." Ava sat up straight and took a deep dramatic breath for her proclamation. "Zara and I have agreed we want you to become a partner in the company alongside the expansion." Ava grabbed both of Jen's hands, presumably believing Jen needed support in light of this joyous bombshell. "We want you to share in the success, because you deserve it, because you'll be family and because it simply makes sense."

Jen experienced new levels of gobsmackedness, causing her to sway slightly.

"I know, darling," Ava squeezed her hands kindly, "you don't have to thank us, you've earned it. It's not everyone we'd allow to buy in, but we know an asset when we see it. You should be very proud of yourself."

Wait, what? *Buy* in?!

44

Chapter 5

Jen's finely-tuned nose was almost exploding with all the scents. *Re:Love*, Alice and Max's florist-cum-salvage shop was a riot of blooms and a joyful assault on her senses. Jen often dropped in after work for a chat, today however it was an emergency. The shop was situated at the end of The Arches, adjacent to the arch Jen's dad had worked in. Alice and her girlfriend Max had made the most of the exposed brick walls and concrete floor with Max show-casing select pieces around the shop – fireplaces, old furniture and some up-cycled items – while Alice's flowers brought a sea of colour to the space.

"They'll *let* you buy in?" Alice asked, incredulous. "I don't know why I'm surprised, the pair of them are nutters." She sat on the front desk, legs swinging as she chomped on a stack of chocolate digestives. She wore her staple of a homemade tea-dress, bobby socks and saddle shoes, which she only ever changed up by adding a cardy and Doc Martens with opaque tights in the winter. Other than the fabrics, Alice's sole variables were her bright lipsticks and her hair styles, which ranged widely from a fully-spherical afro, to two Bjork sprouts when it was hot. Opposite, Jen was taking the opportunity to lie down along the length of an old church pew.

"I know," Jen groaned, unsure how she had managed to get to this stage in her life. Four days ago she was happily tapping her beer, minding her own business and here she was being press-ganged into being part of someone else's. And she hadn't told Alice about the engagement yet. It didn't quite seem like the right time, not when she'd come storming in, mouthing off about Ava's offer-slash-decree. It felt like one of those double-edged honours dictators bestowed on people which invariably lead to a difficult demise. "It's bad enough with the inco pads, but crocheted tampons? I keep asking myself if this is what I got a degree for?"

"I'm guessing you didn't," Alice agreed. She'd always been a good ear for Jen, but normally for Jen letting off steam about Lydia's teenage antics. As the eldest of four girls Alice understood. "And good of them to decide how you want to spend your savings."

"Which is ridiculous, because there are none. The house is paid for, sure, and there's this place, but the rents are supposed to fund Lydia's future prosthetics, not to mention a pension for her." Jen felt her pulse beginning to race. This was the stuff of her 4 a.m. worries.

"Lydia's got her head screwed on. She'll be fine in her job, and she'll get her own pension."

"But what if she doesn't?" Jen whispered, "what if the leg holds her back? People can be so mean and judgey and dismissive."

"Jen? Stop. There isn't much to hold Lyds back. Trust me. You're too close to see it, but she'll go a long way." Jen wished she could be so sure. Alice didn't see the worst days, when things became too much and Lydia retreated to her bed. Her tenacity was impressive, but she was still only human, not a superhero. Not that Lydia remembered this either sometimes; she would make all sorts of mad decisions if Jen didn't keep a rein on her. She'd even mentioned skydiving some months ago, but Jen had put the kibosh on that. Some things were way too dangerous. "Besides, missy," Alice fixed her with a beady eye, "haven't you got something of your own to be worrying about?"

Jen sighed. "The bloody tampons. Ugh. No pun intended."

"Gross," Alice said with a grimace. "But no, something of a more personal nature that should have been the thing you came to tell me about, maybe yesterday?"

Jen looked at her blankly, until Alice picked up a posy from the counter and waved it at her.

Oh.

"How do you know about that?"

"*That?* Your impending nuptials? Because Robert paid for a skywriter and told the whole town." Alice looked at her po-faced.

"What?! Really?" She hadn't seen it. Oh crap.

"No, don't be ridiculous," guffawed Alice. "Could you see Robert doing that?" Fair point. "Lyds texted me Sunday night, ranting. Believes you're making a mahoosive mistake."

"She may have shared that sentiment with me. I think she's worried about me leaving her."

47

"Yeah, no." Alice seemed sure of this, but then she didn't live with Lydia. "She's definitely convinced there's someone better suited out there for you."

"She's been watching too many rom-coms, Alice," Jen said with a sigh. "She's a sucker for those."

"What's wrong with that?"

"Sorry," said Jen, "I forgot you're an enabler." Alice and Lydia regularly saw the chick-flicks together because Jen refused. "They're fun – *fluffy* fun – but they aren't real, Alice. Life doesn't work like that. They give people unrealistic ideas. Either the set-up is ridiculous, or when the characters do get together, the relationship will never sustain itself. All film romance is idealistic and improbable."

"You really think that?" Alice looked appalled, her current digestive frozen halfway to her face.

"Sure," said Jen, looking back to the ceiling, totally clear on this. "It's a life partnership. You have to think rationally and long term, you have to make compromises and be practical, and I don't think meeting on the Titanic or during an impossible mission is a sound basis for that. Those intense scenarios make people overlook the realities and the enormous flashing warning signs that their relationship is doomed."

Jen stopped to look back at Alice, who was still looking at her aghast.

"That's your honest belief?" Her tone was a blend of dismay and moral outrage.

"Deffo," Jen said, nodding along with her own argument. "I mean, I like a good Mills & Boon now and again – who doesn't? – but you know it's as much fantasy as *Game of Thrones* or *Star Wars*. I just think, because they're set in real life, people confuse fantasy with reality."

"Jen!" Alice was fuming. "I should wash your mouth out with soap. This is a haven of romance and dreams. Shame on you. I'm going to fill this space with old romance novels to ward off your bad vibes." Alice was small but she was feisty and right now Jen was aware she'd riled her, but she stuck to her guns.

"Doesn't make it less true." Jen's mind was set.

"But what does that say about you and Robert then? Why are you apparently engaged?" Alice thought she'd nailed the flaw in Jen's argument here, but Jen was ready for her.

"Because we're going to be a sound partnership. That's what Lydia can't get her head around. We're very compatible, like a good business partnership. I've known him since my teens and we've had a steady six years to see that we meander along at the same pace in the same direction, which in business is a good plan. Lydia seems to think that's wrong, that we should be bouncing off each other with mad sparks flying. Where's the harmony in that? Equally, basing a lifetime on someone you met for a mad moment, be it in a pub, on holiday or in a high-octane, life or death scenario, well that's a madness. Lydia just isn't old enough to see it."

"Lydia is twenty-two, Jen, you forget that sometimes."

"Lyds is a special case, Alice. The leg makes it different." People didn't always get this, but Jen knew better.

"Only in your eyes."

"Well, I know her best. That's my job." Jen's voice had become harder. She bristled when she perceived anyone criticising her parenting. She'd done okay, all things considered.

Alice knew to back off. "Well, coming back to your surprise wedding, Lydia thinks we need to stage an intervention."

Jen pulled herself up to sitting, so Alice could see she was clearly of sound mind.

"I do not need intervening."

Alice gave her a long hard stare. "If you say so." Jen didn't get the feeling Alice was convinced. That was rom-com fans for you. "Not everyone's like Danny, Jen," Alice said, gently.

Danny. There was the most humiliating event of Jen's life to date and one which generally lived under a universally accepted seal of *Don't Go There*. She, Alice and Max had taken a week's holiday to Ibiza right after her finals, where she'd fallen for fellow traveller Danny, who'd immediately whisked her off her feet, straight from the transfer bus. They'd even had a meet-cute where she'd mistakenly tried to walk off with his matching suitcase, until he twirled a pair of her knickers at her. He came from her uni town and obviously this had been a cosmic sign to forgo all sightseeing and live in his bed for the week. He was a DJ, booked solid around the Balearic clubs for the following week apparently, he'd even waved his Facebook page past her, giving her a quick glimpse of him at various decks, sweaty in the strobe lights, fans' hands stretching for him in the edges of the numerous grainy shots.

He said he'd never felt this way about anyone before and lulled by the warmth and the sun and the sex, she'd believed him. And yet, once home, her texts and WhatsApps went unanswered. She'd tried to call him, but the number went nowhere. She took a closer look at the Facebook page, a pretty poor marketing job if she was being professionally critical, but also fake when she took a closer squiz at the DJs who, with the benefit of daylight, weren't quite the same man in each pic. Only then did it dawn on her she'd been duped. The realisation that he'd tapped a false number into her phone was a breath-taking blow.

"You weren't to know, Jen. We all thought he was for real," Alice said, seeing Jen running through it all. But Jen was less lenient with herself, because she'd been a clichéd idiot, falling for a holiday fling and believing his invented persona. She was one of those girls who fell for a "shark trainer" only to find out he was a call centre operative from Croydon.

That blow had only been the starter course however. On top of feeling so foolish at the time, all hell had then come at her. While the news of a job in a brewery had briefly buoyed her, the loss of her family had taken her far, far deeper into the pit of grief shortly after. She might have properly dealt with the feelings of being ghosted, had she not had ghosts of her own and saving a sister to contend with. She remembered the humiliation and hurt later, but by then pain was a relative thing and instead it steeled her against getting carried away ever again. Some people just didn't turn out to be who you thought they were. It wasn't a mistake she'd make again.

Alice tactfully changed the subject. "How's your list coming then?" she asked.

"What list?"

"Ha! Don't give me that, Attison," Alice's eyes narrowed at Jen's deceitful attempt.

"There's no way you haven't started a project list for this. What's the app called?"

Dammit they knew her too well.

"ChAPPel," she mumbled, faintly annoyed at being so predictable.

"Show me." Alice did a karate kid "come hither" hand gesture.

"It's a surprise," Jen said, her blush adding a useful, if fake, bashfulness to her bride's plans.

"Hmmm." Alice let her off. "There's your get-out with the sister-in-laws. Tell them you can't buy in as you're throwing all your savings at this wedding." Ooh now there was an idea. "And don't worry, you can put 'mates rates' next to my name for the flowers on your app list there."

Jen made a grand show of gratefully doing exactly that, keeping the screen close to her chest – supposedly to keep her "surprises" to herself, but really so Alice couldn't see there wasn't a single other item listed.

Chapter 6

Jen's front door swung open before she got the key in the lock. Lydia stood with one pot of Ben & Jerry's and two spoons and Jen knew an olive branch when she saw one. She plucked one of the spoons out of Lydia's hand and followed her into the lounge where they performed a perfectly synchronised slump onto the sofa.

Jen dug into the ice cream and savoured her spoonful with her eyes shut. "I hate it when we argue," she said, quietly.

"Me too." She had no doubt Lydia was sitting in exactly the same pose. Ice cream had been used to process many things; grief, phantom pains, exam stress and now ... well Jen couldn't quite name this, other than simply disagreement. "I just want you to be happy, Jen."

"Me too, Lyds. We simply disagree about what that looks like, currently. But that's okay. I appreciate your concern, and I'll just have to show you over time that it's unfounded."

Lydia didn't reply to that, but the sisters continued taking it in turns to snaffle a spoonful of the ice cream until the pot was forensically scraped.

"Can't beat an ice cream dinner," Lydia said, holding up her spoon which Jen clinked in agreement. Cooking was the last thing Jen felt like facing this evening. An evening curled up, watching TV-tat with Lydia sounded divine.

"Beer?" Lydia asked. Her mood appeared to require one. Jen doubted beer on ice cream was a particularly balanced diet, but it had never stopped them before. Jen moved to go, but Lydia hauled herself up and went to the kitchen, returning with two glasses of Barley Wine. It was a rich pudding of a beer, a perfect fruity toffee-ish chaser to their main course.

"*Brew*tiful," Lydia stated after the first sip, and an appreciative groan.

"*Keg*cellent," Jen countered with an equally bad pun. Beer puns were another thing their Dad had nurtured and neither sister ever tired of them, no matter how bad they got.

"Hope you've got the next batches planned," Lydia said nodding towards the County Show-bound boxes which flanked the telly like some bizarre mantel. "When that lot sells, there's hardly any left. The odds and ends shelf is fairly depleted." Jen had made Lydia responsible for stock auditing as soon as she was old enough to drink, with weekly reporting.

"Mmm," Jen managed, non-committal. She had a Mild and a Stout going, but after those, well ...

"What's it to be next? My vote goes for a session beer and Charlie said he'd buy a crate next time you did that one." Charlie, her dad's old business partner was consistently happy to buy a crate of everything she made next. While she'd waved to him as she left *Re:Love* earlier, she knew Lydia often stopped in at the Arches to chat to the sixty-year-old.

"How is he?" Jen asked as Lydia started to surf through the channels, bypassing anything involving hospitals, blood, gore or death, finally settling on a wedding-disaster-themed candid camera show. *What a comedian.* Jen wasn't rising to that, so ignored it. She was keen to maintain the current truce and besides, the beer in her hand had her ruminating.

"His back's playing up again, and he's on about retiring. As if we haven't heard that before." Jen mmmm'ed in agreement. "So which beer shall I promise him?" Lydia prompted.

"I um ... I haven't exactly got the next ones planned."

"Really?" Lydia looked at her in surprise. Jen normally had the next beers chalked up as soon as one was fermenting, both for shopping purposes and to evolve the recipes in her head. In fairness, she had the beginnings of a Golden Ale formulating, but since her discussion with Robert, the impetus had rather lapsed. It dampened her mood and she took another swig of the beer for comfort.

She stared at the TV screen, as the grainy home video showed a reader in a church reciting bible verses, just before fainting and landing face first on the stone floor, with a sickening slap and copious canned laughter. She'd heard the same passages at every wedding she'd ever been to and always wondered who these Corinthians St Paul was writing to were. Each time she determined to investigate when she got home, but then promptly forgot during the reception drinking. But here it was again, and she found she almost knew it; the "love is patient, love is kind" bit and then the next bit about putting away "childish things" when growing up. A creeping recognition drew over her; she was about to be a married woman and the brewing, much as she loved it, was a childish thing.

"Jen? Hey Space Cadet, you've zoned out."

"What? Sorry. Yes. The beer. Right," she said with a shake. "I'm going to start trapping it down, Lyds. Bring it to an end." Jen kept her eyes fixed on the telly, but saw Lydia's jaw drop from the corner of her eye.

"You're doing what?"

"It's time. Time to move on. I'll have a wedding to plan and a new life to build."

"But it's what you *do*, Jen." Lydia's voice, rather than the explosion Jen had been expecting, was raspy and confused.

"There's all sorts of things I can do. There's other creative outlets out there. I could bake for example."

"Pff," Lydia scoffed. "Cupcakes? Do me a favour. You're more badass than that. You *love* your beer, Jen." Now Lydia was getting het up, but so was Jen.

"And I'll find something else to love instead."

Lydia drew a sharp breath to blast her, but suddenly, remarkably, let it go. The silence between them was both hostile and awkward. Jen, not wanting another fight, took the initiative and diverted the subject back away from the beer.

"Look, you might not be up for this, knowing how you feel about the entire wedding thing, but I'd hoped you'd be my Best-woman and maybe give me away. Alice and Max could be lady-ushers, because there's no way Max will wear a frock, but Alice and her sewing machine will make them match somehow ..." Jen saw she was beginning to ramble in her panic about Lydia's response. What if she said no? "... so anyways that is what I was hoping."

"You want me to give you away?" Lydia's expression wasn't giving anything away itself, but when she said it like that, Jen instantly knew it sounded bad.

"Yeah, so no, not *dispense* with me. What I meant was, I was hoping you'll walk me up the aisle as part of Team Jen, and head of my girl squad. You won't ever be able to give me away, we're like this." Jen twisted her index and middle fingers together in front of Lydia's face, and then poked them up Lydia's nose to punctuate her point.

"Girl squad?"

"Head. Of." Jen confirmed.

"All right." Lydia took a mouthful of beer and went back to watching four hammered grannies dancing to YMCA at a reception, the deal apparently done.

"You will?" This had been much easier than Jen had expected. She'd foreseen a diatribe about principles and Lydia not taking part in an event she didn't support.

Apparently that was not the case.

"Not that I for one second believe in this marriage," Lydia stated clearly, "but I will always be your wingman Jen, so if leading you to the pit of doom is something you want, then who am I to deny you?" Cow.

"Well, thanks for that, I think." Jen would take what she could get.

"Of course, it means I'm in charge of the hen-do." On cue, the footage switched to a group of women, dressed in clashing and outdated bridesmaid dresses and paint-balling masks, shooting the hell out of each other in a muddy forest.

"Oh God, no. I don't want anything." Jen couldn't think of anything worse than being paraded along the promenade in a Learner-plated veil pinned with condoms. There was a conveyor belt of those every weekend in town and she was too old and too sensible for it.

"Um, sorry. Not your business," Lydia lorded grandly. "*My* domain." Jen sighed. This was not a battle to have now. Not when she already had a bomb to drop into the mix.

"Yes well, on that note," Jen pulled out a sheet of folded paper from her pocket and handed it to Lydia. Unfolding it Lydia's eyes scanned the memo Ava had pinged Jen, neatly listing dates convivial to her and Zara's diaries for the hen-do. Jen braced herself for the fireworks.

"Oh. That's handy. Thanks," Lydia said, refolding the paper into her own pocket. Weird. Lydia really was becoming harder and harder to read.

Saying no more, Lydia turned up the sound on the wedding disasters, just as a gust of wind lifted a bride's entire meringue skirt and a big comic-book X, complete with klaxon, was superimposed to cover her lack of knickers. Oh, how the surrounding groomsmen laughed! As did Lydia.

Well, two could play at that game. Jen dug out her

phone and opened ChAPPel. She added Bridesmaids to the top of the list above Flowers, typing Lydia as confirmed and Alice and Max as additions below. Lydia tried to sneak a look, but Jen pulled the phone closer. Her sister could stew.

Looking at the app and its meagre contents, Jen expected the ideas to start sparking. Nothing came. She considered taking a step back and using her mind-mapping app to see if a spider diagram jogged anything. Taking glimpses at the clips on the TV screen, there were many weddingy things she knew she didn't want. Balloon arches could do one, for a start, and those sugared almond favours could go too – you never knew which of them represented fertility, and not everyone might want that one. She did list Favours though and then Jen experienced a small spark of joy; *there* was the thing she'd thought of already; her wedding favour beer. And suddenly her fingers were racing as she listed ideas for what she wanted in it and how best to brew it. She might even name it *Wedding Beerlls*. Her dad would have approved. *Finally*, she thought, looking at her app with a smile, she was off. Looking up, she saw Lydia sneaking a peek at the screen, and wearing a smug smile Jen couldn't quite fathom.

In hindsight, Jen should have investigated the sound from the office entrance, but engrossed in her incontinence data, she'd assumed it was just Aiden returning. He forgot something every evening, and given it was Friday it made sense he'd return for it. Eager not to get into conversation with him, she didn't even turn around to check. So the black fabric bag over her head did come as a proper surprise, and she did scream in a way befitting a kidnapping.

The giggling took the edge off somewhat, but she still didn't know what the bloody hell was going on.

"Shhh," soothed Alice's not-remotely disguised voice. "Chillax. You're being abducted." Yes, yes she'd gathered that bit. She just didn't know why.

She heard the computer being shut down before she was manhandled to the door, where she had to talk them through setting the alarm. This was not her usual standard of "locking up" protocol.

Thankfully they took the hood off her when they'd set off in the van – it had been rather air-starved under there. Getting her in had been interesting, given the too-many cooks scenario, but they'd only banged her head off the door frame once, so she considered that a win. Alice and Max owned a Mazda Bongo campervan, which doubled both as Alice's delivery van and their weekend love-nest. They'd had it sprayed hot-pink with *Re:Love* written down the side, which was always an ice-breaker for them on campsites, though they now avoided lay-bys at night after a close call with some inquisitive doggers.

Lydia sat next to Jen in the passenger seating, with a self-satisfied smirk. Alice was hanging over the back of her seat, also wearing Smug, and Max was driving, looking very serious, but then the milk-bottle lenses of her round glasses always made her look comically studious and her buzz-cut afro hair left no room for frivolity.

"Right, you loons, where are we going?" Jen sighed, resigned.

"Hen-do. Weekend away. Hurrah," Alice sang.

"Nooo," groaned Jen. "I didn't want a hen-do." She thought Lydia had let go of the idea. She hadn't mentioned it at all in the ten days since it had been broached.

Lydia leaned towards her and reminded her with a touch of menace, "My domain."

Oh crap.

"But what about the shop?" Jen asked, weakly. "Maxine, tell these two children this is mad behaviour."

"Alice's mum's covering the flowers, my dad's got the salvage," Max said, though even her calm Mauritian lilt was unable to relax Jen, "Alice is thinking the two of them might get it on. Wouldn't that be lovely?" Jeez, there was that rom-com thinking again. What was the matter with everyone?

"We're going somewhere you've always wanted to go," teased Lydia, bursting to tell.

"You're taking me to a CAMRA event?" Lydia had always said No to the Real Ale association dos. Too many beardies. She was surprised Alice and Max were up for it as well. The only events they attended were swing dance related.

"Nope, even better than that." Lydia sounded exceptionally pleased with herself.

"Think further afield," Alice chimed in, "we're going on a plane."

"A plane? Wait, what?" Jen hadn't packed anything.

With an evil smile Lydia extended her pointy finger at

four cabin bags in the corner. Argh, no. They'd packed for her. Jen was very meticulous about her packing. She had various pre-devised packing lists for trips on her laptop, neatly divided by location, season and duration, but they didn't work if she didn't actually get to pack.

"Relax, Jen," Lydia said, knowing full well Jen hated surprises, yet blatantly appearing not to care, "We're taking you to Copenhagen. We've packed your bag, we've got your passport, you don't need to think about a thing. We're totally in control of this."

OH. GOD.

Chapter 7

In Jen's experience hen parties normally stuck together for activities and yet the next morning Lydia, Alice and Max were keen for Jen to enjoy the Kronegaard museum alone. Apparently they weren't as excited about experiencing over a century's worth of global brewing dynasty as Jen was. The museum had for years been firmly top of her "Copenhagen Trip" list, a list Lydia had inexplicably never asked to see in spite of planning this hen-do.

"We'll disturb your homage," they insisted and suggested meeting up again two hours later. Jen suggested four, allowing for travel time, in accordance with her *VisitCopenhagen* app. The others immediately and unanimously agreed. Jen suspected their hangovers were pushing them away from the more cultural pursuits. There had been some lively bars just over the bridge from the hotel Lydia had booked for them; a converted boat moored in the harbour that ran through the city. They might have visited one too many. Not that Jen was going to let a seething hangover stop her. She knocked some paracetamol back with Berocca and ventured out while the others psyched themselves for their shopping with more sleep. Scarfing down a *kanelsnegl* cinnamon swirl as she beelined through the streets, Jen considered how ridiculous this hen-do was. But then, if it helped Lydia come to terms with things ...

The red-brick brewery building was everything Jen had hoped for. Its location on the wharf was impressive, and while actual beer production had expanded out to the suburbs now, there were still parts of the business running from the majestic old buildings, along with the museum. It was exactly as she'd imagined a nineteenth-century factory to look, but without the smog-billowing chimneys. The cobbles remained, as did the grand wooden gates with their carved Kronegaard crown emblem at the entrance. Walking through them caused her to pause and run a hand across them with a lament for something beyond her reach. She shook off the thoughts, keen for nothing to spoil this, and took a brisk look around to check no one had seen her wobble. Apparently not, and thankfully nobody was batting an eyelid at her attire either. Lydia had packed her a weekend bag of charity shop wonders, including the purple sequined Converse knock-offs on her feet. They garishly comple-mented the yellow peasant blouse and elastic-waisted orange gypsy skirt. Her office clothes had mysteriously vanished during the night. Copenhageners, who had designer styling nailed and exclusively wore black and grey, were clearly used to all sorts from visitors.

As she followed the course of the displays with the Chinese tourists and the English stag parties, the story of Kronegaard unfolded, from way back in the 1800s when

Henrik Krone started brewing in his home and then expanded to his outbuilding. Jen couldn't help but feel a link with this man. He'd then started selling to the inn at the end of his street and within fifty years was the biggest exporter of lager on the planet. *Hello* global domination. And here was the thing that surprised her: disparaging as she might – *regularly* – be about Kronegaard beer being unexciting blandness for the masses, once, way back, Henrik had been a *craftsman*. He'd developed a beer people liked and would buy, he'd been a hobbyist like her.

Jen emerged, having sampled more than she perhaps should have, utterly swept up the story; the humble beginnings, and the drama of the choices that had to be made, the holding onto standards and the compromising of principles. Surely there had to be a TV mini-series there? It had all the ingredients. Not that the family had done badly, not by a long shot. They were the next step to royalty now, and certainly well entrenched in those circles; regular private dinner guests at the palace as friends, not just as captains of industry at the state bashes. The family had become celebrities and icons of how a sound work-ethic could get you places. Jen was sure she detected PR spin in the museum boards, but that was marketing, wasn't it?

"All beered out?" Lydia asked as she met them for a late lunch. The restaurant was very old and purported to serve the best *smørrebrød* open sandwiches in the city. Jen's was a roast beef on rye bread extravaganza, loaded with yellow remoulade, pickled cucumber and crunchy onions. (Lydia had had a eureka moment at that – "They're *crunions*, Jen," she'd hooted, passing Jen a second schnapps – or *snaps* as the Danes called it – from the waitress, ready to be downed in one, "you can call the crocheted tampons *Crampons*!" Jen had ignored her, unwilling to let work taint her weekend of joy.)

"It was *culture*, Lyds. And yes thanks. It was un*beer*lievable." Lydia gave her a flick for that one. "You should have come. You could smell centuries of hops and malt."

Initially on reaching the others, sitting at the pavement table, Jen had resumed her slightly braced stance. She'd expected them to crack open the nightmare hen accessories any second, but nothing had happened – not even willy-straws in their drinks. In fact, her mad clothes aside, the four of them were having a lovely time, chatting and continuing their normal banter. No one mentioned the wedding (which was turning out to be the norm as nothing had happened on that front in the last week, given both she and Robert had been madly busy.) The general consensus was also that it was a bloody good thing Ava and Zara hadn't been able to make this trip either. Lydia was still stubbornly insisting she'd already booked the tickets by the time Jen had given her the dates memo and Jen conveniently chose not to call bullshit. In the interest of not hurting feelings, by which Jen meant not raising two she-devils, they all readily agreed to keep this trip secret.

"What happens in 'hagen, stays in 'hagen," Lydia tried with a smutty wink, but the others were adamant it didn't work as well as Vegas. Jen prayed there wouldn't be any strip clubs involved later. And *that* was another thing; she had no idea what the plan for later was and that never sat well with her. The others didn't appear as concerned by this as she did. Thankfully their *Copenhagen Card* travel passes came with an app, and she started paging madly through the screens, the *snaps* now making her feel slightly light-headed.

"Put the app away, Attison," Max growled, "we're in Lydia's capable hands."

"What? Really?" Jen couldn't hide her dismay. There were things she wanted to see and only two days in which to see them. She'd cobbled together an emergency list on her phone during the flight, but she had a full Copenhagen plan on her laptop at home. Other people did that, didn't they, devising fantasy trip itineraries? Sort of mood-boarding, but in words and lists.

Lydia disregarded the dismay. "My hands are very capable, Jen," she insisted, slurring slightly. Clearly beer and *snaps* in the sunshine was having its effect. "I can give you a list of guys who can vouch for that."

"Sometimes, Lydia, you say things I'd instantly like to unhear. That was one of them." The bill being paid, Jen figured it was time to move on. "What's next?" At her best in a proactive role, Jen concluded if she couldn't be the one deciding what they saw, at least she could take a role in making sure they got there.

"Seriously, where are we going?" Jen asked again, after thirty minutes of seemingly aimless wandering through the streets. Her own itinerary, had Lydia only asked her for it, had everything for a weekend break broken down hour by hour. There was a glass-topped boat tour around the canals, trips up spiralling church towers, dinner in Tivoli Gardens which had inspired Walt Disney to start his theme parks.

"Somewhere." Lydia was being annoyingly obtuse in answering her questions.

"I'm sure we just passed the Round Tower. That was on my list." Jen waved her phone at Lydia. "No stairs all the way up, just a winding ramp, so the king could stay on his horse to the observatory at the top."

"Lazy arse," Alice said, still walking, "we're not encouraging that sort of thing."

Jen threw a small hissy-fit insisting she had "Bridal rights", until the others relented.

Never had the seventeenth century tower been scaled so quickly, nor the view of the city's rooftops, towers and entwined-dragon-tail'ed spires admired so briefly. To be fair, the height wasn't conducive to the amount of booze in her belly. Hoofing back down, getting dizzy with the perpetual turn, the others acknowledged the lack of stairs as a boon. Alice reckoned all olde worlde towers show be retro-fitted with no stairs. The *snaps* was definitely having its moment.

Back on the street, Jen was keen to know the next port of call. "Is it something on my list?" she asked, brandishing the screen in Max's face. Max would give her a sensible answer.

"Relax, Jen. You'll see." Well, how was that helpful?

At the next corner Alice and Max ducked into a grocers while Jen sat with Lydia on a bench in the shade.

"Leg all right?"

"S'fine," Lydia answered, head thrown back, eyes closed, enjoying the sun on her face.

"We can stop more often if you need to." Lydia had her everyday leg on – a micro-prosthetic; a far more robotic looking piece of kit, its shiny metal pylon connecting the socket and foot. While she wore her cosmesis – her "fake leg" cosmetic prosthesis – on dates and if wearing skirts to the office, Lydia rarely hid her prosthesis and today was wearing shorts.

"Jen? Stop fussing. I'm fine. Try doing what I'm doing, it's lovely." Jen looked at her sister. As far as she could see she wasn't doing *anything*. She took a look at her watch. It was nearly five. Touristy things would be closing soon and here they were dawdling. Jen really hoped they weren't just killing time before Tivoli Gardens opened. The mid-city park and funfair was the thing Lydia seemed most fired up about and while Jen was keen to eat in one of the many restaurants there, she drew a line at the fairground rides. Rollercoasters were beyond her comfort zone. That kind of control relinquishing was impossible. Even for kicks. She wondered if she'd played her "Bridal rights" card too early. With this hen-do being Lydia's "domain", she doubted she had any rights of veto.

For want of anything else to do, Jen scrolled through the pictures she'd taken at the Kronegaard museum, especially those of the main building. They made her feel slightly melancholy. She'd once been about start work in a place like that, to be part of that industry. It felt a world away and a lifetime ago. The feeling made her lean back and close her eyes just like her sister.

"Wake up, you lazers," Alice commanded, giving Jen a light kick to the foot, "hurry up or we'll be late." She and Max stood in front of them with two bulging carrier bags. *Seriously*, thought Jen, this group behaved unlike any tourists she'd experienced before. They weren't bothered with guidebooks or visiting the obvious sights. They were NOT doing it properly.

Surveying the little GoBoat in front of them, Jen wasn't convinced. It was like a blue plastic bath toy, except grown-up sized, with a solar-cell motor and a picnic table bang in the middle. She'd seen groups pootling along the canals in these, all having a cheery time with their food and drinks in the sunshine. Seeing other people in them was one thing, actually venturing out in one herself was another thing entirely.

Thankfully, Max was up for driving it. She'd once spent a school trip on a narrow-boat and could at least steer the thing. Meanwhile, Alice and Lydia gleefully unloaded the bags, and suddenly their table was adorned with snacks and beers. Trying a bottle of *Mikkeller*, Jen was touched they'd sought out local indie beers. They knew her so well, and all of a sudden she realised the joy of a hen-do. It was time away with the women most precious to you, who knew you best and who had your happiness at heart. She swallowed the lump in her throat and whacked her sunglasses over her eyes so the others would be none the wiser.

Their boat was launched from the jetty by a baby-faced attendant and they commenced their route into the canals. Begrudgingly, Jen conceded this was a fine way to see the city, puttering along between the old buildings with beers in hand, hooting and faking echoes as they passed under low bridges. Crossing the harbour got a bit choppy, but they'd necked a couple of bottles by then, so nobody panicked. Instead they cheerily waved at the tourists in the glass-topped tour boats, at the cyclists on the bike bridge and at the commuters on the yellow water buses. And there was singing. Any song they could remember with a water theme was mauled by their astonishing lack of musical talent. Jen couldn't remember the last time she'd sung. School perhaps. Dreadful as it might be on the ears, she wondered if it wasn't actually rather good for the soul.

Following the map, Max steered them into the calmer waters of the Christianshavn canal where tall colourfully-painted houses lined the streets on either side and boats of all kinds, from small yachts to hydrangea-laden house-boats, were moored.

"They modelled this part of the city on Amsterdam, you know," Jen said, dreamily. The warmth of the day and the beer had sloughed the efficiency off Jen's sightseeing needs. She was feeling quite idle now and more surprisingly, she was rather enjoying it.

"Who's *they*?" asked Alice, who was leaning into Max, face to the sun.

"The King. Christian, I think, or Frederik." She'd seen this on a BBC4 documentary. All Danish kings were alternately

71

called one or the other since the 1500's, which had struck her as rather tidy. "Duh," she slapped herself on the forehead, "must have been a Christian, he named it after himself." But annoyingly she couldn't remember which one had established this gorgeous part of the city and in her tipsiness, it suddenly seemed imperative to know. She dug out her phone and started swiping to locate her Copenhagen app.

"Put the phone away, Jen," Lydia murmured, "we can look it up when we get home. Just enjoy it." She was laid back along the side of the boat, sun bathing. Her prosthetic lay discarded at her side, the socket liner next to it, leaving her scarred skin free to the warm air. She seemed in a state of bliss.

"Won't take a second," Jen insisted.

"Seriously, Jen. It'll keep." Without opening her eyes, Lydia tried to swat the phone aside but misjudged both her aim and velocity.

The phone flew from Jen's hand into the canal.

Heads from the surrounding homes and boats turned towards the ensuing squawking. Jen was instantly hanging over the side trying to reach the phone which currently floated on the surface but was beginning to take in water and start its descent into the murky depths. Jen saw her whole life descending before her.

"Nooooooooooooo."

Max thankfully cut the engine, but they were drifting nonetheless, necessitating Jen to stretch further than was comfortable as she willed her fingertips longer. This could *not* be happening.

Suddenly a small net appeared in her field of vision, deftly scooping the phone up. Thank god. Jen's eyes followed the attached stick up to the deck of a long black barge moored to the quayside. On the deck, her eyes met with a pair of bare feet, travelled up the blond-haired legs to baggy navy cargo shorts, via the bare torso, to, wow, back to the torso because *ripped*, and then reluctantly further on to the face.

"Well, *hello*," Jen heard Lydia say in a salacious tone entirely inappropriate to the urgency of the moment. "Hottie alert."

He was clearly a Scandi; straw blond hair, blue eyes and very tall from what Jen could see from her contorted position. There wasn't time to consider what he made of them ... of *her*. She needed to rescue the phone. Who knew how much water had got in? She stretched for it, but they'd drifted further, and even as he scampered to the end of his boat and hung off it himself, they couldn't reach. Lydia held onto Jen as she leaned herself out beyond what felt logistically possible or sensible.

"I can meet you further along the quay," he called. And Jen was about to say yes, that was a marvellous idea, when Max decided to restart the engine. The jolt sent Jen's momentum forwards, and surprised, Lydia didn't have a firm enough grip on Jen's hips. Aided by the high nylon content of her skirt on the smooth plastic, Jen sailed headlong into the water like a liner descending the slipway on her maiden voyage.

Coughing and spluttering Jen surfaced and took a

moment to gain her bearings between the barge and her GoBoat – which seemed to be moving away in the opposite direction.

"I don't know how to reverse, Jen!" Max shouted. Looking around, Jen saw the canal was too narrow for Max to simply circle the boat. A horn blared from behind her as a tour boat made its approach. The man on the barge shouted for her to grab the net. She didn't need telling twice and she felt herself being pulled towards him. Once she'd grabbed onto the barge, the net was pulled up and a hand grasped hers before she was yanked up to lie like a flapping fish on the hot deck.

The first thing she checked, as her cheek dripped on the tarred felting, was that her phone was safely aboard. Turning her head then to the canal, she saw the GoBoat, with the three other girls watching them. They weren't looking particularly worried. More amused, in fact.

"Keep her!" Lydia called from the back of the disappearing boat. "She's staying at the boat hotel." Looking up, Jen saw him nod, clearly understanding where she meant. "Jen! We'll be in Tivoli if you want to join us for the rides. Don't worry, it's on the itinerary!"

Jen stared aghast as it dawned on her that along with taking the mick, they really weren't stopping. It appeared, primarily by the enormous grin on Lydia's face, that her hens were abandoning her, sopping wet in bad clothing, in the hands of a topless stranger. That was NOT normal hen-do practice either.

The chill of a breeze hit the back of her thighs at

approximately the same moment she registered the sodden orange fabric Lydia was waving at her. Apparently, Lydia had made a final grab for her, and hung onto her skirt.

Ah bugger.

Chapter 8

She wasn't sure she could style this out.

"Yes, so, hello," she mumbled, shuffling around to sit on her bottom, obscuring her knickers and unpeeling the wet peasant blouse from her skin. Bloody, bloody Lydia.

"Hello," he replied. His voice had a highly amused tone to it. "Your friends seem to have left you ..."

Jen looked back at the canal. The boat had turned a corner and gone. "Those women are not my friends. Those women are dead to me," Jen said deadpan, "especially the one I live with and who calls herself my sister." It made him smile and she didn't feel so pathetic.

No longer flailing in the water or on the deck, she took a proper look at him. Aside from the blondness, his face was an impressive construction of planes and angles, and he had that fine layer of stubble, more style than laziness. His shortish hair was rebelling, but against what, she had no idea, and the complete package was what she'd class as Exquisite. However, it was his eyes which had her fixed. They were a soft cornflower blue and calmly focused on her. Which brought her consciousness back to her own face, which she was sure looked bleeding awful. She gave her cheeks a quick swipe in the hope of clearing any running mascara. Alice Cooper wasn't a look she was going for.

He looked her up and down, but with concern as opposed to a leer. "Would you like some dry clothes?" Yes, so he had just suggested she get her kit off, but it hadn't felt untoward, more like common sense. He grabbed a folded fleece blanket from a garden chair perched on the deck and handed it to her. "I think I can find a t-shirt and some shorts." He nodded towards a set of glass doors, which Jen supposed to be the galley and wrapping the blanket around her middle, followed as he led the way. He stopped abruptly, causing her almost to walk into him as he turned.

"I'm Yakob," he said. There was the merest hint of an accent, but really only just.

"I'm Jen."

"It's great to meet you, Jen," he said with a smile. It was a friendly smile; he had nice teeth, with one slightly crooked incisor which she particularly liked. Jen was quite happy with flawed perfection. Especially in lieu of those eyes. Being a realist, Jen knew she'd be scouring *Well, Honestly!*'s Pantone reference book until she found its match. She had plans for that blue. "It was nice of you to drop in."

She couldn't help but roll her eyes. "That's very funny, Yakob." He laughed lightly, as he moved on again towards the galley, picking up her phone as they passed. A small piddle of water poured from it, and Jen tried not to sob.

*

Apparently she'd just walked into a magazine spread. Think designer apartment, minimalist, white walled, but with the smooth curves of the ship's hull to soften the starkness. The floor was covered in a pale wood and all the soft furnishings were in various greys, right down to the soft wool blanket hanging over the side of the wooden-framed sofa. Aside from a black cast iron wood-burner, every piece of furniture was modern, but it worked with the old walls. Jen knew she shouldn't be surprised: she'd been seeing it all day around the city – modern and vintage design blended together with ease to give the city a guise of being comfortable in its own skin. Here, in his home, it appeared obscenely smart while still being unspeakably cosy. And it all looked so infuriatingly effortless.

"Wow," she breathed. "Makes my place look like a charity shop." Years of curation by two floundering girls, desperate to hang on to every scrap their parents had ever touched, had rendered their home a showcase of shabby chic, with numerous projects they'd started but not quite finished. This place made her embarrassed about it. She so needed to sort it out when she got home.

He'd walked into a room while she stood gobsmacked in the centre of the lounge area. Considering it was a boat, the space was still bright and airy owing to the full length of the ceiling being bisected by one long strip of glass, showing the early evening blue sky above along with glimpses of the tallest buildings on the canal side.

"That's amazing," Jen breathed.

"I wanted to have a feature window along the end wall," he explained from the room beyond, "so I could look out at the canal, but then the tourist boats would also be looking in. So we did this instead. It's very pretty at night too with the lights from the houses. I have blinds if I don't want them to see in." Jen's mind wandered to what Yakob might be doing at night that he didn't want the neighbours seeing. She felt some heat rise in her face. Dear God, what was the matter with her? She wasn't normally prone to inappropriate thoughts like this.

Blushing and flustered, she hustled to the pristine white and chrome kitchen. It was smart and functional rather than an ostentatious showpiece. A narrow window in the wall gave her a view up onto the quay and cobbles. The whole space had her enchanted and amazed, not least because he was a bloke and this place was immaculate. "*We?* That explains the tidiness. You're married?" She thought it was a fair question, then checked herself with another blush – she was an uninvited guest and a complete stranger at that, it was none of her business.

"Ha! No. No wife, no husband, no children," he insisted, walking back out. She did her very best to keep her eyes on his face, not on his abs, but some things in life are tough. "I meant the architect and me. It's tidy because I'm not here very often. I've left you a towel and some clothes. You can use the shower in there. The canal water isn't the cleanest."

The thought of a shower was highly appealing – until

she realised she was going to be naked in a stranger's home. She tried to suppress her eye goggle: the Scandies were so much more relaxed about their bodies and she didn't want to come across as a prude.

"Great, thanks," she managed, trying to sound as if she de-kitted in people's houseboats all the time.

He handed her his phone. "Text your sister, let her know you're safe." Jen looked at her own phone, a small skirt of water surrounding it on the counter top. She appreciated his tact at this difficult time.

"Am I safe?" she asked, looking at him. *Man*, those eyes. She'd meant it to be jokey, but realised it came out slightly flirty and Jen did not generally deal in flirty.

A slow smile spread across Yakob's face making her suddenly scuttle off into the bedroom, to send her short, but not remotely sweet thoughts to Lydia and to take that shower – in this case a cold one.

He wasn't in the main room when she came out, damp clothes in hand. He'd found her a pair of drawstring shorts and a Kronegaard promotional t-shirt to wear, it's huge logo now emblazoned right across her chest along with an image of the iconic green bottle uncapped and spraying foamy beer from the top. While advertising their wares was the last thing she wanted to do, requesting alternative clothing seemed rude and she already wasn't feeling on her strongest footing.

Creaking from outside told her he'd headed back out on deck. Following him, she saw a drying rack was optimistically primed in the setting sunlight and at the end of the deck, feet dangling off the side above the water sat her host, a cooler box and a bottle opener at his side. He looked back and sent her a beaming smile. It completely took her mind off wearing his clothes. She'd kept her underwear, having hung them off the open porthole handle as she'd showered. Thank god for the minimal fabric in underwear. For once she didn't curse the extortionate pennies to fabric ratio.

"Hello again," she said, registering with a little dismay that he'd pulled on a short sleeved shirt in her absence.

"Hello again." There was that smile as he looked her over, assessing her as she wore his clothes. She was just going to have to accept he was amused by her. Shuffling aside he made space for Jen to join him in his twilight sun spot. She noted that he hadn't done the buttons on his shirt. Well, it was a warm evening, so totally understandable and Jen approved.

"Beer?" he asked, taking his phone back as she offered it to him.

"Love one," she replied, following his nod to the cooler. There was a range of bottles inside, all Kronegaard she noticed, but then she supposed it was their home territory, so she could make allowances. She picked one in a brown bottle to match his. It wasn't one she'd seen before. The only Kronegaard beers she knew came in their famous green bottles.

She settled into her spot next to him and at first sat in awkward silence. He didn't appear to feel awkward however.

He seemed completely relaxed, simply enjoying the setting sun and calm of the ending day. Gradually, she tried to follow his lead on the relaxation as they sank the first of their beers. A couple of kayakers paddled past them and a few more GoBoats, the passing picnic tables increasingly stocked with evening drinks. Finally, ready to talk again, she pointed to a Tupperware box at his side which he'd regularly move to be directly in the receding sunlight.

"What's that?"

"Your phone," he said. "I've switched it off, removed the SIM and put all of it in rice to draw out the water. Keeping it warm helps too. In a couple of days, you might get lucky and have it working again."

"Really?" She'd been trying to hold onto her grief until she was back in her hotel room, her panic locked away in her head until then. "Does that work?"

"Did for me when I dropped mine in a toilet. Worth a try."

Delighted there was a plan afoot she held up her bottle to clink it with him.

"Skaal," he said. It sounded like *Skorl*, and she returned it to the best of her ability, which made him smile again. He obviously found her entertaining, and not generally having that role when in company, Jen didn't quite know what to make of it.

"So Jen, is this your first time in Copenhagen?"

"It is," she said with a nod, "it's been on my wish list for years, but you know, 'life gets in the way'."

"And other than the underside of a GoBoat, what have

you seen?"

"Well, I did have a to-see list on my ..." she barely managed to point at the Tupperware box, feeling a lump beginning to form in her throat but reining it in so as not to completely overreach her prat quota for the day by crying in front of him, "however, as you've seen, my travel-mates are a rather unruly bunch and do not respect lists and planning." His chuckle was somewhat disconcerting. Clearly he thought she was being funny and actually she wasn't, not about the value of planning. Robert would have been nodding with her. Perhaps Danes were different. She gave him the benefit of the doubt. "I had a detailed plan on my laptop, but ... well, I had to cobble together a replacement on the plane." She reeled off the points of interest she could remember, which was all of them, probably mangling the pronunciation of some.

"That is very ... comprehensive," he said. She couldn't quite work out whether he was impressed or amused.

"Well, if you only have a couple of days, you need to be efficient," Jen said seriously. Some people – Lydia, Alice and Max for example – apparently didn't get that.

"And what about free time?" he asked. His eyes had a twinkle to them.

She didn't know what he meant. "The whole weekend is free time. It's ... well it's the *weekend*." That was the same in Danish, surely? "Weekend" was one of those universal words, wasn't it?

"Yes," he said, "but I do not hear any time allocated to simply walking through the streets, along the canals, looking and breathing." He gave a light wave to their surroundings.

Jen could only blink at him. It made him laugh. "I am teasing you, Jen." She released a slightly unnerved laugh. Other than Lydia, no one ever teased her. "It is a good list of things to do," he said placating her, "but perhaps you should not walk too fast between the sights. You might miss some lovely things; the buildings, the hidden court-yards, quirky fountains, the balconies."

Well yes, that did make sense, she thought, scanning the canal in front of them and the quaysides. There was lots to see when you took a moment to look. Tall hollyhocks in the cobbled doorways, carved wooden double doors, bicycles meandering along everywhere. Perhaps, she should assign some meandering time in her numerous trip lists at home. She was pretty sure though that breathing would come naturally.

"But most importantly," she continued, keen to move him on from the teasing and regain her footing, "I managed to see the Kronegaard museum this morning."

He gave her an odd look. "Kronegaard? Really?" He pronounced it the Danish way, *krorn-gorr,* rolling the *kr.*

"Oh yes. I've always wanted to go. The guide book said it would take two hours, but I took three. It was wonderful. Have you been?"

"I have," he replied, his eyebrows slightly raised.

"Are you *from* Copenhagen?" she asked.

"Born and bred." It struck her as a British phrase, but then from what she'd experienced so far all the Danes'

English was excellent. "And what did you think of the museum?"

And then she was off; waxing lyrical about how inspiring it had been and how the corporate story had changed her perception, not of the brand per se, but of the business choices. She gushed about Henrik, his hard work and his legacy. Mouth going ten to the dozen, her eyes kept flicking to his face, noting how his expression kept changing as she shared her opinions.

"You've been lots of times, haven't you?" she said.

"How could you tell?"

"Your face. While I described it all, your face was this mix of pride and concentration. Pride at the bits I liked and concentration at the bits I didn't. It was interesting to watch. You could have got all defensive at the criticism."

He shrugged. "It's good to hear what visitors think. I guess when you come from a small city, in a very small country, you do feel a huge sense of pride in a success story. And the criticism? Well, there is nothing to learn by getting angry."

"I think you Copenhageners have lots to be proud of," she said, nodding out at the current view.

"Do you recognise the barge?" he asked. "It's one of the old Kronegaard delivery barges, it took beer across the city's canals, or brought in the raw supplies." He looked up at Jen, his eyes dancing. "Once it would have reeked of beer. In some spaces I can still smell the hops."

"Really? I saw pictures of them in the museum, I just hadn't made the connection."

"So are you a Kronegaard fan?" he asked. He did a very good job of making his interest appear genuine. Lord knew she was rarely faced with any when she talked to her friends about her passion for beer. They were happy just to drink it.

"Ha! No." Was it wrong to enjoy the surprise on his face? It clearly wasn't the answer he was expecting after her gushing about the museum. Jen took another swig of her beer. "From what I saw today, I like the Krone family, their tenacity, their vision, I'm just not a fan of what the brand has become. It's just another conglomerate, chomping its way through smaller brewers and plundering the market for the biggest share. There's no heart in that. It's nothing personal against the family, although before today I figured it was all corporate-owned now. One of the boards in the museum said the family are still major shareholders."

His expression had turned somewhat more concentrated. She liked that look too.

"It's a huge family, many of them have jobs there."

"Well, what's family for, if they can't land you a job?" she said, blithely.

"No, they all have to be fully qualified in some field before they are let in," he said, before adding, "from what I understand."

"Yeah, yeah," she said, leaning back on her elbow.

"It's an established family, Jen, you can't run a business like that, or uphold the standards and credibility in society like they have, without enforcing some tough rules." His voice was slightly tight and it made her look up at him. "I know someone who works there." Fair enough.

"So, the boat?" she prompted him, eager to get him back to his barge story, because she liked the way he talked about it. As she'd hoped his face lit up again as he recounted how he'd got a tip-off the brewery was clearing out an old dock property and a couple of barges were due to be scrapped.

"I fell in love with this one and over three years spent weekends working on her, finally finding a suitable mooring spot and moving in."

"Wait a minute, you mean you did all this? Yourself?"

"Well, no," he said, which sounded more likely. "The hull repairs needed a boat builder, but the water-proofing and the building and the decorating, that was me. And some friends helped, though some were more useful than others. Some I'd make sit in the floor with a beer and a guitar, so they kept their hands off any tools."

"You're obviously very creative," she said. She was still blown away by the interior.

"Ha! I don't know about that." He stroked his hand fondly on the deck as he spoke. "It was a labour of love, though. I've had my happiest times here."

"Oh Lord, it's some secret shag-pad, isn't it?" Jen asked, the beer and the encroaching night curbing her filters. He laughed.

"Secret yes, shag-pad no. I just travel a lot and I'm not in Copenhagen so often. I wanted somewhere special to come to."

"Oh right."

"And I haven't got an ex-wife hidden in the suburbs with

numerous children, if that is what you're thinking. This is it. This is me." He held his hands out from his sides, palms up. Jen was touched by the gesture which was both humble and offering at the same time. And for some reason she was pleased about the no wife thing.

His phone dinged. Glancing at it, he barked a laugh and showed it to her. Lydia had replied to her stroppy text. The message read *Wish you were beer!* It took a moment for Jen to clock it was a selfie. Lydia's mouth was open in a scream, and yet her eyes weren't filled with terror. Her hair was also standing upright. It made no sense, until Jen saw that the background was the ground.

"Oh dear God," she gasped. Lydia was taking selfies upside down on very high fairground rides. Just the thought made her stomach turn. A second message dinged in to ask whether Jen was joining them in Tivoli. Jen shuddered.

"Would you like to stay for dinner, Jen?" Yakob laughed. "I was planning to get sushi delivered."

In her head it was a no brainer. Staying here, calmly enjoying the evening on a beer barge was a million times more appealing than dodging hellish rides with her traitorous sister. Normally, she'd have reluctantly gone to keep an eye on Lydia, but considering they'd ditched her, she figured Alice and Max could have the pleasure. However, there was a nagging in her conscience that perhaps newly engaged women shouldn't be having dinner with strange men. She questioned whether Robert would see it as a necessary part of thanking a good Samaritan. Possibly an old, wizened Samaritan, but not this buff one next to her.

Jen weighed it up. Technically, staying a bit longer, having some food could be classed as part of getting over her canal shock. He was still Samaritan-ing her and such kindness shouldn't be snubbed, in her book. It wasn't like it was a date, which would be a complete no-no. And of course her clothes were still drying, so it made sense to stay until she could take them with her. That was just practical.

She took a moment of looking him square in the face before she gave her answer. "Sounds great," she said. It was what Lydia would have wanted her to do, and Lydia was in charge this weekend after all, not her.

Chapter 9

There was a seating area at the other end of the boat; a bench seat and table, complete with more fleecy IKEA blankets for the cool of the evening. Being quite far north, night had fallen now and the windows around them were illuminating. Table laid, Jen took a seat and watched the canal traffic, in this instance a pair of swans gliding past. The air was full of the laughter of passing groups and the murmurs of hand-holding couples. She wondered when the last time she'd done this was, kicking back during the day without a list to guide her or dictate her time. She couldn't recall. And yet it didn't make her feel anxious, or perturbed. Quite the opposite in fact.

He sat down beside her on the bench and settled a platter of sushi in front of them, before leaning to the cool box and grabbing a couple of beers for them.

At such close proximity she got acquainted with the scent of his aftershave. Pine, lemon and something else. Very nice

"So, Jen," he asked, musing over the food for a moment, before plucking out a California roll and nodding for her to tuck in, "what is it you do for a living?"

"Marketing. In Westhampton. In the UK." Thinking about her real life was suddenly unwelcome. Here in this unexpected cocoon of calm she was feeling a sense of welcome respite. Bullet point answers felt like the best way to deflect, along with turning the question back to him. "You?"

"Corporate Finance, Denmark and the UK," he fired back, clearly taking the micky. She stuck her tongue out at him. He was funny. It was clear he found her funnier. "And what is it you market, Jen?"

Jen wished he hadn't asked. She took a long swig of her beer, but he waited.

"Um, so I don't want to tell you. It's the least sexy thing ever." She filled her mouth with a small maki roll, but that didn't save her either.

"Now I'm really intrigued. Come on. Tell me." Those gorgeous eyes were wide with anticipation and his mouth was mischievously pinched. That and his firm tone was irresistible.

Defeated and wishing the light had faded completely now, Jen hung her head and mumbled, "Inco pads." Marketing manager or not, she was incapable of projecting any pizazz regarding her own job.

His brow furrowed. "Inco pads? What is that?"

Jen could only groan and sink further into her seat, hoping the blankets would swallow her.

"I can Google it, Jen," he said, "or you can put your best spin on it."

She let herself deflate melodramatically.

"Stow the Google threats, Yakob. I'll confess." She took another swallow of the beer as if to brace herself.

"Well firstly, yay for you for not knowing what they are. Inco pads are incontinence pads, personal hygiene aids to save people the embarrassment of involuntary uterine leaks. Heard of *Tena* pants? Well we aren't them, but we're growing, and ours are organic, made using Fairtrade biodegradable materials." There, that was the corporate spiel. The cringe was all her own.

He was stunned. She'd rendered him speechless with talk of disposable pants and wee pads. Jen almost – *almost* – felt a sense of achievement.

"That's very ... commendable," he managed. "That's work that changes lives."

"Don't take the piss," she spluttered, because clearly he was, but he was doing it so sincerely, it made her laugh. He made her sound like the Mother Theresa of weak bladders. "See, now," she scolded, "you've made me make a wee pun."

"I'm not! It is important work, that hopefully I won't ever need, but if I do, it'll be the Fairtrade ones I go for." He was trying to be serious, but he was clearly utterly tickled by the conversation.

"Stop it! Look, it was my first job out of uni and the company is growing, so I can't be doing too badly ..." Jen wondered why she was getting defensive. She wasn't a fan of her job, why should he be? To be fair the job had been in the right place at the exact time she needed it.

He held up his hands in surrender. "I'm not teasing, honestly. It just wasn't what I expected, that's all."

"Don't worry, I haven't taken offence," she let him off the hook, but it was funny watching him back-pedal. "It's a job. It pays the bills. But it isn't a *passion*. God, that would be sad, wouldn't it?" She took the last slug of her bottle and on cue he produced a new one from the cooler and uncapped it for her. She scoffed some sashimi in the meantime.

"And the passion is?" Yakob asked, quirking an eyebrow. No way was she going *there*. It wasn't that she was ashamed of her passion, just that after the inco pad confession, she was reluctant to offer up another opportunity to be ridiculed.

He noticed her reluctance to answer. "Everything OK?"

"I'm just wondering where you get all these different Kronegaard beers from," she said, considering the label, buying time and perhaps a segue to a different subject. "We only have the standard lager in the UK, the one in the green bottle. These are different recipes, more crafty, and in brown bottles."

"Kronegaard sell a wider range in Denmark," he said then added, "you're very discerning with your beer taste." She waited for him to add "for a girl," but he didn't. He made it sound like praise.

Jen dropped her eyes and supplied quietly, "That's the passion," before hurriedly taking a sip and waiting for the laughter.

"Beer?" He wasn't laughing.

"Beer."

"Really?"

She nodded and waited for his response, which when it came wasn't what she'd been expecting.

"What made you pick the first bottle from the cooler? They were all Kronegaard. It's what my local shop stocks."

"Primarily I chose the bottle," she shrugged. "It's brown."

"Favourite colour?"

"No," she said emphatically. "I'm not eight, and who picks brown as a favourite colour? Brown glass keeps the beer better. The flavour that is. Green glass not so much. Beer in a green bottle is more liable to skunking; being lightstruck and going off. Take Kronegaard for example," she went on, pointing to the logo and bottle on her top, then hastily withdrawing her hand as she realised she was drawing attention to her chest, "their green bottle might be identifiable worldwide, but if you're about the flavour, you'll pick brown glass every time." Jen saw a look of interest spread across his face, and it cheered her. In her experience blokes liked talking about beer, and Yakob apparently was no exception.

"Interesting coming from a marketing person. You are in fact saying, in spite of Kronegaard having an iconic bottle, you'd still pick a different beer, *because* of the icon."

Jen had to think about it, but, "Yup. Pretty much. The icon thing – it's all about style not substance. These corporate beers are pretty soulless."

"Soulless? Harsh." She assumed he was playing devil's advocate.

"Oh, don't get me started. Really, I could spout about the corporate giants and their ditching flavour for profits, but it's a nice evening." Turned in her seat to face him, Jen was relaxing into her beer spiel. She'd had this discussion many times with Robert's friends, trying to educate them.

"So what do you suggest they do?" he asked. He was now turned to face her, mirroring her posture. Anyone passing would have assumed they were a couple.

"Oh nothing," Jen replied, surprising him. "They're the beer equivalent of the latest boy-band. The music is pap, but it brings the new audience through for better bands to win over later. So the Kronegaards out there can be the lagers to start their palates – and a low bench mark it is too – and the craft beers can impress them later. The big guns can continue doing what they do, and leave the rest of the market to us. The key is to show them there's better to be had. People like to find 'better' things. It's about one-upmanship and looking smarter."

"Us?" This time his eyebrows didn't quirk – they jumped simultaneously. "You said 'leave the market to us'."

"Oh, so well yes," she said flustered. The focus was back on her. She could pontificate merrily about beer as a concept, but her participation in it had her on less confident ground. And yet, his attention ignited a spark of boldness. She wasn't likely to see him after tonight, so what did it matter what he thought of her? She should put herself out there and own it. "My passion. I brew beer. Craft beer. Just from home, as a hobby in my spare time. I've been doing it for years. My dad taught me, and I'm OK at it." She stopped and reconsidered. "No, actually, I'm good at it. I've won awards."

There. She'd said it, and she'd explained it with pride and honestly, it felt bloody great. Somewhere over time she'd come to feel shy about telling people about it. Mentioning her awards felt like bigging herself up or showing off. Why was that? After all, nobody looked down on women who baked. It was all making, *crafting*, wasn't it? Women had been brewing for over ten thousand years. It wasn't like she was suggesting establishing a unicorn farm now, was it? Unusual perhaps, but ridiculous, no. She looked up prepared to take any flak from Yakob, but he was looking at her with an expression of ... well, from what she could garner, a sort of awe or at least mighty impressed. It occurred to her she should mention her passion was coming to an end, that she was about to pack it all away. But that would have sounded odd, considering her arms had been waving about with excitement during her speech.

"You're right, that *is* passion," he said, carefully. Jen nodded. In spite of working on the assumption she didn't care what he, a total stranger, thought, it turned out to have been a fib, as she was now experiencing some trepidation as to his opinion.

"Come on then," she said, defiantly. "Hit me with the abuse."

"What abuse?" He cocked his head, questioning.

"Whenever I tell guys I brew, they scoff because 'girls don't know about beer', or say I should stick to knitting, or they suggest coming round to sample it and offer their advice. Come on Yakob, just get it over with."

"Nope, not doing any of that, but I have to admit I am

tempted to come around and try it." The thought of him in her home threatened to send her slightly a dither. The silence between them as they gazed at each other was thick and Jen found herself on the verge of extending him a breathy invite. He broke it before she did so. "My *Morfar*, my mother's father, he brewed too." From the change in his expression, Jen could immediately see that Yakob had been very fond of his grandfather, the tenderness of whatever memories he was running through was obvious. "He used to let me choose the hops we would use in his experimenting, talking me through the differences they'd make. He let me have free rein and try whatever I liked." Yakob appeared lost in the reminiscing, his voice almost wistful. "The smell of hops remind me of him and our experimenting. Maybe that's why I love this barge so much."

"I know exactly what that's like," Jen gushed, amazed they were having this conversation. "I have a small brewing shed, and the scents in there, they're the scents of my childhood and sharing that time with my dad as we moved through each step of each brew. It's like … it's like he's with me."

"It sounds like we had the same connection with them, you with your dad, me with my Morfar. It was the purest thing making something together."

For a while they both sat lost in their own thoughts and perhaps the pleasure of a kindred experience. Then Yakob leaned away. For a second Jen thought the conversation had upset him, the memories of his grandfather being too much. Lord knew she could get teary thinking about her parents at the slightest thing. As it turned out, Yakob had other plans to add to the moment. Suddenly, at the flick of a switch she was surrounded with tiny white lights, and for a moment she thought she'd been transported into a chandelier. Several tourists on the opposite bank stopped to stare.

"A bit much?" Yakob asked, his voice a little deeper, than before. The entire deck was covered with fairy lights, it was almost covered in sparkle. "The first sets were gifts from my nieces, and then other family members kept bringing more. It's become a bit of a joke for them now."

"It's magical," Jen whispered.

"Good, my nieces will be pleased when I tell them you thought so. They'll tell me they already knew. They are a precocious pair of ten-year-olds." He popped some rice and salmon in his mouth, still grinning at the thought of them. "Tell me about your family, Jen," he said, once he'd finished chewing. His tone was tender. "I know about your ex-sister."

Jen shovelled another piece of tuna in, stalling for time. She was used to everyone knowing what had happened to them, and if others asked she usually artfully turned the questions on them without really answering. People were generally happy to talk about themselves. But now she thought about that "this is me" gesture he'd made. He'd been open with her, and after the "passion" reveal and the knicker-flashing, she had half exposed herself to him already. Besides, it wasn't as if she was going to see him again after this weekend. Telling him wasn't so very difficult, especially if she focused on the comforting flicker of the tealights on the table.

She told him about the death of their parents, giving up her graduate job at the brewery before she'd even started and looking after Lydia. It didn't sound like a sob story, but she wasn't glossing over it either, like she tended to do, like it was nothing. Because it hadn't been nothing. It had been terribly, *terribly* hard.

"Do you feel you missed out?" he asked. He wasn't giving her platitudes or shying away from the conversation. His plate was empty now, and Jen was mopping up the last dregs of soy sauce.

"The job, yes. A social life? Maybe, but I was never really a party girl." She felt she'd said enough. "And what about you? On the subject of family, you insist there's no partner, and I can't see any signs of anyone here, so why are you single, Yakob?" At first he didn't say anything, like he hadn't really thought about it before. Jen gave him the time. She wasn't in a hurry, enjoying the relaxed cosy ambiance which she instinctively knew was the *hygge* everyone wanged on about. There was music coming from an open window above them, slow and sultry. It entertained her while she waited. However, instead of answering he got to his feet and extended his hand.

"Dance?" She looked around confused, then realised the deck was a perfect dance floor and the lights against the balmy night air made for the perfect mood. She let him off the confession hook. It could keep. Taking his hand she let him pull her up and across to him, where he draped it lightly on his shoulder before loosely holding her waist. They moved slowly in time to the music, his soft tuneful humming by her ear making her skin tingle and yearn.

"I seem to have a knack of attracting women who are less than honest," he said with a sigh. "It has left me slightly burned." That made sense. "Maybe," he suggested, sounding more upbeat, "I'm now only interested in women I fish out of the canal." His smile was wolfish. It made her feel funny in her knickers.

"Understandable," Jen said with a nod, "Copenhagen's famous for its mermaid. They're probably in constant supply."

She was expecting a quick reply, but he didn't say anything. He was simply gazing at her. It made her eyes widen.

He spun her then, making her laugh and feel dizzy all at once. "Jen? Can I ask you something?" He sounded quite serious.

"Certainly," she said, "but I've been drinking so I reserve the right to lie." She was at that tipsy but lucid point where comebacks came easily.

"Fair," he said, with an understanding dip of his brow. "But then I reserve the right to ask you again later."

"Fair," she agreed.

He dipped her, and though surprised by it, she didn't yelp as she felt completely safe in his strong arms. "Would you like to stay tonight?"

She opened her mouth but couldn't answer.

When the moment became too long. He righted her and spun her out from him and then back in.

"Don't worry, Jen. It doesn't matter. It was just an idea." He didn't seem offended.

But it *did* matter, because her head was in a spin and it wasn't from the dancing. Every inch of her body wanted to say yes. She instinctively desired to stay in his company and see where it led. She stopped the dancing, and took a step back, though not releasing his hand. Letting go right then might have felled her.

"That would be lovely, Yakob," she said carefully and faltered a moment as his eyes flared, "but I can't. I'm sorry." His tender stroking of the knuckles on her left hand focused her mind. Dinner with a man she'd just met was dodgy enough, staying over was a not part of her moral code. She'd made a promise to Robert. Jen prided herself on being a woman of her word and she was already walking a fine line. If the tables were turned she'd obviously expect Robert to decline, too.

Looking about her, at the lights, the reflections on the water, at the cosy seat with the blankets where they could sit for hours yet with it becoming harder and harder for her to stick to her resolve, Jen saw she needed to leave. It was all too lovely. All too tempting.

"I should go," she said. He started to protest, but she stopped him. "It's been a wonderful evening, Yakob. More than I can express, but I can't stay." He held her gaze for a short moment, then gave her a tiny nod.

"I'll walk you back." He wasn't cross, or making her feel guilty, but while she didn't feel she deserved an escort, she sensed this wasn't a point he was going to be swayed on.

Which was fine, as she had no idea of the way back to her hotel and more importantly having passed up other things this evening, any extra time in his company wasn't going to be added to that list.

Chapter 10

Jen was worried things might be awkward now, but she needn't have been. She'd ducked into the cabin to change into her top and shoes while he'd packed things away and switched off the fairy lights, and when she returned, they were back to how they'd been before. He said she could keep the shorts and politely didn't mention her garish clothes, but laughed when she explained this was not her usual attire, that Lydia had pranked her with them.

"I already like your ex-sister," he said. Something about that warmed her even more to him.

She followed him down the gangplank, wishing this had been the way she'd boarded instead of the humiliating way it had actually panned out. He stepped onto the cobbles and stopped, bringing her to a close stop too. A light breeze wafted his aftershave at her again. Pine, lemon and *sage*. How had she not placed that immediately? She was off her game, clearly. Jen was exceedingly proud of her nose, it was what had helped her build and refine the flavours of her beer. Jim Arbuthnot for example, her brewing rival at the county shows, *his* olfactory skills were shot, given away by his inability to tell when his shirt needed changing. And while he was able to follow recipes for beer, he didn't have the imagination and flavour appreciation to know which new combinations might work together.

"Jen?" Yakob asked, touching her upper arm lightly.

"Sorry?"

"You suddenly seemed miles away."

"Oh, sorry, I was thinking about the way you smell." His eyes widened. Oh crap, that had sounded stalkery and not a little deranged. She clarified herself quickly. "I mean, I was identifying your aftershave." Was that weird? Would he think she was a nutjob? Probably waaay too late for that already and yes, that was an incredulous look he was giving her.

"Really? You can name it just from sniffing it?" He wasn't weirded out. He was intrigued, as if it was her party trick.

"No, that would suggest I had way too much time on my hands. I mean, I can smell pine, lemon and sage."

"Huh," he shrugged. He seemed slightly impressed, whilst also a little disappointed. "You might be right. I don't know. I just like it."

"So do I." It was out of her mouth before the filter kicked in. Her blush of embarrassment was instantaneous. "I mean, it's a good blend." This was not going as smoothly as she would have hoped for. She bit her lips together, stopping herself from uttering another daft word, while he looked at her as if kindly stifling a belly laugh.

With the Tupperware box of rice and phone bits tucked in one hand, Yakob gesticulated with the other for her to lead on along the cobbled quay.

"Tell me more about your brewing," he said, walking without any haste, at her side. "I've been thinking about it."

"You have? Why?" Oh, the times she'd had her own beer processes mansplained back to her. Or maybe he was about to tease her again. She braced herself.

"Because I am intrigued, Jen." He said it so earnestly that she couldn't help but drop her defences. "I am excited about your excitement about it."

"Okaay," she said, unsure. Perhaps he was playing the long-game on taking the piss.

"Don't you find when someone is as enthusiastic about something as you clearly are about beer, that it becomes infectious?"

"No." Jen shook her head, immediately thinking of Robert. "I can honestly say other people do not share my enthusiasm. They'll drink the beer, but they don't see it as anything other than a pass-time, when actually it's in my veins. I don't eat anything without thinking what beer would go best with it."

The glow of a near street lamp showed his smile as it widened. Perhaps it wasn't odd that he'd been thinking about it, if he liked beer too. How many times had she critiqued a beer without ever being able to tell the brewer?

"Don't stop," he encouraged, extending his hand to her and nodding her on, on their route, "go on." It was almost as if he knew she needed to say these things, to declare them. Taking his hand was both easy and reassuring.

"So, I have a small range of beers that I already make;

IPAs, Golden Ales, a Porter, a Stout and a Barley Wine and I planned to make a seasonal beer for Christmas." She didn't mention the wedding beer. TMI.

"We do this in Denmark, the Christmas beer," he said, "it is extremely popular. Every brewery has one. This was my Morfar's favourite brewing time."

Jen knew he was really listening to her. He wasn't pushing – he waited very patiently in fact, but the encouragement was implicit.

"I've got a new fruit beer lined up for the next County Show too."

"Consider entering the national brewing competitions Jen, just to start building up a profile."

Oh. She hadn't got her head around Nationals, but he appeared sure. And his interest in the entire brewing thing was clearly genuine. It made her think.

"Yakob, you asked me earlier if you thought I'd missed out on things. Do you feel you've missed out?"

He looked at her surprised. "Why do you think I've missed out?"

"Only that, when you talked about brewing with your Morfar earlier, I sensed you loved the creativity and it's freedom, but you say you work in corporate finance and those things don't really marry up in my head. So I'm guessing you made a choice somewhere along the line and while you can let the creativity out on the barge, I wonder whether you might have turned your back on a creative calling?"

He stumbled slightly and Jen saw his expression was

somewhat stunned. "No, no, it wasn't anything like that. My parents saw I was good at maths and encouraged me down that path." The light way he said it, made Jen suspect their "encouragement" hadn't been so welcome.

"Didn't you want to decide for yourself?" she asked carefully, thinking how his grandfather had allowed him that freedom when they had home-brewed together.

His smile was slightly tight. If she hadn't been looking at his face so much in the last few hours, she might have missed it.

"I think my nostalgia has given you the wrong impression, Jen. My family is intense but wonderful. I love them dearly. And my job is good, I enjoy it very much. Much as you might not believe it," he said with a genuine smile, "numbers and business can be creative too."

"I suppose so," Jen conceded. Heaven knew she had to be creative with her inco pad marketing ideas, and the crampons were going to need some act of god. "Crafting is still different though. Like you said earlier, it's *pure*." Jen knew without a shadow of a doubt that what she shared with her dad, and he with his Morfar, was about connections, with each other, but primarily with the materials and your own skills.

"I don't know Jen," he said slowly, shaking his head, "I've heard about your lists and I'd put money on your spreadsheets being a work of art." There, he was back to the teasing and she knew he was deflecting. Considering how kind he'd been in light of her various embarrassments this evening, she left the subject, and also because she was caught in the conflict of having to agree with him about her spreadsheets. They were a particular point of pride. Instead she was content with simply looking down the streets as they passed by on their walk and asking Yakob what the buildings were on the opposite side of the water. In the times between, the low murmur of the continuing canal traffic was accompaniment enough, as they made their way, still hand in hand. She liked the feel of it, her hand warm in his. She wasn't inclined to let it go. Knowing this had her off kilter; it felt right, but she knew there was something wrong about it too. Moreover, she didn't know how this would play out when they reached their destination and the trepidation was brewing in her, causing a tightness in her chest.

They crossed a pedestrian bridge that looked like yacht sails. Her hotel lay just a little way along.

"It's been a magical evening, Yakob," she said, feeling torn as they reached the boat. Their time was running out and while she knew it had to, it filled her with a sense of loss. "One I won't forget. But you know, I don't even know your name?"

"Yule," he supplied. "Yakob Yule." He lightly shook the hand he was holding, making a joke of it. Neither of them felt like laughing. The banter of earlier suddenly felt too superficial for this moment. His eyes fell to their hands and he appeared to be deliberating something.

"Jen Attison," she gave him in exchange. Never had her own name sounded sadder. The skin of his fingers stroked the full length of hers as he released them. Her hand felt instantly cold. He glanced away, appearing discomfited. Was he feeling the same physical deprivation she was?

Spurred by something, Yakob took a step closer. "It has been a pleasure, Jen," he said, his voice low, the deep gravelly timbre resonating in her belly. He handed her the Tupperware box. Their fingers touched and she looked up, suddenly aware that she really didn't want this to be over yet, whatever *this* was.

His eyes searched her face, flicking slowly between her eyes, then down to her mouth and back. She knew her eyes had done the same. The pure want in his face was impossible to mistake and it made her breath hitch and the sensation in her belly grow heavier. His pupils were huge in the dark of the evening, the cornflower blue all but gone. The wind whipped an errant lock of her hair lightly across her face and Yakob tucked it back behind her ear, Jen instinctively leaning into the motion, appreciating the care, savouring the caress. He retook her hand, at first a tentative meeting of fingertips, then, when she responded to his touch, his fingers resolutely entwining with hers. They gazed into each other's eyes, the quiet disrupted only by the thumping of her heart in her throat. Then he leaned in and brushed his lips against hers, the softest of touches, but enough to tilt everything she knew.

Jen held still, trying to steady her breathing, trying to keep a clear head. She might sooner have tamed the tide. His breathing was equally ragged. She felt the heat of him and wanting it closer, cast aside any reticence and leaned in. Only, he moved with her, pulling back, leaving her hanging; wanting but lingering. Her brow pulled together. Had she read this wrong? A blush of embarrassment began to creep up her throat but then a small smile twitched on his lips giving her a glimpse of that crooked incisor that did things for her, as his eyes flicked again between her eyes and mouth. No, it wasn't a slight, nor was he playing her: she could read the desire as clear as day on his face. He *wanted* her. He wet his lower lip with the tip of his tongue. He might not have noticed doing it, but *she* had and it mesmerised her. With his free hand he traced a feather-light fingertip from just below her ear slowly along the edge of her jaw, which threatened to melt her completely. Her want became *need* and it took her a befuddled moment to understand what was detaining them. He was holding back, waiting for her assent.

"Yakob," she whispered. She didn't need to say anymore, the plea in her voice was enough. His fingers slid swiftly back along her jaw to thread into her hair like they'd finally been called home and suddenly his mouth was on hers, his body eclipsing the remaining distance between them.

It started as a hungry kiss, their lips keen to discover everything about the other's mouth immediately, almost as if already fearing it wasn't to last. But with the realization that this was really happening, things slowed down, morphing into a relieved softness as if their lips had just recognized each other like long-lost lovers. Then came a teasing approach from Yakob: he nipped her lips, chased her tongue and faked retreats. Heat shot up through her chest and down to her belly. The warmth of his breath intermingled with his scent making her light-headed. Sensing his breathing rapidly accelerating Jen dropped the Tupperware box onto the cobbles and flung her hand up around his neck to run her hand along his skin. He let go of her other hand to cup her cheek as if she were the most coveted of prizes. The moan that escaped her she could do nothing about and she was forced to steady herself with a hand on his hip. Her hand on his skin under his shirt sent a shudder down his spine which she found as exhilarating as the tilt of his hips that followed.

He tasted of beer and soya sauce. It wasn't just a kiss with this man, but with the waterside city itself. To Jen, this was what *dreamy* tasted like. A low growl in his throat and the fast heartbeat she could feel through his shirt, told her he felt the same, as his hand moved assured from her jaw, trailing a fingertip down her side, to snake inch by inch to the small of her back to draw her closer, deepening their kiss as he did. The clinch of it and his obvious arousal pressing against her caused her insides to contract and her fingers to dig into the skin at his nape, pulling him to her. She basked in his desire, utterly lost in the moment and sensations he was sending through her body. His hand travelled from her back to slowly trace her waist, as if he was storing the contours of her body to memory. Her hand followed suit, from his hip to his face, learning the planes of his jaw and cheekbones, shivering at the light scratch of his stubble on her skin. She drew his face even closer, exploring further with her tongue. He mirrored her determination to know more.

Her every nerve was alive with each touch and shared breath. The breeze off the water did nothing to cool the heat between them. The city around them, the low-level hum of cars and cycle bells, the thrum of the waterbus in the harbour behind, or the murmurs from the GoBoats as they passed below, all added to the otherworldliness of the moment, as he held her in his arms, in a state of bliss which she couldn't imagine ever getting enough of.

This. This was pure heaven. Surely, she thought, there had been no better kiss, in the world, ever.

"I reserved the right to ask you again, Jen," he said, when they reluctantly drew apart, for no other reason than needing air. His eyes smouldered as they searched hers for the answer. Jen could see they were filled with a heady mix of hope, desire and lust, which threatened to ignite things in her all over again. She had no idea how long they'd stood there kissing. Her breathing was just short of panting, her heart threatened to burst out of her chest and her knees wanted to buckle. He pushed her lightly by the shoulders to lean against a lamp post, recognising she needed the support, the smile on his face saying the fact amused and pleased him. He leaned against her, and nuzzled her neck, kissing up her throat to her ear, increasing the pressure as he went, presumably to stop her from sliding down the iron work. The absolute pleasure of his mouth on her skin made it nigh on impossible to give clear thought to anything, but behind her closed eyes her lust drew what little thought there was towards how this might play out back on his boat. Oh man ...

He pulled his face back from her skin to look at her and then stepped back, giving her space to answer. His hair was a mess – more than before. She was responsible for that. The thought made her smile. Her eyes darted between his, her entire body wanting to fling itself at him anew. He took her other hand and she clasped his tight. As things stood, she wasn't sure her heartrate would ever recover. And he was asking her to stay. To do that again. And more.

A clock somewhere across the water struck and broke the spell. It felt like a punch to the gut and she was already breathless. The world beyond their little bell jar came rushing back at her, with a huge side order of guilt. She had a fiancé. She was on her hen-do. She could not be having kisses with other men. Especially epic, mind-blowing kisses like this one. There were rules about such things, and she'd agreed to them. Promises made were promises to be kept.

Shaken, she stood up straight, pushing away from the post. She saw the hope die in his eyes, but he nodded, understanding. He released her hand and now she understood the meaning of bereft. They both busied themselves for a moment, looking elsewhere, righting clothes, composing themselves.

"Well, then Yakob," she said turning back with a small smile, but feeling stricken, "I guess this is thank you and goodbye." Suddenly everything seemed more formal, the intimate moment gone.

"And you, Jen. As you said, it's been … magical." Neither of them thought the word was sufficient now, but for want of something superior it would have to do. "I hope your trip inspires you and that you fall in love with my city." They stood looking at each other for a long moment, both trying to get a handle on their breathing and belting hearts, both watching the other for some sign. Finally, Yakob ducked his head, stuffed his hands in his pockets, and headed off.

He managed a single step. Turning back he planted a swift soft kiss on her cheek and with a smile said, "Have a *beer*lliant day tomorrow."

Watching him leave, Jen pushed her guilt aside, desperate to save a grain of the magic, just for tonight. She considered the last few hours. They might not have been what she'd planned, but they had been some of the most astonishing hours she'd ever had. *And* he'd made a beer pun.

British tourist Lydia Attison became the 3 millionth passenger on Tivoli's *Vertigo*, winning her a Tivoli Gardens human-sized teddy bear. Lydia who is missing a leg, is seen here upside down in a selfie she took on the ride which rises 30 metres above the park, taking 360 degree turns at up to 100km an hour. Apparently unaffected by the 5G, she was unable to give a quote, being keen to look after her unwell friends.

Translated from *Københavns Tidende* newspaper, Copenhagen.

Chapter 11

"Jen, darling? Have you heard a thing I've said?"

She forced her eyes to focus on Ava. She'd zoned out a while back, Ava's voice having just become a wall of noise. "Of course," she bluffed. "That's amazing." *Amazing* was usually the response Ava most cherished.

"I know, right? Zara's a lucky thing. A whole extra week at twenty percent off? Anyone would extend their vacay with an offer like that." Jen wasn't so sure. Most people saw work as something you actually turned up to do. "Anyways, she's looking forward to the hen-do. Give Lydia my number so we can plan. You look exhausted – a spa weekend is the obvious choice."

"Mmmhhh," Jen murmured, keeping her head down. Her head was bursting with all the memories of the weekend, but she couldn't talk about it. She'd had to tell Robert the previous night that they'd broken down on the way back from a trip to the Harry Potter studio tour so would miss their date, when in fact she'd been standing in the check-in queue in Copenhagen, propping up Lydia's ridiculous teddy bear. Thankfully, Robert didn't know the first thing about Harry Potter to quiz her and Ava never asked how anyone else had spent their weekends.

"What. Is. That?" Ava suddenly rasped, horror filling her voice and pointing a perfectly-gelled fingernail at Jen's desk. Jen looked down at the offending article, none too chuffed herself. Having got home, she'd tentatively dug out the SIM and phone from Yakob's rice incubator. It had already prompted a bag search at Security, but Jen had explained about the canal and the falling in and they'd let her go with some mocking but without a strip search. Yakob had recommended leaving it in a warm place for three days, but she needed her phone to live her life, so she'd hoped to fast-track things. Turning it on, the screen had lit up, much to Jen's joy, but then fizzed and switched itself off. After that it wouldn't play at all. It simply wasn't ready yet, Jen reasoned, shoving it back in the rice and sitting the box on a hot-water bottle, all wrapped in her favourite jumper. The SIM though, having been tested on an ancient brick of a phone she'd found in a drawer, a device whose sum capabilities was basic telephony and rudimentary texts, appeared to be willing. So for now, she was distressingly app bereft and relearning how to use paper and pen for her lists.

"Phone died," she mumbled. She couldn't say much more without getting upset. Being without it for a day in Copenhagen had been surmountable; Lydia had steered everything, while Jen's mind had been rather caught up in itself; combating the embarrassment of the turquoise 1990's ruched ball-gown she was wearing and the memories of her evening with Yakob. Coming back to real life was totally different. Functioning was difficult. She'd even had to dig out an alarm clock, for goodness sake.

Ava looked at her, then at the phone and then back at Jen, sympathy and a tinge of revulsion written all over her face. The phone looked like some love-child of Darth Vader and a Teletubby, with its black and grey styling and small screen in the middle of its podgy belly. Jen slid it away under a pile of flyers destined for English Heritage visitor centres. Had she not needed it in case Lydia ever needed her, she would have buried The Phone of Shame deep in her handbag.

Jen wished Ava would go away; she had enough to do and needed some head-space to clear her mind of all things Copenhagen. Especially the tall blond parts. She'd lost plenty of sleep already replaying the view of his back disappearing into the distance as she stood by her hotel, her lips tingling, while her body and head argued as to whether she'd done the right thing. No wonder Ava could kindly point out she looked haggard. Lydia prattling on about him the entire following day had not helped, and she had virtually scolded Jen for being tucked up in bed – alone – when they'd returned from Tivoli, which seemed incongruent coming from her best woman on her actual hen-do. However, no matter how many times Lydia barked "What happens in 'hagen ..." at her, Jen held fast that she was a faithful person and she'd absolutely made the right decision.

Yes, Jen accepted there had been a kiss, *the* most perfect kiss, and she felt guilty enough about that, but it was thanks to her that it hadn't gone further, so she'd convinced herself to draw a line under the entire episode. It had been a holiday blip – didn't she know from past painful experience, that people did unreliable things when away from their normal environments? She deftly tucked aside the thought of Danny and the fact she had previous form in this area. She should have known better. Jen normally prided herself on not making the same mistake twice. And yet ... Feeling the need for self-care, she reminded herself she hadn't made the same mistake twice; she'd curbed it after all and she should give herself due credit. *Yay Jen*, she cheered in her head and sat up straight. She was *engaged* and about to embark on her new life, and she should pack thoughts of Yakob away too. It had been a wonderful moment, on a wonderful trip, but that was all. Thank goodness she hadn't jeopardised her future with Robert on a fling. Lydia simply wasn't mature enough to see happiness was a long-game project and Jen had a sound plan for hers.

Not for the first time that morning Jen's fingers twitched towards the computer. So far she'd deliberately stuck to manual tasks, after checking her emails had already brought her perilously close to Google. Lydia had been pestering her to Google him, to see what he did and discover more about him, but Jen had fended off the temptation, knowing it would be an abyss to fall into. What was the point? It didn't matter whether he had a Facebook page, real or otherwise. She was stowing him away as a nice memory, she'd decided. That was final. Her twitchy fingers hadn't quite got the neuro-message yet, that was all.

The front door of the office slammed open and turning,

Jen's eye-line was filled with a mass of bright floral fabric. Ava had turned too, but immediately knew what to do with this visual assault.

"Mumsie!"

Ava's mother, though short, filled the entire width of the doorway. Her penchant for floral two-pieces did nothing to lessen this spatial illusion, whilst also making her look like a walking sofa. Her enormous blonde curls were immaculately dyed and set, and doubled the size of her head, which might have appeared comical, had it not perfectly matched the size of each of her huge boobs. Height aside, everything about her shouted Big Personality and she hadn't even opened her mouth yet. Jen braced herself.

"Girls!" she boomed, "so glad to have caught you before you close for lunch." Jen wasn't sure what decade Ava's mother thought it was, lunchtime closing hadn't been a thing during her working lifetime.

Ava and her mother were busy doing kisses. "Lovely to see you, darling sweetie, but it's not you I'm here to see." Jen felt the woman's gaze lock onto her like a target. Only at that point did it properly occur to her she wasn't just looking at Ava's mother, and Robert's for that matter, but in fact her future mother-in-law. Her entire insides contracted in an instant spasm. Brain taking over in some autopilot fight or flight mode, Jen pushed herself up to standing, preparing for the imminent close proximity of the floral force of nature that was barrelling towards her. Hopeful, Jen held out her hand. Her hopes were dashed, as she was crushed by a pneumatic embrace, making it almost impossible to get her "Nice to see you again, Mrs Thwaites" out.

"Don't you *Mrs Thwaites* me, Jennifer. We're family. You must call me Mumsie, or Celia." Mrs Thwaites pressed a wet kiss on both her cheeks and finally released her.

Jen dragged air back into her body but managed a "Thank you, Celia." There was no way on earth she would call her Mumsie. Lydia would take the piss beyond endurance.

"It's going to be such fun having you in the family," her mother-in-law started, her face highly animated. "I know you miss your parents, darling sweetie, we *all* do," she cupped Jen's cheek tenderly, as Jen wondered how much they really would have missed their car mechanic and seamstress, "but now you'll have Giles and me as surrogates, you poor dear. You must come to us with any problems, just as you would to them were they here." Celia nodded vigorously as she spoke, her loud voice making it an edict. Jen couldn't stop herself from nodding along, not least because the woman's hand was still on her cheek and moving up and down. "Do you play golf, darling?"

"Um ... no," Jen said, glad the topic had been moved from her parental situation. She wasn't in the market for new parents, she just wanted her old ones back.

"Well, that's what lessons are for. You'll learn quickly and I've put you forward for membership at the club." Jen opened her mouth to say she really didn't feel the need, but her mother-in-law was on a roll. "Bridge? Do you play?"

"No, but I–" She wanted to say, thanks to their mum,

she and Lydia could play a mean game of poker, but Celia carried on.

"Hhmm," she said, her large lips pursed, "disappointing. That's not as easy to remedy. Bridge is a game of extreme skill. But if you study my game carefully, I could apprentice you until we partner one day. Margery, my current partner, has been making mistakes recently." She leaned closer to Jen and lowered her voice fractionally, "I think the Alzheimer's might be starting, so I'm planning ahead. I'll let you know when the next game is so you can attend. Meanwhile, the WI run a beginners course. I'll sign you up, so you can actually hold some cards." Jen could feel her heart rate steadily climbing in panic. She'd assumed she was marrying Robert, not his mother.

"But for now it's the wedding we need to focus on, isn't it?" Celia was doing that nodding thing again, though thankfully she'd released Jen's shell-shocked face.

We? Jen needed to nix this straight away. "Yes, Robert and I need to talk about it all."

"Nonsense, darling," said Celia brusquely. "I've never met a man yet who had the first clue as to how a good wedding works and what's important." She turned to Ava, "Remember Rupert wanted that drinks luge thing at yours, darling sweetie? Thank goodness we vetoed that." Jen knew for a fact Rupert had had one at his stag-do instead, fifty men suckling vodka from the nipples of an ice Venus de Milo. It was still on the homepage of the ice sculptor and Jen had recognised Rupert's drunken face when Ava had asked her to cost an ice bladder for demo use at a health show. "Weddings are for mothers and daughters to plan, and in lieu of yours having passed, I shall step in. This'll be my third now, so I'm very well versed and all the local suppliers know me." *I bet they do*, thought Jen. She'd been to Zara's wedding as Robert's "plus one". She'd assumed Zara had chosen all the twee arrangements, but remembering the hooped floral bridesmaids' dresses, she wasn't so sure now.

"Don't look so scared, darling," Celia barked, failing on the comforting front, "the planning might sound daunting, but as long as you stick to the traditional, and don't try to be all modern and wacky, it's very straight forward."

Had Jen not been so terrified of Celia having a hand in her wedding arrangements, she would have been offended by the suggestion of her worrying about the planning. Jen was a planning queen.

"There's a very good shop for dresses here in town, so we needn't travel up to London, which is a blessing as it's both expensive and dirty. I'll make a booking."

Jen knew she had to stand up for herself. Getting steamrollered by her mother-in-law this early on would not bode well for the future. She needed to lay sound foundations for their relationship and the foundations she wanted involved some distance. She hadn't thought about the dress yet. Her wedding critiques with Lydia hadn't involved imagining her own face poking out of the dresses. She needed to buy some time.

"Actually, Celia," she said firmly, "perhaps you could put that on hold?" Celia was surprised to be stopped in her tracks. It wasn't par for the course. "I was thinking about looking for my mother's wedding dress first."

Ava drew a sharp breath. Celia looked quite put out. A paragon of manners however, she recovered herself swiftly. "Yes of course dear, that could be a charming idea. Sentimental value always supersedes fashion at such occasions. I'm sure everyone will agree it's lovely." Jen bit her tongue – Zara's meringue dress had had nothing to do with fashion. She settled for a small smile and a nod instead. She didn't want to start on a bad foot with her mother-in-law, but some lines needed to be drawn.

Celia delved into her handbag and pulled out a piece of card with holes in it of descending sizes. "Well here's the highest priority job of the moment. I know you're desperate for it. I picked up this sizing gauge from my jewellers. Pop your ring finger though and find the right size. I'll drop Grandmama's engagement ring in with him on the way home." At that she pulled the ring box out of her bag with a magician's flourish.

"Oh, let me see!" Ava said, storming across the room. Celia snapped the box open. Ava recoiled. Jen watched many emotions cross her face as she beheld the monstrosity. "Oh Jen, that's very special," she said, way too sweetly. Ava knew she'd dodged a bullet.

Jen concentrated on the sizing chart, and reluctantly found her size. N. For Nightmare.

"Want to have a quick try on your finger before I take it away?" Celia asked, keenly. Ava watched her closely.

"Nooo," Jen wheedled and both faces dropped, "I'd like

the next time it goes on for it to be Robert sliding it on forever." Their "Awww"s said she'd saved it.

Set on her mission, Celia grabbed Jen to her bosom again, kissed both cheeks and left, promising to be in touch to set up a wedding planning date. Ava went with her to have lunch. It was eleven thirty after all, it was hardly worth starting anything.

Jen sat down in her chair, eyes wide like a rabbit in the headlights. She looked at her ring finger, naked for now, but with a sentence hanging over it. And then she remembered soft fingers brushing over her knuckles not forty-eight hours ago and again her fingers started to twitch towards the computer. She abruptly sat on them. It seemed safest, whether to prevent any Googling or to hide her ring finger from sight, she couldn't be sure.

Chapter 12

"Oh, you utter prat," Lydia groaned, shaking her head at Jen. "Have you seen Mum's wedding dress?" Jen looked up from weighing the cracked malt she'd shortly be steeping in hot water, while Lydia sat in her normal spot on the worktop, bottle in hand. Many hours had been spent like this over the years, talking through school issues, life issues, boy issues. The cosiness of the outbuilding, the comfort of the Horlicksy malt scent, made it a refuge for them both.

"What? Of course I've seen it. It's in the picture on the mantelpiece. It's white, satin, simple." Considering the dress was nearly thirty years old, it could have been horribly dated, but their mother had picked a classic boat-neck neckline, and it was exactly Jen's style. "All it's got to do is fit or else I'm stuffed."

Lydia's face took on a smirk. "When was their anniversary?"

"Valentine's. So Dad could remember."

"And when is your birthday?"

"March 9th. You know that."

Lydia waited for her to join the dots.

"Oh. Oh!" She'd never really done the maths.

"Why do you think all the pictures they had out were 'shoulders up' only?"

"Really?" Why hadn't this dawned on her?

"Enormous bump, proudly presented in an above-the-knee maternity style with empire-line waist complete with a bow. You were a sumo baby. Huge."

"How do you know this?"

"*Elementary, my beer Jen*," Lydia gave her a grin, "Mum and I laughed our way through the photo album." In spite of Jen's new predicament, they fell into a moment of quiet.

"She had a great laugh," Jen eventually said.

"And a wicked sense of humour," Lydia agreed. "I was only just beginning to get it. It felt like I was gaining membership to a club." Jen knew exactly what Lydia meant, their mother had been witty and very dry in her humour. And she wouldn't have been remotely abashed about wearing white for her wedding even if about to drop a baby.

"Well, maybe it's genetic then, Lyds – I see her in you all the time." It wasn't just a kindness, it was the truth and Jen could see it pleased Lydia. She'd tried very hard to make sure Lydia got to know their parents as she grew up, in spite of their absence; keeping their pictures out and saving their things. Despite the sadness, they found talking about them whenever they could helped them come to terms with what had happened.

"She'd think you wanting her dress is hysterical."

"It wasn't so much a *want*, more an escape route." What

was she going to do now? She'd dig it out, but the front would have way too much fabric in it. Celia probably wouldn't be too chuffed about a short dress either. Although, Jen quite liked her legs, so short could be good ...

Lydia took a swig of her beer. "You can still pull out, Jen. The hen-do wasn't binding."

Jen concentrated on the steeping malt, she wasn't getting into this. "I meant an escape route from Celia, Lydia."

"Mumsie," Lydia corrected.

"*Celia*. If I ever call her Mumsie, shoot me."

"Deal." Lydia gave Jen's ribs a slow prod with her foot. "Have you Googled him yet? You've got to be itching to." Such a stirrer.

"Who?"

"Don't you give me that. You know who I mean. Mr Copenhagen."

Jen sighed a parental sigh.

"No Lydia, I haven't. Nothing happened, so there's nothing to pursue. He was just someone I met by chance. Someone who helped me out when I'd been marooned by my nearest and dearest. And again, nothing happened and nothing is going to happen. Robert and I are engaged, we are getting married, so there's no need, at all, to be Googling other men on the internet. *Capiche?*"

Some younger sisters might have got the message. Lydia wasn't one of them.

"You want to though, don't you?"

Jen decided the best plan was to ignore her completely and turned back to the sticky sweet wort of malt, chalking adjustments to the ingredients up on her blackboard, the quantities and the dates. This was it, the last beer.

Staring out of the aeroplane window, desperate to think about something other than a certain Scandi man, Jen had started writing notes on the back of a sick-bag. Gradually, her wedding favour beer had started to come to fruition. She was going for some mellow flavours, picking back up on her ideas from the night Robert had proposed, something crisp, lightly smoky, and slightly salty. She'd chosen her malts and devised the timings for the hops and selected which types she'd use, finally finishing the recipe just as they came to land. She'd also made the decision that this beer would be the last. Not knowing *when* she'd pack it away, but knowing it was imminent, was hurting too much. She was going to pour everything into this beer and call it a day, hoping the smart of a quick plaster-pull would be kinder than a prolonged agony. She'd make several batches, of course – she needed enough to serve and give as favours – but then that would be it and she'd dismantle the outbuilding. Looking at her board now, Jen could only hope nipping things quickly like this would work. The recipe was good, she could feel it – she only hoped it would be enough of a high to go out on.

"You've forgotten the name," Lydia pointed out, waving her bottle at the top of the board which remained blank. Lydia had named a few in her time. *Cheers, Brewnette!* had been a favourite, along with Jen's Halloween stout she'd christened *Beerwitched, Bothered & Beerwildered.* "Call this one *Attison's Ruin.*" Jen gave her a mardy look. She was not calling her wedding beer and final shout *that*, and Lydia could do one if she thought she was being subtle.

"Best women are supposed to be supportive, Lyds. I'm sure I mentioned that already. And *mother's ruin* is gin."

"*Attison's Lament?*" Lydia's tone wasn't so teasing anymore. The mood had become more of a provocation.

"Lyds. Please." This was hard enough already. "All I want, is to know you're on my side, even if you don't agree." She turned to look at her sister. "Help me find the right name, something elegant." Jen held the chalk out to her.

Lydia mulled her words, but still looked surly. Finally she got off the counter and took it. "I'll always be on your side. But let's call this what it really is."

She chalked up a single word, handed the chalk back to Jen and without looking back, left.

Well, OK, conceded Jen, she'd at least nailed the elegant bit.

The name of the new beer, the final beer, her wedding beer was *Swansong*.

Lydia had gone to bed by the time Jen came back in. To be honest, it suited her just fine. Jen hated when they were at odds, but this, her marriage, was one change Lydia was just going to have to deal with. Climbing into bed, Jen told herself time would sort this; there wasn't an app to fix or progress this, she'd simply have to wait it out.

An hour later and still wide awake, Jen plodded downstairs to make herself a warm milk with honey. There was so much marauding around in her mind, the paper lists weren't holding it all in check. The wedding, Ava's business offer, the crampons, the ring, the beer, someone else's interest in her passion, they all spun around in her brain like a vortex and sleep didn't have a chance.

She grabbed her laptop from the kitchen table as she went back up with her mug. If the milk didn't work, then at least she could get some spreadsheets done. Sitting in bed, computer on her lap, Jen found herself staring at the Google home page, fingers poised. She typed in crocheted tampons, squeezed her eyes shut and hit return.

Credit to Ava; she hadn't been sold magic beans. Crocheted tampons were a real thing and Etsy was full of them. White or Ecru, bamboo or cotton, even some with smiley faces crocheted into them.

Dear God.

Jen hung her head. Surely, bringing these to the masses – organically or not – wasn't what life intended for her? She quickly hit the back arrow to remove the images.

She doubted she could talk Ava and Zara out of it, and she was reluctant to buy into it. She was stuck between a rock and a hard place; she was about to join their family, and they wanted her to be part of the company. If she didn't come on board it would be horribly awkward at family events and she had no other job to go to. Argh. Jen flopped back on the pillows, unable to reconcile it all. She was just going to have to take Alice's suggestion and say she didn't have the money to buy in and stall for time until she could come up with a better excuse, or – fingers crossed – Ava and Zara saw the crampons weren't a goer.

Her finger tips were still on the keyboard.

Her nails tapped against the plastic.

Her eyes were drawn to the sound and then to the flashing cursor.

What could it hurt to have a little look in cyberspace, to see if Yakob was there, whether he really existed, or if he was merely a figment of her tipsy, sartorially-tortured Copenhagen weekend?

Keeping her hands distant, as if they'd gone rogue from her body, Jen typed in *Yakob Yule* and held her breath.

Nothing appeared.

Huh.

Maybe she was spelling it wrong. She tried with Yakob Yool. Nothing there either. She bunged an *e* on the end of the surname, and also tried his first name with a *c* instead of a *k*, but neither got any results. She wracked her brains to think what else she could try, but realised she had nothing to go on. Argh, why hadn't she got him to write it down? Bugger.

The door creaked open and Lydia's face appeared.

"I can't sleep. I heard you plodding up and down the stairs." Her eyes dropped to the laptop. "What you doing?"

Jen slapped the lid shut, which only served to snag Lydia's interest. "One might suspect you're watching porn, Jen, given that reaction," she said, crossing the floor on her crutches, "but I know you. My guess would have been a spreadsheet, but not anymore ..."

Oh bum. She'd played this very, very badly.

Lydia burrowed her way in under Jen's duvet and got

herself comfortable. "Let's see what we have here, shall we?" She raised the lid with her index finger. Jen's shoulders sagged. Lydia would make this as painful as possible. "Ah ha! Caught red-handed, Miss Nothing Happened."

"Nothing. Happened," Jen tried, weakly. "Really."

"Then why are you looking him up?" Lydia rudely whizzed back through the search history, emitting a snort when she reached the crocheted tampons.

"I'm not looking him up. I'm just moderately interested to learn who I had dinner with. I was alone on his house-boat, I think it's perfectly natural to check I was safe."

"After the fact."

"I wasn't exactly given a choice on the sequence of events, was I?"

"I was doing you a favour," Lydia said, keenly trying another permutation of his name, squinting at the screen. She got equally useless results. "You needed a little adventure in your life."

"My life is fine, thanks."

"Well maybe I'm testing your resolve regarding Robert. Helping you make sure you're doing the right thing." Lydia sat back from the laptop frustrated. "There's nothing there. He's a mystery."

"I know!" said Jen, equally exasperated and disregarding the resolve thing. She didn't need testing. "He's invisible. No LinkedIn, no Facebook, no online footprint at all. It's like he doesn't exist." An awful feeling began to creep over her that maybe he'd given her a false name. Please not again. But then she dismissed it. There had been no expectation of ever meeting again when he'd told her either of his names. There'd been no need to lie.

"Maybe," Lydia said with a lowered voice, "he's a spy. Oh my God. You fell into the hands of a spy. How romantic would that be?"

"Lydia. Stop." Jen swiftly shut down the computer. Enough was enough. "I have all the romance I need." Admittedly what she and Robert had wouldn't be the strongest definition of romance, but it was kind and respectful and they knew what each other was about. She slid the computer to the floor, safely away from either of them, and lay down. "You're too wrapped up in the rom-coms, and now the spy films apparently." She tugged at Lydia's t-shirt, so that she lay down too. "Real life isn't like the movies, Lyds. I know you want it to be, but it isn't. I'll be happy with Robert. You'll see."

Finally the exhaustion was setting in. And for once Lydia had nothing to say. Jen didn't know what she'd thought she'd get out of the Googling. She wouldn't have contacted him or anything like that. Now however, she was even more sure meeting Yakob had just been a moment, a moment that was done and dusted. Not being able to find him was a sign – had she been looking for one, which she absolutely definitely hadn't. Like the beer, she would pack away her thoughts of Yakob too, because the universe was literally telling her this was a dead end.

Chapter 13

The room did indeed have a disproportionate number of beards for the general public, Jen had to admit.

"Only you would take a day off to spend it with beardies," Lydia had said as they'd travelled into London together on the train. Jen was used to the excess of facial hair at beer trade shows, but she was pleased to point out to her sister that over recent years there were more and more women attending. Lydia rubbed her chin between thumb and forefinger and Jen wasn't quite sure whether she was expressing doubt or suggesting the female brewers might have chin hair too. Either way, she wasn't entertaining it, she wasn't having fellow brewsters mocked.

She'd bought her ticket to *Brewing Live* months ago. She couldn't see the point of wasting the ticket in light of her ending her hobby, and besides she needed to find just the right bottles for her wedding favours. Sure, she could spend an evening in the comfort of her own home forensically searching all the online bottle suppliers for the exact shape and size of bottle she wanted, but there was nothing like examining them in real life, holding them up to the light to check the colour density, even if it meant taking the day off work and spending money on a train ticket. Some things deserved proper effort. Besides, it was a day away from the inco pads and imminent crampons, so she was having it.

The Craft hall Jen was slowly making her way through was a hubbub of noise. The show covered three halls, this one for craft beer tasting and supplies, one for the state-of-the-art brewing equipment and the last for all the large corporate companies to tout their huge deals and spend their promo budgets on freebies. With an air of disdain the Craft brewers stayed safely away from that hall, considering the hordes of visitors in there as mere tourists. The halls were connected by a central hub of conference rooms, offering a rolling buffet of panel talks, demonstrations and lectures. Jen had already been to a couple, one on rediscovering hop varieties and another on revisionist brewing techniques, but only because she'd already signed up for them a while back, no other reason. Her copious note-taking she could only put down to reflex. Three years at uni would do that to anyone, she was sure.

Generally, Jen was on the other side of things at trade shows, handing out samples and flyers for *Well, Honestly!*, becoming exhausted from standing on her feet all day and having the same conversations over and over again. Today however, as she wandered along the stands, saying hello to the people she knew from previous years and other events, she was enjoying being a punter. Having tasted several beers already, as one did, she was feeling quite relaxed. Normally, she would have spent the previous evening looking through the delegate listings, planning the most efficient walk route through the halls so she wouldn't miss a thing. However, in light of her only needing the bottle of her dreams and perhaps some ingredients, she'd decided to adopt a more Yakob approach this time, and meander her way around. It was proving quite enjoyable. Of course there was no need to be efficient about it anymore, given she was drawing it to a close. Next year she would just be a tourist herself. Instinctively, she straightened her Kronegaard-sponsored lanyard and show ID. Next year she supposed she needn't attend at all ...

Feeling her buoyant mood ebb, Jen focused on the stand she'd arrived at, one which was on her to-see list. (Yes, *of course* she still had a list. She was just taking more time getting between the points on it.) Bottles of all shapes and colours stood on display, some designed for capping, some with ceramic swing caps. She was in two minds about having those or whether to have personal caps made for the day, perhaps with a *J & R* insignia and the date. She picked up a brown one. Brown was a given.

"Hello again." She heard the voice over her shoulder at the same time as she felt the light tap on it, but it still took her a while to process the words were directed at her. That voice, those words.

She spun, and there he was. Yakob. The internet man of mystery himself. She felt her head instantaneously heat in her confusion. What was he doing here?

"Hello again," was all she could say in her befuddlement. What a muppet.

"It's good to see you, Jen." Yakob looked like he meant it, his eyes were bright and his smile wide.

"You too, Yakob." Oh God, her conversational skills were lacking, but it really was the truth. She'd felt so sad about sending him away on the bridge that night, after that kiss, even though it was absolutely the right thing to do. "What are you doing here?" She'd expected never to see him again and here he was. Shocked didn't quite cover this.

Jen looked him over. Sadly the abs had been covered with a pristine white shirt, but open enough at the collar to give a repeat view of his fine collar bones and he wore a pair of tailored navy suit trousers, the jacket presumably having been ditched elsewhere. If he'd come in wearing a tie it had been dispensed with and whereas she had dutifully donned her lanyard on entry, he'd apparently stuffed his in his pocket, the end of the lanyard peeping out. He looked neither like a tourist nor a brewer. He almost appeared corporate if it hadn't been for the hair still walking its own line. Regardless, Yakob looked equally fine in his business wear as in his weekend cargo shorts. She thanked the heavens she was in her own clothes as opposed to Lydia's charity shop styling.

"Working. Finance things. Very boring. But what about you?" He eyed the bottle in her hand, which she swiftly put down.

"Just browsing. Ingredients and materials. You know." She shrugged a bit, hoping they could move on. He leaned past her and picked up the bottle.

"Are you sure brown isn't your favourite colour?" She

plucked it out of his hand and replaced it. Sixty seconds he'd lasted. Sixty seconds and he was teasing her again. It didn't irk her though, it said he bore her no ill feeling about her refusing him and it made her so glad.

She got a waft of his aftershave, its scent instantly igniting her memories of their evening in Copenhagen. That pine, lemon and sage mix was perfect for him.

"I have some time before my next meeting, Jen. Would you like a coffee?" he asked, then added with a smirk, "do you have a coffee break timetabled?" Why did he find her being organised so funny?

"Actually Yakob," she said with mock indignance, "I haven't timetabled today. I am *meandering*." A to-see list was NOT the same as a timetable. FACT. And yes, she was aware how imperious she suddenly sounded, but he seemed to bring that out in her, along with the pratting, but there wasn't much she could do about that.

His lovely blue eyes showed his delight and she chose to believe it was at her accepting the coffee as opposed to in amusement, though she wouldn't have bet on it. Having a coffee was acceptable, wasn't it? Having coffee in a public space was normal friend behaviour and given he'd saved her from the canal and clothed and fed her, she felt she could easily justify him as a friend. He definitely wasn't a stranger. She safely parked the memory of The Kiss far far away at the back of her head. *What happened in 'hagen ...* although her treacherous eyes did flit to his lips every so often. Unless she was much mistaken, his eyes were doing the same.

Unlike in Copenhagen, he didn't hold a hand out to her this time, safely putting them in his pockets as they walked side by side towards one of the cafés. At one point she fell in behind him to allow for oncoming foot traffic, and watching him she remembered how tall he was. Admittedly the unruly hair added another inch on him, but his legs were extremely long and led up to a very neat bottom. He really had invested in some good tailoring there.

Jen gave herself a mental kick. What was she doing ogling other men? That was Lydia's MO, not hers. And it certainly wasn't the behaviour of an engaged woman. She forced her eyes up to the back of his rumpled head until there was room for them to walk two abreast again, though not so much room that their arms didn't rub together as they made their way.

Jen found the seats while he bought the coffees. As she'd recently learned (and having a crappy phone that didn't do browsing), she took the time to take in the things going on around her; him standing in the queue, him ordering, him paying and returning to her cups in hand. She was getting good at this – although her breathing might be a little off.

"It is not the same, seeing you without the Kronegaard t-shirt,' he said with a grin. "I am sure I saw them giving some out today." She'd had a go at saying Kronegaard like he did, rolling the *Kr*, but she'd sounded like a cat with a furball in its throat.

"I wouldn't know," she said primly, ignoring his jibe, "I don't usually hang around that hall." They both knew she

139

had to pass through it from the entrance to the other halls, the corporates having paid for the central showcase positions.

"You mean they are not on your list?" He was taking the piss again and heartily enjoying doing so, by the looks of it. It didn't feel in the slightest bit malicious, just that he found her slightly hilarious. She still had little idea why, because her planning was what held things together. Sure, the "taking time to look around" was nice, but it was bonus activity, not useful activity.

"I think I might have mentioned, Yakob, I haven't time-tabled today," she said, passing over the mention of a *list*, unwilling to let him win, "I don't have time for or interest in those brands. I'm a craft beer girl through and through." He tilted his head like he wasn't sure he believed her free-style approach, but changed his line of attack.

"You don't think," he asked slowly, but with a look of mischief, "and I only say this to play devil's advocate Jen, that you might be a beer snob?"

Jen's eyes widened at that. She had never been called a snob before. But then she thought about it. "Yes. Totally," she agreed and without a hint of shame. Yakob sat back at that. "What? You think I should be repentant? I'm not. The corporates are all about the money, not about the beer." He opened his mouth to say something but feeling feisty given the strength of her conviction she waved a hand in his face, "And you can tell the devil's advocate from me that my snobbery is in fact promotion of standards, skill and creativity." She wasn't done yet, enjoying having the floor.

"Which, by the way, I think you secretly agree with, given *you* found me in the Craft hall. Lost were you? I suspect, Mr Finance, you are a closet creative. I think your hours with Morfar, instilled a love of the brew in you, but you've buried it under the numbers. Only, the truth will out."

Yakob's expression had changed from amusement to enjoyably challenged. "You think so?" He raised an eyebrow at her.

"I know so."

"Maybe I was spying?" he said, leaning in towards her at the table. Oh, not him as well. Lydia would be delighted with this suggestion. Jen rolled her eyes. His tone was low so she was forced to lean in too. "Maybe I was conducting clandestine research to sell on to clients."

She looked in both directions, then back at him. "Maybe," she agreed in a loud whisper, "but you'd be a crap industrial spy as everything on display here is for public consumption, so there's nothing to sell. Not to mention decent spies probably don't tap people on the shoulder to say hello."

"Only the polite ones." That made her smile. She would have been gutted to learn he'd seen her and not said hello. They stayed still for a moment, both smiling at each other, faces not very far apart. And then on an unspoken beat they both sat back in a truce. Only their eyes were both firmly fixed on each other's faces, specifically eyes and lips and she knew, without a shadow of a doubt that The Kiss was on both of their minds. So much for parking it in the back of her head, which was where she needed it to be, given it absolutely wasn't something she could pursue.

"So how's the brewing?" he asked, just as she leapt into her question of "Which company are you here with?" There followed the polite negotiating of who should go first, although neither of them seemed willing. The negotiating evolved into a stalemate and eventually she caved.

"The brewing's fine." He raised an eyebrow at her response, somehow able to see it for the lie it was. Perhaps it was the lack of her normal effusing. She knew the way she'd spoken about it in Copenhagen was a million miles away from this lame "fine", and something about his generosity, both as a host in Copenhagen and a supporter made it impossible not to tell him the truth.

"I'm um ... I'm bringing it to a close." She took a long sip of her coffee, then instantly regretted it as the heat removed the lining of her upper mouth.

He looked confused. "What do you mean?"

"The brewing. I've got some life things going on, and the brewing has come to the end of its time."

He laughed, and then stopped when he saw she wasn't joking.

"What? Why are you here then?"

She shrugged. "Final ingredients, kit, I don't know, a last goodbye?"

His eyebrows raised as he blinked several times and then shook his head in disbelief. "But you were just at the museum. It's *in your veins*, Jen. That's what you said. Your *passion*."

"Well yes, but there comes a time when some things have to be packed away, don't they?" She hoped he'd understand, but he wasn't nodding along. Not at all. She blew on the coffee and had another sip, hoping he'd do the same and they could change the subject.

"It's not a passion then, is it?" he said, sounding deeply disappointed.

"What? Yes it is. I love it. But it's a practical thing. I can't fit it into my life anymore."

"Passions are things you cannot pack away, Jen. They are the things you shape your life around. They are the things that make your heart *sing*."

His disappointment was quite devastating. She opened her mouth several times but no words came out. But really, what was there to say?

Keen to smooth things over and get them back on to amicable ground, Jen came back to her own question. "What's got you here on business then, Yakob? I never asked you what company you work for." It seemed like a much safer area of discussion than hers. She liked the idea that his employer had links to the brewing industry.

His eyes lifted from the table to dart between hers. He took a breath to speak and – both their telephones rang at once, hers the most scorned of all historic ring tones, his some pop song she didn't recognise and suspected was Danish. Jen evil-eyed her phone, and he appeared somewhat relieved at his, while both of them looked embarrassed at their respective tones.

"Mine only comes with that," she said, hating The Phone of Shame more than ever before, as much for the tone as the timing.

"My nieces picked mine," he said simultaneously.

Reluctantly, they each took the call.

"Jen, it's me!" said Robert. Instinctively Jen looked about, in case she was in some film where the fiancé watches his bride-to-be have coffee with another man. "Hang on a sec, Jen," Robert interrupted himself, before telling someone to go ahead and tee off, he'd just be a second. "About date night tomorrow. Mumsie's hosting dinner for us."

Jen swallowed a groan. Dinner with Robert's parents wasn't quite how she wanted to spend her evening.

"Ava and Rupert are coming too with the kids." Jen's groan now felt like a huge sinkhole in her gut. "It's an engagement celebration. Isn't that nice?"

Jen considered what she was doing, spending time with a man she had kissed recently, on her hen-do. How exactly could she justify this to her moral code? She watched Yakob as his brow furrowed at whatever he was hearing.

"Diarrhoea?" he asked his caller. "Really?" He listened and then looked at his watch. "Ah shit, I hate those things Dave ... yes ... yes ... OK, I'll do it, but you owe me. Next time don't eat the kebab." He looked at her as he hung up and got to his feet.

"Jen, darling?" Her attention was drawn back to Robert, although her eyes remained on Yakob.

"Yes, still here."

"Isn't that nice? The engagement dinner." Jen swallowed hard, as she saw Yakob search for the route he was about to take.

"I'm sorry," he told her in a loud whisper. "My colleague

can't do the panel thing he's supposed to chair. I have to go, I'm sorry." He rubbed his hand through his hair, then said resolutely, "The panel lasts an hour, Jen. Meet me after?"

"Jen? Is the line dodgy? What do you think?" Robert tried again.

Torn yet again and heart hammering, Jen felt her head moving in a nod to Yakob as her mouth finally gave its answer to Robert. "Sounds good."

She spent the next half hour trying to find the right bottle for her favours, in a fidgety daze, quite uncomfortable with her decision-making skills. Her conscience was decidedly unhappy with her. In the end she settled for a swing-top bottle, which she could get a design printed on to, saving her the faff of capping. It didn't lift her spirits. Despite being early, she took herself off towards the conference room doors. Reading the signs for what was going on inside she saw most were marketing seminars, but the last was a panel, with the title of *Brewing Giants; Corporate branding, expansion and domination*. The sign listed the panellists, with Diarrhoea Dave noted as Chair along with his company name. It made her catch her breath.

Sticking her nose inside the door, Jen saw Yakob up on the stage, holding court. Stand-in or not, the audience and other panellists listened rapt.

"Sorry madam." A steward blocked her view. "Do you have a ticket? It's ticket holders only."

Jen backed away. This afternoon had offered her one surprise on top of another and as she'd always said, she

145

didn't like surprises. Yesterday, she'd wanted to know more about him, now she did she didn't feel happier for it. Yakob, it turned out, worked for Kronegaard, something he hadn't deemed worth mentioning the entire time they'd spent together, in spite of her mentioning the company a gazillion times. Jen turned The Phone of Shame in her hand, over and over, as she walked out of the show towards the train that would take her back home and to Robert, Robert who she knew everything about, who didn't keep secrets other than hiding ugly rings in desserts. What the hell had she been thinking?

Chapter 14

Robert collected Jen on Wednesday evening to take her to his parents' for dinner. She'd offered, his flat being on the way, but he'd insisted. Jen suspected he wasn't a fan of her Ford Capri, her mother's pride and joy – he didn't seem to appreciate its retro charm. Or its quirky rattling. Or its pleather upholstery. He couldn't have an issue with the colour – his convertible Jag F type was racing green too, only without the speed stripe. He had aluminium trim instead, which wasn't her cup of tea, so they were probably evens.

Jen had worn another dress, anticipating Celia being the kind of woman who would expect it. Indeed, peering into the drawing room where the rest of the family, bar Zara, stood waiting for them, champagne in hand, Jen knew she'd been right. Celia was wearing a floaty chiffon extravaganza, featuring a riot of hibiscus and bird of paradise flowers. She clashed with the large print Laura Ashley curtains, which in turn were at odds with the busy carpet.

"Jennifer darling sweetie," Celia boomed as Jen took her first step into the room. "We have lots of wedding business

147

to talk about. I've been so busy on your behalf and I need to update you."

Jen looked behind her, hoping for Robert's assistance. And there he was, his calm hand coming to rest on her shoulder, a touch of support, showing them to be a team. As his thumb stroked the base of her neck, Jen knew he'd sense her need – *their* need – to wrest control of their wedding day. He was dependable, a quality she prided in herself too.

"Oh look at you, Mumsie," Robert grinned over Jen's shoulder, "you're in your element when organising a wedding." He gave Jen's shoulder a squeeze and let her go. "No need for a wedding planner here, Jen, Mumsie is on the case." Jen didn't know what made her heart sink more, that he was encouraging Celia, or his fake American accent for "on the case".

"Briefly darlings, I've spoken to the vicar at St Jude's; he's waiting for your call with the date and to set you up for your marriage class programme. There's two folders on the hallway table with reception packages from both the golf club if you want a summer marquee or the manor if you want autumn/winter. I've booked some menu tasting dates with both of those and a caterer, remind me to give you the dates before you leave. Ava agrees her cherubs will make the most adorable pageboys, I've teed up Henry the photographer, he's expecting your call too, as is the horse and carriage place, for transport to and from the church."

Jen had to admit Celia had been extremely diligent, but that didn't help when the help wasn't wanted. Jen struggled to formulate her answer but was thankfully saved by Giles Thwaites grandly presenting her with a glass of "champers". Her weak thank you to him was taken as acceptance by Celia.

Jen turned desperately to Robert. "Didn't you mention a golf friend having got married in Calabria, Robert? The old monastery that was now a hotel? Think of it; just immediate family," Lord knew her side of any church would be sparsely filled, "year-round warmth, dancing beneath the stars?" She'd only just thought of it, but now it sounded perfect.

"Ha ha!" Robert laughed. "The women at the bridge club would have a field day if we did that and denied Mumsie her glory. Plus dancing is not in my skillset." Jen wondered if she was the only one expected to take classes for this marriage, as Robert accepted his glass of champers, the subject apparently settled. Then she noticed how deeply happy he looked, surrounded by his family, seeing his mother so wrapped up in his nuptials. How lovely and kind was that? Jen chided herself. Perhaps weddings were really for the mothers. She didn't have enough experience, of weddings – nor mothers, she supposed – to know. Perhaps she was being uncharitable; both Celia and Robert wanted the best for their day. She saw that. Only she didn't find it easy to relinquish the control of it. Jen decided she needed to relax and that nature had invented champagne for a reason.

Her glass was knocked out of her hand before she'd even managed a sip as Ava's sons provided a military salute with their Nerf guns during the toast. Jen insisted it was fine, her dress was navy, so the champagne probably wouldn't stain. She clenched her glass stem harder second time around, as the four boys deployed into a full-blown Nerf-war around them. It made it rather hard to hear what her future father-in-law beside her was saying, so she had to concentrate.

"Celia and I are terribly pleased, you know. We know a good egg, Jennifer, and you'll fit in beautifully."

"Thank you, Giles. That's very kind."

"Robert's been telling me all about your plans."

"Oh really?" She wondered which he meant. She'd only seen him three times since the proposal, and they'd only tentatively and unsuccessfully looked at wedding dates, navigating his many golf matches and trips.

"A holiday home is an excellent investment, especially when you have rugrats." Giles looked fondly at his grandsons, currently mounting a skirmish across the sofa and Celia who sat on it. Both Ava and Rupert appeared oblivious. Ava was FaceTiming Zara and Rupert was discussing cricket with Robert. "Once you pop out more than two, hotels are a nightmare. Ava and Rupert know all about that." Jen suspected their boys were blacklisted from hotels the world over.

Ava's head poked up. "Was this the holiday home? Fabulous idea, Robert," she said, sending her brother a smile, "but nothing too far away darling, or else it'll be a pain for us to get to on a weekend. If they're cooped up for too long the boys are hyper by the time we get anywhere."

In Jen's view, the boys were currently hyper and they only lived five minutes away. Ava went back to Zara, while Jen fought hard to contain her shudder. A holiday home was very low in her priorities and now even more so if Ava was booking in.

"The house hunting started, has it?" Giles asked with a nudge. "No doubt you're both eager to get under the same roof?" She almost expected him to wink at her.

"Well I ... We haven't ... there's Lydia to consider too, you see." She really hadn't got to this bit yet. She had no plans to leave Lydia alone, she simply hadn't got to discussing it with Robert yet.

"Ah yes, your sister. How is she, poor thing?" Jen hated it when people referred to her as *poor* anything. Lydia was doing all right, thanks very much. She was one of the most positive people Jen knew. Except regarding Jen's marriage, of course, but otherwise.

"Lydia's fine, thank you," she said primly, but getting distracted by Ava's son Beckham standing next to them for no reason at all. He didn't even look at them, concentrating hard instead on the floor. After ten seconds he scooted off again. Six-year-olds could be very odd.

"I suppose being handicapped is difficult at her age." Jen's toes curled, knowing Lydia would have gone ballistic if she'd heard him. She saw herself as physically challenged, that was all. And Jen imagined it would be difficult at any age.

"Lydia's actually very active, Giles. She runs three times a week." Once a promising gymnast, Lydia still took her fitness very seriously. "She does all sorts of regular things. In fact, she's off camping with friends this coming weekend." Jen's nostrils began to twitch as they were attacked by a rank eggy stink. Holy crap, that was unnatural. Giles clearly didn't have her finessed sense of smell as he wasn't reacting at all, while she wanted to double over choking. Bloody Beckham. Little shit.

Instead Giles' eyebrows raised, impressed. "Good for her. Yes, bravo. Camping with just the one leg must be a struggle. But I suppose her friends will muck in and take up the slack."

"Oh, you'd be surprised what Lydia can do with her prosthetic leg," she coughed, desperately trying to stop her eyes from watering at the stench. She turned to refill their glasses, keen to gasp in some non-farty air and drop the conversation. People like Giles only ever saw her sister with pity, but Jen was tremendously proud of Lydia. Her friends were a good bunch too and while she wasn't going to say so to Giles, she knew Lydia would be safe in whatever field they'd picked for the weekend.

"She's an inspiration, that's what she is," Giles expounded. "If ever I'm feeling sorry for myself, I only have to think of your Lydia and I see life's not so bad after all."

Enough! Lydia was not some base measure of how good other people had it and who was he to judge her life as worse than his? How *dare* he? Still struggling with the hideous reek, Jen opened her mouth to say so, starting with the basics that Lydia's life was not there to be an inspiration to others either.

"Now then Dad, no more monopolising my bride-to-be." Robert appeared at her shoulder. He didn't mention the noxious odour either. What was the matter with their noses? He squeezed her in to his side for a kiss on the temple, only for Ferdinand to smash into him and it became more of a headbutt.

"We were just discussing the house hunting, Robert," Giles said, any thought of Lydia gone.

"Ah yes, I've got plenty of particulars rolling in. I know the estate agents from the conveyancing, so they're sending me the crème de la crème, hot off the press." Both men laughed. It was exactly the same loud bark. Jen had never really noticed it when it was just Robert. Now, in stereo, it was quite alarming. Standing side by side, she could see how similar they really were. She wondered whether it was just in looks and lack of nasal aptitude.

"What do you have in mind?" Giles was exclusively asking Robert now. Jen could only follow his lead and look at Robert. She too was curious what he had in mind, seeing she hadn't been consulted.

"Nothing too grand, but large enough for hours of hide and seek for the kids and running races on the lawns in the summer." Robert suddenly looked wistful and nostalgic. Jen pondered whether he saw himself mowing those lawns and whether the labyrinthine house came with a cleaner. Robert abruptly looked at Jen and smiled. "And, of course, some space for Jen to have a hobby."

Giles turned to Jen. "Oh yes? What do you have planned? Women are happiest when they're busy." Annoyingly, Jen actually agreed with him – she hated having nothing to do – but she didn't need him telling her so.

"Well, if we find a doer-upper, Jen'll have her hands full with the refurb." Apparently ventriloquism was her newly-acquired skill – she hadn't even opened her mouth. "And then there'll be the babies." Robert had the good grace to touch wood then. "Plus, there's Mumsie's bridge plans."

"Ahh," said Giles, conspiratorially. "You'll have your hands full then. Excellent." He gave Jen a pat on the arm, genuinely delighted for her.

"I currently brew my own beer too." She didn't know quite why she'd said it. Possibly to have her own say in the conversation. Possibly to see how supportive Robert would be.

Giles' face took on a blank look. "Beer? You?"

"Yes. Me," Jen said. A touch of the feeling she'd had when confessing her passion to Yakob was rising in her tummy. Not that she was giving Yakob any further thought. She didn't know whether he was a liar or a player, only that she didn't need either in her life. "I've won shows with my beer." Saying it out loud again gave her another boost of pride. Giles looked as if she'd just informed him Churchill was a burlesque dancer. "Celia?!" he said brusquely, "since when did the WI competitions have a beer category?"

Celia gave him a withering look as she roughly wiped a stalactite of snot from Rooney's pug-face. "Don't be ridiculous, Giles. Women don't make beer." Giles turned back to Jen, his expression confused, as if suggesting she'd been pulling his leg, or worse still, blatantly lying to him.

"Actually, women brewers – *brewsters* – have been brewing beer for over ten thousand years," Jen started, just as Robert said, "It was her university hobby. Jen's considering baking now, so wherever we find has to have room for a decent kitchen." With that, Giles looked much happier, which irked Jen in many ways.

She raised an eyebrow at Robert. "Is that what you have planned, that I'm in the kitchen?" His brow furrowed, savvy enough to sense he was on unstable ground. "No, of course not, I just meant–"

"She's not going to have time to be in the kitchen, are you Jen?" Ava slid her arm inside Jen's and pulled her closer, rendering Jen suspended between the two siblings. Robert's grip reflexively tightened. "Jen's buying into *Well, Honestly!*"

All eyes were suddenly on Jen, with various expressions.

"Since when?" asked Robert, put out. "First I've heard of it."

"I'm thinking it over," Jen began, willing a natural disaster – tsunami or tornado, either would do – to rip through the house right there and then.

"See?" said Ava and Jen half-expected her to stick her tongue out at her brother.

"But, to be honest, Ava," Jen said, sensing her opportunity, "I don't have the funds. But I do appreciate the offer. It was terribly generous."

Ava's pout was huge and Jen felt her arm sliding away. There would be some bridge-building needed there. *If* she still had a job. Robert's face was filled with triumph over his sister.

"Surely you understand Jen needs her savings for our home, Ava?"

Jen wasn't sure what savings he thought she had. It seemed like now was the time to utilise Alice's time-buying excuse.

"Actually, Robert, I have a wedding to fund, so the money's already spoken for. We'll need to talk about the house thing." Having managed her economies for the last decade, his making plans for her money bothered her, but she understood marriages came with adjustments and this would have to be another of hers. He opened his mouth, but she cut him short with a pointed "Later." She wasn't discussing her finances in front of his family. For now though, her wedding-funding ploy appeared to have done the job, as Ava huffed off to the velour chaise longue and began texting furiously on her phone.

Eager for things not to be awkward between her and Robert, Jen clinked her glass to his with a "To us". They each took their sip and with a twinkle in her eye Jen leaned in to say "Mm, the champagne tastes *grape*." There followed a small satellite delay as Robert looked confused, then finally got it.

"Aha!" he said, "I see what you did there. Great/grape." He awarded her a short unconvinced laugh. "Although, strictly speaking, champagne isn't actually the grape. It's named after the region. The wine itself is an extremely complex blend, not only of grape varieties, but from different vineyards across the region—"

Robert was interrupted, and Jen saved, by Celia moving

to the mantelpiece and banging a brass mini-gong. Jen supposed this was to announce dinner. Actually, she'd lost her appetite and wasn't looking forward to sitting through a meal with a surly Ava and four boys who preferred bogies over vegetables. She'd always suspected Zara was work-shy, given how much she travelled. Now, looking at her forth-coming "new" family, she began to wonder whether Zara wasn't, in fact, hiding.

But Celia didn't usher them all through to the dining room. Instead she offered Giles her hand which he clasped, taking his place next to her.

"I was going to announce this over dinner, darlings, but the time seems prescient given the conversation. Giles and I funded both Ava and Zara's weddings, and given your parents aren't here to give you yours, as our beloved new daughter, Jennifer, we're going to pay for your and Robert's nuptials," Celia pronounced, basking in her fairy godmother status. "Your funding worries are no more!"

Jen stood stunned, until Celia pulled her into another crushing embrace, almost smothering her in her cleavage, while Robert vigorously shook his father's hand and Ava whooped that they could be bizzy-buddies after all, none of them acknowledging Beckham having dropped another one.

This should be a godsend, Jen thought, her eyes watering again. Why then, did it feel like she was brewing a small panic attack?

Chapter 15

"Bummer." Alice, though not one for swearing, wasn't one to sugar coat things either.

"I know." Sitting on Alice's shop counter while her friend arranged flowers was calming and Jen needing calming. Ava had forced her through a day-long brainstorming session for marketing the crampons and Jen, normally a fountain of ideas, had pretty much dried up. Zara Skyping in for thirty minutes from an infinity pool, complete with cocktail in coconut, hadn't helped. "What's more, Celia thinks I was crying tears of joy. Seriously, something had died in that boy's bottom and no one else batted an eyelid."

Alice snorted a laugh, but Jen couldn't see the funny side.

"How am I going to get out of the business now? I don't want to sell crampons. I don't want to sell inco pads either, but this is the limit."

"It could be a sign," said Alice, tying off a peony posy and setting it nicely on top of a wooden cabinet from Max's salvage. Jen noticed a small stack of romance novels on it. A swift scan of the room showed it wasn't alone. *Jesus.*

Alice didn't say a word.

"A sign of what? That I haven't had enough kickings in life?" Jen wasn't really prone to self-pity, but she couldn't quite see how to evade this.

"The need for a job change?"

Jen's shoulders sank a little. "Yes, I suppose. Robert's got it all planned out. Refurb the house, then fill it with sprogs."

Alice came around to the front, jumped up to sit next to her friend and took her hand. "Do you not want a house of sprogs?"

Here we go, thought Jen. Another "intervention". "I do. Maybe. But not right now."

"Fair enough," conceded Alice, which surprised Jen, as she'd been prepared to defend much harder. "You might take ages to find the right house, or have the babies, so surely Robert can't take issue with you finding another job?"

"Believe me Alice, I've lain awake thinking about this, but there aren't many marketing jobs in town, not decent ones anyway–"

"In spite of the bar being pretty low," Alice helpfully interjected.

"–and I'd still have to explain it to the family without them hating me."

The shop door opened, its bell jingling. Max reversed in, carrying two bulging jute bags.

"I've cleaned out three charity shops now, babe. The romantic mojo's got to come back." Turning and seeing Jen, her smile dropped. Jen sensed she'd heard something she shouldn't have and cocked an eyebrow at Alice, who was looking sheepish.

"Um, so, last time you were here and dissing the rom-coms and true love? Business has been a bit pants since."

"You think I've jinxed your shop?" Alice had always been a bit woo-woo, but this? Jen felt bad. Had she really been so negative? To be fair, no one had graced the shop in the hour she'd been there, and the going-home traffic normally held at least one boyfriend who'd arsed-up, needing to make amends with flowers. Alice gave her hand a squeeze.

"No, I don't think you've jinxed my shop. I'm just bringing more romance in." Alice took a look around and genuinely seemed pleased. Max was keeping her head down, neatly stacking the new books onto some repainted bookcases and a couple of brocade reupholstered chairs. It added to the boho feel. "I like the way it looks; blooms, romantic furniture and love-stories. Who wouldn't want to buy flowers in here?" Max finished her task and made a show of bowing to Alice, who blew her a kiss as she wandered to the back end of the shop and her salvage store.

"Are things difficult, Alice?" Jen asked, suspecting Alice was putting on a brave face. It didn't help that as landlord, she took money from them every month.

Alice sighed. "Foot traffic has always been touch and go around here. Some of Charlie's customers stop in now and again. But three of my corporate clients just cancelled their regular orders. They get flowers for the reception desks or for employee gifts – you know, birthdays or anniversaries etc. One is merging with a bigger company that's got its own supplier and the other two are moving out of town. It was steady money. Meanwhile the funeral homes find us too untraditional."

"OK," said Jen, her mind already whirring on how to promote Alice's business. "Have you asked to pitch for the merging company's contract?" Alice's face showed that she clearly hadn't. "Al, you have to be more forward. Shy bairns get nowt."

Alice wrinkled her nose at Jen. "What does that even mean?"

"It's northern. You have to ask for what you want."

"Yeah well, I'm not really pushy like that." While Alice could be plenty feisty with her mates, and chirpy with her customers, she had never been comfortable cold calling strangers.

"Well, we'll have to work on that. Meanwhile, what are the other options?"

Alice shrugged. "I'll keep an eye out for new companies moving in and leave them a card?" Jen thought they had to do better than that. "Otherwise I'll have to start looking at spaces closer into town, but they're more expensive, less quirky and most importantly can't house Max's stuff. I love working in the same place." Looking around her Jen saw that it would be tragic if they were forced to split up. *Re:Love* was all about the mix of the two of them and the mix of the flowers and the pre-loved salvage.

Alice's phone binged. Jen didn't look at her own. The Phone of Shame did not warrant the constant checking she'd been used to. It currently sat ignored on Jen's teenage Filofax which had been resurrected to hold her lists, now she was app-bereft. She wasn't feeling as inclined to fill her lists in, either. The wedding to-do list was as thin on the ground on paper as it was on ChAPPel.

Alice checked the notification, then jumping down sashayed to the computer. Today's tea dress was one she'd sewn using old fabrics Jen had found in her loft. While Jen's mother was a dressmaker, Jen had just never learnt how, spending hours with her dad instead, honing their beer. If Jen wasn't mistaken, Max's short sleeved shirt was the same material. Max dressed exclusively in 1950's US boys' style, with turned-up jeans, and white t-shirts under various short-sleeved shirts created by Alice.

"PanFlora order incoming!" Alice announced with an operatic flourish. Jen looked at her watch. She needed to be off. Lydia would be home soon.

"Ooooh!" sang Alice. "This is interesting."

"Is it *Romantics Anonymous* ordering a room full of flowers?" Jen asked, still slightly stung about the mojo insinuation.

Alice ignored her. "I have an order here for tomorrow. For a Jen Attisen."

"What? Really?" Jen had a rush of excitement. She *never* got flowers. Ever. Except once, when Lydia robbed some from a garden returning from a pub and left them on the kitchen table with an "I wuv you" note.

"Yes indeedy. Only, it can't be *you*," Alice said smugly, "your surname is Attis*on*, not Attis*en*. Can't be the same.

Shame, it's a lovely bouquet; all reds. Zinnias, roses, and Hypercium berries. Fabulous."

Jen was disappointed and confused. She'd been excited that they might have been for her – who didn't like getting flowers? It didn't make her a hopeless romantic or anything, it just meant someone was thinking of her and that was always nice. But like Alice said, the spelling *was* different. Robert knew how to spell her name and would have called the shop direct. He took pride in promoting local business.

"Where are they going then?" Jen tried to sound interested as opposed to envious. She wasn't sure she pulled it off.

"Hhmmm," murmured Alice, pottering between her flower buckets, pulling out some stems and beginning her assembly. They did look lovely. Lucky cow, that Jen Attisen. "To some company." Oh. Robert wouldn't send flowers to her work either. He'd think it was impractical for getting them home, whereas really all women wanted the chance to lord their flowers over their co-workers.

Alice worked fast and fixed the flowers into a spherical bouquet. Looking at them, Jen couldn't help but sigh.

Then she held up two cards, for Jen to pick one, which she obediently did, but without enthusiasm. Alice checked the computer and wrote the message.

"You know, I think she'd rather have them today than tomorrow, don't you?" Alice said. It was after hours, so it seemed like a moot point.

"Is it local?" Jen asked, glumly.

"*Well, Honestly!*? Pretty close."

163

Wait, what? "But that's ... that's me!"

Alice laughed at her, and handed her the gorgeous bouquet. Delighted and intrigued, Jen whipped the card off and read it;

Follow the passion!

Jen was conflicted. On one hand she wanted Alice to hack the PanFlora mainframe immediately for his number and email address. She was well-mannered, so she should thank him. On the other hand she was still angry and disappointed with him. She'd walked away from the show and their rendezvous for a reason. She wasn't about to put all of that aside for a bunch of flowers, even if it was the most stunning bouquet she'd ever received.

"So," said Alice. "I'm guessing it isn't Robert."

"I ... um ... I don't know Alice." She didn't know what to say. She didn't want to incriminate herself in anyway – not that there was anything going on, of course.

Alice guffawed then gave her a hammy whisper, "I think Robert knows how to spell your surname."

"I mean, I'm not sure *who* they're from." Well that was true. She was ninety-nine percent sure given the passion comment, but there had to be room for doubt in the world and he hadn't signed the card. It gave her the leeway for sidestepping the question.

Alice's eyes lit up. "Ooooh, a *secret* admirer. How very *romantic*. Good job you aren't one of those non-believer types, eh Jen?" Jen sensed she was being mocked and that she was on dodgy ground here.

"Gotta go, Al," she said, cack-handedly pulling her coat on while not letting go of her lovely flowers. "Lydia's off camping. A weekend of singing around the campfire. She'll need some help packing."

Alice gave her a smug smile. "Run away then, avoid the question."

Jen scarpered. As the door closed behind her she heard Alice shout "Good job, Max! The mojo might be back!"

Jen placed the flowers on the workbench of her outbuilding. They *were* gorgeous. But they didn't change the fact she was annoyed with Yakob. Sitting on his deck, talking about their families, especially about his Morfar and her dad, she'd thought they'd had a connection, an honesty between them. There had been numerous chances where he could have said *Oh Kronegaard? I work for them.* And he hadn't. He'd definitely *hidden* it. There was no two ways around that. He'd let her trash the company in all sorts of ways and he'd let her run her mouth off about her brewing like he wasn't already well informed about such things. How stupid she must have sounded. Instinctively Jen put her hands to her heated cheeks. Oh God, she'd talked him through glass colours like he was a novice. How cringey. There was no way he couldn't have been laughing at her behind her back. Just like Danny must have been too after she'd left Ibiza. It all made her feel a little bit sick.

Neither Danny or Yakob had turned out to be what she thought, and while the red of the flowers reminded her of the red and white Danish flags she'd seen all over

Copenhagen, they also reminded her that it had all happened in a holiday environment and she was adamant in her belief that people didn't think straight on holidays. Regardless of having met him again, Yakob was definitely a holiday thing and Jen immediately realised that she absolutely wouldn't let it destabilise what she had with Robert. Robert was a *better* thing. He was a decent bloke, just as her dad had said. She'd known him for years, not just a fleeting few hours. Having just been talked through all of his baby photos by Celia after their dinner, Jen was pretty sure she knew everything about him. Her life with Robert would be straightforward and uncomplicated and she could stay in control of it. OK, so he was making plans without her, but what they needed was a dedicated meeting, a sit-down to discuss and plan things out. They could set an agenda and work through the points, until they had a clear mission statement they could stick to for this marriage, which she believed would be a success. Within a framework like that, Jen knew she could function and go forward and most importantly stay in some semblance of control. Not of Robert; she didn't want to be *controlling*, but of them as a team and partnership. However, above all else she needed to know she was part of the steering, because she'd been in a position of floundering helplessness before in her life and she would do everything she could never to be there again. Letting go of the brewing was surely a small price to pay for that stability, wasn't it?

But.

Looking at her brewing paraphernalia, surrounded by the aromas of the beers and the yeast, the barley and the hops, the entire atmosphere in the room was tugging at her soul. The joy she got from brewing, the memories she had with her dad, knowing she was good at it, all those things gnawed at her. The thought of packing the vats and the bottles away made her feel sad to her bones. Not jotting down notes for recipe ideas was a notion that made her anxious. There was a helplessness to those thoughts that scared her.

She sat upright and took a resolute breath. She was going to ignore who the flowers came from. Whether an encouragement or an apology, it didn't matter. At the end of the day, they didn't change anything – she'd made her decision on the plane coming back from Copenhagen. Packing it away was a huge change for her, but that was probably why she was finding it hard. Many things in life were hard; that didn't make them impossible, nor the wrong thing to do. She'd sell her stock at the show, she'd finish her wedding beer and that would be it, as she threw herself headlong and blissfully into her sustainable married life with a decent man who she knew and was clearly in tune with, who didn't tease her, who indulged his mother and tolerated his obnoxious nephews lobbing sprouts at him over a dinner table, and who her dad had approved of.

Resolved, Jen tied the flowers upside down from her awards shelf for them to dry. It was too beautiful a bouquet, too rare a thing in her life, for her to bear seeing it wither

167

and die in a vase. It bookended her shelf of beer accolades and mementos like a big, fragrant red full stop.

She had a plan, and being a stickler for plans, Jen knew she was safer, less exposed to trouble, if she followed it.

Chapter 16

"They've totally filched your ideas," Lydia hissed indignantly, handing Jen a paper-cup of steaming coffee, while giving a couple of other entrants milling around the tent flaps, the stink-eye.

It was a cold morning for July, or maybe simply being out of the duvet at aahhmmaaggaahhdd o'clock made it feel Baltic. The craft tent had been buzzing from very early-doors, with people putting the finishing touches to their entries. There had been some argy-bargy going on around the cakes display, proper "piping bags at dawn" stuff, but that was cake-bakers for you; vicious.

The Home Brew category was somewhat more sedate, there being no more than eight entrants, six of whom were retirees and all, bar Jen, male. None of the others had much sense for the creative display element. "There's two others displaying their beers in a tin bucket," Lydia detailed, with a sneer. Jen had done that the previous year, salvaged tin bucket, fresh straw and three bottles for tasting. She'd plumped for a cracked butler's sink this year, filled with dried flower petals. It was different and had been free. It was amazing what Max had in her salvage rejects and Alice was happy enough for Jen to root through her offcuts.

"When's the judging finished?" Lydia asked, slurping her coffee and burning her tongue. Burnt or not, it didn't stop her swearing.

"Another half hour," Jen groaned, eyeing the closed-off tent. She hated this bit. No, in fact the bit she hated most was walking away, having set up the display. The brews were like her babies going into school for the first time. She'd done her bit, now they had to stand on their own two feet. That made her feel queasy. What if the judges failed to appreciate their brilliance? All mothers experienced that, didn't they?

Jen had first won two years before, when she'd lifted the title off Jim Arbuthnot, who after years of winning thought he owned it. While Lydia and Jen hopped around in a deranged happy dance, old Jim had had a face like a smacked bottom. Jen didn't know which was worse for him, that his run had come to an end or that he'd been beaten by a woman. He stormed out muttering about India Pale Ale being the easy option, but even if Jen said so herself, that brew was the smoothest thing this side of smooth and packed with flavours. The following year Jen easily won again, with *Clink and you'll miss it*, a copper-coloured American Pale Ale, which she'd spent ages perfecting to get the right bitter hoppiness using three different kinds of hops, giving it aromas of citrus, mango and flowers. It was the most expensive brew she'd made yet, but thanks to the win she sold out from the stall, giving her enough profit to overhaul the coal shed into her brewhouse, using YouTube tutorials to guide her with the hammer and nails.

This year, she'd gone for a light yellow fruit beer using elderflower. It was light and summery and Lydia had declared it her favourite ever, naming it *Hoppy Days*.

The crowds were arriving in droves which immediately pepped the spirits of the stallholders. Jen often spent her Saturdays working a stall at the local farmer's markets. She did a decent trade with her beers, especially, like that day, when she could wangle a plot next to Fenella the cheesemaker. The two products went well together; it was all fermentation after all. Sales had taken a leap when Jen had suggested they collaborate on a Ploughman's gift pack. She wasn't quite sure how she was now going to break her news to her stall mate. She decided to wait until later. No need to spoil things from the off. Fenella, though a good thirty years older than Jen, was a spritely woman, happily widowed and polar opposites to Jen when it came to facing life, living by a mantra of *Que sera sera* much to Jen's mystification.

"It's colder than a witch's tit out here. So much for fucking July weather." Fenella had always had a mouth on her too, which enamoured her to Lydia, who also had a coffee for the cheesemaker.

"I'm not sure anywhere in this country is warm at nine in the morning, Fen," Jen said, unpacking another box of bottles onto her trestle table. She'd rented a van for the weekend, the Capri not being built for delivery driving, and it had been rammed full. Fenella pulled her knitted Peruvian hat down over her ears. Her fluorescent yellow puffa jacket was zipped to the hilt.

Jen had another scan of the stall, and surveyed the boxes. "If it'll just get a bit warmer, and if I can win a commendation or more, then I'm hoping these'll all shift." She prayed she had enough for the day. She'd held some back for tomorrow. She could go back to get those and spend the rest of the night replacing them if she had to.

"Relax," Lydia said mildly, blatantly eyeing the passing bottom of a young farmer. "You know the drill. You've got enough stock. And none of this commendation bollocks, you're going to win." Sometimes Jen thought Lydia's confidence in her was slightly indecent, surely she had to grant the other contestants a modicum of skill or chance? "Where's Robbie?" Lydia added, causing Jen to purse her lips slightly. Lydia thought she was looking innocent, but Jen knew she was stirring.

"Robert will be here," she said confidently. "I texted him the announcement time." She busied herself with the merchandise and stall so as to ignore Lydia's customary eyeroll.

Attison's Beers, locally brewed with love, it said on the banner behind her. She'd added a sticker for each of the past two years stating she was the beer category winner. Surveying the table top and its many, many bottles, Jen was so flipping proud of all of it. Was that wrong, she wondered? Pride was supposed to be wrong, but in this instance she didn't care. *I made that. I made that with my recipes, my ideas, my time, my hands.* And it gave her a thrill. Until she remembered that she was stopping this, that the end was in sight. Then it gave her a lump in her throat.

"That's six bottles gone already," Lydia said with a grin, dropping some cash into the unattractive money apron around Jen's waist. Jen hadn't even spotted Lydia's patter-come-flirting with a couple of farmers, being so caught up in loving her wares. Lydia was a born saleswoman. "Gotta love beer drinkers. Any time, any place, any where."

"You stole that line," Jen pointed out, marking the sales down on her spreadsheet. She liked to know what had sold best. She was still working on paper, The Phone of Shame not knowing the meaning of spreadsheet.

"So? It's a motto I hold dear." Lydia replied and Jen rolled her eyes at her.

It was hard to stay nonchalant when the judging tent reopened. Word rushed around the showground like wild-fire, a gushing relief to all those who'd spent the last hour clock-watching and sweating.

"I've never seen geriatrics move so quickly," Jen observed wryly, watching the flurry of competitors sprint to see if there was a certificate by their entry, "unless it's at the supermarket and a checkout's just opened."

Only, Lydia wasn't behind her as she'd thought. Lydia apparently had no qualms about racing for results, and was barging through the tent with an impressive use of her elbows. Thankfully the strewn straw was keeping the ground solid enough for Lydia's leg so far. Jen worried how long it would be before things got slippy.

"You did it, Jen!" she shouted over the thronging mass as Jen approached the tent with feigned calm. Jen heard a small groan from her left and turning, saw Jim, brow deeply furrowed and shoulders now sagging. As if that wasn't awkward enough, Lydia then appeared at her side, slung an arm around her and planted a huge kiss on her cheek before pronouncing, "Three years in a row. Woohoo!" *Bless her,* thought Jen with a pained smile to Jim, *but I want to slap her silly sometimes.*

Making it to the beer display Jen got only the briefest glimpse of the gold-coloured card before Lydia swamped her into a second hug.

"I knew you'd do it. I am so proud of you." Jen decided not to slap her silly at that precise moment, the reality and joy of the situation beginning to sink in.

The judges notes, scribbled onto the card, were exactly what she was looking for; *a fruity light delicate beer, perfect for summer, hoppy days indeed!*

"Congratulations." The voice jogged her out of her vain-glorying. She looked up into the face of a tall well-built man, black and silver tufty hair, mid-forties. She recognised him, but couldn't place him, but it didn't matter either way, as she was smiling at him like a fool, because she'd WON!!! and he seemed happy for her.

"Anthony St James!" Lydia exclaimed, her jaw roughly around her knees. Yes, that rang a bell with Jen, but out of context she was still at a loss. "I love your show. I watch it in bed on a Sunday morning, if I'm by myself. Sometimes, even if I'm not – they never seem to mind. I'm Lydia, by the way," she gushed, vigorously shaking his hand, "and the mute grinner here is my sister, Jen. Three times winner of the beer class." She elbowed Jen sharply in the ribs.

"Anthony St James," he repeated, shaking her hand. It was a good handshake. Strong and firm, but without crushing her bones. Jen's dad had taught her to shake hands. It was something she always noticed.

"Off the telly," Lydia hissed in a bizarre pantomime hiss, which Anthony St James Off The Telly could definitely hear but chose to ignore.

And then, with a startled *Oh*, she got it. It was *Anthony St James. Off. The. Telly*. He'd opened a posh restaurant in town the summer before, but she'd never seen him. She'd assumed he only put his name on the menu. But here he was.

"The TV chef," Jen babbled, "right here. In real life. I'm such an idiot. I'm sorry. I couldn't place your face. I'm used to seeing you this big." She indicated the size of her TV screen which was embarrassingly small "and here you are, this–," she raised her hand to just above his head and realised that she was being an idiot. Whipping her hands behind her back she chewed her own lip for damage limitation.

"I wanted to congratulate you on a really good beer," he said graciously ignoring her muppetry and subsequent blushing. He probably encountered starstruck muppets like her all the time.

"You've tried it?" she asked slowly to control her effusiveness. She wanted to claw back a modicum of dignity, but on the other hand she was so desperate to hear what he thought, that it hurt.

"I was a judge this year. I've spent the morning scoffing sponges, chutneys and beer."

They all winced in unison, which made them laugh.

"Well, thank you," she managed, pulling herself together. "I'm honoured." He looked at his watch and his smile pulled into a "must go" smile. Jen realised she should probably be making her way back too, given Fenella was covering her stall for her.

"Wait!" Jen grabbed his arm in a pique of high drama, causing Lydia to think she'd lost the plot. Jen grabbed three unopened bottles from her display and handed them to him. He had to hold them to his body, slightly awkwardly and enough to draw attention.

"A gift from Attison's Brewery." Jen might have been lacking in the blowing-her-own-trumpet department, but she knew a marketing opportunity when she saw one. A celeb walking around with her bottles, was tantamount to an endorsement.

"You have a brewery?" he asked, a brow arching. Jen looked from him to Lydia and back again, conscious that her face was getting hot.

"Just a small one," she squeaked, and instantly felt more stupid for squeaking. Squeaking was not cool. Squeaking did not say she was a serious brewster, brewing the best of British craft beers. But then again, she wasn't; she was just a hobbyist, and one about to pack it in at that. He didn't need to know that though, while she had stock to shift and wasn't above taking advantage of poor unsuspecting celebrities. "But a good one," she added, thankfully without a squeak this time.

Ambling arm in arm back to the stall, Lydia stopped to buy two homemade liquorice pipes, handing one to Jen. They walked along smoking them like two old biddies. Jen could tell, even without the pipe, Lydia was pondering.

"How can you give this up?" Lydia finally asked. "Really, Jen. This win, it's a sign. You're gifted. Your talent is recognised, if not by Robert, then by the rest of the world." Jen wasn't sure the county show constituted The World, but she understood the sentiment.

"Robert knows I brew well." It seemed right to defend him, she just wasn't sure it was absolutely true. No, actually that wasn't fair. He *did* know she was good at it, he was a man who dealt in evidence after all, but the fact was it simply wasn't part of their future. "It just doesn't fit into our new plan."

"*His* plan. I can't believe you'd have signed it off willingly."

"Times change, Lydia," she said, dodging the question and speeding up a bit to reach the stall and end the conversation, not least because there was a germinating part of her that agreed. She *was* good at this. Much as she was trying to convince herself it was the timely thing to do, it didn't quite add up in her head. She didn't seem to be able to click with other crafts – her attempt at knitting had almost killed her, meanwhile she couldn't stop herself thinking about new recipes or flavours. Looking at the rosette she'd taken from the display to perch on her stall, she wondered whether Lydia might be right. Was it a sign?

News had filtered out about the win and the customers had started arriving. Clearly they seemed to like cheese too, as Fenella didn't have enough arms to handle it all. She didn't disguise her relieved sigh when Jen retook her spot behind the trestle. Fenella wasn't subtle like that.

Lydia started messing with the banner behind her.

"Lyds, give me a hand, please," Jen groaned. The queue – yes a queue! – was getting longer. "What are you doing?" She turned to see Lydia had added a sticker onto the vinyl, listing this year's win. "Where did you get that?"

"I had it made," she smirked.

"But you couldn't have known the result."

"Pff. Of course I knew. *Faith* Jen, faith."

Jen had to bite her lip, because her eyes suddenly stung a little. She loved this girl. She was indisputably the best cheerleader.

Speaking of cheerleaders, she looked about, but there was no sign of Robert. *Her fiancé*. The Phone of Shame showed no messages. She told herself he couldn't have got the message, reception out in the showground was dicky at times.

Lydia looked at her watch. "You going to be OK handling the sales? I need to go."

"I'll be fine," Jen said, hoping that was true. The queue

wasn't abating. "Ready for a night of campfires and guitar strumming?"

"I've packed my music and earphones if they try the strumming," Lydia said, pulling her stuff together.

"Call me if you get stuck, or if your leg is giving you problems or–"

"I'll be fine, Jen." Jen noted Lydia's change in tone. It was snippy. She told herself to relax. It was just a night in a field, for goodness sake.

"Right. Yes. Only, make sure they pick somewhere not too muddy. They don't see how mud pulls at your leg, or that it can be slippy."

Lydia took a breath for her retort, but released it, unwilling to get into it. She gave Jen a kiss on the cheek, said she'd see her later, and headed for the car park, where allegedly her friends were waiting. Jen decided she'd send her a text to check she'd found them in a little while.

"Have fun!" Jen called, hoping it might smooth things over, but Lydia simply waved without looking back. Jen watched her disappear with her usual sense of trepidation for her sister. It took the beeping of her phone to distract her.

Srry darling.
Was asked 2 sub in a
4ball match at last min.
C U 2morrow.
Robert

Robert religiously signed his texts with his name, as equally religiously as he corrected anyone who shortened it. She wondered who else he thought she'd think it was from. After all, she didn't know anyone else who'd let her down for a game of golf.

Chapter 17

"You've got a good business there, Jen. Thought about expanding?" Fenella asked, as they packed their trestle tables down, both stalls depleted. *Every day,* Jen thought. She decided to postpone the news that she was packing it all in, until the end of the show. Given her mood with Robert, she wasn't currently inclined to think about accommodating his wishes. And having spent the day next to Fenella's fromagerie, she knew which aroma she'd prefer to live with.

Driving home, she was still narked with him. Was it too much to ask that he came to see how she'd done? Even if he saw her hobby as something that was ending soon, he was a competitive man and should have been rooting for her. And yet, he'd neither wished her good luck, nor asked her how she'd done. The disappointment inside Jen ran deep. She was still muttering about it as she stumbled through the front door, arms laden with bags and table cloths to be washed.

As always, she was met by her parents' beaming faces. A large framed photo of them hung at the end of the short hall, directly opposite the door. They'd hung it there themselves, "to remind us not to be miserable gits when coming in from work." Jen and Lydia had unequivocally agreed to leave it there after the accident, in spite of it breaking their hearts. Over time, it had become easier to look at. On numerous occasions Jen had found herself asking their advice as she passed, generally regarding Lydia.

To free up her hands, she stuck the rosette onto the frame for the moment. It made her feel like a child, bringing a prize home to show them. They would have been so proud. Given it was for beer, her dad would have been over the moon. She could imagine all the questions he'd be asking her; about the beer, about the display, about the competitor's entries. Actually no – he'd have known all of that already, as he would have watched her brewing it and he would have worked the stall with her. He would have kissed her good luck as she went to see the results and he would have celebrated with her after. Jen hustled to the kitchen to off-load the table cloths, and to clear the welling in her eyes.

The wash cycle with the table cloths was just kicking off when the doorbell rang. She wasn't expecting anyone. Lydia was probably Kumbaya-ing in her field already.

Opening the door, she was met with a face full of white flowers and a fist proffering a bottle of champagne. Alice's face appeared from behind it all.

"Delivery for the victorious Jen Atti*sen*."

Jen ushered her in, as Alice unloaded the bouquet in her arms. White roses, freesias and jasmine, surrounded by pale green eucalyptus. They smelled heavenly. Alice knew her way to the kitchen and placing the bottle on the table, found two mismatched champagne flutes. "I've had it chilling all afternoon," she said, pausing for a moment, "but do you want to save it?"

"Open it," Jen said, immediately. Lydia wasn't around, Robert could get stuffed right now, and Alice was one of her favourite people, so it seemed exactly right to celebrate with her. Jen unlocked the door to the courtyard and set two faded patchwork cushions on the doglegged wooden bench which her dad had built into the near corner. The evening sun hit perfectly in over the outbuilding, warming the little suntrap.

"Read the card," Alice commanded, setting the glasses on the table and settling herself onto the bench.

Congratulations, Jen!
Follow the passion.

Dropping down into her seat, Jen was mystified. How could he have known? He was in a different country for goodness sake. How could he know about the win, and arrange flowers so fast this time? How? Dammit he was making it hard to not think about him or stay cross at him. He was certainly persistent in his encouragement, it made her wonder whether he could really be laughing at her brewing. That he'd acknowledged her win, where someone else hadn't, wasn't helping either.

Alice gave her a nudge. "Want to talk about it?"

"I ... he ... actually, no, not really, Al." How could she

talk about it without being disloyal to Robert? They were beautiful flowers, just as lovely as the red bouquet, but they hadn't come from her fiancé, and that had her conflicted when it came to squeeing about them. Which was difficult as she was now pissed off with both men and she really, *really* wanted to squee about the flowers. Apparently she loved receiving flowers. "They're gorgeous, Alice. You did a beautiful job." Jen popped the cork on the bottle. Much as she loved beer, the pop of a fizz cork was a wonderful thing; one compact little sound announcing to a room that something marvellous had happened.

"The instructions were pretty clear; white and fragrant," Alice said, as Jen filled their glasses. "He obviously knows you have a fine nose." They both knew they weren't talking about Robert. Alice was one of the least judgmental people Jen knew, but she still couldn't bring herself to talk about Yakob other than to enquire whether there had been a name with the order.

"Nope. Sorry," Alice said, holding up her glass to toast Jen. "Follow the passion," she toasted, with a knowing smirk. Jen had no choice but to clink her glass and agree. "I knew you'd ask me though," Alice went on, after a long sip, "so I've pulled a favour at PanFlora, and someone's on it. You'll be the first to hear if we get anywhere."

Jen relaxed into her seat and allowed herself to bask quietly in the glow of the day, gazing at her bouquet. Alice told Jen about her day at the flower shop, still lamenting the decreasing flow of customers but being entertained by the increasing madness of the few who did come. Jen took part in the conversation, but her focus was on the words on the card as she spun it on its corners, between her fingertip and the wood of the table.

She was rather amazed by the efforts Yakob had made. He'd tracked her down for starters, when really all he'd known was her name, her town and the fact she worked in inco pads. Google could have helped him there, she supposed. He knew she'd won the show though, which meant he'd not only remembered her talking about it, but he'd made time to find out the result. Perhaps it might be mentioned already on the show website. He'd then reacted immediately to arrange the flowers and the—

"Was the champagne in the order too?" she asked, interrupting Alice's flow about someone's dog weeing against one of her flower buckets in the shop.

"I love you Jen, but I can't afford this stuff." She poured them another glass and carried on about the dog, not remotely bothered that Jen wasn't fully engaged.

Jen continued with her pondering. He'd arranged flowers and champagne to celebrate her win. How nice was that? How supportive. His insisting she "follow the passion" made her feel he saw something in her, when really that was ridiculous. He didn't really know her, and he hadn't tasted her beer, but nevertheless he was encouraging her dream. His belief in her was heart-warming. And generous – he wasn't asking anything in return. It reminded her of her dad.

Worried she'd get teary, Jen forced herself to look away from the flowers and to focus on Alice. They spent the next hour discussing Alice's marketing options and everything unrelated to the fragrant white elephant in the room, until Alice said she had to go and Jen remembered she still had a re-stocking situation and that she was dog tired.

Alice, slightly squiffy, took her hand at the door.

"I know we aren't talking about it Jen, and I totally respect that, and I know they're only flowers, but I see the shine in your eyes when you look at them and I see your brain working overtime about what they might mean. I also see your conflict and I get that too, but here's the thing; the conflict says you have *options*. Your head and heart knows there's more to think about. You aren't married yet and even if the flower-sender isn't something long term, then perhaps it's still a sign you need to be reconsidering your current choices?" Alice didn't hang about, having said her piece, she gave Jen's hand a squeeze and headed off down the path before Jen could say anything about how she was wrong, or in defence of Robert.

Closing the door and leaning against it, Jen turned to face her parents. They were smiling as if they had forever in the picture, but she knew how short their lives had actually been. What would they think now of her choice, if they knew she was about to pack her talent away, for a simple safe life?

She wasn't so sure they'd be so proud of her after all.

Probably not helped by the champagne, Jen's mood took a turn for the worse and for once she was glad Lydia wasn't in the house. While her sister convened with nature, Jen slammed about the house, banging doors and stomping up and down the stairs, soundly ignoring the protesting wall-walloping of the neighbours, as she prepared for the early start the next day and tried to sort out her life. Jen was proud of her multi-tasking skills, but this was hard.

Coming across her failed attempt at knitting, she slapped it into a drawer. She wasn't going to be picking up a golf club either and Celia could stick her bridge too. There wasn't any other hobby she wanted. Three rosettes was a clear sign. The Universe had made its point. Jen stopped her angry marauding, the words sitting primed on her tongue. She took a moment before she let them fly, their release hurling her across a precipice; "I am not giving up the brewing!"

At once a layer of anxiety lifted from her. She felt a smile rise to her face, and she said it louder.

Better.

She said it again, this time technically a shout, and it made her feel euphoric, in spite of the annoyed 'Oi' from the other side of the wall. She locked up for the night and hoofed up to her room, where she flung herself backwards onto the bed.

She was keeping the brewing. Two hundred percent FACT. It made her happy and she *needed* to be happy, because life could be short, so she had to accommodate it. That was her brief. Jen liked a brief, as it was a starting point for a list, and now she could start building her action plan, because she was going to need one.

Somehow she was going to find a way to grow her

brewing business – because she wasn't just in this for the hobby now, she was going see her goals through – and show Robert it could all work and hopefully work well, to their long-term benefit. So she was cross with him right now, but such things passed, everything would smooth out. All couples had spats. Once he saw it could turn a proper profit she was sure he'd be on board and more supportive than he was currently. In spite of what Alice was wrongly alluding to with the flowers, she'd accepted a future with Robert and she believed this new strategy would be a sound underpinning. The kids could wait and when they came, they'd be fine seeing Mummy had a career too. She wanted her kids to see their mum had goals and ambitions, not just wiping their noses and bottoms. She'd still be depend-able to all of them, she'd just have something of her own too.

There, that was decided, and she felt immeasurably better for it. She'd have to thank Yakob one day if she ever met him again. Not just for the flowers, but for pushing her to hold on to her passion. She would always be grateful to him for that.

Daredevils came out to play on the south coast this weekend, with the annual Extreme Sports expo welcoming over 10,000 visitors. Adrenalin junkies had the opportunity to try many of the extreme sports, ranging from Paragliding to Aggressive Street Skating, Soapbox-racing to Parkour.

Local live-wire Lydia Attison (22) is seen here

impressing spectators with her newfound Street Skeleton skills. The gorgeous Westhampton resident was fearless as she took one of the fastest times of the day, in spite of being a leg down on other riders in the sport, which is essentially racing at high speed, face-down to the asphalt on a wheeled tea-tray. A scout for the British Bobsleigh and Skeleton Association said he was keen to spend some time with Miss Attison regarding ParaSkeleton, which is seeking to become a Paralympic sport.

Unfortunately, Lydia was unavailable for comment despite continued efforts by the Echo.

-Neil Finch, Staff Reporter,
Westhampton Echo, page 5

Chapter 18

Jen was deliberately late to the restaurant. Robert preferred eating out on a Sunday – less noise, more service, apparently. It was, in his mind, another genial part of their Wednesday/Sunday date night routine. This evening however, it would also mean him sitting alone, waiting, which would be more obvious, more awkward. She reckoned twenty minutes was enough to make her point. Maybe it would dawn on him that it wasn't nice to leave people hanging or take them for granted.

"Something happen?" he asked, getting up from the table to kiss her hello. He took a look at his phone too, in case her distress message had just pinged in. Perhaps he was making a point of his own. She was having none of it.

"No," she said, leaving The Phone of Shame in her bag. Funny, now she didn't have her iPhone with its apps, she wasn't remotely inclined to have it sitting out on a dining table, and she was noticing how others religiously did, and how often they looked at them during conversations. Had she been like that? If so, things were changing once she got a new one. "I was tidying up from the show and lost track of time."

He gave her an odd look. Losing track of time was not something they did.

"Right," he said slightly unsure of her, but was side-tracked by the waiter arriving to take their drinks order. Robert began to suggest a wine for them both, but Jen asked for a beer instead, earning her another disconcerted look, before he ordered his by the glass. Jen took a look around the dining room. It was a calm modern space, the decor kept to creams and whites. Jen imagined during the day, when the light came in through the white wooden shutters, it must feel like part of the beach that lay beyond the glass. "So, the show," he started and she was pleased he'd taken the hint. Sometimes people just needed prompting. "Sell out? Clear the stock?"

"I did," she said with a smile, waiting for him to ask about the competition. It suddenly dawned on her she was sitting in Anthony St James' place. She wondered how he'd managed, navigating the showground laden with her beers. She on the other hand, with no beers left to sell had simply given Fenella a hug and carried her earnings, banner and trestle table back to the van.

"Excellent. That'll give you some space back in the house and money in the coffers. Can't market a house properly with a lounge full of boxes."

Jen felt her entire body bristle. So many things about that sentence bothered her, she didn't know which to tackle first.

She decided to back-burner her beer for the moment as there was something more pressing to address.

"Robert, have you forgotten Lydia owns half the house?"

"No, of course not," he said, tearing off some of the sourdough roll on his side plate and buttering it, "but is she able to buy you out?"

"No, of course not," Jen batted right back.

"There you go. So she'll get half of the sale value." Robert sent her a smile, as if they were on the same page now. "You know, properties in the old town are getting exceptional prices; there's the competition with the second-homers and holiday-lets, too. I asked around with the estate agents. She'll be able to buy something of her own with half the cash. In fact," he paused to taste the wine and having swilled and considered it properly nodded to the waiter, in spite of it being a full glass already, "if we can time everything right, she could even buy my place. How neat would that be? Minimal chain. Fortuitous and practical." Jen could see how it wrapped up neatly in his head, and had it been anything other than her childhood home and her sister, she might even have agreed – at least to its practicality – but it wasn't and she didn't.

She took a big swig of her beer. "Robert, your flat is on the third floor."

"Which affords it the sea view."

"That's six flights of stairs for her."

"There's the lift," he pointed out.

"Which is temperamental and to be honest it's not really in a part of town I want her living in."

"She's a big girl now, Jen. She can choose for herself." He was looking at her like she was being stubborn in her arguing. He was also overlooking that he appeared to be choosing for Lydia himself.

"Good," said Jen, "then you'll understand if she chooses to stay in our parents' house, which she is used to, and which," Jen fixed him with a determined eye, "I won't be forcing her to sell." Jen wasn't going to be forced into selling anything either. She wasn't a push over.

"But Jen, how will we buy the house we want, if we don't pool our resources? I know my sisters have their eye on your money for their business, but I'll persuade them to make you partner based on your paying for your shares over time with the dividends and–"

"I'm not taking the partnership," she interjected. She'd better get that on the table now. She didn't want to work for the sisters forever, and she didn't want to buy into the products. Saying it aloud felt good. A huge smile spread across Robert's face.

"That's wonderful, Jen. I'm so glad."

"You are?"

"Absolutely. It would have been a waste of time setting the partnership up, just to get you back out of it again once the babies come. Can you imagine?" There was very little in the crampon scenario Jen wanted to imagine, that was true, but she didn't share his motivation. She had to tell him about her beer plans. Walking over, she'd decided she needed this laid out clearly, so they could proceed with their future planning knowing what was what. "But coming back to the house then, Jen, that only leaves selling the Arches ..."

"I can't sell the Arches, Robert. Apart from the sentimental value, the rent the units bring in has funded Lydia's healthcare and prostheses. Do you know how much a leg costs?"

"An arm and a leg?" he ventured with a smirk, hamfistedly trying to lighten things. She was definitely in an odd mood this evening.

"Not funny."

"Sorry," he said contrite and sipped at his wine. "Surely the settlement from the haulage company covers that?" Robert had been part of the compensation case. It had been uncontested given three CCTV cameras recorded the lorry ploughing through her family.

"I want Lydia to have the best legs possible, and nowadays they cost more than the case calculated. It's tens of thousands per leg. They only have a five year shelf-life and then you either refurb, or pay again to get a new one. Hoping, as I am, she's going to have a long life, I need to account for that, plus an old age where she'll need extra facilities and help. That doesn't come cheap either, and I can't afford to overlook it now." Jen wished she had her iPhone, so she could show him her spreadsheet of things required to ease Lydia's life.

"OK," Robert acknowledged, but he didn't sound too chuffed about it. "What about selling one of them? That would help."

Jen considered it might appear as if she was being uncompromising in co-funding their future. She didn't want it to look like that. She wanted them to be equal partners in their life together, but she was in the position of having to consider other people too. She didn't want to boot Charlie, Alice or Max out either.

"Do we need a new house straight away?" she asked. "You can move in with me. We could rent yours out, if you like. Start a portfolio or sell later?"

Robert tried very, very hard to disguise his wince, but failed. Jen raised her eyebrow at him, keen to know what the problem was. She loved her home.

"I was thinking, we should be *together* – by ourselves – in our first home Jen, no disrespect to Lydia of course, and also that I might need somewhere to work. I can't see a room in your house to do that."

Jen had to agree there. It was a Victorian two bed terrace with a lounge, dining room and kitchen downstairs. Definitely little study potential. She nodded to say she understood, but he took it as encouragement to go on. "Plus we could move now to something big – if you release the equity – and stay put there. Our forever home."

A forever home. She'd never given that much thought. Thinking about it now didn't give her the goose bumps she thought it should. More the chills.

"Don't people have a first home first? Then save for a forever home?"

"They can, but we could skip that." He seemed so keen, and normally that might have carried her along, but given all the other things she needed the money for, Jen didn't buy into it.

The waiter came to take their order and Jen decided to

park the issue. She wanted time to think it through. She didn't want to sell anything her parents had worked so hard for, she didn't want to turf Lydia out or disadvantage her in any way given it was largely Jen's fault she was facing a lifetime of challenges, and if that meant she had to live more modestly, then fair enough. But she could see, having agreed to marry Robert, she was going to need a plan which satisfied his life expectations too. She felt a sudden yearning to be in her outbuilding, working on her beer. She did her best thinking when her hands were busy and she was creating.

"Ahh, the brewing maestra, Jen Attison." The voice made Jen look up. The waiter had left the table and in her place was a figure in chef's whites. Robert was looking between them surprised.

"Hello Anthony," she said, hoping to get away with the familiarity. She was a customer after all, so she could probably take the liberty. Meanwhile Robert was looking decidedly on the backfoot. "Can I introduce my fiancé Robert?" That still sounded strange on her tongue. "Robert, Anthony judged the brewing at the show." Jen kept a blank face. Robert still hadn't asked her about it.

"You must be very proud of her *and* her beer, Robert," Anthony said. "They really are quite exceptional flavours she can conjure. You're a lucky man." Was it appropriate behaviour to kiss a relative stranger in front of your fiancé? Jen forced herself to err on the side of caution and remain seated. She couldn't stop her face from beaming though.

"I, um, yes, of course." Robert looked at her. Jen took the expression to be shame.

"Lovely to see you again, Jen. Enjoy your meal." At that the chef nodded and headed off to greet the few other diners, leaving a pregnant silence between them that over-rode the room's low-level jazz music. Given her feeling from this afternoon, she let him stew in it, until he caved.

"You placed then?"

"I did. First place." There seemed to be something else going on here, as he didn't seem as enthused as she might have hoped. Anthony had been more effusive.

"Well done."

"Thank you."

"We both had a winning day, then," he said perking up. "Toby and I won the Fourball."

It took everything Jen had to calmly congratulate him in return, when really she wanted to yell that her being awarded first place for the third year running was light-years away from him winning a Saturday morning golf game. The crossness in her wouldn't be curbed though, not entirely, and so she found herself blurting out the thing she'd role-played all the way to the restaurant.

"I'm continuing with the brewing, Robert." She held her breath to see what he'd say. He was busy buttering another bite of bread, so she carried on, taking a conciliatory angle. "The beer I'm on now is one I've planned for the wedding. I want it to be a one off, just for our day. We could give the guests a bottle instead of favours. I'll design a label with our names and wedding date on." She looked at him expect-antly, hoping the wedding idea would ease this through. She'd always found in her negotiations that giving the other

197

party something they'd like took the sting off the thing they didn't.

He gave her a benign smile, one that suggested she'd overcome a hurdle.

"Jen," he said, raising his wine glass to her, "I'm totally on board with that."

"You are?" Jen was delighted. Didn't that go to show that talking about things was always best? Being honest and expressing one's thoughts often moved things along and unblocked stalemates. Maybe there had never been a stalemate at all, maybe she'd misunderstood him.

"Absolutely. If it's what you need to let it go, of course I'm with you. Go for it. Weddings are all about the bride, aren't they?" He clinked his glass against hers as if sealing the deal. The wind knocked right out of her, leaving her speechless. Which went unnoticed, as Robert was animated again. "I meant to say the ring will be back in another week. The jeweller rang. He had to send it to London. That ivy effect was a nightmare to work with." Jen instinctively retracted her left hand from the table top to her lap and cradled it safely in her other hand. The ring was a nightmare full stop. "And Mumsie has been on my tail too. Wants to know how you're getting on with the dress, or whether she can book the appointment at the shop?"

The rest of their meal was rather subdued. Jen had promised to talk to Celia about the dress and thereafter feigned exhaustion from the weekend's stall-tending to explain her lack of conversation. She was too tied up in her thoughts to make the effort. And she didn't really want to talk to him right now. Married couples had disagreements, maybe they were having one early. She just didn't know how to deal with it, and he didn't appear to be hearing her anyway. Had he always been like this, had she simply not noticed? Jen supposed that she too might get bull-headed about things when she had a plan in her head. That was possible, so perhaps she should make allowances for him. Partnerships were about compromise, weren't they? Jen sighed. If business had taught her anything it was the value of a tactical retreat and so she took one now.

Jen focused on her food, enjoying Anthony's flavours, playing her usual mental game of matching her beers to the dishes. At least it zoned out Robert's account of the Fourball. She declined dessert, legitimately desperate for her bed now. She was having an internal battle of whether to accept his lift home to get there quicker, or whether to walk, to give herself some space to grumble in private. She didn't need Lydia to be party to it. That wouldn't be helpful. However, as they reached the restaurant door, she stopped.

"I've forgotten my phone, Robert." He saw it wasn't in her hand where it normally lived. Jen knew it was safely buried in her bag.

"I'll pull the car around?"

"No need, darling, I'll walk. Helps my digestion," she said, keen for them to part on good terms, but also keen for them to part ASAP. She'd had a brain-wave and needed to execute it before she – or he – talked herself out of it.

Chapter 19

"What's got you so perky?" Lydia asked. She was sitting at the kitchen table, mug of hot chocolate in hand. Jen had virtually bounced into the house, her exhaustion from the day and her dinner with Robert overridden by an adrenalin rush.

"Just landed myself a supply order on my beer." Jen dropped down into the seat opposite Lydia with an air of pride, only just refraining from punctuating her announcement with jazz hands. Her eyes fell on the new edition of *Brewing Times* on the table. The headline heralded a US corporate having bought a smaller craft brewer. Distracted she pointed at it.

"Bloody corporates," she sniped, "buying their way into the craft market." She batted away the immediate thought of Yakob chairing his panel of bloody corporates. "Where's the honour in that? They should stick to their own bland game."

"Pssh. Enough of that." Lydia plonked her mug down on the paper, eyes bugging. "The *supply order*, Jen. What? How?" Her smile was as large as Jen's which was back to out-spanning her entire face. Jen still couldn't quite believe she'd done it. She'd get more worked up about the corporate thing tomorrow when she read the full article, but for now it wasn't enough to dampen her euphoric mood.

"So Robert and I were at Anthony St James' place and he comes over to say hello, and mentions I'm a brewing goddess and then as we ate, I was thinking about which of my beers would work with the food and it sort of came to me; "local restaurant serving local beer" and I should give it a go, because maybe I met him this weekend for a reason. So, when we left, I went back in and asked him, and he liked the idea." Jen slumped back in her seat, breathless.

"But Jen," Lydia said with mock dismay, "you're stopping the brewing." Lydia raised a taunting eyebrow at her.

"Hmm, yeah, no. I can't," Jen said lightly and scrabbled for something else to say to mask her massive U-turn. She wasn't a U-turny person. *Have a plan, stick to the plan, complete the plan* was her normal MO. Additionally, she didn't want Lydia questioning her departure from Robert's vision. Lydia would see it as some chink in their relationship, and it definitely wasn't that. She was simply having to work a bit harder to show him what was important to her. Once this got off the ground and hopefully turned a profit, she'd no doubt change his mind. It could help fund their future home. The celebrity connection couldn't hurt either. That was a useful name-drop for the golf course, right there. "Anthony's currently in negotiations to open two more restaurants, along the coast, eventually with a view to more, and if I can get the quantities going, then I can supply those too."

"That's amazing, Jen."

"I know!" Jen was simply over the moon. There was an excitement in her stomach, the heady cocktail of anticipation and self-belief, she hadn't felt for ... well, not since she'd been offered the job at the brewery years ago. The memories of that came back vividly; the opening of the letter, the euphoric happy dance, the squeeing call to her parents and their being truly stoked for her, hooting down the line. She felt her smile slide a little. They'd planned to come up to her uni digs, they'd told her to book somewhere to celebrate. Only they'd never arrived and her life had taken another mighty turn.

"Jen? Earth to Jen?"

Jen shook herself out of her memories. She wasn't going to think about that. This was a moment to enjoy.

"Sorry, what did you say?"

"I was asking, not to put a dampener on things, but you know, logistics and that, how are you going to up your quants? The shed is only as big as it is." The fermentation and conditioning tanks she had on a constant go were enough to supply her farmers markets and a pilfering sister, but not a steady supply to an eatery open six nights a week.

"I was thinking about it on the way home, *as it hoppens*," Jen said, moving to make herself a cup of Ovaltine and ignoring Lydia's groan. There was no way she'd sleep given her current pulse rate – she needed some sedation to reconnect her mind to her show-tired body and she had work in the morning. "I should probably have covered that before I hit him with the idea, but it was one of those seize-the-day things."

Another thing her marketing experience had taught her was, in business, the universe sent you all sorts of opportunities – you just needed to spot them and exploit them. "I'll need to rent a space somewhere and invest in the kit. I'll take out a loan to cover it – I'm hoping the three years of show wins and my stall figures are enough to convince a bank manager. I'd start with a small unit somewhere. Nothing swanky, just clean and functional, with room for the vats and storage for the ingredients and the finished bottles." She dreamed of a bottling machine, but that would have to be on the wish list for now. They cost a packet.

"Take the leg money," Lydia said.

"What? No."

"Jen, I'm sorted for a while. I'm not growing anymore, so I don't need so many prosthetic changes. I know you're saving the Arches rent for the next ones, but you can take some then replace it later when things are up and running."

"No," Jen was insistent. "That money is ring-fenced. It's for your future."

"What about *your* future, Jen? You're just as entitled to the rent as I am. It's *our* inheritance. So use some of the accumulated money now when you need it. Set things up, and then repay the account if you like – but without the interest."

"I'm not using your money." Both women had stopped smiling now and brows were creased as they each tried to out-stern the other.

"I'll be a silent partner then," Lydia conceded, "if it helps you get your head around it. I'll shoulder part of the risk. I've got two shoulders and I'm willing."

"But it *is* a risk, Lydia, and I can't let you do that."

Lydia got up and using her crutches, moved across the kitchen to put her cup in the sink. "Jen, it's a risk that I'm up for, because I and all our friends love your beer and I believe in you." Jen thought it was ridiculous. Sometimes Jen felt Lydia deliberately overlooked her leg when it came to life decisions. Working in London was one example.

"Are you going to leave work?" Lydia asked. She obviously thought they were in agreement over the money, but Jen was simply pausing the discussion for now. She'd still go and see the bank. Lydia couldn't make her touch the Arches money. "Surely you'd rather have the beer over the crampons?"

Jen shook her head. "Not while I'm starting up. I still need the income. I'll just have to work a double shift until it's up and running."

Lydia gave her an emoji-worthy sad face. "You'll be knackered."

"Maybe, but I'll be doing something I *want* to do with the aim of stopping doing something I don't."

"Fair enough," Lydia said, heading towards the door. Then she stopped and turned. "This is what I was hoping for. This is what you were supposed to do, Jen. I'm really pleased and excited for you." There was no doubt she meant it, her face was aglow.

"Thanks Lyds. That means a lot." And it really did. For

all their bickering and disagreements, Jen never felt happier than when she had Lydia onside and at her side. There was someone else who she believed was on her side too. "I wish," she murmured, thinking of the two bunches of flowers which now hung drying from the outbuilding rafters, "I wish I could let Yakob know." It seemed OK to say it to Lydia. She'd met him after all, and it wasn't like Jen was declaring undying love for him or anything, just that she'd like to share her news with him. Not least because Robert's joy had been minimal. It was impossible to stay angry with Yakob when she'd just had good news regarding something he'd been telling her to do. "He was really encouraging when I met him. I think he'd like to hear about it and I'd like to thank him." Jen supposed she could go 'old school' and send him a letter. Between her memory and Google Maps, she could probably estimate his address. She could describe the boat in the address and hope the postman could work it out. Or she could go full GCHQ and see if Google Earth could magnify a name on it.

"Well, Cinders," Lydia said, reaching for her back pocket, "that's an easy do for a Fairy Godsister like me." Lydia waved her phone in front of Jen's face as if it was stardust from a wand. "You texted me from his phone remember? His number's on here."

Jen had a moment of jaw flapping and hand waving.

"Oh my God Lydia," she screeched, "why didn't you mention it?"

"I didn't know you wanted it. *Nothing happened*,

205

remember?" Yes, that was Jen's line and she was sticking to it.

"But we looked for him on the internet. You could have mentioned it then." Couldn't Lydia see how she'd let the side down?

"What? And you would have texted him to say *Who are you??* Don't be daft."

"Well, I need it now," Jen said crossly.

Lydia's eyes narrowed at her tone. "Which is why I just offered it to you. Chill the fuck out, Jen. Considering 'nothing happened'," Jen scowled at Lydia's annoying air-quoting, "I don't see why you're having a hissy-fit." Lydia was displaying a mix of outrage and amusement. Jen was definitely on the back foot and didn't like it.

Ominously unwilling to let Jen see her contacts, Lydia dictated the number, although she disclosed he was listed under 'Jen c/o Boat Hottie'. Jen doubted the Copenhagen police would have been impressed with Lydia's sisterly concern had anything untoward happened to her that night. With jittery fingers she typed the number into The Phone of Shame. Looking at it with disdain she knew she needed to get a new one sorted, but then the logo for ChAPPel loomed into her mind and she side-lined the thought. It felt like a symbol of her failure on the wedding project. She really needed a proper planning session where that was concerned, but right now, she had some Thank You's to make.

Lydia pocketed her phone again and said goodnight. The salacious smirk on her face was one of triumph.

"Don't get ideas, Lydia," Jen said tersely, keeping her eyes on the crappy grey screen, "it's just a hello and thanks. Nothing more to it. Nothing happened."

Jen thought she heard a "yeah right" as her sister disappeared up the stairs.

For the next fifteen minutes she composed and erased messages, until she groaned a frustrated Argh and decided she was too tired and too flustered to do this right. She headed for bed, phone still gripped in her hand. Once under her covers, she told herself she should go to sleep. It was too late to text anyone anyway and he was an hour ahead too. But her mind wouldn't settle, so with a huff she had another go. She could always wait until morning to send it.

> **Hi, Just wanted to say a big THANK YOU for all your encouragement on the beer. A local restaurant wants to stock it and I've decided to follow the passion and try making a business of it. Jen X**

There. It was a tad long, but it told her news, it said her thanks and it wasn't too sappy. She'd ummed about the kiss, but figured one was acceptable – they had kissed for real, after all. No kisses would seem cold, two would be too effusive and possibly open to misunderstanding. Engaged women had to be careful about such things.

Her thumb hovered over the send key. She really should leave it to the morning, so she could revise it if necessary. But she wanted to tell her news to someone – someone not related to her and duty-bound to be wowed.

What if he was asleep and it woke him? Well, Jen reasoned, he shouldn't have his phone on when sleeping, so this could be a lesson.

She hit send and it was gone.

Dropping the phone on her quilt, Jen flopped back on her pillow, wondering if she'd done the right thing. On top of the excitement of the evening there was another feeling creeping up on her, a trepidation, but a good one. She wanted to hear back from him, she knew she did. Thinking about him and their night in Copenhagen, always (yes, it had happened more than once) gave her an exhilaration she couldn't really understand. Even her anger over the Kronegaard thing hadn't quite slewed that off, if she was a hundred percent honest.

She grabbed the phone to switch it off. He might not even respond. He might simply accept her thanks and be done with it. The very thought made her shudder. Or rather, it made her *hand* shudder.

The phone was vibrating with an incoming call. The number was the one she'd just sent her text to.

Chapter 20

"Jen?"

"Yakob?"

"Hello again." She could picture his face clearly, she could hear him smiling. Which was good as her own face was suddenly filled with an enormous grin. For starters he'd responded to her, which gave her an enormous sense of relief.

"Hello again." Hearing his voice again, knowing she'd found him made her so so happy.

And then there was silence. Nothing awkward, just calm, as if they were listening to the other breathe, or simply content to be connected.

Eventually she broke it.

"I wanted to let you know. About the deal. And that I'm doing it. The beer. I haven't packed it in." She knew her sentences weren't brilliant, but they were tumbling out.

"I'm so glad. It was ridiculous that you should stop." There was a touch of admonishment in there, but she'd take it. He was right. What had she been thinking?

"I know, I know. I think I just got ... well, *misdirected* I suppose." She was going have a think at some point why she allowed herself to even consider it.

"What? You?" he scoffed, "with all your spreadsheets and plans? How is that possible?" Yes, he was definitely grinning at the other end.

"Shush," she said, "enough of the teasing. Sometimes people are mistaken about things." It reminded her of something else she'd be mistaken about or rather *misled* about and it brought a curt end to the lightness of her mood.

He picked up on it instantly and in a quiet tone said, "You didn't wait for me at the show, Jen." Was it wrong to be pleased that he sounded disappointed? It was simple statement, not an admonishment in this case, simply an opener for an unavoidable conversation. Jen thought about it. This had started as a nice call. She didn't want to sour it. She could lie, say that her train was earlier than she'd thought, or her call had necessitated her return. But considering how upset and dismayed she'd been, Jen felt she deserved answers. Honesty felt like the best approach.

"I found out who you worked for Yakob. I didn't know what to make of it, why you hadn't mentioned it." She felt her face warming at the memory. "I felt stupid for not having put the clues together, and I felt embarrassed for having talked to you about my brewing and things like that, when you work for a giant like Kronegaard."

"We never discussed my w–" he started calmly.

"You had many opportunities to put me straight, Yakob," she cut him off sternly, he wasn't getting out of this. "I spent most of an evening slagging off your employers and you could have stopped me at any time to tell me. I even slated them wearing one of their own t-shirts!"

"They won't mind," he said.

"I'm serious, Yakob, please be serious for a minute. I felt like such an idiot, and a rude one at that, having landed on your deck, accepting your hospitality and then sounding off about the company you work for. Why didn't you say?"

He took a moment to compose his answer and she suspected he was rubbing his hand through his messy hair. "Because you are entitled to your opinion, Jen. And it's an informed opinion. Plus I enjoyed listening to you getting excited about the industry I work in. It was refreshing. Had I told you, you would have felt awkward and maybe clammed up and I didn't want that." None of that sounded malicious, she had to admit.

"And you weren't laughing at my tinpot brewing?"

"Not for a second. Do you think Henrik Krone started with more?" Fair point. He was sounding very reasonable.

"You should still have told me," she said again, sounding slightly petulant. "I felt like a fool."

"That was never my intention, Jen. I've never thought you were a fool." Well, that was good as he'd had ample opportunity in Copenhagen.

He waited. The choice was hers whether to hold it against him.

"OK. Fair enough." She thought she heard him release a sigh at the other end. "Maybe I shouldn't have left. I just don't deal well with surprises, or people not being honest." She thought back to something he'd said on the boat, about dishonest girlfriends. Perhaps they had that in common too. "Same as you." She took his silence for contriteness. Her actions were clearly not a point of hilarity for him – for once. Good. She liked that. She decided to let him off the hook. "So are you really a corporate shark?" she asked.

"Ha! That makes it sound far more exciting than it is." He seemed to like the description and she really hadn't meant it as a compliment. She'd been hoping for a straight No.

"It sits weirdly with me," she confessed. "As a beer *snob*."

"Doesn't with me," he said, blithely. "It's just numbers and shopping."

She was pretty sure it wasn't. "You eat up companies."

"I sustain and generate jobs," he chipped back.

"You're all about profit."

"And we pay our taxes on it, which improves global economies." He didn't seem remotely apologetic. In fact he seemed to be enjoying this.

"You aren't about the craft." That's what her dad would have said.

"Does that matter? You and many others seem to have that covered." What?! Now he had to be messing with her.

"I don't think you believe that. That it doesn't matter."

"I work in the numbers department, why should I care?" Jen saw this might be true, but her gut told her no.

"Sorry, Yule, I call bullshit," she said, with a sly smile. "I saw the way you talked about brewing with your Morfar. I know love of the craft, when I hear it. I hear it in my own head. You *do* care, you might just not be in a position to do anything about it."

"Ha! You think I am held hostage in the finance sector?" He was chuckling now.

"I think somewhere along the path you turned to the dark side, but the goodness is in you."

"Maybe I *chose* it, Yoda." For a second he didn't sound quite so cocky.

"Or maybe your parents did."

The lack of immediate response was a jarring halt to their flow. What had she said? Maybe his parents were dead too. Jen started to formulate her retreat and apology, but then he was back. "So, what do you think Jen, how will my creativity burst through these corporate bonds?"

"Well, that remains to be seen Yakob, creativity is a curious thing," she said, relieved to have him back on track, "but right now, with all your recommendations to follow the passion, I'd say you're living vicariously through me." It felt true as she said it. What was more was she *liked* it.

"Hmmm, it's certainly an interesting experience. I don't know Jen, I'd say I'm far too ingrained in the business side of things to tinker with The Craft." The grandiose way he said *The Craft* told her he was back to teasing and deflecting. Somewhere she'd prodded a nerve. Ha! "We'll just have to wait and see, won't we?"

He wasn't denying it, she noticed and she liked the fact that the "wait and see" implied knowing each other in the future.

"I'm glad you texted," he said, changing the subject.

"I wasn't expecting you to call back. I didn't want to disturb you. It must be late there." She looked at her clock.

It must be half eleven in Denmark, far later than she'd normally ring anyone.

"I'm not usually asleep at half ten," he said with a laugh. Such a nice laugh. Throaty. Genuine. "I'm not that old yet." She didn't know how old he was, not much older than her though, maybe mid-thirties with a boyish face.

She looked at her clock again. She still had the analogue dinosaur on her bedside table. Perhaps she hadn't wound it properly, so she checked her phone. Also ten thirty.

"Did your clocks change? Denmark's ahead, isn't it?" She imagined him lounging on his sofa, looking up through the glass roof, the summer night and the lights from the surrounding buildings melding above him. The image made her sigh.

She sensed a hesitation. "I'm in the UK, Jen."

"You are?" Well, that would explain the time thing.

"I am. I live here too." That, on the other hand didn't make much sense to her.

"Wait, what?" Jen sat back up in bed. Reclining must be making her thinking sloppy.

"I work in the UK, Jen. I go home most weekends and stay on the boat, but this is where I work."

At first she couldn't think what to say. This was huge. She'd thought of him as being far, far away and now, well, apparently not. "How did I not know this?" She thought back to their chatter in Copenhagen. She'd just assumed that the boat was home for him. "See! I did just talk about me on the boat. What a lousy guest."

That made him laugh again and she relaxed. "I liked

not talking about myself," he said, "and you were interesting. You probably thought I was interviewing you." No, that wasn't how she remembered their evening at all. In her head it had been perfect. He'd been interested in what she did. He'd listened to what she had to say and engaged her in good conversation. The only downer had been having to leave. No actually, her body now told her, the bigger downer was not accepting his offer to stay the night. But she'd had decent reasons for that, her head threw back.

"No, it didn't feel like an interrogation," she said, "but now it's my turn. Seeing as you withheld information before, now I get to ask you some things."

"Can I reserve the right to lie?"

"Have you been drinking this evening?"

"No."

"Then no." She was sounding quite school ma'amy.

"Go on then." He didn't sound totally open to the game.

She settled back down, ready to make this last a while. "Where are you right now?"

"In bed." Oh. For some reason that made her blush, which was silly as she was in bed too, but it made the conversation feel more intimate. Also, it hadn't been quite what she'd meant.

"And where is that?"

"I'm in Halesford." Kronegaard had a huge plant in the town. Anyone with an interest in the business knew that, and anyone who'd driven along the ring road had seen the enormous tanks on the side of the building holding the

215

beer. Once when they'd been stuck in a jam beside it, she and her dad had tried calculating the number of bottles they'd each fill. The numbers had been beyond them.

"That's less than hour an away." She wasn't sure what she meant by that, but it was out of her mouth faster than she could stop it. Was she just showing off her geography skills or was she suggesting something else?

Thankfully, he sorted her predicament. "That's correct, Jen. I have some evenings free early this week, and I have never been to Westhampton, so I was thinking I should visit."

"You were?" she gulped.

"I hear it's a nice place."

"It *is* a nice place," she agreed, stalling for time, panicking. Presumably he was proposing a visit *to see her*, not simply a tourist excursion to behold the lesser-known towns of the English south coast. Part of her wanted to jump on the bed with glee and the other was asking where she was going to get an invisibility cloak for them at such short notice.

"I am also interested in seeing a particular microbrewery and tasting their beers." Oh Lord. He was making her sweat a bit. She kicked her covers off to get some more air to her skin. It didn't help.

"Are you sure you aren't coming to spy? My award-winning recipes are not for stealing." She was teasing, but also still a bit disgruntled he hadn't 'fessed up to his job, before.

"You have my word. You can blindfold me if you like."

216

OH LORD. She fanned her face with her hand. It really was a warm evening. She'd have to open a window soon.

He seemed determined and she was reluctant to put him off. She wanted to see him, though she knew she probably shouldn't. How would it seem to others?

But then, he *had* hosted her beautifully when she'd fallen into his neighbourhood, shouldn't she host him properly when he made the effort to come to hers? She could control this. It was just a matter of proper manners and spending an evening with a friend. She was reciprocating his generosity, that was all. Who could have an issue with that?

"Tuesday?" she said. "I'll show you the delights of Westhampton."

"It's a date," he stated, "I'm looking forward to it. Good night, Jen." She bade him goodnight too, but he hung up before she could assimilate what he'd said and clarify it wasn't a date. It couldn't be a date.

So much for controlling this.

Chapter 21

Monday was a wreck. Jen's usual diligence was woolly to say the least. Her head was filled to bursting. Ava had called in sick – which was a good thing as Jen had plenty of work without the distraction of deflecting any discussion of the crampons – but Ava was keen for the jobs on her own desk to keep moving in spite of her absence. "The world can't stop turning just because I'm not there Jen." As if. She didn't sound remotely unwell either. Being convinced her work was considerably more important than anyone else's, Ava asked Jen to prioritise it. Oh and Zara wouldn't be back for another week. Her husband had surprised her with a stop-off week in Dubai. So there was plenty to be getting on with in the office. Meanwhile Jen set Aiden on boxing deliveries far away in the back cupboard.

Not that the office work was really what she was thinking about, although she did have an idea for targeting cruise companies to get some inco pad samples left in the cabins. Two things were filling her head. She needed to get things moving on the production front to deliver regularly to

Anthony. She'd agreed to start with the IPA and a Golden Ale to test the waters which was easy enough, but she needed to expand somewhere to accommodate the quantities. What was more, if she was going to do this after work and on the sly, she'd need it close by and all the properties on the rental websites were miles away.

And then there was Yakob. Her thinking was all over the shop when it came to him. For starters she couldn't stop trying to visualise his face properly, although why that was important to her, given it was just dinner and showing him around town, she couldn't explain. The dinner itself was a worry. She'd decided it would be better to eat at home; sitting in a restaurant with another man would make it look like a date and Sod's law said someone she knew would see her. They were a known family in Westhampton. Tragedies had that effect. Exactly what to feed him though, had her in a quandary until hoofing through Pinterest she thankfully found a beer-braised summer stew she could whack in the slow cooker in the morning and leave to get on with it for the day. There, that was one thing off her list and ten minutes later she struck the online shopping off too. Able to marshal her thoughts a little better now, Jen drafted a quick itinerary of places in town to show him, assigning some time simply to walking around and viewing, because she knew that was important to him.

She waved at Alice and Max as she passed the shop on the way home. The tenant of the neighbouring unit was pulling the wooden bi-folding doors across the arch to close up.

"You weren't about to pass by and not say hello were you?" he asked with a big smile. His beard was snowy white now, where once it had been jet black. He used to piggy-back her around the workshop when she was a little girl, shouting every now and again as she'd grabbed his ears to cling on.

"Hi Charlie." She gave him a hug. "How are you?" Her dad's best friend had continued the business after the accident, fixing anything that involved an engine and could be driven into the workshop. He was the perfect tenant; never a problem he couldn't fix by himself and always on time with the rent. Jen suspected he saw it as a point of duty to their parents not to cause the girls any further grief.

"Tired." Normally Charlie was upbeat in spite of his constant retirement threats, but when Jen looked at him now, she saw he was looking much older. "My back's done in and the work isn't helping." He nodded for her to follow him in, which she did through the door in the last of the wooden folds. It had been a scorcher of a day, so the cool of the brick arch was welcome. Stooping with a wince, Charlie set about making them tea in the little kitchen. Tea only came one way with Charlie; with lots of milk and four sugars.

He dealt best with one thing at a time, so she sat quietly while he tinkered with the mugs. The workshop was a fond part of her childhood. It smelled the same way that her dad had when he came home; a comforting mix of diesel, petrol and WD40, with base notes of grease. The space was functional with two large recessed bays in the floor for cars to drive over and so Charlie could work underneath them. Really the workshop was far too big for his needs now, but once there had been two of them and an apprentice. The far wall was still racked out to hold a multitude of parts and fixings, the office area was stacked with ring-binders of paperwork, Charlie not being the sort to appreciate computers.

He handed her her mug of tea, which she politely sipped, waiting for her teeth to start furring.

"What about getting someone in to help, Charlie? You could take more of a back seat and they'll eventually buy you out of the business?"

Charlie shook his head. "I've been asking around for a while and the younger lads aren't interested. They want the modern franchises out on the industrial estates. They either don't have the moolah to take it on, or the balls." Jen nodded along, keen not to veer him onto his pet subject of "Young People Today ...". "I know it might need some updating," he continued and Jen bit her tongue from asking "you think?", "but it's been a good business. I'm just not up to it anymore."

"Really, Charlie? You're looking to stop completely?"

"Sorry, love." He looked properly apologetic and she realised he meant the rental income.

"Don't you be worrying about us, Charlie. Your health is more important. We'll re-lease it."

"You might have a job with those things," he pointed at the maintenance pits in the floor. She supposed they could be filled in somehow. "Most mechanics just hire a unit now and kit the place out with the modern hydraulic lifts. Those places come with more parking too." The Arches had never been designed for a raft of waiting vehicles. Jen leaned back against the brick wall. She loved this place with its rusticity. The floor was concrete and there were no frills anywhere. Alice and Max had used it to their benefit; Alice as a juxtaposition to her pretty flowers, Max to cope with the scuffs and blows of the salvage items that came in and out with fast turnaround. If she leased it to something corporate, that would all have to change. She'd hate to see it decked out as an office with plasterboard partitions and false ceiling. Maybe she was averse to seeing it change *at all* – it was so full of memories for her. Finishing her tea in large gulps, hoping the sugar might bypass her teeth altogether, Jen reasoned that perhaps she was letting nostalgia get in the way of good business practice. She knew what Robert would say.

"Well, I won't do anything until you've properly decided, Charlie," she said getting up, "it's all yours until then."

"Thanks, love," he said, standing up with a groan. "I'll keep you posted, but I doubt it'll be long."

She gave him a hug and left, running her hand sadly down the door frame as she did so.

"Get a grip," she told herself, continuing her walk home. She wasn't losing the place. Not yet. It wasn't for sale, and she and Lydia could decide who they rented it to. Maybe there was someone out there who wanted "rustic industrial with minimal allocated parking". Alice and Max were evidence of that. Alice relied mainly on phone calls and foot traffic, while Max's salvage suppliers and customers were the types who didn't bat an eyelid at double parking.

As if she didn't have enough going on, Jen considered what might work in the space. If it didn't go to another mechanic, it might do for storage. It had character which was a selling point, but it wasn't the character many shops would want. It was rather too industrial for that. A gallery maybe? It wasn't quite the art-buying end of town, though. She wasn't sure Westhampton even had one of those. She looked around the street and her eye fell on a wine merchants. Nothing exclusive, just a chain shop. Their set up was pretty basic with wine boxes stacked high on the floor. That would work. They might fancy expanding. The Arches would give them double the space, floor-wise and to the loft – not all businesses could get best use out of a high ceiling. They didn't need it. It was the loft height that was one of the issues in her outbuilding. She couldn't get bigger tanks in there.

She stopped in her tracks.

Oh man, she was a prize idiot. The answer was obvious.

She met Lydia from the train which in itself wasn't unusual, but she came on foot. Normally she'd take the Capri, ostensibly to keep it "ticking over", but really to spare Lydia the extra walk. Tonight Jen hadn't been home yet. After her brainwave, she'd sat herself down on the nearest low wall, dug out her Filofax and started a list, soon covering four pages with what she'd need and what she'd have to do, and what the timings might look like. She listed the people she'd need to talk to and questions for the internet. The first thing was what planning permissions she was going to need to change the arch from a mechanic's workshop to a brewery.

She didn't know why she hadn't thought of it instantly. She was normally much better at ideas than that. Ideas were her thing. The arch was perfect – maybe not now exactly, but it could be. It was industrial and functional, she could spool it down with a hose for starters and nothing would be ruined. And it was going to need plenty of spooling down before she could get anything started. But it had the space, nearly two-thousand square feet and the ceiling height for the tanks. In fact it might be much too big for what she needed, but the space was hers, *theirs*, and that made things easier when it came to the finances. In the back of Jen's head she was pleased it was big, because it could allow for expansion – but she didn't think about that too deeply, it wouldn't do to tempt fate.

Her head was whirling with all the ideas and rough sketches of where things might go without having to change too much. She was definitely going to have to take that loan though. "Bank appointment" got added to the list. As did "Update Business plan". She wasn't starting from scratch. In her downtime, between the brews being ready for tapping, Jen had already spent hours planning her fantasy brewery. It had its own file on her laptop, between her library of travel itineraries and folder of beer recipes, which she tinkered with when she'd read a new brewing magazine, incorporating good ideas others had had, or learning from

224

their words of caution. This wasn't dullard time-usage at all, no matter what Lydia said. Other people played fantasy league football, or built Pinterest boards with their dream homes or secret weddings, how was this any different? Not weird at all.

She saw her evenings evaporating in front of her; this was going to need lots more research. She was already registered as a brewer with the taxman for her farmers' market sales. Jen was a stickler for the rules; rules allowed control. Beer duty still had to be paid even if you were a teeny weeny micro-brewery, and now she'd need to look at the quantities to see when her discounts would disappear, as well as all the other changes upsizing would invoke.

Her eye inadvertently caught her watch. Bugger. Lydia's train was only a couple of minutes off, which necessitated some harried bag stuffing and a dash to the station. She desperately missed her phone and its extensive line-up of alarms. She resolved to sort a new one as soon as she got in – only, thinking about her industrial shopping list she wondered whether she could even afford it.

Lydia had already started off down the road as Jen rounded the corner to the station in full sprint.

"Lyds!" She caught her, but spent the next moments bent double, trying to breathe. It felt like her lung lining had been stripped.

"You know, some might suggest you lead an unfit life-style," Lydia said. She wasn't presenting well on the sympathy front. "You should come running with me."

God no. The thought of running for pleasure was an

oxymoron to Jen. Lydia tended to run around a prepared track as it was kinder to her running blade. It was her pride and joy and as far as Jen could see, the only time she would be sensible was when she was wearing it. It hadn't come cheap either, which was another reminder to Jen why she ring-fenced the Arches rent. It gave her a pang about what she thinking of asking.

"No car. Came from work," she said, still rasping. "Just ran a bit faster than normal."

"Than ever," Lydia pointed out and started walking. She didn't seem remotely bothered not to have the car. Jen, not so much. "What's kept you at work so late? Crocheting the tampons?"

Jen took another gulp of air and following her, started telling her all about Charlie, his retiring and her idea. Lydia's face clearly said she liked the idea.

"It makes perfect sense. Use it."

"I'll defer the rent for six months, but you will get it back."

"We've been through this, Jen, take what you need. I don't mind. I get a decent wage." She did. Jen had to admit Lydia had got herself a good job when leaving uni. When she was being self-depreciating Lydia would say it was because she upped the company's disability quota, but they both knew she'd won it based on her smarts and personality. Even with the commuting costs, she came out well. It just didn't cover her leg costs.

"I'll pay it back with interest when I'm up and running."

"No need."

"Yes need. And I'll get a set-up loan from the bank."

"We went through that too. Take it from the rental account." Lydia stopped and turned on her before she could interject. "Jen, just do it. That money isn't all mine. You've sacrificed so much, now it's your turn to have a chance. You've given me mine, let me share in this adventure." She walked on, as if the discussion was closed. Jen stood with her hands on her hips, flapping about what to say next. Of course she'd rather use their money, but she'd work out some way of replacing it, with interest, so Lydia's faith and gamble was paid off. If she failed, then fine, she'd have tried and she'd dedicate herself to the inco pads or the crampons or whatever madness Ava and Zara discovered next.

Lydia was hoofing ahead and it took Jen another effort to come level with her.

"Thank you," she said quietly.

Lydia looked at her askance. She'd been prepared for a fight. "Good decision. And you'll take a year, not six months. Can't get anything done in six months. It could take a year to get the place re-rented, it's a niche market that'd want it anyway. So we'll take a year's hiatus on the rent and revisit after. That's the deal."

It felt more like a command than any deal-making, but Jen took it with a nod. A year would give her so much more leeway for trial and error. She kept her eyes on the ground, unwilling to see Lydia's smug smile at calling the shots. Her gaze slid to Lydia's leg. Checking her gait and posture was second nature to Jen, keen to detect signs of discomfort Lydia was refusing to admit to. She was wearing her micro-prosthesis, the metal shaft reflecting the evening sun with each step. She normally didn't wear it with a skirt, favouring the more leg-like cosmesis, and today, considering the heat, the skirt was the obvious choice where the leg was not. Naturally, the anomaly alerted Jen's radar.

"What's with the prosthesis?"

Lydia bristled, but kept walking, eyes front and centre. "Two legs beats one, I find."

"You know what I mean, Lyds. You normally wear that one with trousers."

"You're reading too much into it." Lydia's face was tight, and Jen knew she was on to something. Something Lydia didn't want to talk about.

"Is the cosmesis hurting? We can get it looked at. The money is there. If it isn't fitting right, or the socket is faulting we need to get it looked at fast before you do any damage to your residual limb–"

"Stump," Lydia snapped, "it's my *stump*. Let's call it what it is, 'residual limb' sounds wanky. And I am well aware of all those things. I am aware of my health care, I don't need you to keep reminding me."

"Alright, stroppy," Jen said, keen not to have an argument in the middle of the street. But she did need to get to the bottom of this. "You do sometimes leave the care late though and if you'd taken preventative measures earlier–"

"I lost it."

Jen stopped in her tracks. "What?!"

"The leg. Saturday night. Long story. I took it off and then it was gone. I've been to the police and they'll call if it gets handed in." Lydia restarted her walk, forcing Jen to follow.

"Where?" Jen was bewildered. How could she lose a leg? "Why did you take it off?" Jen understood why she'd taken that one, the silicone cosmesis was the easiest to clean. Mud in the exposed joints of the prosthesis was a nightmare. But she couldn't see how she'd lost it. You'd spot an errant leg in a field, surely?

Lydia scowled at her. "I lost it at the place where I was, and I took it off because I wanted to. Just leave it, Jen. I said I'm on it." Lydia's pace stepped up a gear. They were close to home and she was obviously keen to get in and away from the conversation.

By Jen's reckoning Lydia was not remotely as concerned as she should be. That leg was key to her having as normal a life as possible. Yes, she had the other legs, but this was the one she wore when she wanted people to notice least. It sustained her self-confidence. Lydia unlocked their front door without further explanation or remorse. The cosmesis wasn't her most expensive leg, but it was still vital nonetheless. It was a clear sign Lydia couldn't look after herself properly. Who lost a leg in a field? Jen understood her wanting to take it off while they sat around the campfire, but she should have put it somewhere safe. That was just basic skills. Good Lord.

"How did you even get home?" she called up the stairs. Lydia hadn't phoned her, or even told her about it when she'd come home. They'd talked about the beer deal. She should have told her then.

"I do have friends, Jen. They carried me to the car, and they drove me home, and they brought me in to my crutches. My whole world does not revolve around you."

Lydia's bedroom door slammed. There it was, her answer to everything; hiding herself away. She might think she was an adult, but she had a good line in showing herself up to still being a surly teen.

Well, she could stew in her mood. Jen had work to do, and plans to make. She parked herself and her laptop at the kitchen table, grabbing some fruit from the bowl in lieu of dinner. It was going to be a long night, and somewhere she was going to have to find time for sleep, because from now on she was working double shifts.

Chapter 22

The Capri caned it down the side streets of Westhampton, like something out of a 1970's car chase, Jen swearing at the cars in front to get out of the way. She didn't have time for their dawdling. Yakob would be arriving in an hour and she still had a humongous to-do-list. Having to drive twenty miles to fetch a leg was the last thing she'd needed, and in the end she'd been forced to blag the afternoon out of the office to do so. She'd told Ava she was off out for some tampon and mooncup research. "Knowing The Competition" was key to affective marketing. Ava had been impressed. Jen would have to scour the internet later for some facts to spout. She didn't know how the sisters were going to take her turning down the partnership, she could at least try to soften the blow with some market research and a decent marketing plan.

On the upside, getting out shielded her from all the emails with wedding dress suggestions Ava was now bombarding her with. Clearly Celia had enlisted her to her cause. It only served to steel Jen's resolve to wear her mother's dress. She'd have to ask Alice what she could do with it. But not now. Right now she had a rush hour to cleave her way through and preparations to make.

Stifling a yawn she briefly considered stopping to buy an energy drink. She'd woken up at 3 a.m., with her face on the keyboard. She wasn't sure all the indentations had properly gone by the time she'd reached work. The house had better be in some decent state, she'd need the full hour to sort her face. But stopping for stimulants now would allow these slowpokes to get back in front of her and she'd had to employ Formula One thinking already to get past them. She ploughed on.

Thankfully, an early-morning delivery, some assassin-speed chopping and the slow cooker had the dinner sorted, the aroma of the stew now a comfort as she came storming in through the door, slinging her bag and coat in the cupboard, and manically checking for mess as she tornadoed up through the house to her room. God, she needed a drink. Just something to take the edge off this nervousness.

"He's just a friend, Jen," she sang under her breath. It was ridiculous stressing about it. Friends didn't judge. He wouldn't care what she looked like. He wouldn't be expecting her to have some swanky home like he did. She'd described where she lived. He wouldn't be expecting *haute cuisine* either. She'd texted him the address and said she'd cook. It was the nearest she could get to clarifying it wasn't a date. Anything more overt would sound rude.

Flicking through her clothes rack for the third time she stopped and shook out her arms, to get a grip. What was the matter with her? What a prat. This was a simple meal.

Why was she feeling so out of control? The thought brought her up short. She *would* keep control of this. Enough of the pratting about. She pulled a loose short-sleeved black top off a hanger and a pair of black jeans out of the drawer. She hastily hoiked on her best underwear, but purely for confidence purposes, nothing else. A long necklace finished the look; casual but smart. Way better at least, than the yellow and orange he'd seen in Copenhagen. She dragged a brush through her hair and wanded her lashes a couple of times with mascara. That would do. Jen shimmied at her reflection. She was back in the game.

The door slammed downstairs. Oh crap. The one day she'd told Lydia she couldn't collect her from the station was apparently also the same day she'd come home early. Somewhere in Jen's head she'd thought she could feed Yakob and have him out for the local tour before Lydia got home and that she might have gone back out by the time they returned. Damn the plans that didn't work.

She trundled down the stairs, mentally prioritising the things she needed to sort in the kitchen. She had her beer tasting plan fully sorted too. She planned to show Yakob all her wares.

Jen came to an abrupt halt as she rounded the door jamb. Lydia stood holding her cosmesis.

"You got it back." Lydia's expression was more confusion than elation, but she hugged it to her body. Jen moved on again, past the table and dug about in the cupboard for the steamer. "How did you find it? I looked everywhere. The police station and I are on best-buddy terms."

Jen nabbed the broccoli out of the fridge drawer while she considered whether to have this conversation right now. She was trying to stay composed, going head to head with Lydia wouldn't help that. But she couldn't help herself. Perhaps leaving the issue festering wasn't helping her nerves.

"Some spotty student had it in Kingsley. Two whole towns away. Practically pissed himself when I showed up asking for it."

Lydia looked questioningly at Jen, her leg-reunion happiness moving aside.

"Right, but how'd you find it, Jen?"

"Can you explain how it got from a field to his house?" Jen deflected the question, trying to keep her annoyance at bay, channelling it into slashing florets from the stalk.

"Dunno?" Lydia's defences were raising. "Thieving rambler?" *There* it was, the snark. Jen doubted this lad had known one end of a walking boot from the other. His skin suggested he rarely saw daylight.

"I asked him where he'd found it and he grunted something about an extreme sports event."

"Weird." Lydia was refusing to get into it. Well, Jen knew exactly where she'd been, she knew all about the Xtreme Sports expo. They tried tapping her for advertising every year, as if inco pads were for people peeing themselves with fear. Arguing about Lydia being there wasn't going to help. Jen decided to climb down, but she needed to state her position and explain her concern.

She stopped her aggressive prepping to give Lydia her full attention. "Look, I don't mind if you go to watch people doing mad things, but can you just let me know? That's not too much to ask. I need to know where you are in case anything happens. *Anything* can happen. Those loonies trying those sports have no idea what they're dicing with. Surely you must have thought that when you saw them?"

Lydia's eyes were bright but her mouth was tightly pursed, clearly holding back.

"Actually, they looked like they were having the most amazing, liberating, heart-stoppingly fabulous time, like life had no limitations or big sisters telling them what they can and can't do, even if they're adults and capable of making their own choices." Jen sensed Lydia was trying to make a point.

"All I'm asking is that you don't lie to me, and you let me know where you are. Then I might not have to go fetch your leg."

Lydia was very still, but it wasn't a calm stillness, more the seething kind. "You still haven't said how you found it. How Jen?"

Jen looked about the room. Her face was rather shifty. Bum. She shouldn't have started this.

"I, umm, there's this website, lost things, I ..." her explanation trailed out. "I'm expecting a guest. I don't have time to discuss this now."

"Fine," Lydia said crossly, grabbing her bag from the table, "but the subject isn't closed, Jen." She whipped out of the room, allowing Jen to exhale slowly in private and take a moment to try stilling her heart.

"You're welcome," she said to the empty room.

The doorbell rang and she almost dropped the floret she'd been crushing in her hand. She tried to walk in a composed fashion to the door, slowing further to check her hair in the mirror. "Calm, calm, calm," she told herself like a mantra. It wasn't a very good one. It didn't work.

And there he was. On her doorstep. So close she could touch him. Looking every bit as delicious as he had in Copenhagen. His smile was warm and not remotely nervous as far as she could see, which put her more to shame. Why was she blushing? Her entire head felt hot.

"Hello again," he said smiling, hands in pockets, looking the epitome of relaxed. His pale blue work-shirt had lost its tie somewhere and the sleeves were rolled up to the elbow, giving her a good view of his tanned forearms. His hair was as rebellious as ever.

"Hello again." She stood gazing at him, taking him in, until it dawned on her she should ask him in. Flustered, she ushered him past her, which he did, but stopped to kiss her firmly on both cheeks, leaving her frozen for a moment in his wake, as he headed into the kitchen. Befuddled by the evocative reminder of his aftershave, she felt her inner prat resurfacing. Oh crap.

Chapter 23

Sitting opposite Yakob at the kitchen table, Jen's assess-
ment was so far things were going well. She'd dreaded
their conversation being stilted, but it hadn't been at all.
He'd made all the right sounds in response to her food, so
hurrah for that. He'd even had seconds, which was a firm
sign of approval, or incredible politeness and she was willing
to take either. And he'd liked her beers, at least the two
she'd given him before and with the meal. He'd tasted and
considered each carefully, while she'd sat with her heart in
her throat, until he'd given her a detailed and thankfully
favourable critique of each. She was conflicted as to whether
she could have taken a harsh verdict from him; he knew
his stuff, so no doubt it would have been fair and constructive, but anything other than "It's wonderful" would possibly
have crushed her. It dawned on her how much his approval
meant to her. She was so keen for him, as her newest
supporter, to be impressed. Feeling faintly embarrassed by
her neediness, she sought to direct the subject onto himself.

"So Corporate Shark, how was the show for you? Enjoy
the panel? The title was very aggressive."

"The show was busy, I hate those panels – which is why my rule is not to do them unless a colleague is welded to the toilet – and those panel titles are just to stir people up."

"You don't think Kronegaard is a 'Brewing Giant' set on global domination?" It looked like it to her.

He took a swig of his beer and lips pursed, took a long look at her. "OK. Probably." His following smile said he wasn't remotely repentant, the ridiculously cute lip-pursing thing had purely been for being caught out.

"You're still in my bad books for not having told me, by the way" she grumbled, getting up under the guise of fetching a couple more bottles from the side, but really to hide her face. "I would have kept my criticisms to myself." Yeah. That probably was a lie. "Well, toned them down a bit perhaps." Jen knew her limitations on such subjects.

"That's precisely why I didn't say!" he exclaimed, amused. "I like hearing what people think. I like knowing what people think about beer. Telling them what I do, who I work for, doesn't generally help that flow of information."

"Oh, man, is that what I was? A one-woman focus group?" She said it in jest, but what if?

"No, of course not," he laughed. He really had a great laugh there. "Trust me, I don't entertain and kiss women for research purposes. That would be too much dedication to the firm."

There. Now he'd done it. He'd acknowledged the kiss and she didn't know what to do with it. It needed addressing somehow, didn't it? Even if it was to say it had been lovely, thank you, but it was a mistake and one she couldn't

238

elaborate on. Jen's mouth opened a couple of times as she tried to work out what to say. Instinctively, she couldn't bring herself to call it a mistake. It had been incredible. Looking back – and she did, *often* – Jen knew that kiss, the way it made her heels lift off the ground and the blood roar past her ears, had been the icing on the cake of her trip. In the end she wussed out and changed the subject as she returned to the table.

"Tell me what it is you do there, exactly." She really wished he wasn't a corporate shark. She couldn't help it. Her dad had brainwashed her on the subject.

"It's very boring," he said and then paused, taking another swig of his beer. She deliberately waited for him to go on, which he eventually did. "I focus on the stability and longevity of the company." She raised her eyebrows at him for a translation. "The way I see it, my job is to make sure the company stays strong and our employees' jobs are safe." That sounded more decent.

"Like how?"

"So, for example, our plant here in the UK; we need to keep the right balance of employees to beer output, and to make sure it still makes financial sense to have local plants rather than import the beer from elsewhere. It's the same in all of our overseas territories, so I try to safeguard both in all of them."

Within the realms of working for the evil corporates, it sounded to Jen like he'd picked a worthier area to work in. Maybe not the sharkiest of sharks then.

But then she remembered that he hadn't been bothered

by her spouting at the show – more amused in fact – he certainly hadn't denied their activities.

"But you *do* buy other breweries, don't you? You are responsible for companies disappearing." That copy of *Brewing Times* had instigated some colourful language.

Yakob seemed to pick his words carefully. "Jen, do you remember Ross brewery?"

Yes, of course she did. A middle-sized macro-brewer, Kronegaard had swallowed it up some years ago. The beer had been the usual insipid blandness, but it had plants in various countries. "We bought that to increase our business around the world, but it allowed most of the workforce to keep their jobs. Every job loss was voluntary redundancy – that's rare in mergers and acquisitions. That was a good thing." It placated the look of alarm on her face. "So the brand name disappeared, but it firmed up the future for us and the employees – both theirs and ours."

Jen relaxed a little. Corporates eating corporates was fine by her and she didn't want people to lose their jobs. And besides, she told herself, it wasn't like it was *him* dominating the brewing world. It was the company, his bosses, the Kronegaard family. It was just his job. Lord knew, she understood that. She was a slave to her bosses too. Sometimes you just had to do what it took to pay the bills. She certainly wouldn't have chosen the inco pads.

"Speaking of futures," he said briskly, placing his cutlery together on the mopped-clean plate, "I have a gift for you." He pulled a package out of his pocket. A little smaller than his palm, it was roughly wrapped in newspaper. It reminded her of how equally crap her dad had been at wrapping. She cocked her head questioning. "Something to bring you luck for the new venture," he said, with a slightly shy smile.

Thanking him, she carefully unwrapped what could only be described as an amulet, an oval golden engraving of a woman holding barley. Jen smiled widely.

"Ninkasi. Goddess of brewing." Her smile grew further as she turned the metal over in her hand. It was old and hand-worn. It was beautiful. She loved it.

"It seemed apt," he said gazing at her, which made her blush all over again. This blushing thing was something only he made her do. It certainly wasn't anything she had any sway over.

She stood up and moved to open the back door, clutching Ninkasi to her chest. Instinctively she held out her hand. "Wanna see where the magic happens?"

By brewery standards, the outbuilding was of course tiny – it could probably have fit inside one of the vessels attached to the building he worked in – but it wasn't minuscule. But standing in there with him, as he took it all in, Jen suddenly felt the compactness of the space and the close proximity it put them in. She made room for Ninkasi in the centre of her awards shelf, then slid up on the counter like Lydia normally did, to put a little distance between them, lest she faint. It allowed her to watch as he slowly turned, assessing the room, observing her neat organisation, her chalkboard planning and the actual brewing that was happening right here, right now.

He struck her as a different man from the Yakob she'd seen at *Brewing Live*. There he'd clearly been a business man, aware of how he appeared to others, more formal as he nodded briskly to people they passed. But he was also different from the Yakob she'd met on the boat, so relaxed in his home. This Yakob, looking at all the elements of the space, breathing in the scents with clear intent, was both lost in memories and also more relaxed than ever she'd seen him. Compared to her, he had always been the epitome of chilled, but this was a new level. It was like he'd come home. Watching him almost felt intrusive. Her sanctuary clearly had some similar meaning for him.

She could hardly breathe waiting to hear his appraisal.

"It's perfect," he said, pulling himself out of his daze, leaning back against the opposite counter, crossing his arms, flexing the muscles in those lovely forearms of his. *You're perfect*, she thought. Catching herself, she pulled two bottles from another shelf, hoping her hair might hide her blushing face.

"This is the show winner," she said uncapping them and passing him one. He studied the label before taking a swig. He closed his eyes while he thought about it. It gave her a chance to run her eyes up and down him. He was really here, in her brewery, as opposed to in her memories.

"*Hyld*," he said in Danish, "elderflower."

She nodded to show he was right and to go on. She was grinning like a fool already. "It tastes like summer." He gave her a big smile, clearly proud of his skills and also impressed with what she'd done. "It's refreshing, but comforting," he went on, talking as much to the bottle as the brewster. "Like lazy days. That's brilliant." She wanted to fling herself at him. He *got* it. He understood what she was doing with that beer.

He bounced up on the counter next to her, their shoulders almost touching. His hands gripped the edge as hers did.

"It reminds me of my Morfar's brewing room. The smells, the equipment, all of it."

She took a punt. "Admit it, Yakob, you want to have a go. It *calls* to you."

"It's nostalgia, that's all."

She didn't believe him. "Strange. Your eyes don't light up in the same way when you talk about the numbers. Some things you can't hide. *It's in your blood*," she whispered.

He took a moment to think about it. "Some doors in life close as you get older, don't they, Jen?" There! That was tantamount to an admission. She was right and Jen felt duly smug. "You were correct on the telephone the other night. My family wanted me to take a different path and I did not want to disappoint them." Oh. Her smugness switched to sadness. Her parents had always encouraged her to pursue her interests. "So I followed the numbers as they wished, but I get to use them in a brewing environment. That is a win-win situation, no? And I am good at what I do." He wasn't bragging. He had always owned his numerical adeptness and more recently his corporate sharkiness, and yet Jen felt he was trying to convince himself that he really was in a win-win situation, having turned his back on the actual alchemy of brewing. She wasn't quite sure what to say.

Yakob turned abruptly to face her. "Jen, this has to be one of my favourite breweries, but you know you can't stay here, yes? It is too small for what you need if you are going to supply other people."

"I do," she conceded, but knowing she'd still keep this for testing new recipes. This would still be her lab. It was also her link to her dad, his framed photo on the shelf where Ninkasi now stood. They were both brewing gods to Jen. "I've been doing the figures based on what I sell at the markets. I'm going to invest in a six-barrel kit, with mash tun, the lautering system with a heat exchange and three fermentation vessels for a start. So, a big outlay, but you have to speculate to accumulate, right?" He was nodding along, listening to her thoughts. "I upgraded from a small kit to this kit when I started selling at the markets, I'll just have to do it again. More spend, more paperwork, more permits, but I'm not scared of that."

"And a location." He looked from the ceiling to the floor. "Those vessels won't fit."

"I'm on that one too, smartarse." She deliberately knocked him with her shoulder, and felt the skin of their little fingers touch. Neither moved away. "I found somewhere. Somewhere totally perfect."

"Tell me."

Reluctant as she was to remove her hand, she grabbed the photo behind him.

"So this is my dad. I think he and your Morfar would

have got on." She gave Yakob a quick smile. "I owe him all of this. But what you need to look at here is the workshop behind him ..."

She told him all about it, somewhere along the way setting the picture back, freeing her hands to illustrate her grand plan. Her heart was hammering from her excitement. Just as it had when she'd been telling him about the beer on his boat.

"And you own this already?" he asked when she finally finished.

"I do. *We* do. Lydia and I."

"It's perfect," he said, looking her right in the eyes.

"Perfect," she agreed, caught in the depth of the cornflower blue and desperately trying to regulate her breathing as it was still recovering from her enthusiastic expounding, but also rather wobbly at their faces being in such close proximity. "I could show you the arch. If you like," she said in a low husky voice she didn't quite recognise as her own. The atmosphere had changed somewhat. There was a charge there she couldn't put a name to.

"Do you want to leave?" he asked, his own voice suddenly rather hitched.

She slowly moved her head from side to side, eyes still locked on his, and giving in to the need to swallow. Her mouth was parched, but in spite of having a beer in her hand, she couldn't bring herself to use it.

"Show me another time?"

She nodded this time, equally slowly. She found him hypnotic. Good grief. She sensed perhaps she should shake herself out of this, but then his eyes flicked to her lips and back and then his gorgeous face and lips were moving closer and closer to hers.

And closer.

The tour would definitely have to wait.

It was a kiss unlike the other but equally perfect, at first a whiling of time, softly gentle but with purpose, as if they'd both been waiting to do this and now was simply the moment. There was no rush, or desperation, but it was passionate none-the-less as it grew in intensity, each of them matching the pace as if it was the most natural thing in the world. He lightly held her face as he slid off the counter and moved to stand between her knees, sustaining the kiss throughout. Jen pulled herself forward, so they were closer still, interlocked. The movements were utterly in tune, they fitted together just so.

"Jen, can I ask you again?" he murmured into the skin on her throat, his hand sliding down her side, teasingly skirting her boob. Fingers in his hair, Jen briefly wondered whether her knickers were fireproof.

She didn't need him to ask. She had this.

"Yakob, will you stay?"

Chapter 24

The bed space beside her was rumpled, but empty. His scent still lingered, the aftershave and the olfactory ghost of a sweaty sexy night. Mmmm. She wanted to bottle that somehow. Looking beyond the bed, she could see his shoes strewn where he'd kicked them off. He hadn't gone then. Good. Not that she thought for a second he'd have slunk out, never to be seen again. The things he'd whispered to her last night, intimate things he planned to do with her in the future, told her he hadn't done a moonlight flit.

Getting up was an interesting experience, some muscles whinging from unusual usage. Not *abnormal*, just not what she was used to. It had been thrilling and lived up to everything his kisses had promised.

The clock said it was 7 a.m., but the lightness of the summer morning made it feel earlier. She was exhausted too. That didn't help. There hadn't been much sleeping going on. It was a minor miracle she could stand. Now she understood Lydia's dedication. Exhaustion and muscle aches aside, mentally Jen felt supercharged; confident and glowing. She pulled on her ancient dressing gown, realised it wasn't fit for human eyes, and quickly dug out the slinkiest of her nightshirts.

Whilst trying to finger out the mess of her bed-head sex-hair, Jen trod carefully down the stairs, keen to avoid the squeak of the fourth step. She hadn't been so careful last night, as they virtually tumbled up the stairs, fumbling at buttons and zips as they went, lips locked the whole way. The house had been still when they'd come in from the outbuilding and she'd assumed Lydia had gone out. In spite of her recent lecture, last night she hadn't cared where her sister went or what she did, as long as it was *out*.

Hearing chatter in the kitchen, she abandoned her stealthiness.

"What's your busking skill?" asked Lydia's voice.

"Busking? Like street entertaining? I don't have one."

Lydia drew her breath through her teeth. "Everyone needs a busking skill, Yakob. What if you completely hit the skids?"

"Good point. I don't know. Perhaps I could whistle." He genuinely sounded worried at his lack of proficiency. "You?" Jen spied on them through the gap between the open door and frame. Lydia sat on the counter as Yakob made coffees. She was dressed for work, a short-skirted suit showing her cosmesis back in situ.

"Well, Jen's let me down on my upbringing there, really. I reckon I'm good for spraying myself gold and standing very still in public places. Maybe that. Or I could charge little kids to touch the robot leg."

"Eight-year-olds would think that was awesome. You'll be a hit. And your apocalypse skill?" he asked, turning the tables. It struck Jen how comfortable they were with each other. Granted Lydia was no shy child, but it wasn't every day – or ever, actually – that she woke up to a strange man in the house. This could have had awkward written all over it.

"What?!" Lydia asked.

"Come the apocalypse, Lydia, what skill will ensure your survival?" There followed a silence as Lydia brooded the question.

"I can use my leg to smuggle things or whack people with. They won't expect it."

"Good one." He took a slurp of his coffee and handed Lydia hers, before picking up the last which Jen assumed would be for her. Their chatter was so easy, if ridiculous in subject matter. She envied the ability for frivolous chat. She was more about facts and getting to the pertinent points.

"That," continued Lydia, "or I can sell sex to get more rations. You?"

"Morning!" Jen interrupted. It was time to shut down the conversation. She'd have to discover his apocalypse skill later. She wanted to know, only she needed to think of her own first. She supposed Excel spreadsheets would fall by the wayside, come the apocalypse. "I see introductions aren't necessary." She could probably dispense with any of her own awkwardness too. It wasn't like she hadn't shared the kitchen with a million of Lydia's visitors, often just in their

Pernille Hughes

under-crackers and besides, these two already appeared to have bonded. She couldn't decide whether she was narked or pleased.

Placing his cup, Yakob reached out an arm and reeled her in for a kiss to the temple. He kept her against him as they stood. Jen wasn't sure what to say. Lydia jumped down from the counter. "Gotta go."

"Lydia needs to catch her train to London," Jen explained.

"*Lydia*," corrected Lydia to Yakob, "needs to stop by Boots for a bumper box of ear plugs. I'm going to need them if you're staying again." Lydia didn't look back as she left the kitchen. "Honestly, all the sex noise – it was like having Mum and Dad back in the house. Gross." The front door slammed moments later. Jen wasn't sure where to go from there.

Thankfully, Yakob did, launching a slow volley of kisses across the back of her neck. She felt her legs go wobbly again. She looked up at the kitchen clock. Maybe ...

"No," he said slowly, against her throat, "I have to go." Her low moan was either dismay or want, she was too away with the sensation to be sure. She felt his low laugh at her nape, which did nothing to diminish the sensitivity of her skin. She had never looked at the kitchen table in this particular way before. Surely just five ...

"I'm sorry." He dropped his forehead against her hair. He seemed as disappointed as she was. In fact, there was something pressuring her hip which suggested she wasn't alone in the wanting. "I have a meeting and a flight to catch. I'll be back though, Jen. Soon. Yes?" The first sounded

250

apologetic, the second certainly hopeful and the last, endearingly asking for permission.

She stepped away and kissed him. Not a full-on snog, because morning breath, but definitely one that held intent. "Absolutely, yes."

He left the kitchen and she heard him head up the stairs to retrieve his shoes, then the thudding as he returned. He slung an arm around her waist and pulled her to him as if they were in a film. "Leaving is un*beer*able." She rolled her eyes and admonished him with an *Oh beer me!* which earned her a laughing kiss. "See you soon, Jen."

Feeling her euphoria beginning to ebb, she followed him to the door, stopping to hand him his Copenhagen shorts, which she'd washed, rolled and bound with a red ribbon, before opening the door to let him out. The day looked set to be another scorcher, but Jen was feeling her blood cooling and with it a sense of loss. He turned on the step and planted another kiss on her. "Get brewing, Ninkasi. I'll be back to sample the goods." Man, he made that sound filthy.

He was in his small black Audi before she could think of a sexy answer. Sexy answers did not come naturally, and she would have sold her hair to have had one just then. With a wave he was gone and it was as if he'd gone back to being a dream.

Deflating fast Jen headed into the kitchen and held her coffee, surreptitiously sniffing the mug, his aftershave having left its trace on the sides. She supposed this was the fabled "drop". She didn't much like it. Looking at the clock, she saw she'd need to leave for work shortly. She didn't much like that either. The doorbell rang and she nearly threw the coffee in the air in celebration. He was back. He'd reconsidered the table-top quickie. He could drive at double speed after.

She swung the door open, trying for a sexy pose, face beaming. And caught the beam from crashing as she realised it was someone else entirely standing in front of her. Someone who must have passed Yakob's car moments ago. Someone she hadn't given a second's thought since before leaving the office yesterday.

"Morning Gorgeous," Robert said, stretching in over the doorstep to give her a fleeting kiss, as her stomach crashed through her feet. "I thought I'd give you lift in."

Jen stumbled like a zombie through the shower and around her room getting dressed. The nausea she was feeling was dreadful. Her head was pounding with guilt. What had she done? And why hadn't she thought of it? She was *engaged* for goodness sake and it hadn't even crossed her mind while she'd been busy kissing Yakob, or undressing him, or watching him mesmerised as he slowly divested her of her own clothes, or while they'd been swept up in all the deliciously lovely and heart-thrashing, exhilarating things they'd done. Not once. How could that be?

She came shamefaced down the stairs, convinced he'd be able to see the deceit on her. Or smell it. She must surely reek of betrayal.

Jiggling his car keys, Robert headed out of the door

oblivious to her turmoil. It made her feel even worse. He was so trusting and she should have been worthy of that trust. She'd let their relationship down. She'd let herself down. She'd been a poor ambassador for the Attison family. As the door closed she took a quick look back at her parents' faces in the picture. She expected them to be frowning, appalled. Strangely, they were still beaming at her. Well, parents were supposed to love you no matter what, weren't they?

"Are you all right, Jen?" Robert asked, as they drove down the street. "You're looking pale." She was trying to quell the gut-twisting nausea again, but it might also have had something to do with his over-powering air-freshener. It was cloying in its sickly-sweetness, but he seemed unbothered by it.

"Not much sleep," she murmured, keeping her eyes straight ahead. She was too ashamed to look him in the face. He deserved so much better. More than once she opened her mouth to confess all and beg his forgiveness, but something stopped her. She should discuss this with someone first. Alice perhaps, but that would involve sharing her shame with another person, whereas Lydia already knew. She was working on some judgement limitation here. She could take Lydia lording it over her, if it spared her the disapproval of her friends. If she was honest with herself, she didn't want anyone to know she'd lost control of things – loyalty and decency for starters – for a while there, either.

"This'll perk you up," Robert said excitedly, reaching

under her seat. He lifted a small white paper bag up onto her lap. "Happy three and a half week engagement anniversary." Oh God. Could humans die of shame? Was that a thing?

She wanted to give it straight back with a "No no, I don't deserve it", and she should offer him the option of annulling the engagement. That would be the decent thing. She should give him back the ring – although that was actually a plus point. Perhaps she should see the ring as her penance now, a symbol of her ugly nature to carry until death did them part, in lieu of a scarlet letter.

"Go on, silly billy. Open it."

Smiling weakly, only wanting to please him, she did so. A new iPhone box lay in her lap. A big fat tear rolled down her cheek and splashed onto the box.

"I knew you'd love it," Robert said, grinning as he steered through the traffic. "Back to your apps. No more bits of paper." Jen nodded with a sniff, trying to hold back further tears, stroking the box with her fingers. "And now I can send you all my diary notifications."

He pulled up outside the office and leaned over to her. "There's another surprise. But you'll have to wait for that." He took her face in his hands then, a move that nearly broke her as his hands overlaid the imprint of Yakob's. He kissed her, firmly and succinctly, then released her.

She waggled the box at him with a wan "Thank you, Robert," then let herself out of the car, trying not to stumble under the weight of her guilt.

*

After an entire morning of wretchedness and self-flagellation, entirely unnoticed by Ava because the first consignment of crampons arrived and instigated a Skype party with Zara, Jen got her other surprise. Still sniffling, she had miserably switched the SIM from The Phone of Shame, briefly thinking how apt it was now and she should be made to keep it. Forever.

The new phone flashed to life and she spent an hour resurrecting her old apps. ChAPPel provoked a sob from her as it loaded and she couldn't bring herself to open it. As WhatsApp took its rightful place back in her life, a message pinged in from Robert.

> **Golf weekend at the**
> **end of the month**
> **cancelled, Jen.**
> **Let's get married!**
> **Robert**

The calendar notification setting the date popped up immediately after and Jen's nausea finally won.

Chapter 25

Almost three days had passed since Charlie had called Lydia to come and help Jen. Normally, when she'd sought sanctuary from life's stresses, she'd go to the outbuilding, comforted by the hoppy smells. But the outbuilding couldn't be that place any more. Not when every inch of it would now remind her of Yakob and realising this made her chest hurt unbearably. She'd never known guilt could be so painful. She assumed this was guilt. What else could it be?

A panicking Ava had sent her home at first puke. Apparently, there was nothing worse on earth than four boys vomming in synch, so Jen was immediately quarantined under school regulations, not to return until she'd been clear of any sick or potential squits for forty-eight hours. It was a blessing. She went to the only place she could think of to get her head straight; the workshop at the Arches and its comforting scents. And there she'd stood, blubbing, telling Charlie about all her plans for the place in lieu of confessing what really had her howling, while he'd stood there slightly scared, telling her she could have the place as soon as she liked, because his back was buggered and his wife would be delighted. He'd then scuttled off to phone Lydia, suggesting Jen might be having a small breakdown.

"It's all right Charlie, I've got this," Lydia said, when she arrived. "To be honest, it's not a shock she's imploded. I was wondering when it would hit." She took the near-catatonic Jen by the hand, away from the corner she was sitting in, out into the light of the rear yard. It was a tip, a general dumping ground for spare bits that would never be used, but hoarded "just in case". A small area had been safeguarded however, with a rusty table and two chairs, and an overflowing ashtray crafted from an upturned hubcap.

"Robert came by the house," Jen said, like an automaton. Lydia could do the maths.

"Before or after Yakob left?"

"After. But that's not the point, is it?"

"Well, silver lining; less awkward," Lydia said, with a shrug.

Jen felt another breach in her tear dam. She'd been trying very hard not to upset Charlie further in there, but it was impossible to keep it up for Lydia's benefit. "I'm such a bad person," she whispered.

"Jen, you aren't bad. You've just made a mistake."

"I know," she sniffled, staring at nothing in particular. Looking anyone in the eye today was a no-no. "I know it was a mistake, but it was amazing Lyds, and he just gets me." She needed to say this. She needed to tell someone.

In the event that she did die of misery, then at least someone could whisper to Yakob that he'd meant something to her.

"Jen." Lydia's voice was stern, like she wanted her sister to snap out of this. "The mistake wasn't sleeping with Yakob. From what I heard, that was a gift from God. The mistake was accepting Robert's proposal. The sooner you see that and break it off, the better."

Jen opened her mouth to say *not this again Lydia*, but found her sister's flat palm in her face, stopping her. "It's not just that I think he's a dullard and all the things I said before, though they still stand. I saw the way you were around Yakob this morning. Even for those few minutes you were a different person. Happy. Relaxed. Smitten. And that's the thing Jen; even if Yakob isn't the one, Robert definitely isn't either. That's what you have to see. That's why marrying him is a mistake. I don't know if you've fallen head over heels in love with Yakob, but what I do know is you don't love Robert. You think of him fondly, but not once have you said you loved him." Jen thought back. Lydia was possibly right. She hadn't ever said that. Not about him, or *to* him. But he'd never said it to her either. They just didn't use words like that.

"Robert's a good man, Lydia. We've known each other for years and he's good and kind and ... Dad said he was a decent man. Dad knew him. Dad approved of him." Large tears started to spill as Jen tried to make a cohesive argument.

"Oh my God, Jen," Lydia said with a disbelieving laugh, "Dad saying he thought Robert was a decent bloke wasn't the same as him giving his blessing as your life mate."

"We'll never know," exclaimed Jen, "it's the closest I've got." Learning to adult had been hard enough without her parents to guide her, so she had hung on to the few remnants she had of what they might have advised. This one had seemed to make sense to her when accepting Robert's surprise proposal.

Lydia shook her head firmly. "You can't steer your life by a throwaway comment. Dad thought the postman was a decent chap too when he helped him down from the roof when the ladder fell. Remember that? Should we go looking for him for you?" Jen made a blubbing snort, which could have been a snotty laugh or sob. Lydia carried on unhindered by the snot. "Dad would want you to be happy Jen, of course he would, but you're putting words in his mouth and he isn't here to confirm them." Well, that sort of made sense she supposed, but that didn't change the facts as they stood.

"But ... but I made Robert a *promise*. I committed. He proposed and I accepted. That is a verbal agreement, Lydia. How can I go back on that?" It was her being a woman of her word and seeing things through, that made her trustworthy and reliable, and if she wasn't seen as such by those she loved and valued, Jen didn't think she'd know what she was.

"For fucks sake, Jen," Lydia barked, shaking Jen's hands, "this isn't a contract, it's your *life*. You're allowed to change your mind."

Jen stared at her, stumped. There was something that rang true in what Lydia was saying. And Lydia wasn't finished. "I know you, Jen. I know how this has you conflicted because you need to be seen as dependable, but I'd put money on what's actually upsetting you most is the thought of having to let go of Yakob. That's what's tearing you apart, right up there with the terror of the feelings you have for him, because you aren't used to them and you can't control them."

Jen burst into a fresh volley of wracking tears. Lydia's words weren't just ringing true, they had klaxons going off and neon lights flashing around them too. Of all the awfulness of the day, the thought of not seeing Yakob again was the very worst.

"How did you get so wise?" she asked Lydia as she was escorted home, feeling pathetic because her little sister was both looking after her and was apparently infinitely smarter when it came to this kind of thing.

"I read lots of romances when I was recovering," Lydia sighed, pulling her along by the hand, "and just from watching you fuck up, I suppose."

Jen chose to let her "vomit bug" continue, allowing her to stay off work and cancel her date night with Robert. He stayed away as *there's no need for two of us to come down with this, is there, darling?* He'd already been feeling a bit iffy since he'd seen her, according to his texts. Her new phone lay discarded on her bed, where her original phone would have idled in her hand, ready to grant her wishes at a moment's notice. Instead, Jen was surrounded by paper, lists and forms to fill in. She had come to re-love the feel of paper. It didn't ping messages at her for starters, giving her panic pangs. She almost dreaded that ping now. The funny messages from Yakob kicked her spirits sky high, the check-in notes from Robert flung her straight back down into the hell of guilt and worry about what to do. The opposing feelings were exhausting and as Lydia kindly pointed out, she looked wrung out. Ava's constant texts regarding how to run the office didn't help either – so much for being on sick-leave.

After the first afternoon of simply staring at her ceiling, looking for hidden messages of advice in the Artex swirls, Jen started to reject the helplessness. The following morning, she did the only thing she knew how to do to combat it and that was to adopt a project and take back the control, little by little.

The brewery expansion couldn't have come at a better time, nor could the free days off. They allowed her to make the required phone calls to the council and HMRC, without the threat of Ava catching her. Steadily, she got more and more of a grip, pushing her focus onto the paperwork and the growing shopping list and budget excel sheet. She even ventured out into the outbuilding, to tap the current beer which was ready. This was supposedly the first batch of the wedding beer. Rather than brewing another of the same as scheduled, she spent her afternoon setting up one of her staple beers, to deliver as a trial batch for Anthony. She wanted him to know her full range. Boiling the water and malt, adding the hops to the wort at the right times, Jen engaged with her true self, closing herself off in the task and not worrying about anything beyond the door.

It was dusk by the time she'd transferred the cooled beer to the fermenting tank and washed out the mash tun ready for next time. Looking at the room, trying hard to compart-mentalise her thoughts of Yakob for now, she saw that whatever happened now with her love life, this was one thing she would not, could not, give up. The beer was her constant, her touchstone. It was her creative release and it was where she most felt herself. Like Yakob said, it made her heart sing. The board above the counter still held the recipe for the wedding beer. *Swansong* it said in Lydia's angry script. Jen took the cloth and rubbed it out. She'd tried it as she'd tapped it; it was strong and robust, but fresh and full of hoppiness. She had her own title now and chalked it up. *Heartsong*.

Chapter 26

As soon as the clock struck five on the Friday, Jen was out of the house. Now officially the weekend, she felt "recovered". Charlie was smoking at the door when she arrived at the Arch.

"Sorry about the other day, Charlie," she said giving him a kiss on the cheek, dodging the smoke, hoping he could see she was in better shape, "I've done as much as I can on paper, now I need to measure up and calculate and no doubt revise and adjust. I'll try not to get in your way and I don't want you to see it as me pushing you out. You must have jobs still booked in and lots of things to wind up, but I need to get my brain working on this." Walking in however, she came to a grinding halt.

Various men were milling about the place, pulling boxes from the wall racks and putting them in what appeared to be designated piles. Some were even pulling items in from the crap-pile in the yard.

"I'm having a garage sale," Charlie said behind her. Looking around, the workshop was looking pretty sparse already. "I put the feelers out as soon as you left on

Wednesday, this lot have always had an eye for a bargain. It was like flies to shit down here yesterday. Bloody piranhas."

She turned to look at him. "I meant what I said about not pushing you out, Charlie. You have a month's notice on your contract. I was expecting you to take it."

"Don't need it, don't want it," he said with a grin. "The wife booked a holiday as soon as I told her. Over the bleedin' moon she was." Charlie wasn't looking half as tired as the last she'd seen him either, well, perhaps not the last time, where he was scared by her crying, but the time before. There was a spark back in his eye. "The shelving comes with the building." That was a blessing, she was going to need the racking to store boxes and kit.

"I'm leaving you something else too."

"You are?"

"You could call it a house warming gift," he said with a smirk, "but the thrill might wear off pretty quick." He waved his hands in a ta-dah fashion at the corner by the office.

She looked at him with feigned excitement. "A pressure hose. For me? You spoil me."

He was grinning now. "Don't worry, love. I'll give you a hand."

"That's OK, Charlie. I'll do it. You have an excited wife waiting for you. I've got this." Now she could envisage having the place to herself, she couldn't get him out fast enough. And she wanted to do the power cleaning herself. If she was going to be the one adhering to the food and drinks regulations, she needed to know she was abiding by the cleanliness stipulations. She was only going to know that if she did it herself. Scanning the space, her beautiful if dirty brewing space, she tried to work out how long it would take her. If she started as soon as the last guy left, and dispensed with sleeping–

The "vehicle reversing" beeps interrupted her frenetic calculations. Charlie went to investigate, with a "What's this then? I ain't ordered nuffink".

He called her over to the door. A lorry with its own forklift on the back was parked out front. The driver jumped out and they stood silently as he lowered the forklift and finally pulled open the doors.

"You been shopping already?" Charlie looked amused. Jen looked gobsmacked.

In the back of the lorry stood three large fermenting tanks. But she hadn't bought them. How?

"Lads!" Charlie shouted back into the arch, "the lady's gonna need a hand here."

She couldn't help stroking them. The tanks. Not the lads, although they and the driver had done a sterling job, as she'd hastily hosed down the area she had planned for the fermenting, along the right hand wall. It wasn't quite the immaculate job she'd intended, but they'd left enough space between each to access for later cleaning. This was the thinking she knew how to do; the practical thinking, the implementing of plans, firmly pushing aside the emotional stuff she clearly was inept at. The lads hadn't minded helping, in fact they were highly interested in the idea of the town having its own brewery. She told them about her market stall, but it also got her mind working on other possibilities, as she gave the new tanks a polish. She'd have to look at the regulations for selling at the front door. As long as she declared it, surely it couldn't be an issue? She made a note in her Filofax, and got back to the wiping.

The tanks weren't new, but she didn't need them to be. The scuffs and little dents gave them character, helped them fit in with the building. She'd need to build a platform around them so she could get into them for cleaning, but a stepladder could do for now. What was most pressing however, was the phone call she needed to make. She had a man to thank for some tanks.

Just bringing up his number made her smile goofily. She was glad no one else was around to witness it. Just before hitting the dial button she had another idea. This was a smartphone. She hit FaceTime instead.

And lo, his heavenly face appeared before her.

"Hello again," said the slightly pixelated Yakob. His eyes were wide and he seemed delighted to see her. "You have a new phone!"

"Hello again, Santa," she said, batting away the pang of guilt that she was using Robert's gift to call him. She was too pleased to succumb to it and she'd already done worse.

"They arrived then?" His image was moving with a slight lag as if time zones away, but she could easily make him out. It was lovely to see him.

"They're beautiful." She leaned against one of them,

feeling slightly delirious at sort of being with him. Since when had she become such a sap?

"They're steel tanks, Jen," he said, clearly not seeing the beauty. She gave the one she was at a quick caress in case it had heard his derision.

"A departure from the flowers, aren't they?"

"Maybe a little more useful?" His lovely blue eyes kept flicking across the screen, like he was taking all of her image in at his end. She doubted she looked her best, but it was too late to care and he didn't seem repulsed.

"Such a thoughtful gesture, Yakob, but I can't let you buy them for me. I need to reimburse you. They're in my budget."

"Jen, they were being removed from a building at work and I thought recycling them was more environmentally friendly. Really, you did us a favour."

"But you could sell them."

"Jen," he said, with an eye roll that the pixels didn't disguise, "we're quite a big company, we don't have time for eBaying."

"Fair enough." That did make sense. "Well, thank you for thinking of me."

"You were top of my list of start-up breweries." And there it was again, the blushing. She couldn't hide it, and he clearly noticed as his smile grew wide.

"You don't have a list." She said it as a statement, but a teeny tiny part of her wanted assurance.

"No, I don't," he said kindly, "but you know, as soon as you start using them, you'll be a competitor, so we'll be enemies."

267

"Obviously," she agreed, "especially when I start kicking Kronegaard's butt." She liked hearing him laugh.

"It's all going well then?" he asked.

"Well it's early days yet, but I have it planned." She walked them over to the far wall to show him her flow charts and excel sheets, setting out what was happening and when.

He whistled at her. "That's pretty detailed, Jen," he nodded, though she doubted he could really see and appreciate the meticulous logistics through the pixels.

"It's the six Ps Yakob; Proper Planning Prevents Piss Poor Performance. These sheets keep me in control of all this," she said grandly, turning three-hundred-and-sixty degrees so he got a proper look at her Queendom. "Where are you, by the way?"

"Sydney." She was right about the time zones then. But that would mean ...

"Ah no, did I wake you?" He didn't look nearly bleary-eyed enough, but then his hair always looked kind of bed-heady, so she couldn't be sure.

"Ha! No, it's morning. I'm just leaving for a breakfast meeting."

"Oh right, what are you up to? Wheeling and dealing or saving lives?"

He grinned. "Don't know about lives, but hopefully some livelihoods."

"How are you doing that then, Super Shark?"

"We're buying a brewery that's in trouble. Merging it with ours will save quite a few jobs and help us out here with our grants." *It's just his job, it's just his job*, she reminded herself.

"Fine. The less of you corporates there are the better for us craft brewers. But did you hear that Fenby & Clegg got taken over by a US competitor last week?" *Brewing Times* had been all over it happening again as another craft brewer was swept up by a corporate giant. Bang went their authenticity.

"I did." He didn't seem as appalled as her. "As things get more automated Jen, jobs become redundant and fewer employees in a foreign plant put the international grants at risk."

"Oh, so it's really about the cash the countries will give you?" He had the good grace to wince at that.

"*Grants,* Jen, and it works both ways; companies can afford to come to a country, and people get employed. But they have to sustain the employment numbers. Branching into the crafts beers does that." What? He condoned buying into the craft beer market?!

"No, Yakob, it's completely wrong," she insisted. "Craft beer is about being independent, it's *anti*-corporate. It can't be that if they've sneaked their way in. They should look somewhere else for their numbers."

"Nobody's sneaking," he said with a laugh.

"Right," she scoffed "and they'd have 'Artisan's Beer by Enormous Corporate' clear and up front on the label, would they?"

"Well, no, but in the small print."

"Exactly. Sneaking!" Jen felt like she'd won the argument.

But Yakob was still up for discussing it. Fine. She was enjoying the debate.

"Jen, you're looking at this wrong, it's about giving people a range of beers and keeping people in jobs." He seemed up for the discussion too, he certainly wasn't in any way abashed by her attacking his job.

Jen shook her head, "That's just spin, Yakob. You'll never convince me the macro-brewers are some kind of hero. Corporate brewers should leave the craft brewers alone. It's unethical." That might be over-egging the pudding, but she felt strongly about this. "Your bosses know it too but proceed anyway."

They stared at each other for a long moment. Some thought passed across Yakob's face, but he let it go, seeing that Jen's stern expression wasn't about to budge. It left him looking slightly sad. Well, the thought of corporates muscling into the craft beer market left her feeling rather volatile.

"It's wrong for the corporates to take ownership of those beers, Yakob. Corporate beers are long established and bland."

"So, you're saying corporate brewers can't have new beers? That's ridiculous." Was she getting him a little riled? Ha! She had him on the run.

"Sure, they can have new beers, but they should make their own, like those other beers Kronegaard have but don't get seen elsewhere. They should use those rather than taking ownership of someone else's work. Craft beer is about authenticity, recipes that have stories; how the brewer came to put the ingredients together, what inspired them. Your bosses might not know what I'm talking about, but *you* do Yakob, don't pretend you don't – think of the stories behind the beer flavours you and your Morfar made together. You can't have that legacy, if you just buy someone's work." Het up or not, Jen was finding this rather exhilarating, discussing the industry as an equal with an insider. Lydia never bothered fighting the opposing corner when Jen was spoiling for a rant.

For a second he was stumped by that, but rallied. "You're over thinking it. The customer doesn't care."

"*That's* what we're trying to change. The customer does actually care, many just don't know it yet. It's the corporates that don't care. That's why I hate them," she rounded off with a flourish.

The wind seemed to be taken out of him. "You *hate* them? They bother you that much?"

"Totally." Well probably not that much. Hate was a big word. But she was making a point. That's what hyperbole was for.

"Wow." Yakob was looking slightly wide-eyed across the pixels.

Jen shrugged. "Well, I guess it was the way I was brought up. My dad was quite outspoken on the subject." She'd enjoyed this sparring. It felt … sparky.

Yakob nodded, the atmosphere between them calming again. "I guess families can have that effect." He looked away at something she couldn't see. From what she *could* see, the room behind him looked pretty plush. "Have you got a good view from the room there, Yakob?" she asked changing the subject. Sydney would be on her bucket list.

He looked back at her then with a smile. "The entire harbour. It's magnificent, but this view," he nodded towards her, "is pretty special too." Awww. He suddenly checked his watch, "I have to go, but I'll be back next week. Can I come and see how it's going?"

"Spying?"

"Yup. I'll definitely be delving around for your hidden secrets." Oh God, she felt things clench in her nether regions.

They began to say their goodbyes and instinctively Jen touched his face on the screen with the tip of her finger. It took her a second to be aware of it and how it must look to him, but also to spot he was doing the exact same thing. It made her breath hitch. Hanging up, missing his face already, Jen stood for a long while after with the phone clutched to her chest, slowing her breathing. This wasn't a holiday blip, this wasn't her being a fool. They obviously had a genuine connection. They had common interests and could discuss things. Everything about him was genuine, from his enthusiasm to the way he looked at her. And he was coming to see her, so if she needed more incentive to get this place shipshape, there it was. She considered how she was feeling and knew for sure Lydia was right. The way he made her feel, and the way Robert didn't, was enough to confirm there was a hard conversation that was long overdue and a hideous ring to be placed firmly back in its box.

Chapter 27

"Are you supposed to be out of bed already, Jen? You look grim." Nice. Robert looked reluctant to give her a kiss. That was OK, she wasn't really hankering for one. What she really needed was a stiff drink. A double perhaps. She'd taken the walk up to the golf club to clear her head and to practice what she needed to say.

She probably did look tired to be fair, she'd worked at the Arches the entire weekend, pressure-hosing the walls, sealing them once to stop any brick dust and then again along with the floor to make everything washable to meet the food prep regulations. Her tanks had been lovingly wrapped in tarps to shield them. Tomorrow she was ordering the brewing kit. For now, the aim was to get the beer up and running and that couldn't happen fast enough. She'd mapped it out on another Excel sheet to get the timings right, with the beers maturing at different times to allow for bottling.

Jen was also sporting a slightly sweaty glean from the uphill walk. She probably looked like she was running a fever, especially as she was fidgety too. The foyer of the golf club was exceptionally old-fashioned with maroon carpets, dark wood furniture and the scent of Mr Sheen and mothballs, populated predominantly with older men in V-necked jumpers with a whiff of cigar. She was feeling antsy all round. She wanted this over with.

Gate-crashing the end of his Sunday golf game was supposed to allow her to do this on neutral ground. It seemed unfair to break up with someone in their home or when a dinner had been bought. This needed doing decently.

"I'm fine, Robert. No barfing for days."

"I was about to drop in to see you," he said, guiding them towards the door.

"You were?"

"Yes, of course. Date night." Ah, yes. She had sort of remembered, only her need to see him for other purposes had superseded any thoughts of it being a date. Walking out of the club, Jen hot on his heels, Robert looked around for the Capri and seemed rather relieved not to spot it. He pressed his key fob and the lights on his car flashed while the boot opened simultaneously for his golf clubs. "Jump in, Jen. I have a surprise."

Oh no. Not more surprises. Please.

She took a breath to start her speech as she fastened her seat belt and he folded the roof away, but reconsidered. Was it a good idea, upsetting someone when they were at the wheel? No probably not.

"How's Lydia?"

"Good thanks. I think. I haven't seen her this weekend."

"Out gallivanting?"

"Well, you know Lydia," she said, not mentioning she'd hardly been home to see her. Lydia had left her a note telling her she was seeing a friend and she would be on her phone, as she normally was, in case Jen felt the need to check on her. Honestly, what was her problem? Jen didn't have an issue with her seeing her friends, she didn't even comment when the friends were of the one-night variety, but she thought it was reasonable to expect some honesty. Lydia was still peeved by that apparently. "Where are we going?" He'd pulled out of the club in the opposite direction of town.

"Surprise, remember?" he teased. Well that didn't help her antsiness. What if he'd heard about her infidelity and was driving her off to a remote shallow grave? She told herself to get a grip. This was Robert. He wasn't about to bludgeon her with his golf clubs, he loved them too much for that, plus it would spoil his chances of becoming Club Captain. *And* he was a lawyer, so he saw first-hand that crime did not pay. Except the lawyers; they got paid ... She shook her head. She should be concentrating on what she was going to say to him.

As her hair whipped about her face, she was vaguely aware they were circumnavigating the golf course, and after five minutes they pulled into the driveway of a large mock-Tudor house.

"Whose house is this?" she asked, as he got out.

"You'll see." He was sporting a very particular aura of self-satisfaction. Jen joined him mid-gravel, where he was gazing at the building, his hands on his hips, like it was the promised land. Jen was looking at it with increasing dismay. She knew where this was going. Robert caught her hand and pulled her towards the house, extracting some keys from his pocket. Unlocking the front door, he swung it open grandly. The hall beyond was wide and imposing. The decor was very dated, but Jen was more concerned about the *why* than the what.

"I could carry you over the threshold," he said. What was he on?

"People only do that when they've got married and it's supposed to be into their own homes, silly." She deliberately skipped inside before he could act on his thoughts.

"It's for sale, Jen," he said moving behind her, placing his hands on her shoulders. "Take a look around."

She was stuck. He'd clearly arranged this viewing, it would be rude to simply refuse. But on the other hand she needed to tell him there was no point. On practical grounds she didn't want a row here in someone else's house. Without saying anything, suspecting Robert might assume it was pure awe given his own delighted face, she perused the ground floor. Natural curiosity and her sense for planning made her brain start ticking over the possibilities it could offer. The wallpapers, carpets and kitchen were decades old, but those were replaceable. The space was there, and if the dark wood went, the light would be there too. She slid her hand up the long banister as she scaled the wide staircase, imagining children's bottoms sliding down it, and a bright runner on the wooden steps. The bedrooms were huge too, and the views were fabulous, out over the golf course and the sea beyond.

Still she didn't speak, nor did Robert press her to. He was letting her take it all in, assessing the possibilities for herself. Clearly a family had lived and thrived here. The house deserved a new one to fill its walls.

The back garden had children's games written all over it, though perhaps not the rusting slide in the corner, which had more of a death-trap label. Whoever lived here next would change it out for some modern wooden climbing-frame-fort construction. She could see where a trampoline would go too, and judging by the light, there should really be a seating area over there to the right to catch the afternoon sun, perhaps with a pergola ...

"This is the barn," Robert interrupted her visions, nodding towards a long building backing onto a wooded copse to the side of the property. Venturing in, Jen saw the high-lofted space was filled with a world of things, from all sizes of bike, to an old wheel-bereft Morris Minor, a work bench that was impossible to get to and a million boxes. But if it were to be empty, it could be a decent space for something ...

"I've been thinking about what you said, at the restaurant, about your brewing. Why not keep it as a hobby, and not finish after your wedding brew?" Jen turned. Robert was looking back at her quite earnestly. He seemed to think he'd come up with the idea. "I do see that you need to fill your free time, Jen, in addition to Mumsie's plans, and I thought that perhaps you could move your brewing

277

paraphernalia in here." Jen's jaw dropped. She hadn't expected a turnaround like this. He'd seemed so adamant. She'd never have considered stopping if she hadn't been convinced by his earlier stance. The building conditions were as suitable as her own outbuilding, except bigger ... "It's away from the house, but still close, yes?"

"Well yes," Jen said, quietly, a little lost, "it could be perfect." Jen was utterly thrown by his consideration. She possibly owed him an apology on that front.

Robert's smile widened in response to her wonder. He sensed he'd got this right. He took her hand again and guided her back out into the evening sunlight.

He stopped in the centre of the lawn and took her other hand too, rubbing his thumbs across the backs of her fingers. "Look at this place. It's perfect. For *us*, I mean. I can see it, and I saw you getting it, in there. It needs gutting, but you and your spreadsheets will manage that in a jiffy and then it's a forever home." Jen looked back at the house. It was definitely a forever home. But not hers. She couldn't quite find the words though to start on what she knew had to be said. He mistook her reticence as concern. "We can afford it, Jen. Just. If we stretch a little, but that's what you're supposed to do with property. I've got a small inheritance sum to use, and the workshop can be sold now."

Her head snapped back towards him at that.

"I received Charlie's notice to end the tenancy on Friday," he said, "I've asked about and no one's renting those old places now, not for workshop purposes. You'd be better off selling his and keeping *Re:Love* for a regular income."

She still didn't say anything. He had it all planned out. He fished about in his pocket and brought out a little box she was already familiar with. "Look what's back." Fiddling with it, still trying to hold onto her left hand he cack-handedly managed to extract the ring. The box fell to the ground. They smacked heads as they both tried to pick it up, something he chose to ignore, as he got his moment back on track. "I wanted to put it on your finger here, in the grounds. I thought it would be a lovely story for the grandkids." She could see how much he wanted this. It was clearly everything he dreamed of, all laid out just so. Could she stamp on it? Break up with him in the middle of his dream scenario? She didn't know if she had it in her. He was a decent man. He wanted good things for her, for both of them.

"But Robert," she said, eyeing the ring that was coming perilously close to her ring finger now. Jesus, it was truly as awful as she'd remembered. She could almost feel her finger retracting into her hand. "The house isn't ours." She said it kindly, because he seemed so swept up in the scene he'd constructed, he'd apparently forgotten that buying houses required some negotiations and paperwork. His smile bloomed across his face.

"Well, see I've actually put an offer in. *And* it was accepted." Oh, he thought he was the very height of clever. "Derek's a member at the club – see the gate at the hedge there, it leads straight onto the twelfth tee – anyway, I've recently settled his wife's will and he's looking to down-size, so he gave me a preview before the agents and it was too good a deal to pass up. It's perfect for us."

It took her breath away. He nodded at her gasp, assuming she was wowed by their luck. Until she withdrew her hands from his and placed them firmly in her pockets. He still held the ring, primed for placing.

"Robert, do you see me as an equal partner?" This had never really occurred to her before. She'd seen them as well-matched in their ways, but perhaps they weren't equal in each other's eyes.

"Of course I do." The way he pulled his head back ruled it an unusual question.

"But you're making enormous decisions without me."

"But you don't *like* making decisions, Jen," he said, like it was a known fact. She didn't know what he meant by that. "Remember the distressed state you were in at the hospital with Lydia? It was too much for you. I want to spare you all that." He came forward and held her by the waist, gazing into her eyes. "I can make all the tough decisions for us. I'm happy to do that."

She was aghast. Was that what he thought? Was that what he'd *always* thought?

"Robert, I'd just signed off her *leg*. Of course I was distressed. And later when she regained consciousness and found it gone? I'm sure we'd all be screaming in shock, and who wouldn't class that as distressing? Yes, the doctors made it clear there was little choice, but it didn't make it less horrific for her and devastating for me. I felt *helpless*.

Helpless like I'd never known before. *That's* what I was so upset about. My parents were dead, my sister had to lose a leg or I'd lose her too, and there was nothing I could do about it. Do you see?

"I *can* make decisions, Robert," Jen went on, "I *do* make decisions, both at work and at home so Lydia is safe and I can manage things for us. I don't need a husband to make them for me. I need to be an equal voice and partner in my marriage." While she'd already decided this wasn't a marriage she could enter into, she still thought it bore expressing. He could learn something for the future.

He removed his hands from her waist to his own hips. He studied the ground for a few moments, pondering her words. *This is it,* Jen thought, *this is where he sees this can't go on, and I'll agree and it can all be amicable.*

"I see what you're saying, Jen. Your point is duly noted." He did look suitably chastened. "I'll endeavour to amend my thinking. I'll stall Derek and you can decide on the house."

Gah.

Even thinking about losing this place was killing him, it was written all over his face, but credit where credit was due, he was still doing it.

But Jen was on it now; riled up and focused. Even if he could change his thinking, on the beer and on their partnership, it didn't change hers. Jen took a couple of steps away and turned to look at the golf course, the sun growing low across it, the last of the golfers speeding up to make it to the last hole before the light gave out.

"What if I asked you to put a hold on the house for the foreseeable future, Robert?"

"Really?" Gutted didn't quite cover it. "But *why*? These houses come up so rarely."

Turning back she asked, "What if I said I needed my savings and income for the next few years to set up my brewing as a business?"

Now it was his turn for his jaw to drop, and he looked between the house and her a couple of times as he tried to compute.

"But it's just a hobby, Jen." And there it was. He simply couldn't see it as more. He couldn't see her potential to succeed at this, or even her need.

"It's not just a hobby, Robert, it's part of who I am. It's my passion and my ambition, and I don't think you've ever quite seen or allowed for that."

His head jerked as if slightly offended. "Not sure that's fair, Jen, there's the barn there. That was my idea."

"It's not about the barn, which is safely away from the house so things don't smell of beer. It's about you not recognising my passion. Brewing makes my soul happy, and I want to make it my career. I always did, though the last few years have put that on hold. I want my life partner to understand that and support me to pursue it."

He kicked a stone around considering her argument.

"I see. I *do* understand – and it isn't that what marriage is about, *compromise*? If it means so much to you, darling, then yes of course, I'll work with it." His expression was slightly tight and Jen could see him mentally sorting through which of his plans would be affected by this. "We can look at a business loan for you and we could maybe still cover the house? And Ava's nanny might be available once you've got things going and we think about family." He shot her a desperate smile. "There, that's supportive, isn't it?"

Jen took his hand.

"I don't want you to 'work with it', Robert. I want my partner to support it willingly, to cheer me on."

"I am. I just said."

She shook her head sadly.

"I want someone who gets me, who gets excited by my passion, Robert. And you aren't excited by it, or that part of *me*. You don't really want to back it, not fully, so ... I don't think I can back 'us'. I can't fit into the life you have planned."

He blinked, stunned.

"So that's it? You want to call off the wedding?"

The ring lay in his hand, still on offer. Jen gently, but firmly, folded his fingers around the ugly thing.

"I do."

Alluring, but elusive Westhampton adventurer, Lydia Attison (22) was finally tracked down by the *Echo*'s roving reporter this week, as she took part in a wake-boarding challenge. Wake-boarding's governing body is keen to promote the sport to all abilities, and Lydia easily demonstrated her inexperience and disability wouldn't hold her back as she

gave other wake-boarders, both able-bodied and
non, a run for their money. "It was an impressive
start," said Pete Chivers from the committee, "I'd
certainly like to see more of Lydia," he added with
a leery, slightly inappropriate, wink. The *Echo*
caught up with Lydia, who, with that lovely smile
of hers, said the day had been "exhilarating."

–Neil Finch, Staff Reporter,
Westhampton Echo – Page 4

Chapter 28

In all her time working at *Well, Honestly!*, Jen had always made it in before Ava, the only exception being the day Jen came for interview. Now, first thing Monday morning, Jen found her in the middle of the main office, arms folded crossly, fingers drumming on her arms and foot tapping on the floor. Call her Sherlock, but Jen suspected Ava was miffed. As soon as Jen was through the door, Ava hit the dialling button on Skype which she had primed on her laptop. Zara's face appeared on the screen. She looked as mardy, if not a little hungover, as her sister. She also appeared to be skiing. Indoors. Yes of course, that's what one did when in Dubai …

Jen dropped her bag onto her seat and turned to face the music, wishing she'd stopped on route for a coffee. The sisters were far easier to deal with when jacked-up on caffeine, but she'd stopped in at the Arches to check on things, in this case that the wall sealant and floor paint had dried. This would be her new routine and her coffee-shop time had evaporated. Jen wondered whether she could convince Alice that an espresso machine would be a great mix with the flowers and salvage. It might bring in new trade too.

"Something you want to tell us, Jen?" Ava asked. Jen detected some snark there. Ah, they'd heard. Obviously the sisters were upset by her spurning Robert. She should have expected it. The Thwaites were a close-knit bunch. Even Zara, who seemed to stay away as much as possible.

"Well, yes. I'm sorry." She wasn't sorry about the break up per se, but she was sorry about hurting Robert, and also any offence the family may have taken. It wasn't personal. Well, maybe not being Celia's bridge apprentice felt like a win, but it wasn't about them, not really.

"You gave the distinct impression you were up for it." Ava was livid. Zara stared at Jen, clearly in agreement, like some cyber henchwoman.

"Yes, yes I know I did," Jen agreed, ashamed. "But it was a genuine change of heart on my part. It wasn't maliciously meant. I didn't want to hurt anyone."

"Well, I feel totes let down," Ava stated, flinging her hands down to her sides, where they hung in fists. There was a risk she'd fling herself on the floor and tantrum.

"Totes," Zara agreed, as a skier passed behind her, sending a spray of snow over her. Some swearing ensued, and her mood was not improved.

"And you should have told us yourself, not left it to Robert," Ava added. "I'd thought more of you than that."

Wow. They were taking this really badly. "Well, I rather thought it was best coming from Robert, and it's quite recent." She didn't want to say she wasn't *that* close to them.

She'd only mentioned it to Lydia this morning as she'd walked out the door. Lydia had spun back into the house to envelope Jen in crushing hug and a brisk "thank fuck for that", which was far more accepting than what she was getting here. She hadn't told Alice and Max yet, and they were infinitely higher on her list than the sisters.

"We have so many plans," Ava lamented with a wail. "You're crucial to them, Jen. It's going to be such a blast." Ah yes, the hen-do. The official one. Jen couldn't say she was too upset about giving that a miss. She wasn't the spa-day sort, least of all with these two preening away and spaffing champagne on drinking games.

"I am sorry. Truly," Jen said, which she genuinely was. She was slightly touched they were this upset. Lord knew it meant something for Zara to get her face in gear. "I just never saw I had other needs. And while it would have been fun going with you, it wasn't the right thing to do in the long run."

Ava looked incensed. "Well, I think you're wrong. It's a winner if ever I've heard of one. You're making a huge mistake." She was adamant and sounding quite snarly. Jen appreciated her faith in her and Robert, but ultimately she couldn't agree.

"This isn't about you Ava, or you Zara. Being your sister-in-law would of course have been lovely, but this is about Robert and me, and it just wasn't going to work." There. She didn't think she could be plainer than that, and it wasn't any of their business, anyway.

Both sisters looked confused.

"What?!"

Jen didn't quite understand their reaction, but then she was slightly bewildered about how personally they were taking it all. "I broke off the engagement?" Ava turned to look at Zara on the screen. Both their jaws were hanging. That didn't make sense given the last few minutes. Jen looked between them, equally confused. "What did Robert tell you?" It had been amicable. Sort of. A bit frosty, yes, and the car journey back to her house had been one of the more awkward trips of her life, but it had been civilised and polite. She couldn't imagine him going home and ranting about it. He was more the stoic type when it came to loss of face. Unless of course he'd gone home and told them he'd dumped her, in which case she had royally stuck her foot in it now.

"But that's what you needed your money for!" it exploded out of Ava. "The house by the golf course. That's what he told us Friday night. He said you'd decided you couldn't be partner here because you were selling the workshop and you'd rather invest your money in the house." Oh. That was a whole different conversation. Now things made more sense to Jen.

"That's not quite what I'd said," she began, knowing they'd made no such agreement. She'd definitely told Robert she wasn't going to take the partnership, and probably she should have got in there first to tell her bosses, but, given all the recent events, it had rather got back-burnered. And of course she hadn't relished the conversation she knew would follow.

This one, in fact.

"Right. The partnership," Jen acknowledged, "that's not what I thought we were talking about."

"So the house thing is off then?" asked Zara.

"Well, the wedding is off, so yes." Jen had thought that was quite obvious.

Ava's face filled with relief and she dropped into a chair. "God, you had us going there, Jen. Didn't she, Zaz?" Jen noticed neither of them seemed particularly gutted on Robert's behalf.

"Totes." Zara started looking around her, no longer invested in the conversation. "Aves darling, you can handle this now, can't you? The situation's over. We're off to Wild Wadi. Jonty loves a water park. He's booked us a few more nights, by the way sweetie, so we can try out Aquaventure and Atlantis too." She blew air kisses at the screen and disappeared before Ava could get a word in.

Ava pulled out a coffee cup from behind a stack of papers, steam still rising from it. She hadn't been pacing the office since dawn then.

"Panic averted," she said, having a sip, and laying a hand on her chest to calm her breathing. "Of course, I'm sad about Robert. Mumsie is going to be devastated, and personally I think you've passed up a gem there, but I would say that, given he's my brother. But you're a grown up Jen, and you make your own choices, so I'll have to respect this one. I'm a grown up too, and that's what we do, isn't it?" She seemed quite proud of her own magnanimity.

Jen tentatively pulled her own chair out and sat down

to her work. She was rather hoping Ava would disappear into her office leaving Jen to get on with things.

"So, how quick can you get the Arches sold, do you think?" Ava asked, going nowhere. "And don't worry – we're going to have you so busy as partner, darling, you won't have time to think about the pain of the breakup. I know Robert will throw himself into the golf. And the work, of course. He can draw up the partnership docs for a start."

Jen came to a slow freeze. There was so much going on there, misconceptions that needed tackling – not least that Robert could throw himself *more* into the golf. She stared at her screen, instinctively knowing she stood on a precipice here. *Do it*, she told herself. *Tell her. Be honest. She'll understand*. She was a "grown up" apparently, whose choices would be respected. Jen almost laughed at her attempt to delude herself.

She spun to face Ava, hands clasped between her knees. "So here's the thing, Ava ..."

She told her about her dream to brew, stressing she'd absolutely be doing it out of hours and that *Well, Honestly!* wouldn't feel any adverse effects (at least not while she still worked there, but she didn't add that bit), and she'd be doing it at the Arches, which meant not selling and by the way it was actually half Lydia's anyway, and so, unfortunately, there wasn't any money to buy in with, nor would she feel she could give the partnership the time it deserved because of the beer, which was her passion and her dream, again not that it would impact her work here, and had she mentioned the passion?

Ava stayed quiet for a moment, after which Jen noticed she was shaking. Jen checked her face to see if she was crying, but the laser stare from her eyes said "not so much". Then the tremors erupted into a full volcanic blast.

"But what about MY dreams?!" Ava flew to her feet from the chair like some geyser, the force making Jen sit back in her own. "The tampons are already arriving. Surely that trumps your brewery thing which you haven't started yet." Jen chose not to point out she'd been making beer for years already. Ava needed to vent. "We need your input. You're spoiling everything." She sounded like she was six and Jen could see one leg trembling, itching to stamp.

"You'll have my input, Ava. I've already done a marketing plan, haven't I?" She understood Ava's disappointment. Perhaps doing the marketing research and plan had given the impression she was committed. In her own head, she'd given the impression of still thinking about it. Either way, she hadn't been completely honest, had she? "I'll do the marketing, you just won't have to share any of the profits with me."

"No!" Ava was angrily waggling her finger at her now, steam virtually coming out of her ears. "If you aren't prepared to take a stake, then you can't play at all."

"What?"

"No. You can't stay." Ava was livid, almost foaming at the mouth, teeth gnashing. "If you aren't with us on this, then we need to find someone who is. This is an all-or-nothing deal." Ava clearly wasn't thinking straight, the high pitch of her voice supporting Jen's opinion.

"What happened to respecting choices?" Jen asked, bewildered. "I can still work on your products. I just can't invest in them." Jen was having a panic. She needed the job here. She needed an income. She didn't know whether the brewing would work, and while she would willingly work two jobs to give it a go, the thought of banking everything on a risk was beyond scary.

"That isn't a 'choice'," Ava hissed with a snarky air-quote. "It's an *insult*. And I, *we*," she jabbed her finger to the blank screen beside her, supposedly representing Zara, "can't – *won't* – stand for that. If you're not in, you're out. Pack up your stuff."

Jen looked at her stunned. Was she serious? The silence between them said apparently so. Aiden walked into the office, took one look at them and walked straight back out again mumbling something about needing milk. Neither woman moved.

Come on, thought Jen. *Back down. I need the money.*

It dawned on her that Ava was thinking the exact same thing. Her money was what they really wanted. Not her. It rather put things in perspective, stripping away any senti-ment and loyalty.

"You need a marketing person, Ava," Jen tried, hoping to calm the tension. "Someone who knows the business." Neither sister could market for toffee and Jen was key to the business. But Ava's angry aura said she'd never admit it.

"And we'll find one who recognises the post of Partner & Marketing Director is a dream job. Someone with *vision*." God, she was stubborn.

"You're putting me in an impossible position, Ava."

"It's not impossible," Ava scoffed. "We're offering you a fabulous opportunity, and you're rejecting it. But you seem to be on a roll this week, passing up fantastic things. Clearly you aren't the astute business woman you think you are."

"Don't you want to discuss this with Zara?" Jen asked, sensing they were at an impasse.

"No need. She's with me." Sounded about right. Zara was happy not to make the decisions or do the work.

"You know I have rights, right?" Jen asked, feeling she should be sticking up for herself out of principle but, given she hated the job, not finding the conviction.

"Ugh!" Ava exclaimed, with a look of scorn. "It's all about the money with some people! You'll have your wages at the end of the month. Consider this gardening leave. I don't want to see your face around here and we don't need you." Jen would give Ava two days to see that it wasn't true; Aiden could barely open the post.

Jen shook her head, knowing there was no point trying to reason with Ava and finding it bizarre she was about to leave work before it was even 9 a.m. on a Monday morning. Though the fear was building inside her about the lack of income, she knew in her heart there was no way she was putting Ava's bonkers dream ahead of her own. Maybe she *was* on a roll – finally understanding which arrangements weren't right for her.

Jen turned to her desk, dropped the framed photo of her and Lydia into her bag before pulling it onto her shoulder. Realising Jen's intention, Ava's eyes grew wide and she poorly stifled a shriek, then stormed into her office slamming the door behind her.

Walking out, Jen hoped she never saw an inco pad again. Even if the brewing didn't come off, if she ran out of cash or nobody wanted the stuff, she was done with them. She'd bloody find her busking skill first. For once she was putting herself foremost.

Only, rather than being a euphoric moment, stepping out onto the pavement had her feeling highly vulnerable and far from in control.

Chapter 29

Trying to keep the unemployment issue as low-key in her mind as possible, and only stopping for two espressos, Jen headed for the Arches. No, she wasn't floundering aimlessly without a job to anchor her or give her day shape, stability and general security in life. Of course not. It wasn't like she didn't have other things to do. She had a brewery to establish and beers to create and customers to conjure out of thin air. None of that was a shock, it was all planned and under control. She'd just lost her long, comfortable lead in, that was all. Nothing to worry about. It was all stuff she was going to do anyway, lalalala, not worried, not worried ...

She texted Lydia the news and by the time she reached the Arches she had a string of Lydia's immediate thoughts ranging from party emojis celebrating this *Golden Hopportunity* to a sad haiku lament over their lost free crampon supply. She ended with suggestions for where Ava and Zara should stick their crampons and a note to Jen of *Don't stop Beerlievin'*, complete with backing track.

Espresso-fuelled and denial-led, Jen threw herself into

her to-do list, relishing crossing things out on the pad as she went. Deleting things on the phone lists had never offered quite the same pleasure. Still in her office clothes she stuck to the cleaner jobs, initially making files with the permit paperwork, the council applications and receipts. The first receipt was for the twenty-something grand she blew in the space of thirty minutes, purchasing a six-barrel brewing kit which would make her over nine hundred litres of beer with each brew, and then for the further five grand's worth of ingredients and bottling supplies. The price tag would have been worse if she hadn't already had Yakob's reconditioned tanks. Giddy-shocked from her purchase, she optimistically made a file called Sales, which she placed mid-shelf ready and waiting. Aarrmmaaggaahhdd, she was doing it. The hysteria was bubbling in her, a queasy mix of caffeine, glee and bum-clenching fear.

Looking out through the office window at her new workspace, she experienced the absolute joy of being part of an entity as it began. Ava and Zara had – somehow – already established *Well, Honestly!* when she joined, but this was brand new, starting from scratch, utterly in its infancy. Robert could keep his babies, right now this was all the baby she needed or wanted. But thinking of babies … Jen grabbed her keys, swiftly locked up and nipped next door.

There was no two ways about it, *Re:Love* definitely sported a more inviting aroma than her place. For now. Currently it smelled of tyres, fuels and Charlie's cigarettes beneath the newer, stronger scents of her own brick and floor sealants, but Jen knew with time, and weeks of airing, it would come to bear the fine scent of beer, yeast, malts and hops.

"Skiving?" asked Alice, popping up from behind the counter.

"Nope, setting up next door. For good. I got canned." For the first time she could properly smile about it. So what if she didn't have a guaranteed income now, and no firm sales and nothing concrete to work with other than three recycled tanks and her know-how? It was all hers and for today at least she decided to enjoy it.

Alice's jaw dropped. "Max! Emergency meeting!"

Max appeared from the back carrying a mantelpiece, which she propped against a wall, placed two buckets of flowers on either side and joined them at the counter. She was, as always, wearing her resting serious face. Jen briefed them on the details, both on the sacking and the break up. Neither friend seemed overly upset on her behalf. For either event. Alice was looking positively pleased.

"I think you've got some employment rights there, Jen," Max pointed out, sensibly. "They can't just sack you from one second to the next without some gross misdemeanour. You weren't watching porn in the office, were you?"

Jen gave her a look. "No, and yeah I know," Jen said, though she suspected Ava felt she had indeed committed a gross misdemeanour in rejecting their offer. "I'll think about that in a few days when the dust has settled. Right now, I want to get the brewery going. I'm running on the adrenalin." Which was true. She was raring to go.

"Well, I for one am delighted to have you as a new neighbour." Alice always had lovely things to say. "It'll be nice to have more life around the place. Checking on you will give me something to do. Another local company just cancelled their order. Cost cutting."

"I was just thinking about a business op for both of us actually, Alice," Jen said, excited, ignoring the suggestion that she needed checking on. "You'd be my customer, Alice, but it would work both ways."

"I already drink your beer," Alice pointed out.

"I know, but I meant the shop. I had this idea. You know how you're allowed to deliver champagne with the flowers?" Alice nodded. "I was thinking about how people buy flowers for new mums and I thought you could try a gift set with flowers and a couple of beers for the parents. A stout's supposed to be good for breastfeeding, isn't it? Anyway, that was what I was thinking, a baby gift set. I know it isn't going to solve all the finances, but who knows where it might lead. What do you think?" The words came tumbling out of her mouth and she held her breath, hoping Alice might think it was a goer. Alice mulled it over, looking around at her accessories.

"I could cellophane the bottles and tie them off with the matching ribbon to the flowers." Jen nodded eagerly, pleased Alice was thinking along with her.

"I'd do you a small batch from home so the stock's not too big and we can name it something relevant."

"*Daddy's Financial Drain*," Max chipped in.

"Or something positive," Alice chided with an eye-roll.

"*Daddy's Darling*, perhaps? Or something gender neutral, we'll work something out. It's worth a shot, Jen. We'll soon see if it tanks." She stuck out her hand and they shook on it. "I'll look at the wholesalers to see if there's some baby-handy container for the flowers."

Jen looked around the room, eyes settling on the flowers Max had moved. "A bucket. Like a small beach bucket. Something for everyone then."

"Perfect," said Alice, making a note to source buckets.

The bell at the door tinkled and a customer came in needing Alice's attention, so Jen made her excuses and left, trying not to obviously skip, delighted as she was with her new deal.

A car was parked outside her workshop. That in itself was not unusual, people blocked the access all the time. But this was a black Audi she recognised. The owner leaning against it, checking his phone, was also a giveaway. Seeing him, combined with the skipping thing, made her come to a grinding halt as the dopey grin spread across her face. He looked up at the bang of the door behind her.

"Hello again," he said. God how she loved those words. Today was just getting better and better.

"Hello again." He held out a hand to her which she took, before reeling her in towards him. Not being averse to such a direction, Jen found herself standing against him. Yakob blinked at her, before ducking his head slightly with a tilt and placing a long slow kiss on her lips, irrevocably convincing her of the newfound delights of PDAs.

"What are you doing here, Yakob?" Jen asked. She supposed she should ask him how he found her, but there weren't many arches in town. He'd seen the picture and you only had to follow the railway.

"Having a late lunch break," he said, wrapping his arms properly around her waist now, making her sigh.

"I seem to remember you work about an hour away. Wouldn't that lunch break be over just getting here?"

"Hmm, probably," he murmured, stealing another kiss, sliding a hand up her back. He could do that any day of the week she decided, barely keeping hold of the moan threatening to escape her. "I'm jet-lagged and don't know what time it is, but I had lots of lunch meetings last week, so I'm due an afternoon off." The whole afternoon. In spite of the volatile start this was now, officially, a good day.

"How was Sydney?" she managed, his lips back on her.

"Successful but exhausting."

She pulled away to look at him. "Too exhausting to help me out in there? I've got a long list of things to do."

A very wolfish smile met her. "Me too." Oh. She sank a gulp and clenched her thighs.

"You'd–" she stopped to clear her throat again as it was rather claggy, "you'd better come in and have a look then." She didn't know if his list was best covered inside or back at home, but the sooner she'd given him the tour, shown him his tanks in situ, the sooner they could get down to it. Down to *things*. The jobs. *Oh whatever*.

Aware her heart rate was belting along, she reluctantly

stepped away, delving into her pocket for the keys. "How did you know I'd be here? Not that I'm complaining."

"I was going to surprise you at your office, but got lost. I passed these arches and recognised them, so stopped to check my phone map. And then here you are."

"As if by magic," she trilled, thankful for so much, not least that he hadn't showed up at work. That had Catastrophe written all over it.

"And why aren't you at work?" he asked. Jen headed for the workshop door, trying to work out what to say, in the end deciding she'd rather he knew the truth.

"Long story." This time it was more of a resigned sigh. "Bullet point; I lost my job today. Irreconcilable differences just about covers it." She looked back at him. He was still leaning on the car, hands in pockets now, one eyebrow keenly arched. "It's a really boring story, but it's all good, as now I can focus on The Passion, can't I?" She sent him what she hoped was a seductive smile, and then added a cheeky wink, then worried it was too much and it'd looked like she was having a facial seizure. Moving things on, she prompted, "Speaking of *passion*..."

Thankfully he twigged quickly and immediately stood to follow. *Game on.* Jen rammed the key into the lock, then spent a frantic moment trying the get it to turn smoothly. She'd be WD40-ing that first thing tomorrow. Finally it turned, as did she, to see where he was, just as a large beige car pulled up to a screeching halt.

The window lowered.

"Jen darling sweetie, I thought it was you," Celia called

loudly from the driver's seat. Her outdoor voice sounded like a parody of the Queen. The floral headscarf, quilted jacket and Range Rover completed the homage. Jen felt her entire insides contract in dismay. Not now. Please not now. "Darling, I'm so glad I've seen you. Saves me phoning." Celia's eyes flickered to Yakob, then back to Jen disregarding him as of no consequence to her errand. "I know you're still considering wearing your mother's dress, but speaking from vast experience, a girl needs choices when it come to her wedding dress. I've taken the liberty of booking you a bridal fitting this weekend."

Not knowing where to look, Jen glanced at the roof tops. Where were the snipers when you needed one?

Chapter 30

The workshop had never felt so silent, even though there were two of them in there. Yakob was examining the tanks in their pride of place, as she entered, but his movements were unsettled and his hair was more mussed than before. She'd let him in so she could talk to Celia. *There* was a conversation she didn't want to relive, telling your not-to-be mother-in-law what her son had failed to convey. Celia had presented four of the five stages of grief ("acceptance" being a far-off thing) within the span of five minutes, before crossly putting the car into reverse and insisting she was going to sort this with Robert. Jen had the distinct impression Celia truly believed she had some say in this.

Still, it was at least a conversation she'd known how to handle, as opposed to this one, which had her trying out various openers in her head, none of which were acceptable.

Eventually she went with a simple "I'm sorry."

He faced her, hands in pockets. His expression was inscrutable, but his cornflower eyes had lost their sparkle.

"Sorry you're getting married? Or sorry you got caught out?" His voice was measured, but he swallowed deeply before speaking and Jen sensed he was keeping a tight rein on his feelings.

"No," she said clearly, walking towards him, but halting a little way off. "Neither of those. I'm sorry you were put at a disadvantage like that." And she truly was. That must have been hurtful and humiliating, neither of which she would ever have wished to cause him.

At first he didn't quite know what to do with that, then his expression hardened. "So what was this? A distraction, a laugh? Something you do regularly? I didn't have you down as a liar, Jen. I've met my share, but you had me completely fooled." His voice was less than measured now, angry in fact and Jen noticed his eyes skitter to the door assessing whether simply to leave. Instinctively she took a step to the side, blocking his way. She understood his anger. She couldn't imagine a scenario where this would look good. And yes, he'd told her before he'd been burned by dishonesty, so his reaction was even more justified. She'd been fooled once and she knew how that felt. The panicking side of her brain was scrabbling around for anything it could think of to appease him, but thankfully the more sensible side, the one she brought to confrontational business meetings, deemed that if she hoped to rectify this, the only chance of quenching his anger and disappointment – because that was written all over his face too – would be with absolute honesty.

She took a deep breath and drew herself up for the full confession he deserved. "I *was* engaged. Until yesterday evening. Robert, my ex, has apparently yet to inform his family. I thought it was best coming from him."

Jen faced an agonising wait as Yakob scrutinised her face for any tells. She didn't flinch. He had to take the time he needed. His hands remained firmly stuffed in his pockets, his body language rigid and defensive. Finally, just as she was about to abandon her resolve and succumb to the panic which wanted to beg his forgiveness in a pitiful show, he came to some conclusion and gave her a chink of respite. His curt nod said he understood, but his expression remained passive and his body remained several meters away from hers.

"You should have told me. Maybe in Copenhagen for example." His tone was still abrasive. He would still be thinking she was an unfaithful skank, she reasoned. Fair enough. She'd have to ride out his questioning and just pray by the end he could see this was a case of circumstance rather than malice.

"I didn't think anything was afoot in Copenhagen, Yakob. We'd just met. You kissed me as we were parting and it knocked me for six." Jen's heart was beating a full military tattoo in her chest as she exposed her feelings and hoped it was enough. Having him angry with her was excruciating.

A small smile twitched on his mouth and the relief was almost too much. She held it together though, knowing she was far from out of the woods.

"You could have mentioned it when I stayed over? I seem to remember you giving me a hard time for withholding information." He rocked on his heels, and then took a couple of steps closer which she took as encouraging. He wasn't storming off and she was taking the wins where she could.

"Hand on heart, Yakob, the only thing I had in my head that entire day – and night – was *you*. I only remembered the engagement after you'd left and it had me reeling. I felt so dreadful – towards all parties. That's not the kind of person I am. You don't know me well enough to take my word for it, but Lydia is my witness. I was beside myself."

"With guilt?"

"Partly," she readily admitted, and his eyebrows rose in surprise at her candour. She knew she was on the right track with the honesty though, whether it appeared ballsy or not; it was the only way she could show him she wasn't dishonest like previous women he'd met. "Robert's a decent guy. He deserves to be treated decently, and I don't think I did." She wasn't proud of it.

He moved closer to her, so they stood nigh-on toe to toe. His voice was low. "You said 'partly'?"

Their close proximity warranted nothing but the truth. More to the point, Jen was fast learning she had no desire to tell him anything *but* the truth. His enthusiasm, his support was what was giving her fledgling ambition its wings. In spite of the recent events in her life, she felt she was sailing on his belief in her, that it was underpinning her passion. To protect all that she wanted it wrapped in trust and truth.

Yes, she should have mentioned being on her hen-do in Copenhagen, she supposed other hens might have been shouting it from the rooftops. But something in her had kept it back, even if it wasn't deliberate. In hindsight, perhaps that should have told her something earlier.

The image she had most clearly from that trip, was Yakob sitting on his deck, palms up, saying 'this is me'. She knew how it had made her feel then, how it was the honesty she craved and how she wanted to meet that honesty now, not just to convince him to trust her, but to satisfy her own need to lay herself completely bare to him. "Well the other part, which had me terrified," she began slowly, her low tone matching his, not quite able to look him in the face, "was that I couldn't hide from the fact I have feelings – for you – that I'm not used to, and I'm not in control of." He stepped a little closer and taking a hand from his pocket gently trailed his fingertip from her ear along her jaw. Jen sank a deep gulp as her nose was enveloped in his scent, barely managing not to lean closer to take a long hard sniff of his lemony piney sageyness.

"What kind of feelings, Jen?" His tone was still low, but firm; he wasn't letting her out of this until she'd told him everything he needed to hear. It was seductive. The heady feeling had her tongue tied. "Tell me. What feelings?"

Well, she didn't know what to call them. At least not by any name she'd used before. But she knew what they felt like.

She raised her eyes to his. "Feelings that make me think about you constantly. All. The. Bloody. Time. Feelings that make you the first person I want to share news with. Feelings that are not conducive to marrying another man. Feelings I definitely didn't have for that other man and which I've only recently realised I should have had. Feelings that have me wanting to do this constantly." She tipped her chin slowly upwards, so her lips were within a hair's breadth of his. Then she rose up on her toes and made the connection, praying he wouldn't pull away.

Some prayers get answered.

Jen had always been circumspect about the term "one thing led to another", but this and her last encounter with Yakob was changing that. Things just seemed to flow between them. There was no awkwardness, no bumping noses pre-kiss, or heads, or elbowing the other in the boob or things like that which Jen could attest to being totally possible. They shared a sense of timing and awareness of the other, their pace was keenly matched and simply, one thing *did* lead to another. They naturally gravitated from the middle of the workshop floor to the wall behind the tanks, Yakob caging her in with his hands against the wall, while hers were entangled in his hair.

"This is all I've thought about since I last saw you," he growled between their kisses. She already had a sweat on from his earlier grilling, but this was sending her skin into overdrive.

"Pff. You've been in meetings the last week," she rasped out, lifting her jaw for him to continue down her neck. What a fibber. Not that it mattered. She liked hearing it.

"I didn't hear a word the managers said. I was embarrassingly useless. I might have single-handedly dropped the share-price," he murmured against her skin. Business talk was surprisingly sexy. *Share-price* was particularly tingly. She'd put money on *Presentation* being a good one too. It was getting her hot. *Hotter*. Could she ask him to describe an Excel sheet? Not yet. Too soon.

"Keep going," she groaned, her fingers now beginning to tackle his shirt buttons. She had a faint idea where this was heading and the idea had her blood rushing. Christening the brewery hadn't even been on her to-do list, which just went to show the naysayers that she could be spontaneous. Yakob pressed himself further against her body. Oh yeah, now she definitely knew where this was going. And without being the one to take control or steer this, Jen was happy to go with the flow of her emotions and desire. Right now, she wanted this. She wanted the spontaneity and embracing the passion. She trusted him to be the guide in this moment. *This was him*, so now this was her. She'd already exposed her feelings, she was ready to do so with the rest. She slid her hands inside the shirt, stroking his side and to the front, where her fingertips came to rest at his belt buckle. His fingers took their marks at her bra clasp. His eyes drew to hers and they took a moment before they came to a clear easy agreement. Go, go, go!

The door banged open at the street end of the workshop.

"Jen! We've bloody found him," Alice shouted into the room. "PanFlora came back to me with his name and guess what, it's spelled with a J."

Behind the tank, Jen and Yakob froze, eyes fixed again on each other, only this time with dismay as opposed to lust. Quickly, deftly, they redid buttons and buckles and righted hoiked garments.

"Jen?" Max's voice. Oh bum, it was both of them. Holding

309

his arms, then giving the biceps a gratuitous squeeze, because *oh man*, Jen turned them so he was against the wall.

"I'll get rid of them," she mouthed and letting go, stepped out to face her guests. Yakob obviously wasn't convinced. He looked worried, which she found both cute and flattering. His lovely eyes seemed to be pleading with her. Well, she'd heard erections could be painful if left, poor guy. Speed was obviously of the essence. She'd do what she could.

"S'up, guys?" she asked, nice and blithe, hoping she didn't look too dishevelled. There was nothing to look guilty about, it was totally feasible she'd been busy behind the tanks.

Max had some sheets of paper in her hand. Alice took some steps towards her, and Jen hurried forward to head her off, lest Yakob's hiding place be revealed.

"You've been Googling the wrong name, Jen," Alice said, thoroughly delighted with herself. "Or rather, right name, wrong spelling. Yakob Yule, right? Danes pronounce a J as 'Y' apparently. Who knew? Anyways, it's written Jakob Juul."

Foreplay-dazed while trying to be deceptive at the same time, it took Jen some moments to suss what Alice was on about. Max stepped in, holding the papers in front of her face. "We searched for him under the correct spelling. Google lit up like a bloody Christmas tree. Thousands of hits. You'll never guess–"

Alice couldn't keep it in anymore. "Jakob's a Kronegaard, Jen!"

Chapter 31

Jen's brain wasn't properly computing what Alice was saying, but then Max put the papers in her hand and suddenly she was seeing headlines about beer-heirs and playboy high-jinks and pals with royalty, all of them illustrated with pictures of Jakob Krone-Juul's face, either beautifully kempt in official photographs (he was godfather to a baby prince apparently) or poorly dodging the paps with a baseball cap and stubble-beard. She felt like she was having an out-of-body experience. It wasn't pleasant.

"You OK, Jen?" Alice asked placing her hand on Jen's forearm.

Sitting down seemed like a good plan, but chairs hadn't made it into the building yet. She'd made do with an upturned bucket so far.

Jen saw their eyes flick to behind her, and their jaws simultaneously form into identical O's. It might have been comical, but Jen had lost all capacity for humour. Turning to follow their focus, Jen saw Jakob had stepped out from behind the furthest tank. He had both hands in his pockets, and his mouth was pulled up to one side. His eyes were firmly fixed on Jen and what she might do next. Good question.

Turning back to her friends, Jen found them looking sheepish. Max reached out to retrieve the papers, but Jen clutched them to her with a brisk shake of her head. Max backed off sharpish, and spun Alice towards the door.

"I've just remembered that thing we forgot, babe," she said, propelling Alice out of the building at lightning speed, Alice still questioning "What thing?"

Which just left the two of them. If she'd found the earlier silence difficult, then this was a whole new ballgame.

"Jen?" she heard from behind her, but she didn't turn. Her eyes were running back over some of the headlines. He was constantly being linked with various gorgeous women. Or rich women. Or gorgeous and rich women. So no wife, or ex-wife, just lots and lots of high-society girl-friends. But it wasn't really the women that were killing her, it was that feeling of the rug having been pulled out from under her feet.

She felt his hands gently settle on her upper arms, but she resisted his turning her.

"Jen. Look at me." She stepped out of his grasp, but did as he asked. He looked miserable. Good. That's how she felt. "I was going to tell you," he began.

"Sure." She didn't believe him. Plain and simple.

"Really. I was planning to tell you today. I thought about it all week. But then there was your mother-in-law, and then there was the kissing." Ah yes, the kissing. That all seemed very far away now.

He held out his hand for the papers and she handed over a couple without a word.

"Latest headline there says you just bought a craft brewery in Australia, Jakob." It was all making her feel very sick. She'd thought they were debating on FaceTime. Turned out he'd been lying.

He scanned the sheets, his expression hardening as he sifted through them.

"Don't judge me by what you see there."

"I'm not. I'm judging you by what I know, here." His eyes flicked up and he looked hopeful, but Jen didn't share his optimism. She didn't know the guy in the photos, but they told her how little she knew about the guy in front of her. In fact, she knew even less about him than she'd thought. He read it in her face, but he didn't give up.

"See this picture?" He pointed to the baseball hat shot. "It says I'm sneaking into a building for a liaison. In fact, I'm attending my niece's Science fair. That one with the royal family? The christening? He's my best friend from school, he's just born to a particular family. He's still just a good bloke. No airs, no graces. Those pictures can't show that. Likewise, I'm still just an ordinary guy Jen, I was just born to a particular family." But he hadn't told her about it, had he? He wasn't who she'd thought he was. She'd been there before and her alarm bells were ringing.

"And the Australia deal?" She'd assumed he was buying another corporate, he'd never put her right.

He rolled his eyes at her. "Get over it, Jen. It's business." Wow. He wasn't denying it. "They were having difficulties

313

and we saw an opportunity. They approached us." That took the edge off her disapproval, but then his eyebrow raised and he added, "But we'd already identified them for a takeover anyway." He wasn't ashamed at all. "My job is to make the company money. I make and keep jobs. That's what I was doing. My job." Well, it was a *bad* job, by her reckoning. He wasn't apologising for it either, which irked her. His demeanour shifted to something less bold. "But my job isn't me. You know *me*."

He was standing now with his hands out from his sides, palms up. That supposedly honest gesture. It had her well and truly fooled then. It had her riled now.

"You gave me a false bloody name!"

"I didn't," he said, shaking his head, then hesitated. "Not really. I'm a Krone on my mother's side. Stefan Krone was my Morfar. But I drop the Krone most of the time." How was that not sneaky?

"What bloody happened to 'This is me'?!" she snapped.

"This *IS* me!" he snapped back. "You met me, without any back-story or gossip. You know me as *me*. Nothing more, nothing less. None of the crap they print about me in the papers; the speculation, the conjecture or the lies. Can you imagine how refreshing, and appealing, that is? How amazing to meet someone who didn't pre-judge me, or hang around for the fame, or money, or hold back their thoughts on my family?" No, she hadn't held back there, at all. Apparently, she hadn't just insulted his work, but also his family. Bloody hell.

"I live on a boat, Jen. Know why? Because in the back

314

of my head I need to feel I can escape all of it. I could slip the ropes and float away from it." That sounded like a sorry way to live one's life – though admittedly the boat *was* gorgeous. Jen understood what he was saying about his not picking his family, but knowing about it just upset her further. These were more things she didn't know about him. More things he hadn't trusted her with. More things that said this man, who she'd just admitted to having feelings for, whose existence had moved her to throw away another life, was simply a figment of her imagination. Just like Danny.

He took a deep breath, gearing up for another attempt at diffusing things.

"I know you're angry with me for keeping this secret, Jen, but you kept secrets too. You said nothing about being engaged. Why was that?" His eyes were flicking between hers, urging her to think, but he answered for her. "Because the time wasn't right, or you didn't know how to start. You know how that is. It's the same."

"It is NOT the same!" she roared. Was it? No, no she was sure it was radically different. Not that it mattered as she was on one now. She'd been blindsided by this and she was fighting that feeling of being at a disadvantage she normally strove to avoid. "I didn't hide who *I* was. I simply didn't mention something that was happening to me at the time. But I told you who *I* was, Jakob, about my family, about where I work and how I feel about it. I told you about my *passion*. You? You omitted all of that, or cloaked it in vagueness."

As she spoke, more and more reasons for her being a fool piled on her. She'd spent a morning in his museum and not spotted the resemblance in the family photos on the boards. He hadn't at any point in her espousing about the brilliance of the place said "oh yeah, that's mine, by the way." There had been plenty of chances. Tipsy or not, she would have remembered him doing that. In hindsight she should have noticed him deflecting the questions about himself. There was the barge from the factory and he'd sent her the tanks. Obviously, regular workers didn't get to take home the cast-off equipment. Duh. She should have spotted it all, but she'd just been swept up and blinkered by the bloody romance. Just like with Danny, she hadn't seen the details behind the facade. So stupid. What a prize prat. It made her want to cry. He must have thought her so gullible. It gave her another sickening thought; "You must have been having such a laugh at me, with my little brewing ideas."

"What? No–" He looked alarmed at the turn in her thinking. His hands raised to in front of him in an "I'm innocent, I'm hiding nothing" gesture, but she knew now it wasn't true and not to trust his gestures.

"Don't give me that," she spat, all the anger coming up in her now, the disappointment, the embarrassment and the shock boosting it on, "did it give you a kick to donate the tanks to me?" She looked at them and felt bad about dragging them into this venomous shout; she bloody loved those tanks already. "Was I some comedy charity case? Pathetic little me, having a go at what your family has already conquered years ago and made mega-bucks from."

"Stop, it," he said firmly, but keeping his distance, because there was every chance she might swing for him.

She'd never felt this before, this bilious rage that had her unable to move. Casting it out and in his direction was the only thing her body could do, and yet she didn't feel in control of it. She didn't feel in control of any of this. His eyes were intent on her face, trying to read her. *Yeah, good luck with that Jakob,* she thought. Right now she was a cocktail of emotions. The Molotov kind.

"I will not stop," she raged on, trying hard not to sound like a tantruming five-year-old, but feeling every bit of one. "I showed you my brewery ... and other private places," she could not bring herself to say it, but he knew what she was talking about, "I made myself vulnerable to you, and obviously my trust was totally misplaced. I'm not particularly high-maintenance, Jakob, but I do have a basic bar of trustworthiness."

"I was never laughing at you, Jen, not once," he said, the frustration making a vein in his temple throb. "I have been excited about your beer venture from the first second you told me about it. I have never been anything but encouraging–"

"To my face," she interjected, worried his voice would start persuading her, "probably not behind my back."

"Never. I've not discussed you or your beer with anyone. I only ever wanted to see this work. I was looking forward to seeing you grow this." *Was.* He knew where this conversation was going. That made things easier. "And as for your other private places?" Jen felt her head start to get even hotter. "If you think I went *there* as part of some game, then you are right – you don't know me at all – but that wouldn't be because of me, that would be because you are an awful judge of character."

"I am not!" She had lovely friends. She really did. Though she had misjudged Danny, but that was years ago. And she might have almost married into the wrong family, but she'd dodged that bullet. And she'd got him wrong, hadn't she? Ugh, maybe he was right..?

Apparently he wasn't convinced by her denial either. He simply shrugged. Well, she wasn't going to stand here stating her case for reading people, especially not to people who portrayed themselves as something they weren't. Time to bring this to a close.

"I don't trust you, Jakob. I can't trust you. I'd always be wondering what else there is to know, what surprise might come and whether you're telling me everything."

He ducked his head, shaking it. She could actively see him giving up, and something vaguely around her heart area began to ache.

"I think you're scared, Jen," he said, abruptly righting himself, eyes blazing. "I think the way you feel about me, about us, frightens you, because you aren't in control of it. You can't app it or make a list or an Excel sheet for it and it terrifies you. So it's easier to trash it than let it flourish and make yourself more vulnerable."

"That's rubbish," she whispered, unable to shake the feeling that he'd just flayed her.

"*That's* the truth, Jen. When I look at you, when I think

about you or talk to you, I feel helpless – and it's the most exhilarating, scary, wonderful thing. I suspected you couldn't be single when we met on the boat, Jen – I could have asked you then – but really, I didn't want to hear it, I was already signed up to follow my feelings. I don't care about the engagement, I believe your intentions weren't dishonest." He ran his hand through his messy hair and shook his head in dismay before carrying on. "Look, we've both with-held information, we both now know. We're quits. Can't we draw a line under it all and take each other for what we are?"

Jen stance was rigid. "I don't think so."

"Then you're a chicken." The words shot out of him and his eyes burned cold at her in a challenge.

Really? He was calling her names now? She wasn't having that. And she wasn't *scared*, she just knew when she needed to defend herself.

Incensed Jen's brow drew in and she hoped her eyes looked as steely as his. If he was slinging ridiculous psycho-logical "insights" at her then she had some home truths to come his way.

"Here's the thing though *Jakob*, I don't know *what* you are. And what's more, I don't think you do either. You play the role of being Corporate Shark yet I can see – I've always seen – it isn't where your heart lies. You push me to follow my dreams, but what about yours? Don't stand there saying 'this is me' when we both now know that's a lie. All your encouragement about my brewery is really you living vicar-iously through me. I joked about it before, but now I see

I was right. The real Jakob, the man you're supposed to be, is the one who explored his creative desire with his Morfar, not this corporate suit who pushes numbers and takes over other people's creative endeavours thinking that it's enough to make him happy. Your Morfar was trying to show you something, something he saw in you. Instead you let your parents press you into something else. You might say you're good at being a shark Jakob, but I don't see it making *your* heart sing. The lecture you gave me at the tradeshow? Well, back at you Juul, you hypocrite. If anyone here is the chicken it's you."

He looked stunned, and somewhat uncomfortable. It was the first time she'd ever seen him look like that. Unless she was very much mistaken, she'd hit a nerve. Well good. It was probably long overdue.

"I'm part of a big, old family, Jen," he said angrily, "I had a role to take, a duty to fulfil. I love my family and I would never risk their disappointment.'

Jen looked at him hard, then nodded. "Fine. It's your life and your choice. I think you might be underestimating your family's capacity to allow you your happiness, but hey, you know them best and obviously I don't know them at all. But you'll have to excuse me if I say I can't draw the line as you ask, because I honestly don't know the man I'd be left standing with, not least because he doesn't even know himself." Every sentence felt like a spear and her hurting soul was taking a malicious joy in hurling them at him.

Fire flared again in his eyes and it wasn't the sexy kind, more molten and spewing. His jaw was set hard, not something she'd seen before either, having always been used to his lovely smile.

"One day you might look back and consider the decisions you made Jen, and wonder whether there was more to be had in life. You might regret some of the things you didn't think were worth the risk, that weren't worth the fight or stepping out of your comfort zone for." He fished his car keys out of his pocket, and walked past her to the door. "Good luck, Jen," he said. "I hope the brewing is everything you dreamed of."

Chapter 32

Their front door slamming shut was generally a thing to put Jen on edge; it was a portent for Mount Lydia about to erupt; a bad date, a selfish co-worker, a guy on the train who was hot, but didn't succumb to her seductive glance. Jen was surprised the door was still hanging on after all these years, given the force it was shown, but then it was an old house and the door had been made in stronger times. Tonight though, she was glad to hear that slam, as she'd been waiting to tell Lydia. She was going to be as outraged as Jen about this.

When Jakob had left the workshop, Jen had simply stood frozen for many minutes with an enormous sense of dismay. But she'd been right in her reaction – she was sure she had – and so decided the dismay could only possibly represent the disappointment of being so let down by someone she was so interested in. For now the howling outrage was holding back her tears of being utterly gutted. Having locked up, she'd stalked through the streets towards home, replaying it all in her mind, her head placing the spotlight firmly on the deceit and Google images, to subdue the kissy scenes her heart naturally defaulted to.

Lydia stormed into the kitchen without so much as a "Hi", and started to sort herself a cup of tea, her back to Jen. Excellent. This was exactly the mood Jen wanted her in, the indignation and commiseration would be at precisely the standard she was looking for. Jen fully expected some ripe swearing, but the occasion undoubtedly warranted it.

"You won't believe what I found out," Jen began.

Lydia grunted something nondescript, as she pelted the teabag into her mug. She didn't ask if Jen wanted one, which was fine, as Jen had just been through this same pelty procedure.

"Jakob, of Copenhagen fame, isn't some random worker at Kronegaard. He's actually Kronegaard. Or at least one of them."

She sat back, arms folded and waited for the *What the fuck?!* Then she would reply with an incensed *I know, right?*, and so it would begin, the Jakob take-down. She so needed someone to help her take him down, as something in the cavern of her chest was still ignoring the memo.

Instead, Lydia took her sweet time pouring the milk, and stirring her tea with a less than delicate tinkle. Perhaps she was processing. Fair enough. Jen could do the filling-in in the meantime.

"He lied to me. He deliberately withheld the details of his identity, details that are somewhat pertinent to my career. He totally played me, Lyds, he *slept* with me, he could have been laughing at me behind my back the whole time, plus and – this is the cherry on the bloody cake – he buys craft breweries and it doesn't bother him!" There. Lydia now had the full briefing. She could take her pick which bit to launch into first. Jen had all evening to work on this, weeks in fact.

Still Lydia kept her back turned, though she did straighten up to have a long sip of the tea. Did she need more info? Jen went on to tell her what had happened, how he'd turned up and how Alice and Max had exposed his heinous player-ing, how he'd tried to defend his actions-slash-deceit. "And then he had the gall, THE GALL – to suggest I was overreacting, that I wanted to destroy things, because I was scared. Ha! Hahahahaha!" She was sounding a little manic now. She knew that. But it was all too very ridiculous, utterly and totally.

Finally, Lydia turned to face her. Her expression was grim. How apt.

"He's right."

"What?!" She waited for Lydia to laugh and show she was kidding. But Lydia's face remained stony.

"That's what you do. When you get scared you shut things down. You liking him is scaring the pants off you, so you're shutting him down on a daft pretext."

Jen had to blink a few times. She pulled her earlobe to see if wax was making her hear weird things. Daft pretext?

"He lied to me! He made himself out to be someone he wasn't." Jen had never told Lydia about Danny, but she couldn't see how the basics of this, the deceit, wasn't enough for her sister to get it.

"No, he just wasn't at the right place to tell you yet."

"He had loads of chances."

"What, you think he tells people as soon as he meets them who he is? How arrogant or stupid would that be?"

"There were other opportunities," Jen barked. This, amongst various things today it seemed, was not remotely going how she'd imagined.

"Give him a break. He hadn't found the moment yet. Had you found the moment to tell him about Robert?" Lydia gave her a laser-pointed look. *Jeez.* Not her too. "And as for the job. It's a business, that's how businesses work; investment and expansion."

"But it's the principle," Jen hissed. "It's unethical."

"Get a grip. It's just beer. There's room for different brewers and not everyone can afford your fancy beer. You need to stop being the beer police and just get on with doing what you do and leave other companies to make their own decisions about whether they sell out."

"But he knew how I felt about corporates buying craft brewer–"

"Jen! Listen to yourself. Could you be more self-involved? It's his job. He's been doing it for longer than he's known you. He's part of a global firm. Looks like he's quite good at it."

"It's not even what he dreams of doing. He should be on the brewing side!"

"Again, not your business. He's a grown-arse man, he can make his own choices. Who the hell do you think you are, telling people what they should or shouldn't do with their lives?"

Why was she defending Jakob? Jen had assumed they'd be safely ensconced on the sofa by now with a tub of ice cream and two spoons, maligning all men, but particularly Scandi beer heirs. And now Lydia was having a dig at her too. She parked Jakob's job for now, they'd have to agree to disagree on that. Jen had something else she needed to set straight, given Lydia seemed to agree with Jakob on that as well.

"I don't shut everything down."

"Right," Lydia agreed rolling her eyes. "I fell over in week three of Explorer scouts, which was some of the most fun I'd had in years, and because I gashed my good leg, you withdrew me."

"They'd made a mistake with the intake. You weren't supposed to have been there," Jen insisted. They'd already had this discussion.

"Now who's the liar? I emailed and they told me what really happened." Dammit.

"It wasn't safe for you." Jen was not going to be critiqued for things she did to keep Lydia out of harm.

"You shut it down because you were scared. I was in no more danger than any of the others." Lydia's eyes were hard and angry and her voice was rising.

"Your situation is different." Jen held back from nodding at her leg. They knew what she meant.

"You know what, Jen?" Lydia took a deep breath, "there is no one who makes me feel more disabled than you. No one. You think you're protecting me, but you're preventing me from living my life." The venom in her sister's voice took her aback.

326

"What?" Jen stared at her sister astounded, stunned at both the turn in conversation and the sentiment. How could she even say that? She had changed the whole course of her life to raise Lydia. She'd done her best. It suddenly dawned on Jen that Lydia's attitude had come with her through the door. She was already angry about something. "What's the matter with you?"

"*You*. You are the matter with me," Lydia growled, clearly seething now. She dug in her pocket, pulled out an item and slammed it down on the kitchen table.

Jen stared at the small patch, no bigger than a ten pence piece with a QR code on it. "I've got patches like that on all of my prostheses. I'd always thought they were some factory quality sticker. Imagine my surprise when Alison at work tells me about her ugly divorce, where amongst other overbearing things, her husband had stuck these in all her handbags. He wanted to know where she was at all times."

Oh. "I know it looks bad," Jen started, "but–"

"You put GPS stickers on me!!" Lydia shouted at her. "You were tracking me! How controlling can you get? I had our IT specialist confirm it was the same kind of sticker, because I couldn't believe you'd really do something that shitty to me."

Jen raised her hands flat to Lydia, trying to calm her down. "I wasn't tracking *you*. Don't be daft. It's the legs. You know how much they cost. Those stickers were just an insurance policy in the event of them going missing," Lydia did not look like she was buying it, which was pretty harsh when Jen only ever had her sister's best interests at heart. "Which, as it happened," Jen pointed out, "was a good thing, wasn't it, when you lost the cosmesis."

"And you tracked it on what?"

"I borrowed Alice's iPhone and used my SIM. Took me straight to it. See, it was for a good purpose."

Lydia looked like she was counting to ten.

"It's strange, Jen, how you didn't say 'S'all right Lyds, I can get your leg back with this, lend me your phone, will you', or tell me how you did it when you got it back. It's also odd how you didn't feel the need to consult with me about this gross invasion of my privacy."

"It's hardly that," Jen scoffed. Lydia's murderous expression said otherwise.

"You are totally out of line. Ten quid says you didn't tell Alice what you needed her phone for either." Jen examined something on the floor.

"I'm just looking out for you Lydia, seeing as you seem unwilling to do so. You seem to deliberately overlook your predicament and you can be reckless."

Lydia pushed herself away from the counter and leaned both hands on the table so she could look Jen in the eye. It was not a friendly gaze.

"You know what? Every time you remind me I've only got one leg, I go out and do something adventurous. To be clear, those are the things you consider reckless. If you ever read the *Echo*, you'd know I've recently been skydiving and Team GB have invited me to skeleton bob trials because turns out I am pretty bloody good at it."

Jen felt the blood draining from her face. She'd done what?!

Lydia was still going. "Last Saturday I was wake-boarding and I'm learning to paramotor. I can fly, Jen. Up in the air, soon by myself, and I love it. Your bloody GPS didn't show you that, did it? No, all it shows you really is the nights I stop out with hot blokes. Those nights show *me* that being an amputee isn't the sum of me, which is what you seem to think. Those guys don't see my leg. They see *me*. And I let them see *all* of me and they are quite happy with that, probably because I'm bloody good at sex too. All those things make me feel free, when you don't."

Lydia stood upright, on a roll now. "I was so pleased when you met Jakob, Jen. I saw you gawp at his bod from the boat and it was the first time I'd seen you following your own desires, rather than repressing them so you could look after me. That's why I left you in the canal when fate chucked you a lifeline. That's why I've been texting him ever since, including the news of the show win." Jen's jaw hit the floor. She'd had no idea Lydia had been orchestrating this. But Lydia didn't look like she was wanting any thanks for it. "But, don't think it was to make you happy – although you actually became more bearable for it. It was to get you off my back." Lydia's words felt like a slap. Lots and lots of slaps, one sting right on top of the other.

"And now you've gone and fucked that up too, Jen. So no, I'm not going to tell you he's done wrong, when I know it's you that's shut it down. *You* did wrong. He's the best thing that's happened to you in so long and you've arsed it up."

It had been a crappy day; she'd got the sack, she'd had to deal with the disappointment and shock of Jakob, and now Lydia was hurling all sorts of ridiculous accusations at her. She seemed to think she was some kind of romance whisperer when in fact she had no idea what Jen had experienced before, so her expert credentials were worth diddly-squat. Well no. Jen wasn't bloody standing for it. Who did Lydia think she was? Jen had done everything for her since they'd lost their parents. Everything. Jen stood up, feeling rabid rage coursing up through her body.

"You've got a nerve, standing here saying things like that to me. I've given up so much for you, put up with your teenage tantrums and trying to raise you single-handed, while clawing together some semblance of a life of my own. You have no bloody idea how hard that is. Not one clue. And here you are saying it isn't good enough and I've ruined your life and necessitated you being a slapper for your own self-esteem. Bollocks to that. Take a look at yourself, Lydia. You're here, surviving quite comfortably, so I think I've done my basic job OK, thank you. Shame I've failed when it came to your character, clearly you are one ungrateful and apparently disloyal, meddling cow."

"Says *she*, who puts tracking devices on her sister! How meddling is that?" Lydia shouted back. This was quickly escalating into one of their full-blown rows, but there was an edge to this one there had never been before. This was far too close to the bone. And Lydia wasn't done yet. She seemed to have grown an inch from the anger radiating out of her. "You know what, Jen? Finding theses patches couldn't have come at a better time. They're the last push I needed. I'm not sticking around to see you wallowing in your self-pity over Jakob, when screwing it up is your own doing. I'm not sticking around to have you turn your attention back on me, making me feel half the person I know I can be and am going to be."

"God, that is so self-involved and totally untrue. Don't give me that crap. I've made you the woman you are today."

"Only by making me rebel against you – not that you can see it, as you're so fucking blind to anything that isn't about your struggle. I will not be your charity effort anymore. I'm outta here."

"Here we go again," Jen sneered, "another of Lydia's hissy-fit walk-outs. Like I haven't seen a million of those in the last few years."

Lydia fixed her with a hateful eye. The force of it made Jen flinch.

"I've completed the first part of my training. I can now transfer to any of the international offices and finish the graduate programme there. That's why I picked this company in the first place and I'm going."

What? Lydia had never mentioned this as part of her grad scheme – not that it mattered as she was bluffing. "Don't be ridiculous, Lydia–"

"Right now I'm waiting to hear back from Singapore and San Francisco. Fingers crossed for whichever is furthest away from you. I need to live for myself without you making it harder. And maybe you can get on with living your life, without hiding behind me as some martyr looking after your crippled sister."

Jen's jaw hit the ground. "Those are awful things to say."

Lydia walked to the door, scooping up the GPS patch as she went. "Truth hurts."

Jen forced herself to stand her ground. "You'll be back as soon as you're hungry. That's your usual. You don't know how to take care of yourself." She'd seen this all before. Lydia needn't think she was fooling anyone.

"Newsflash, Jen. I'm twenty-two, and I've been an adult for a while. I can look after myself just fine when you actually let me. More to the point, I can do what or who I like, wherever I like. Like right now, I'm getting a bag and leaving. I'll be back for my stuff when I get something sorted. Don't call me. Call Alice if you need to get a message to me."

Jen sat down and drank her tea, crossly. She wasn't bloody rising to this. Lydia could be an utter bitch sometimes. Many times, in fact. She was sick of her moods and being the one she took them out on. Those GPS patches were simply to safeguard her legs. She was blowing it all out of proportion. If anyone should be sounding off here, it should be Jen, for Lydia being in cahoots with Jakob. But that thing about her moving abroad? That had to be a bluff, surely..?

She listened to her sister stomping about in the room above, and then to her coming down the stairs, crutches whacking the walls as she carried them under her arm. A horn beeped from outside and Jen listened to Lydia organising her bags being taken. And then the door slammed, followed by a loud smash.

Probably the Best Kiss in the World

Jen found their parents' portrait on the floor, the glass cracked across their faces. Their smiles were gone under the crackle. Jen looked at the door grimly, the silence in the house becoming smothering. The awfulness of the day finally took its toll, with Jen sliding down the wall clutching her parents to her chest.

Lydia would be back. Of course, she would. And Jakob? She was better off without him, she whispered to the picture as her sobs echoed around the hole in her chest.

Chapter 33

Lydia was being particularly stubborn this time, still not having returned after three weeks. According to Alice she was safe. That was all Jen needed to know. Beyond that, Lydia could stew as far as Jen cared. She wasn't going be treated like that by her younger sister.

Jen was fine. F.I.N.E. Totally fine. The beer was fine. Everything was bloody fine.

She reaffirmed this every day as she tended her tanks in the Arches, focusing on her venture and avoiding all thoughts of the things that had gone shitwards. The first thing she'd done the morning after Lydia's walk-out was to grab her phone, offer up a prayer that Robert hadn't wanted his gift back, and open her *List*IT App. Her sobbing over the smashed picture had just been all the pent-up shock and frustration of the day, nothing more. The glass would be replaced and she'd carry on as she knew best; working to her lists. Things needed to get back on track. This was what she'd been missing. This was what had disrupted the order in her universe – not sticking to her lists or meticulously devising plans on her laptop. Obviously she deleted ChAPPel from the phone. She wasn't sad to see it go.

She had a portable master-list of all the things she needed to do, and then sub-lists breaking the original task down. This was so much better. She felt on course to something. Being on course suited her. None of that randomness. Spending most of her time in the Arches was conducive to her productivity, the house being disruptively quiet at the moment. In the workshop there was at least the murmur of traffic, the rumble of trains above and Alice's chick-flick soundtracks filtering through the bricks. Not to mention Alice's singing along, which while initially painful, now offered Jen a degree of comfort. Yes, the Arches was exactly what she needed at the moment, to focus on the newly arrived kit, setting her brews, her lists and building her business. Building her new life, in fact. She didn't need any distractions, such as suitors or siblings.

She was delighted with the new phone. Over the moon. Only, that too was annoyingly quiet. Before, she used to take calls all the time, inco pad contacts or just Ava whining about something or other, or dumping more work on her. Well, she could live without those. Robert used to text her, but there was radio silence there. She couldn't blame him for that. Lydia's numerous snarky texts about the people she came across in her work were missing, but as Jen was still seething from their argument, she was awaiting an apology before she'd be open to any joviality. There was nothing from Jakob either. Not that she was waiting for anything there. Jen had angrily closed down all thoughts of him. That relationship was done and dusted. She'd sworn not to give him the time of day. Not one minute. And every time he'd since slunk his way into her head, she batted the thought away, with a swear. Her swear jar was filling up fast, but if nothing else, Jen was a determined woman and she vowed to purge herself of this stupid tendency to think about him. She didn't need him to make her dreams come true.

Jen tucked the phone out of view. She knew what she was doing for the day, she didn't need to see her lists for the time being and she didn't need reminding that no one was calling her. She was waaaay too busy for that. She was getting back in control of things.

The brewery was her life now, and far more reliable it was too. She'd got the change of building usage through superfast, along with her permission to brew, having called the council and found the Environmental Health Officer was a beer aficionado. The workshop had been rewired and re-plumbed for the waste waters and was now legally a brewhouse. New signage had been commissioned for the frontage, neatly announcing it was *Attison's Brewery*. Jen had taken herself off on a three day commercial brewing course to cover all the business aspects and now, having her evenings to herself and uninterrupted by a ranting sibling, she had all her tax paperwork up-to-date and submitted. She'd even found a local farmer wanting to buy the spent malt from her as animal feed. What had Lydia been on about, saying she had no life? Her life was crazy busy and as complete as anyone else's.

And the beer was brewing. Hurrah! The six barrel kit had been delivered, installed and demonstrated. Two fast-fermenting beers were already tapped – she'd barely been able to lift her arms for several days after having bottled one-thousand-eight-hundred litres, so outsourcing the job was looking appealing. Meanwhile the boxes were stacked neatly on the shelves, with a couple of new brews in the tanks. The Golden Ale and IPA were due out in the next week, and then she'd have a basic array to deliver and the supply cycle could properly start. After that she could start building up more stock to sell elsewhere and even at the door. Since the sign had gone up she'd noticed cars slowing to check it out as they passed. Even the most reticent people became curious when it came to sourcing beer. Which would all be a good thing, as she'd had her last pay packet from *Well, Honestly!*. She'd spent huge amounts already and given the current sisterly climate she wasn't quite sure where she stood on the loan from Lydia's leg account, but once she'd sold this stock to Anthony, she should be good for a little while longer, although her shopping list was growing. There was all sorts of kit she'd like, and eventually, when her brain got over the new-recipe block it was strangely experiencing, she'd need more ingredients too.

There was a knock on the door.

"Ha, Ha! Knockers!" she said to herself. Out loud. She was doing plenty of that recently.

Alice stuck her head in the door. "I need more of the baby beers. The *Hoppy New Baby* combos are going like shit off a shovel." Nice.

"Hmm, I'm sure you mean something more nectar-like, as opposed to shit, right Alice?" Jen couldn't help but match Alice's grin. The thought of *Re:Love*'s business returning was heartening.

"Right deffo. So have you got any?"

Jen took great pleasure in carefully perusing the few boxes on the entire wall of otherwise empty shelves, finally pulling one out. This one had come from home. Not having to store boxes around the house anymore made the place seem much roomier. Lydia not careening around increased the space too.

"One box of twenty-four left."

"Perfect. Do me an invoice, yes?"

Jen nearly flew to her laptop. An invoice! Her very first. "And don't forget to put that first batch on there too." Alice added, almost making Jen swoon. "Foot traffic is picking up. People are having a nosy at yours and popping in at ours on the way. Got any more ideas?"

She did, as it happened. "You can do engagement packs with *Hopposites Attract* or wishing them *Health, Wealth and Hoppiness*. Or *Hoppy New Home* for the new homers. Who wouldn't like a bunch of flowers and a couple to beers for the first night?" Really, the beer didn't need to change, just the labels.

"On it," Alice beamed and Jen could already see her thinking about the flowers she'd use. "Brew more and we'll do it."

"You know Alice, we could flyer local companies, suggesting them as employee gifts?" Jen grabbed the phone and added it to her list. "How's things?" she asked, trying to appear nonchalant. "Up to much?"

"Hmm, not really. Swing dance, cinema, book club."

There'd been a new rom-com released recently, Jen had seen the posters. "Watch the film by yourself?"

Alice stooped to take a very close look at the dial on the nearest tank. "Not really." They both knew Max would rather poke her own eyes out than go to the cinema. So many people in a dark confined space was beyond her.

Jen decided to go with a silent stare, as if expecting Alice to expand her answer. Alice caved pretty quickly. "You know who I went with, Jen. She's asked me not to tell you what she's doing. I'm only allowed to say she's fine. Which she is. I'd say if she wasn't."

"How long do you think she's going keep this huff up, Al?" Jen grumped. Alice had witnessed hundreds of Lydia's strops. She'd listened to many of Jen's rants about Lydia being a teenage ingrate.

Alice drew a breath. "I dunno Jen, depends how long it'll take you to apologise."

Jen experienced a weird series of pops in her ears as she made sense of what Alice had said.

"Me? *She's* the one to apologise. She said some awful things to me," she spluttered.

"Only in response to your actions, Jen." Alice leaned against the tank, arms crossed. "Jen, you do see that what you did with the tracking patches was a horrible thing to do, right?"

"I wasn't 'tracking her'," Jen did the air-quote thing to

mock Lydia's dramatics, but suspected she looked ridiculous, "it was the legs, they're expens–"

"Jen. It was a horrible thing to do." Alice was brooking no argument here. "It was a total invasion of privacy, which you knew, because a) you are smart and b) you would have told her what you were doing otherwise."

Jen sensed her head heating up. She wanted to defend herself, yet her lips felt knotted. But that was OK as Alice wasn't done yet.

"You might have convinced yourself that you're only protecting her, but you have to recognise now Jen, that instead you're trying to control her. What you consistently refuse to see is that Lydia is quite capable of controlling her own life."

Jen's lips released themselves, but only to flap up and down in shock at her best friend's opinion and that she was giving her a sound telling off.

Alice clearly felt she had said her piece and with a nod to indicate it was over, dropped her feisty stance and moved away from the tank towards the shell-shocked Jen.

"More to the point," Alice asked briskly, perching on a stool Jen had fashioned from some thoroughly hosed tyres left in the back yard, "how are you?"

Jen took a long moment to find her equilibrium. She was slightly bewildered by what had just occurred. She felt like a scolded pet. Her head was retaining its pounding heat, but resolutely she packed the moment away to dissect later in private. She pulled herself together to her automatic response. "Fine."

"Bullpoo," coughed Alice.

Regaining some composure, Jen arched a brow at her. "Look around you. It's happening. The beer is flowing. You just ordered some stock and I could fulfil it instantly." Jen was aware she was sounding a little snappy, still feeling defensive, but Alice ignored it.

"I'm not talking about the beer, Jen," she said gently, "I don't think anyone has ever doubted you could do the brewing." Alice was clearly getting at something. "What about *you?*"

"Couldn't be better," Jen stubbornly insisted. She plastered a smile on her face and tried to widen her eyes as much as possible. "I'm not surrounded by inco pads for starters. Or crocheted tampons, thank god. Plus there's no Ava and Zara in my life."

Alice wasn't buying the perkiness. "Still not what I meant, but now you've brought them up, heard from Robert?"

"Hm? No. I wouldn't expect to, what with the crushing his dreams thing." The guilty feeling started to creep up through her chest, but she batted it away. In the long run, she'd done them both a favour.

"Which leaves ..." Alice prompted.

"I'm fine, Alice. Honestly."

For the second time Alice's usually chirpy little face took on a very stern guise. The reintroduction of the crossed arms backed this up. "You've had an enormous row with your only sister, which you're unwilling to reconcile, and the super-hot guy, who got your knickers in a complete twist, has walked out of your life and you really feel you ernille Hughes

are OK with that? I'm insulted, Jen. Either you think I'm incredibly stupid, or you simply don't mind lying to me. Which is it?"

Jen was about to start angrily defending herself, *again*, but looking at Alice, she deflated. She loved Alice, they'd been friends for years, and, apart from today it seemed, she knew where she stood with her. Alice might be pocket-sized, but she was a giant of integrity and honesty. That wasn't a friendship you took for granted. And besides, she couldn't afford to lose more friends currently, she was down to so few. Any more and she'd have only her hops to talk to.

"No, I'm not completely fine," she admitted sulkily. "On the personal front things are a bit crappy right now, but it'll sort itself, Alice. Lyds and I will work this out when she's calmed the hell down, and the Jakob thing, well it just wasn't meant to be, was it? He came into my life, and let's be honest, he helped me dodge a bullet, but clearly it wasn't supposed to be a long term thing. Not all encounters are supposed to be forever, Alice. Sometimes, they have a single purpose to serve and then life moves on. I know your films lead to Happily Ever After, but I've said before, real life doesn't always work like that."

"You honestly believe you should just let Jakob go? Are you aware what you were like with him in your life?"

Jen just scowled.

"You were happy, Jen, relaxed, and you weren't living your life by app. And your plans came to life."

"And they are still living," she said, wafting her hands around to indicate the entire space. "I *am* doing it. I'm

42

living my dream." And clearly she was relaxed too. She came to work in gnarly t-shirts and worn jeans. What was more relaxed than that?

"Really? I know you have a passion to brew Jen, but for a while there you got to share that passion with someone, and it was the dream *squared*." She held up a hand before Jen could interrupt. "Don't bother. You can't budge me on this. It isn't only the films informing me, it's personal knowledge. I love my flowers. I love seeing people's faces when I deliver my bouquets. But it's even more wonderful to talk to Max about it, to share the joys of wedding bouquets, and also to weep with her over the funeral flowers. Connecting with another human over something you do is a gift, and you just passed it up."

Jen really didn't want to hear this. She'd made a decision and she was getting on with it. So what if she didn't have anyone to share it with? She didn't need that. She was delirious about getting to do her thing. Enough for two. Plus Lydia would be back eventually and she *got* it.

"Alice, I know you want to see me happy. Truly I do. But I've got this. The Jakob thing is for the better. He just wasn't who I thought he was, he wasn't honest with me or even himself and I can't get past that. But I can get past *him*, which is good, because if I'm going to make this happen I don't need any distractions." Secretly, she had to admit he still had her plenty distracted, but it would fade and pass with time. She was sure of it. "Right now, I need all my focus and time for this. Later, when I've got an established and successful business then I'll have time to see who's about."

Alice stood up, clearly cross. "Jen, God knows I love you, but you're a total wally sometimes. Pig-headed and stubborn. You don't get to pick when love comes your way. And that's a real-life thing, not a rom-com thing. Seeing 'who's about' is not good enough. You could have gone down that path with Robert, you ... you utter numpty." Alice looked like she was about to blow a gasket.

Jen's phone rang and she slid it into view again. Anthony St James. She held up her fingers to say two seconds. She didn't want Alice leaving cross, but she needed to take the call from her only other customer. "Stay Alice, it's Anthony. I'll ask him if he has a regular flower order and if you can pitch for it."

Only, Anthony got to his point with minimal small talk and Jen's face paled with each word. She looked at the three tanks in front of her, and the boxes already sitting on the shelves. There wasn't much effusiveness in her goodbye.

"You forgot the flowers thing," said Alice. "What's up?" There hadn't been much to go on with Jen's *yeses*, *nos* and *I understands*. But her face umbrellaed it all under 'Bad news'.

"Um, so, that was my big order. He's got finance issues and needs to cancel. Unless there's a pretty fast boom in engagements, people moving homes and having babies, I'm slightly screwed, Alice."

Chapter 34

Clouds were amazing things, Jen decided, staring at them from the concrete of the back yard. She'd been lying there in a near-catatonic state for the past hour, maybe three, she didn't know. Alice had offered to stay after Anthony's call, but Jen had asked for some alone time to process things. She preferred to do her internal screaming in private. The back yard was perfect for this. Though messy, it was enclosed and warm and quite comforting.

She had rather a lot of beer with no home. There were only so many bottles she could foist onto Alice or Fenella for the Ploughman's gift sets. She couldn't think of more cheese and beer opportunities.

"Come on Jen, think of something. You're an ideas person. What the hell are you going to do with a shit-load of beer?" She was back to talking to herself. That probably wasn't good, but she didn't care. She was claiming it as part of her "process". And who else did she have? She was no longer talking to the obvious choice. Bugger. Thankfully her phone was safely out of reach inside, so she couldn't give in to the temptation. It was currently so strong it might have felled her, making it advantageous she was already lying down.

There were other restaurants in town. Only they didn't have quite the same cachet as Anthony's celebrity-chef signature eateries. The Anthony deal had ticked all the boxes for her brand profile and thinking about the long-game. Except for the financial difficulties bit. He might have thought about that when he commissioned her.

She wanted to kick her heels and wail a dramatic *All is lost,* but her tenacious streak kicked in. "Get a grip, Attison," she growled. "Think beyond." That's what her favourite lecturer had always said, trying to get them to think laterally to find new strategies.

"You all right, Jen?" Max stood in the doorway, looking fairly worried, even from Jen's upside down view.

"Mmmhhhmmm," Jen said, "just brainstorming." Granted, her position in the messy yard might look odd. "The clouds are helping. It's a Zen thing."

"OK," Max nodded and turned to go, having assured herself Jen hadn't done anything drastic and being able to report favourably back to Alice.

"You could, umm, stay if you like, Max. Be my sounding board." Jen wasn't used to asking, but the clouds weren't giving her anything to work with. Max shrugged and sat down on an old engine. Then she waited patiently for Jen to begin, which felt far more awkward to Jen than talking to herself.

"So, um, I have lots of beer."

Max nodded. "Right."

"And I've got nowhere to sell it, not in large quantities

that is, and I rather need some large quantities to go, in order to get the monies."

"Right." Max was definitely taking the "board" part literally. She did manage to blink, which Jen took to be encouragement.

"OK. I think, for now, the restaurant route is out."

Max nodded, now dispensing with words altogether in her listening role, but that was fine as Jen was warming up to it now.

"I could do more of the markets, but they're sporadic and really labour intensive in terms of travel and set up and they take me out of the brewery for a whole day. If I pay someone else to man the stall, that's a chunk of my profit gone. So, I need to look at either something I can just deliver to, or something from the door." Yep, that made sense. Really, the best scenario was selling casks of the beer, as there she wouldn't have bottle costs or need the bottling time. But to date she'd only ever sold bottles. "I could try to sell to some free-house pubs, but I've got no track record on the delivery, and it'll mean quite a lot of door-knocking." Well, she could do that. She wasn't afraid of cold calling, or hard graft, but currently she wanted to be here, nurturing the beer. "Jakob said I should enter the national competitions, to build the beer profile, which would help with the door knocking and maybe bring people to me." She could research that. "I'm not aware of any imminent ones though." Max emitted a low grunt at that. Yes, Jen thought it was disappointing too, but then again her main focus right now had to be on immediate marketing – plain dirty selling, not brand building. This beer needed a home so it was off her shelves, bringing money in and being tasted.

Tasting. Hmm. Part of Jen's issue was people at large didn't know her beer, not unless they were county show-goers.

"What if people could taste the beers here?" she mused, the idea germinating in her head. "What if I had a tap area inside, where people could come and taste and then buy. Not a pub, but a bottle shop with taps; a brewery shop, like a farm shop." Suddenly she could see it, with people milling about, glasses in hand, trying her different beers and perusing the shelves, then buying a few, or filling a reusable growler direct from the tap, taking them home and loving them and vowing off macro beers and coming to her Tap & Bottle shop for ever and ever, amen. "I'll have to check the building permit, but I think I can do that. As a shop or tap room. Not a pub. But I can have tables and chairs for people to sit in as they taste, and I could even have some out here, if I got this pit cleared up." This. This had her excited. A tasting facility in her microbrewery. And she could offer shelf space to other non-local microbrew-eries. And oh! She could have an open-mic slot, for locals like Jim, where each month an amateur brewer could have a tap and people could try theirs too. Now the ideas were coming. Her fingers were twitching for some paper to start the scribbling. "Max? What do you think? Max??" Jen flipped over onto her front to see if her brain-boxiest friend thought it was a goer.

Max was sparked-out against the wall, the warmth of

the sun having lulled her off. Well, that was fine, Jen thought, rolling back unabashed, because she already knew this would work; it was right on her doorstep and she already had the stock coming. She didn't need Anthony's restaurant, she could cut out the middleman. Looking up, she smiled; the cloud overhead, was, if you squinted a bit, trophy shaped.

Jen on a mission was like a tornado in reverse. Nothing could stand in her way as she pulled it all together. It had taken some explaining to the council that this wasn't a pub. The concept of a brewery shop, with a tasting bar in the same space as the brewing tanks was a new one to them. In the end it was her offer of giving educational tours to school kids that swung it.

The fermenting and tapping was going at full tilt. The rows of bottles and stock boxes growing on the shelves were both pleasing and scary; she needed stock, but she'd need it to shift too. Moreover, it was keeping her busy, which was great, because she so needed to be busy. It kept her mind off the things that threatened to break her.

Lydia still hadn't come home. It was well over four weeks now, and still not a word, other than Alice's updates and small signs that she'd been in to collect things while Jen was out. The most Lydia had ever been away was a two week Italian exchange with school, and it had driven Jen nuts. Now though, Jen couldn't quite work out which was worse, having her far away with some contact, or near without any. It made her anxious, and actually teary at times.

Alice's rebuke was rattling around in her head too. Jen still thought the reaction to the GPS stickers was grossly out of proportion, but maybe, perhaps, possibly Alice was slightly right about Lydia being in control of her life. Jen had to admit her sister had managed for four weeks without her assistance now, so there might be some element of truth in there.

That said, Jen was pretty damn sure Lydia had some apologising to do too, and as such hadn't yet taken any definitive action to negotiate a peace deal. She had her pride and knew from experience that giving in to Lydia's sulks would come back to bite her. So for now, she was getting on with things, trying to ignore the growing ache inside her as each day passed without contact. She threw herself at everything, to the point where she could come home at night and fall into bed too tired to think about the house without Lydia in it. Never before had she wanted to avoid her own home, but now she needed the sheer exhaustion to make it bearable.

A task she'd put off was clearing the rear yard, but her mind had started its painful wanderings again, so she'd bitten the bullet.

"We'll give you a hand," Alice said, as she watered some potted hydrangeas outside *Re:Love*. Jen had her eye on some of them. She had an idea of extending the flowery industrial look they'd created in *Re:Love* into her own arch. There was something about continuity between the two shops that appealed to her.

Jen looked at the two knackered tyres in her hands. There

were loads more to go if she wanted the yard available for nice days. "That's OK, I've got it. I need the exercise and you've already loaned me the Bongo." Piling the dirty tyres into the Capri would have required ten times as many trips to the dump. The old car engines were staying at least, she had plans for those.

"Come on, Jen. Max and I can carry some out."

"Really, I'm fine. It's all under control." She needed to do it herself – she wanted the exhaustion. Plus she could do with stronger arm muscles; lugging the bigger sacks of ingredients was more demanding than she'd anticipated.

Alice put down her watering can abruptly and placed her hands on her hips.

"For fuck's sake, Jen, relax the control and let people help. Let them *share*. I promise the benefits are way more than you've ever dared let yourself imagine, and then you can really be living the dream." Alice never swore. Her crossness drew Jen up short. It hadn't really dawned on her that people wanted to help. She'd always assumed it was a bother for others, or she'd be beholden to them. Or they had some other motive. Jakob had helped her by giving her the tanks, but she hadn't asked for them and he'd been wooing her, hadn't he? Or playing her.

Jakob was another subject the exhaustion was supposed to be stymieing. It was hard though. No matter how many times she aired her room or washed her sheets, the ghost of his aftershave still lingered. For once she wished her nose wasn't so sensitive. She didn't want to think about him, but the brewery and her home currently being the sum of her world made it difficult, as he'd been in both. She couldn't help it. To be honest, she wasn't even angry anymore, just disappointed. The previous week's *Brewing Times* had announced the Australian acquisition deal with a huge nod to its saving many jobs and the previous owners gave a lovely quote saying how to all intents and purposes it was business as usual for them. That rather took the indignation out of her. Now, with a little distance Jen had conceded he probably wasn't laughing at her behind her back – she simply didn't believe he was like that – but she still couldn't move on from him concealing who he was. That part still had her gutted.

She considered what Alice was saying, as she stared at the ground, trying to breathe in through her nose and out through her mouth. It helped her focus her thoughts on non-Jakob things and the tyres were making her biceps and shoulders burn. She couldn't put them down – that would make her look like she was struggling. Alice was glaring at her, waiting for a response. How hard could it be to accept?

"I know, Alice. I know. And I will. Just not yet. There'll be lots to do soon and you'll be the first people I ask." She could ask Alice if she had hydrangeas in the same cornflower blue as her new signage. *There*, that was an ask. But not just yet ...

Alice shook her head angrily and returned to her flowers, muttering something Jen couldn't quite hear. She loaded the tyres quickly and scurried back into the workshop and the next stack.

Jen glanced at the post pile, on the shelf by the door,

half of which was Charlie's un-diverted letters, the other hers from home, grabbed on exit and unceremoniously dumped on entry at the brewery. She usually perused them with a strong coffee. The latest *Brewing Times* sat on the top and she grabbed that to avoid the letters and hide from the tyres a little while. Unfurling it, she came face to face with Jakob. *Now* they bloody wrote about him! She could have done with that earlier and she could have done without seeing him now.

It was a professionally shot corporate photograph, formal and posed, but it still took her breath away. She managed a small smile for his hair having stuck to its informal principles. She read the headline a couple of times just to be sure she'd got it right. *Krone-Juul Departure Shocks Industry*. Jen's eyes scanned the story quickly, as it detailed Jakob having handed over control of his division with immediate effect and without public comment. Kronegaard weren't commenting, the family weren't commenting, no one was commenting and that was really annoying as Jen needed more. She tried to overlook the parts where the paper detailed how well-respected he was in the industry and how well he'd done over the years building the company and their profits. *Brewing Times* were baffled apparently and speculated whether there was some trouble within the dynasty. She slid the paper aside, hoping his family was behind him and not against him. It had always been clear he adored his family; his boat had various sleek silver frames of blond group shots on show. She didn't want to think that anything she'd said might have set him at odds with them. She already knew what that felt like what with Lydia not speaking to her, and being without one's family totally wasn't something she'd wish on anyone.

Avoiding those thoughts, Jen looked at the post instead. The top one was familiar. Suspecting she really shouldn't, not right now, not without that coffee, she opened it and felt her stomach drop to her feet. Jen gazed semi-stunned around the room, the credit card bill hanging in her hand by her side. She'd done a lot, but there was still so much left to do. Making this a public venue required additional outlays. The feature wall had two cans of cornflower emulsion on order for it. The gorgeous brass beer taps were booked to be installed at the end of the week, but she still had some form of bar to source. She needed an industrial dishwasher and a gazillion glasses to go in it, all to go into the old office, which was now also her pump room. And then there was the small matter of furniture. She planned to make some kind of banquet seating in the inspection pits in the floor because she liked them as a feature and couldn't afford to fill them. The engines would go down there too, with some reinforced glass on top to make low tables. But the rest of the room needed tables and chairs. Suddenly, faced with what she'd already spent on kit and the beer and the bottles and the lack of money coming in, it all became overwhelming and Jen's heart was belting out of her chest.

Shaking somewhat, she walked zombie-like back out of the door and into *Re:Love*. Alice and Max broke off the smooch they were having across the counter and stared Jen.

Three little words. That was all it would take. Three little words she hadn't used in her adult life. After a couple of failed attempts, she finally choked them out.

"I need help."

Chapter 35

Dreamy blue, Alice had called it. Jen was regretting it, the blue, not the rest of the room. Gazing at the finished space, Jen kept getting teary looking at the fruits of their labour. After another two and a half weeks of crazy-hard work, it was even better than she'd mood-boarded. Max's salvage had produced all sorts of treasures, now beautifully arranged against the backdrop of the Dreamy Blue rear wall. She'd be paying her off for a long time, but thankfully they'd come to an agreement involving reducing the rent by half for a period. Jen's half.

The bar was a magnificent old counter Max had salvaged from a derelict pub. A fabulously ornate old gilt picture-frame surrounded the blackboard with all the available beers and their descriptions chalked onto it, and hung above the row of taps. The front of the workshop was filled with old tables and mismatching seats Jen had found in Max's stash of orphan chairs. Max had relished shifting her stagnant stock, keenly repurposing it into items Jen needed; there were various suitcase tables around the room for starters, and deep seats made from old chests of drawers.

The loos had been spruced too; no small blessing given Charlie's cleaning skills. Both now boasted a fine Victorian bowl with high wall mounted cistern. Alice had discounted her an array of hydrangeas, all placed in planters Max had made from dented milk churns. The old toilet was fully hydrangea'd up too, out in the yard, which now boasted basic benches and round tables made from old cable spools. An old enamel bath had even been fixed upright to the outer wall, to make a seat.

Alice had sweet-talked an art-student into painting a white and silver mural of Ninkasi in the yard, telling Jen brewsters should stick together. Finally, a long length of chain, found under all the removed rubbish, hung, fixed to the brick walls, separating the public and brewing areas. Jen couldn't have people messing with her magic. So it might not have be the sleek urban-chic venue, inspired by a Copenhagen houseboat she'd initially dreamt of, but this revised concept still said *hyggelig* and – crucially – was a fraction of the cost. Jen was pragmatic when it came to budget slashing.

But, it had been a stupid idea choosing that blue. What had she been thinking? At time of purchase, she'd told herself it was just a colour she happened to like. Whenever she looked at it now, Jen could only think of a pair eyes of the same hue. So much for sealing him away in a mental box, never to think of him again. On that front she had been failing so hard. She'd photograph every new or completed item in the brewery, wanting to send it to him as running commentary of her progress, but then she'd remember he wasn't part of her journey anymore and would sadly post it to Instagram instead, like some virtual baby-book. She was even getting followers. Meanwhile, neither the internet nor the papers had further news on what had happened at Kronegaard, which felt more and more ominous. Aside from the clipped newspaper photo she'd pinned to the office noticeboard intending it to wish him well in some good vibes way, he'd vanished off the face of the planet again.

"Where do you want the kegs?" Jen spun away from the dreamy wall to face the gruff voice. Jim Arbuthnot was rolling a metal barrel towards her. He'd been fairly confounded to find her on his doorstep asking if he wanted the inaugural open-mic beer slot, but it hadn't taken them long to agree on a profit split and he'd got to work on his brew pronto, his mistrust of brewsters miraculously evap-orating. Now he was involved, he'd even been willing to offer a hand in the final set up of the tap beers. She suspected he enjoyed having something to do beyond his allotment, and for her part, Jen was finding it easier with the assistance.

Asking for help hadn't proved the disaster she'd feared. It didn't come naturally to her, but she was forcing herself and it appeared to be paying off. She sort of needed to give up control to stay in control. Amazing. Who knew?

Tonight however, the proof would be in the pudding. Tonight she was opening the door to the public – the full arch door, because the weather was glorious and she wanted everyone to see what was going on inside. She had fantasies of the whole town coming – Lord knew she'd put out enough flyers – and people would be spilling out into the street with their half pint glasses, tasting her beers. That was the dream. But she'd also be happy with just a few. Jim, freshly showered, smelling better and wearing a freebie *Attison's* t-shirt was insisting the entire allotment committee were coming, so that would be five at least. She just needed the word of mouth to start. Otherwise she and her cash flow were royally stuffed.

And Lydia. She was desperate for her to be part of tonight. This was Jen's baby, her dream, (her disaster if it didn't work), and she wanted her sister – and silent partner – to be there to see it.

The silence had finally become intolerable – a whole six weeks. Defeated, Jen had accepted that Lydia had proved her point; she could manage on her own. In spite of regular phone checking, there'd been no calls from the police, hospital or Lydia's employers. It may not have sat well with Jen, who suddenly felt parentally redundant, but she couldn't say it wasn't true. And on top of all that, sitting alone in the sofa one night, almost catatonic in her loneliness, Jen had had to admit that she missed her sister beyond measure. The tears slowly dripping into the barely untouched Ben & Jerry's had led her there. The following morning she'd posted Lydia one of the Opening Night invites she'd made for local dignitaries, as an olive branch. She hadn't heard anything back of course, but it would be typical Lydia to want the drama of sweeping in. If it meant having her back in her life, Jen could grant her that. For now though all she could do was cross her fingers and hope she'd show.

Jen pointed Jim in the direction of the pump room, and turning back found a figure in the doorway. A broad-shouldered figure, carrying a small bunch of flowers.

Ah. Here was one invite she hadn't sent, but knew she needed to face. She shouldn't have left it so long, but she'd been a wuss, neatly hidden under the guise of being ri*don*-culously busy. He appeared to converse with someone outside the door, before nodding then taking a breath and moving towards her.

"You did it, then. I should have known it would look this good." Considering he'd never been convinced by any notion of the entire venture, this was praise indeed from Robert. "I underestimated your determination."

She faced him with a smile. A genuine one. It was good to see him. It was good to see him not broken. That took the edge off her guilt.

"Thank you," she said, deciding it was a compliment and happy to take them where she could get them. She waved him to the nearest chair and offered him a drink. She was back a few minutes later, two half pints in hand, confident that tap number one was functioning perfectly.

"This is a new one I'm launching tonight." He took a sip and nodded his approval. "It's called *Heartsong*."

The expression on his face said the name didn't mean anything to him, but that was OK, it didn't have to. It meant enough to Jen. She was disgustingly proud of it and having done more research, was submitting samples to all the competitions she was remotely eligible for, in all the relevant categories. She was going to blow her own trumpet and build her brand.

"I ... um I wanted to see you. See how you were."

"I'm fine. Thank you. I'm sorry I haven't called, but ..." She waved her hands vaguely at the room. Yep, still a wuss. She could do better than that. "I *am* sorry. Really. I should have checked how you were. I never meant to hurt you, Robert." He nodded fractionally, apparently uncomfortable with the conversation.

"Mumsie was heartbroken. She'd signed you up for the beginner's bridge league and onto two WI committees." Jen couldn't honestly say she was sorry about that. "And the girls can't even say your name. They were obviously looking forward to having you as a sister." Well, that was a different kettle of fish and Robert clearly had the wrong end of the stick, but she chose not to put him right. What was the point? Better he feel he had the full support of his family.

"I've been doing some soul-searching, Jen. Some of the things you said up at the house, well, they suggested I needed to revise my thinking." He looked her in the face now and she saw his usual earnestness. It was endearing as it always had been, but Jen recognised that in terms of raw chemistry, Lydia had been spot on all along; there was none there. "You should have your business, I see it's important to you. And you are talented at the brewing, I should have acknowledged and supported that."

"It doesn't matter, Robert, but thank you." Jen was finding the conversation rather awkward. It wasn't helped by Jim's loud whistling from the backroom. "Please don't worry about it."

"Well, that's kind of you, but I wanted to say we could make plans *together*, give you the chance to realise your dream and then later we–"

Jen stopped him with a light hand on his knee and a small shake of her head. It seemed the kindest thing to do. She knew what he was here to ask, and she knew she could no more settle for it now, than she felt the need for its steadiness. She wasn't the same person who'd seen similarity as being better than sparks. She might have neither on her horizon, but she knew now she wouldn't, *couldn't,* settle for less. There weren't, and never had been, any sparks between her and him.

"I can't see it working, Robert. Not in the long run. It's not enough to be suited in terms of manner. I think people might need to be suited in their dreams and needs. I think, for both of us, there could be someone *more* suited out there." A shot of hurt crossed his face as he took her words personally. "Just think Robert, there's a sporty woman out there, who'd love to run with you in the mornings and live against the golf course and play some holes with you after you come home from work." His eyes suddenly took on a wistful look, which egged her on. "That would never be me. The golf club or other local clubs, is where you should be looking. You have so much to offer, you're a steal, but I'm not the right girl to steal you." He blushed a little.

"I daresay," she continued, "with connections in the club and being competitive already, such a woman would be an ideal ally for Celia too, on the charity work and bridge front." OK, so it was probably mean stitching this woman up before she'd even come into Robert's life, but Jen needed to seal this deal. He was certainly nodding. If she wasn't mistaken he might already be mentally perusing the membership list in his head. "I honestly believe Robert, that's the woman who your Great Granny's ring was meant for." Poor thing. Jen would surely drop a rung on the ladder to hell for that one.

He looked at the flowers, then extended them to her. "Have these as a good luck gesture then." She accepted them graciously, recognising Alice's work. She'd picked the exact same flowers of her first bunch from Jakob. Meddling bint. There would be words ...

"Won't you come to the opening tonight, Robert?" She looked at her watch. There was less than an hour until action stations. A quick glance around the room said she was ready, but still she instantly nearly peed in her pants. "I'd like to have you here, and who knows who you might meet."

"Well, Mumsie's outside and there's a club meeting at nine, but we could stay for early doors, make it look like the place is bouncing." Yeah, Jen was pretty sure no one would look at Celia in her twin-set and think the place was bouncing, but bodies were bodies and not to be sniffed at.

"JEN!" Alice came charging through the door, closely followed by Max, looking serious as ever and a harassed-looking young man she'd never laid eyes on. Oh please god, don't let this be some misguided intervention. She had the Robert thing sorted. "Jen, Lydia's missing."

Jen was well aware Lydia was missing. She should be there, being part of it. Jen was unhappy doing something so big in her life without her.

"I know," Jen sighed, "I sent an invite and I'm going to call her. I'll sort this thing out so she can be here."

Alice stood right in front of Jen so she had her full attention. "No, Jen, she's *gone* missing. Neil here's a friend of hers, he'll tell you."

"I'm Neil Finch, a journalist at the Echo," said Neil. He talked very fast. "I'm really sorry to meet under these circumstances. Lydia speaks very highly of you." Jen resisted a snort. That was unlikely given the current emotional climate between them. Journalist Neil needed to check his facts. "I'm not here on a story. Not now, anyway." He was getting upset. Possibly one of Lydia's conquests, Jen decided. He seemed very emotional. She might have picked a clinger this time. "She was having a paramotoring lesson today. I was covering it for the paper – you know, a human endeavour story – only she hasn't come back down to land. She was in a tandem trike with an instructor and some cloud suddenly came in and I think they might have come down in that."

From the point of 'she hasn't come back down to land', Jen's reality had taken on the guise of a slowed-down record. All the blood drained out of her face and the air seemed custard-thick around her. Old memories came rushing back to her of policemen at her door, suggesting she came with them because her sister needed her. They'd left it for her to piece together herself why her parents weren't in a position to do it. Alice clutched her hand to bring her back to the here and now.

"Can you take me to where you were?" Jen asked. The Capri was at home.

"You can get on the motorbike. That's how I got there with Lydia." Jen didn't even want to think of Lydia on the back of a motorbike. Oh dear God.

"Alice, I need the Bongo." If Lydia was injured, then at least Jen could lie her down. Jen found herself in the position of wishing her sister was *just* injured, but it didn't take a maths boffin to work out High Height + Hard Ground = Bloody Hurt.

Alice was already holding out the keys.

"Want me to fold the front doors open, Jen," asked Jim, wandering to their group, oblivious to the predicament. "Sure to be early birds when there's beer."

All eyes turned to Jen. Jen's eyes, wide and twitchy, took a long scope of her baby. She'd worked so hard on this and she needed it to be a success. She needed everything to go right tonight. Lydia hadn't even seen it yet.

"I'm sorry. I have to go." She pulled off her pristine *Attison's* staff apron and handed it to Jim. "I need you to man the pumps, Jim, you know how to change a barrel. Robert, can you help out until your meeting? If Celia could lend a hand too, that'd be grand. All the prices are on the chalk board. Alice and Max know how to work a till."

Jen grabbed Neil's shirt by the shoulder and frogmarched him out past a lurking Celia, to his bike and the Bongo, not looking back as she left her baby in their hands.

Chapter 36

The Bongo speedometer had strained to the far right for the last ten minutes, as it hurtled down the narrow lanes towards the sea. Neil, leading the way on his motor-bike, only fractionally ahead of her front bumper, hadn't mentioned that part. Neither the beach, nor the sea made for improved conditions in Jen's current horror scenario. She was pinning every hope on the instructor having control of the situation, but Neil seemed pretty sure something was amiss. Jen was driving on auto pilot, the tears well and truly blocked off for now. Tears had nothing useful to bring to the party and she needed her sight for the road. If any bleeding caravaner dared to come towards her now she was going to have him.

Finally, Neil pulled into a small woodland car park, the type Lydia always referred to as "Dogging Central", and yanked off his crash-helmet. His distressed hair matched his expression.

"I was over there when I last saw them." He pointed to a low hill, which would have given him an uninterrupted view of the sky and the sea beyond. "I ran around shouting for ten minutes trying to find her, then raced into town to find Alice." Jen kept a lid on the pang it gave her, that someone would consider anyone other than herself as next of kin. *Next of kin, stop it, Jen. She's here somewhere, you'll find her.* Jen took a look around. To the right was a low bluff down to the sea and the stony beach, to the left dense woodland. If he'd been running about for ten minutes and then driven ten minutes to find her and ten back, that was thirty minutes Lydia could have been bleeding out somewhere. Or drowning.

"Have you called the emergency services, Neil?"

He looked momentarily confused, then distressed. "No, I um, sort of panicked." He looked out to sea and then back around. "I didn't know which one to call either. And Lydia says you always sort everything."

The fear she was currently feeling easily extinguished any pride at that.

Jen pulled out her phone and swiped at the screens. There was just a chance ... come on, come on ...

Bloody yes!

"This way!" she shouted at Neil turning for the trees, but didn't really care if he followed or not. She certainly didn't slow her sprint for him.

"LYDS!!!" she shouted under the tree canopy. Jen's eyes were struggling, flicking from the dot on the GPS app to the terrain in front of her, but the last thing she needed was to face-plant on the way. She'd imagined the trees might carry her call from trunk to trunk through the woodland, maybe even amplifying it, but apparently it didn't work that way. There was no reply, but nevertheless she persisted, running deeper into the woods. "LY-DI-A!!"

There were plenty of bird squawks and nature sounds, but nothing that gave any clues. The earthy smell of the tree litter did nothing to comfort either. Jen kept running, hurdling over fallen trunks, ducking under the lower-hanging boughs, her adrenalin glossing over the fact she was too unfit for this. Her body would get the memo tomorrow. But she'd happily take it, if she could just find Lydia in a state where she could listen to Jen whinge about it.

Further and further in she went, the little red dot getting nearer and nearer.

"LYDIA!!" She came to a relatively sparse area, where she could see between the tree trunks for a fair distance, looking for something of a synthetic colour. God, she hoped paramotorers were required to wear high-viz.

But there was nothing. No neatly parked trike, no Lydia sitting calmly whittling or whistling waiting for collection. Nothing. Jen studied her app. She was on the spot. Right on the spot. Bloody thing. Why wasn't she here? Jen refreshed the app with shaking fingers as finally the tears of fear and frustration caught up with her. Lydia was her family. She couldn't bear to have got her this far in life only to lose her. And the thought of never getting the chance to tell her how much she loved and missed her was just about to fell her.

"Fuck's sake, Jen! You bloody tracked me again."

Jen's joy was instant. Lydia's swearing was music to her

ears. Wiping her nose with the back of her hand she looked up into the canopy and then didn't know whether to laugh or sob. The mangled mess of paramotor trike, red canopy nylon, branches and Lydia was an alarming sight. Jen held her hands together at her face, as if praying, but more planning how to proceed.

"Are you bleeding, Lyds?" Lydia sat in the front seat of the triangular trike, the mass of canopy around her obscuring Jen's view of who was behind her.

"Not that I can see. Maybe my head." Lydia felt about on the back of her scalp, then looked at her hand. "No, we're good. I had my helmet on, but I clocked it in the landing. I might have passed out for a bit."

"Is your instructor OK?" She wanted to thank them for bringing her little sister down alive. *Safely* was still debatable.

"He's conscious and moaning a bit. I've checked his pulse, but he needs some help."

Thundering footsteps came up behind Jen, but she didn't turn around. She didn't want to let Lydia out of her sight ever again. Lydia's head followed the sound however and her smile spread. "Hi Neil."

"Hi Lydi." Jen did turn to look at him now, then back up at Lydia. There was something in the way they spoke to each other ... surely not ... good grief. Neil was more than a One-night Wonder.

Now was not the time for soppiness.

"Neil, phone for an ambulance and the fire service. We're going to need a ladder and possibly some cutting gear." Jen squinted at the crushed knot that was her sister, her instructor and their aircraft. They were wedged rather than hanging, so Jen didn't think they were about to fall, but it looked highly uncomfortable. Then Jen saw a limb crushed between metal and wood at the front and her stomach plummeted.

"Lyds?" she asked tentatively, hoping her tone sounded chilled enough not to scare her, "can you move your toes?" She didn't seem to be in any particular pain, but what if she in fact couldn't feel any? What if she'd broken her spine?

"Relax, Jen. It's the cosmesis that's trapped. I wore this one because Neil and I are going out later. I'm just working on releasing my stump, but I'm a tad wedged."

Somewhere in there, was a blessing. Jen was just too close to the brink to value it right now. And perhaps Lydia was delirious, Jen decided; there was no way she was going anywhere this evening. So much for accepting Lydia was in control of things. She was stuck up a tree for goodness sake.

"They're coming, Lydi," Neil shouted up. Jen watched him scope out the trunks for climbing options, before rolling her eyes. His spindly frame wasn't built for scaling anything.

"Thanks Neil," Lydia called down.

Jen's eyes narrowed. Lydia was looking down at him quite moonily. She clearly hadn't spent the last six weeks holed up at Alice's weeping over the state of their sibling relationship.

"How'd you find her?" Neil asked Jen. "They're quite hidden up there."

Could she claim it was a sisterly mind-reading thing? Yes, yes she absolutely could –

"She's got a sodding tracker on my leg," Jen heard from above. "I could have sworn I got them all. Supposedly it's to keep the prosthetics safe." Right. She hadn't let that go yet, then.

Jen considered her sister and the crumpled wreckage around her. Was this truly Lydia's response to Jen's actions and keeping control of things? These reckless, life-threatening things were Lydia's attempt to be free. How *awful* was that? And it was her doing ...

Shaken, Jen sat down. Both Lydia and Alice had been right, she had done a horrible thing. And they didn't know all of it. She saw now she needed to confess, not least because Lydia was at a disadvantage and might be more lenient with her wrath, but also because Jen finally understood what she'd done.

"It's not on the leg," she said, her voice small. "It's inside the socket. Under one of the manufacturer's stickers." Unlike the others, this patch was, as Lydia insisted, purely to keep dibs on where she was.

Lydia didn't speak to her again throughout the entire rescue, not even to answer Jen's cross question of *What the bloody hell is that?!* as Lydia was carried, hero-style, by a fireman. The "*Footloose and Fancy-free*" tattoo on her stump was new.

Given the instructor needed the ambulance bed, the paramedic allowed Lydia to drive with Jen, on the proviso they went directly to A&E to have her checked for concussion. Jen already had that at the top of her to-do list, she hadn't needed telling, in spite of Lydia being on fine form chatting to the fireman as they made their way to the Bongo.

The leg was a goner. As was the paramotor trike, which the firefighters had left in a sheared heap at the base of the tree.

Jen got the silent treatment all the way to the hospital, Lydia continuing her hard stare out of the passenger window. Once in a while she'd turn to check Neil was following them.

Pulling into the car park, Jen flung the pink Bongo into the first available spot, cut the engine and turned to her sister.

"I've said I'm sorry, Lyds."

"Actually, you said 'I *apologise*'. That's not the same."

Jen considered this. She had a point. "I *am* sorry, Lydia. What I did with the patches was a shitty thing to do to you. I ... I'm ashamed of doing it ... I just thought it would help us." Lydia opened her mouth to disagree, but Jen carried on, "I know now that wasn't the case. I am sorry. Truly. And I hope you'll forgive me ..." the contrition had Jen firmly on the back foot, not something she remembered being very often with Lydia. It veered her off message for a moment as she went on, "... given how, as it turned out, it *was* quite fortuitous today–"

"Don't. Don't try to excuse it, Jen. Yes, as it turned out it was handy today, but it won't ever make it right. I don't know what to do to show you that you have to let me be."

"No need. I get it now. Honestly." This still felt uncomfortable. Jen was keen to lighten the mood. She wanted them to be friends again. "The mad sports aren't the best way, though," she said joking, but only half. She did understand why Lydia had been doing them – the thought made her shudder – but surely it was just *caring*, not *controlling*, to point out the dangers of such activities. "Taking off in a hairdryer-powered go-cart *was* mad. Thank God the instructor was there to get you down. Surely you see how risky those sports are? I've missed you so much Lyds, and I almost didn't get to tell you–"

"Stop," Lydia interrupted, brow furrowed. "You think he saved me?"

Jen pointedly looked her up and down. "You could have plummeted into the sea or smashed to the ground."

"I'm aware of that Jen, but *he* didn't get us down. *He* had some kind of seizure up there and *I* grabbed the controls. Granted it wasn't the prettiest of landings, but I did miss the entire sea, there was no smashing and he's alive and in care."

"What? But he talked you through what to do, right?"

"Not unless my name is now God and 'Help me' is shorthand for a manual of landing instructions."

Jen was stunned. "But ... how?"

Lydia gave her a "guess what?" face. "I know stuff. I can keep a level head. I can do all sorts of things."

Oh.

Lydia watched deadpan as the knowledge sank in. So Lydia was the hero here? Slowly, Jen was filled with a huge sense of pride for her sister. She didn't think she could have done what Lydia had done. Remembering a certain flailing panic over a phone in a canal, Jen suspected she wouldn't have had the presence of mind and courage to bring the trike down. Spreadsheets wouldn't have helped her there. She had to admit that while Lydia had proved she could look after herself over the last weeks, she'd gone above and beyond here in terms of capability.

Jen dug out her phone and holding it flat so Lydia could see, swiped to the GPS app and deleted it. Lydia gave a small nod. Then Jen deleted the one showing delays on the trains and then the same for the tube, which garnered her a raised eyebrow. Oh, she hadn't known about those ...

"Thank you," Lydia said with a deep sigh, as Jen repocketed the phone. "That wasn't quite what I was expecting to happen as I flew around earlier."

Jen couldn't help herself.

"I wish you hadn't been up there in the first place." Seeing Lydia's mouth open to respond she raced on, "I *do* get it, Lyds. I absolutely see you can look after yourself and do what you want. But can we agree, you never need to deliberately put yourself in danger again or take those risks?"

"Argh!" Lydia exclaimed frustrated. "I started doing those things in response to your smothering, Jen. And now I do them because I can choose to do them, and I love them. I totally get off on the high-octane stuff. It shows me what it is to be alive." She turned to face Jen square on. "When I woke up from the accident, do you remember the nurse I had? From the Philippines. Lovely lady. Frannie?"

Jen nodded, not quite sure where this was going. She vaguely recalled, but there'd been a whole lot of awful going on at the time and much of it was now a blur.

"When you weren't at my bed, when they'd kick you out to eat in the canteen, she would come and whisper to me that I should live." There were tears running down Lydia's cheeks. "*Live*, she would say, *live because your parents can't.* I heard her."

"Jen, there were days when it felt a lot easier to just roll over and let go. It felt like I had a choice, that if I gave up the will, I could go and be with them. That's what it felt like anyway, but there was this little voice, every day, whispering to me to grab life by the scruff of the neck and hang on." Lydia sniffed and dug around in Alice's glove box for a tissue, gave up and used her sleeve. "She sat with me and told me how I'd been given a second chance and now I had to make the absolute most of it. Not let anyone tell me what I couldn't do, because I'd been kept here to show others I was tough. Those words Jen, those where my real crutch. There were the prosthetics and the physio of course, but they all said the determination was the real backbone. It was the one thing they couldn't provide, but I had it in spades."

That was true. Lydia in rehab had been little short of miraculous – with the exception of her leg not springing back. She had been on a mission, pushing herself to extremes to get on, get moving and get out.

"Which is why Jen, it's so hard to deal with you coddling me, trying to keep me super-safe, when what I need to do is spread my wings, even my damaged one. I need to make the most of this life, because we don't all get a long one, and I got a second go." Lydia was proper ugly crying now. "I've missed you so much these last six weeks, but they've told me what I already knew; I can stand on my own one foot. I need you to see it – *really* see it –so you can let me go and let me live." She was begging.

Jen had never seen Lydia so distraught, not since waking up in the hospital with two parents and a leg gone. She started scoping the car park for the quickest route to A&E, desperate to get her checked ASAP.

"Because if you can't Jen, if you refuse to let me live my life without trying to influence it, I'll never be able to fully live," Lydia gasped out with huge bone-shaking sobs, "I'll be doing it to defy you and I want to do it properly for myself, because this is who I am, and so I can be who Mum and Dad wanted me to be and so, one day, just maybe, I can forgive myself for causing their deaths."

Chapter 37

"What are you talking about?!" Jen gaped at her sister, who was holding her body, wracked with sobs. This had to be shock setting in, surely, but what was that she'd said? "Lydia, you are not responsible for them dying." Jen was baffled. Lydia had had counselling after the accident, they'd signed her off. They hadn't mentioned anything about these feelings.

Lydia was shaking her head violently. "I am. I made them take me shopping that day. I was being a brat. You were getting all the attention with your new job, and I wanted some. So I insisted we stop in town for a new gymnastics leotard. We'd just come out of the shop with it, where I'd been deliberately umming and ahhing about some others. If I'd just got the one I'd liked straight off, we wouldn't have been outside when the lorry came." Lydia had never told her any of this.

Jen got out of the car. The air was balmy again and Jen could hear the hubbub from town. They were ahead of the Friday night A&E crowd at least. Jen headed directly around to the passenger door, yanked it open and pulled her sobbing sister into a hug. Lydia hung on her, and Jen let her continue until she was down to the laboured breathing.

"Lyds, listen to me now. You are not to blame. It was just wrong place at the wrong time. Pure bad luck or fate, whatever you believe in. That's how I've always seen it, that's how I'll always see it."

"But I made them–"

"No. You aren't to blame, Lydia," she repeated slowly. "Mum and Dad were adults, they could have said no. It *is* possible to say no to Lydia, you know," she said, holding Lydia's face in her hands, so her sister would look her in the eyes and understand this properly. "I don't blame you for this. I never have and I never will, and I don't see who else could hold this against you other than me or you." Doubt was beginning to cross Lydia's face. "Really," Jen nodded at her. "No blame. Honestly. Cross my heart." Lydia gave a slow nod and a long snotty sniff. Lovely.

"It wasn't all bad luck," Jen said. "I got to keep you. I prayed and begged and bargained with any power I could think of, to let me keep you." Jen's tears were rolling too now, partly at memory of those days and now for her guilt-ridden sister. "You pulling through was the most amazing thing, but it scared me so much because I'd been so helpless. You wouldn't wake up for so long and all the while your leg got worse. There was nothing I could do. Your leg was a mess from the truck, but we might have managed. Then the bone infection set in and they couldn't stop it. They said I could help you, but by signing off your leg. What kind of a choice was that? I felt even more helpless than before. I can't think of a feeling I hate more than that."

"Jen, it was gangrene! If you hadn't made that decision, I wouldn't be here now," Lydia said. "I don't blame you for that. I know I howled when I saw my stump," Jen shuddered at the memory; those screams, Lydia's battling arms trying to get up and away from her, "but I was fourteen and scared. We both know it was the right thing to do. Jen, you weren't out of control there, you were listening to specialists. You aren't helpless if you defer to others when you need to. God Jen, when will you see that asking for or accepting help doesn't make you weak. It doesn't make you less in control. It makes you human, and it makes you smart, because you're addressing your needs." Not for the first time, Lydia's words rang true with her. Wasn't that what she'd just experienced with the brewery?

Steadying her breathing, Jen thought back to the time in the hospital. "I *did* see I had to do it. It was awful, but I knew they were right, that I had to follow their advice. It was saving your life, wasn't it? *No brainer*, right?" Jen managed a snotty teary laugh, aware that she was sounding like Ava. "And your shock and reaction was completely understandable. In the back of my head I knew that too." Recent erroneous actions regarding Lydia notwithstanding, Jen knew she was and would always be a realist. She'd done what had to be done. Being honest, those weren't the things she felt guilty about. "Only, afterward," she went on, somewhat less sure of herself, "when we started to see what you couldn't do anymore, like your gymnastics, or some crappy

boyfriend dumped you because he 'couldn't deal', well ..."
Jen wasn't quite sure how to say it, "I worry that I ruined
your life."

Lydia pulled her face back abruptly.

"Wow, Jen, ableist much? I've got a good life, I'll have
you know. I'm educated, I work hard, I've got a good job
and decent mates. So I'm missing a leg. I'm more than my
leg, it doesn't define me and the best people see that. All
lives have challenges, this one just happens to be mine. And
I'm OK with that. It's part of who I am, it's my reminder
to live."

Jen stared at the leg for a moment. It had haunted her
for years. And yet here they were, her sister a hero, as well
as a rational adult, who not only valued the life she had,
but actively sought to get the most from it. Why hadn't she
seen and supported that? Finally the cogs all rocked into
place in Jen's head. "I haven't been 'best people', have I?"

"Not recently, but maybe I could have handled it differ-
ently, talked to you about it." They gave each other small
weak smiles, conceding that communication might have
been of benefit, but they were getting there now. Eventually,
Lydia asked quietly, "and you really don't blame me for
Mum and Dad dying?"

"No. Truly I don't. Do you blame me for losing your leg?"

"I didn't and don't blame you for signing off on my leg.
Given what happened today, you did me a favour. Hanging
around in that tree with a crushed leg would have been a
bummer. Being able to detach mine was handy." Lydia gazed
at her for a long moment. "I think we both might need a little

bit of help. Talk things through with someone?" Jen sniffed, her tears drying up now. Lydia could definitely need some counselling on the survivor's guilt, and she might perhaps have some of her own issues that could do with airing.

"You get it now though, Jen, don't you? You are not responsible for me." Lydia remained silent as Jen looked her sister from eye to eye and back and nodded her assent.

Lydia scanned the car park. Following her eye, Jen saw Neil a little way off, leaning against his bike, giving them space. He instantly went up in her ratings.

"He's seems a nice guy," Jen said. The air now cleared between them, the roots of their issues having been addressed, Jen was feeling far calmer.

"He completely is," Lydia agreed with a soppy grin. "He'll keep an eye on me when we're away. I got my international gig."

It was a punch to the gut. "Wait, what? But we're friends again, Lyds, there's no need to make a point by leaving," Jen spluttered.

"Jen, it's not me making a point," Lydia said kindly, aware of Jen's obvious distress, "It's me living and having an adventure. It isn't to spite you, I promise. I think we both need me to do this. We need to reset ourselves to who we should have been before the accident."

The panic was building in Jen's chest, and much as she tried to quell it, she wanted to shout 'Don't leave me'. The last six weeks had been hellish. Had it not been for building the brewery she would have gone batshit crazy. "Where are you going?"

"All over. I'll do my two years in Singapore and then the world is our oyster. He wants to be a travel writer, so he'll freelance while I qualify and we'll take every holiday I've got until then and we'll run a blog as we go. I'm going to judge how disability-friendly places are. I don't know when we'll be back, or where we'll settle. The jobs are kind of transferable or mobile, in his case." Jen was trying so hard to control her breathing, but failing miserably. Thank god they were just outside A&E.

Lydia put her hands on Jen's shoulders and held her gaze. "We both need this Jen. You put your life on hold for me and it's just beginning to start again. I promise it'll be OK. I'll be much, much better at keeping in touch. You'll be sick of me Skyping you." Jen couldn't imagine that for a second. A big fat tear broke over her eyelid and made a bid for freedom. Lydia wiped it off her cheek. "You might not see it now, but you need me to go, so you can get your own shit together. Alice says the brewery looks amazing, but you haven't sorted out your fuck up with Jakob."

Oh, why did she have to bring *him* up? No matter how hard she tried, she couldn't pack him away out of her mind. Every night she'd wanted to tell him everything she'd done that day on the beer and every night she went to sleep sad that she couldn't and hadn't. And somewhere along the line a little voice had begun to whisper, then shout, that she'd made a ginormic mistake. That who he was to the world didn't matter, whereas who he was to *her*, did.

Just. Like. He'd. Said.

And maybe, rather than punish him for not daring to

chase his own dream, she could have encouraged him, just like he had her. It might have been very special to have joined *him* following his passion.

It made a sob bubble out of her.

He was the best person she'd met in years, she told herself, all the regret now tumbling over her. She loved her brewery, she truly did, but she'd love it more if she'd been able to share the experience with him. She already felt he'd helped her build it. Lydia's fingers were getting busy on her face now, trying to staunch the torrent of tears.

"Jen," Lydia said softly, like she was a child in need of solace, "I know you think you don't know him. But, *of course,* you know him. In your heart you know him – you had a connection. You've got a lifetime to get to know him – or check him out and decide no – but give it a proper chance. There's chemistry and the shared interest and I'm not just talking about people liking the same band or something. You knew everything there was to know about Robert, but you didn't have any of the other things. You didn't love him. At least with Jakob it's the right way around, you have the emotions, and the knowledge can follow."

"You think I love him?" Jen sniffed. Did she? Was that what this consuming obsession was?

Lydia smacked her palm off her forehead, which Jen was pretty sure she shouldn't be doing with a possible concussion. "Jen, for someone with a first class degree you can be phenomenally stupid. You've been in love with him since Copenhagen."

Oh. Hearing it didn't make her instantly want to deny

it or call it ridiculous. The words actually gave her a deep-seated sense of contentment. She did love him. She did.

Only she'd sent him packing. She looked at Lydia looking back at her, her sister's expression hopeful this could all be sorted. But Jen was a realist and knew the truth. She'd screwed it up good and proper. But negativity wasn't what Lydia needed right now.

"We need to get your head looked at," Jen said, now keen to get this part sorted so she could drive home and curl up in bed to cry.

When Jen had been little and impatient for a brew to finish, her dad had always told her *Magic comes at a cost*. She was beginning to understand him now. Good things in life came at a price; she got her brewing dream, but she had to lose Jakob; she could find Lydia alive, but she had to let her go. Or maybe losing Lydia to her travels was the cost of having her new business. Whichever, it was heart-breaking, and she needed to hide from it.

"Neil'll help me with my head," Lydia said, sliding down from the seat. Neil pushed himself off his bike and came towards them. He looked pleased to see Lydia, but fairly scared of Jen.

Lydia held out a hand to him, unable, on one-legged grounds, to move from her propped position at the Bongo. He'd have to carry her.

"I can–" Jen started.

"We've got this," Lydia said, with a gentle but firm tone. It felt like a test.

With a nod, Jen stepped back to let Neil past her. "Fine.

But promise you'll get a cab home. No motorbiking. That's just common sense, not me being controlling."

"Done. Now bugger off and tinker with a valve or steep some wort or something –" Lydia cut herself off, with a look of horror. "The opening. That's now!"

"It's fine," said Jen, only just remembering herself and slightly gutted her crying-in-bed plan just got nixed. "I have a troupe of helpers handling it." It didn't hurt too much saying it; she'd thought it would be like shards on her tongue.

"Nooo," wailed Lydia, the most panicked she'd been all evening, "No, it's not fine." She pushed Jen to get back in the car. "You have to go. Be there. Now! Or you'll ruin everything."

Chapter 38

It had gone brilliantly. Or so they said. It had definitely *gone* by the time Jen pulled up in the Bongo, the last of the customers leaving, bottle bags in hand. Being a shop, the opening hours only stretched from noon until ten o'clock, which Jen had thought was an absolute win, but tonight, she wished it could have gone on longer, so she could have been part of it for a moment. She hadn't got to sell a single pint.

Standing in the doorway, wrapped in the scents of a party; the notes of beer, perfume and aftershave mingling with the balmy night outside, Jen watched Jim and Alice clear things away, while Max counted the takings, and had a surreal notion of being superfluous to the action. They'd managed it without her. Nothing, so far as she could see, had come crashing down, and they weren't sobbing, broken beings.

Sensing she was being watched, Alice flicked her head up, then dropped her broom and hurried over.

"Jen? What happened?"

"She's fine," Jen confirmed and winched on a smile to

reassure Alice. "The instructor had a seizure, but Lydia navigated them down. They're both going to be OK."

Alice dragged her over to the bar, placed her on a stool, then poured her a glass of *Heartsong*, while Jen gave them a brief rundown of events.

"They couldn't get enough of that one," said Jim, nodding at her beer as he made to leave. "You're already running low."

Jen squeezed his arm. "Couldn't have done it without you, Jim. Things went a bit haywire there."

"Can't plan for everything, can you, luv? Some things you just have to take as you find." He mopped his brow with the back of his hand. "Nothing's perfect at first, but it can still be worth the effort and I reckon you've got a winner here." Jen was pleased with his praise, but his words resonated more with her than perhaps he knew.

"Let's hope so. How did your beer go?" Jim looked quite made-up.

"I need to put on another batch, if you want a full month's supply. Night, luv." He looked quite invigorated by his evening away from the allotment and there was no trace of the scowl she was used to getting at the shows.

Sipping her beer – oh man it tasted good and bloody hell did she need it – Jen took a surreptitious look around. With Jim gone, there was definitely only three of them in the building, no one else.

Alice held court with her account of how successful the night had been with a steady stream of excited customers and she was particularly proud of herself for having bravely approached both Robert and Celia about the floristry accounts at the golf and bridge clubs. They needed prize and raffle bouquets all the time. She now had some business proposals to pull together. As Jen finished praising her, Max confessed Alice might have also signed all three of them up for bridge lessons as goodwill. Ah nuts.

Jen closed her eyes and leaned back, purportedly savouring her beer in light of how the night had panned out. Alice and Max were tactful enough to let her get on with it. Really, she was keeping her eyes shut to alleviate the sting of further tears. She was officially an emotional mess now. Bridge lessons aside, the Lydia events and discussions had thrown her for a loop and missing the opening was a huge blow, which was only just catching up with her. But it was nothing compared to the gut-wrenching disappointment she was experiencing because she'd got her hopes up for something entirely different.

As Jen had got in the Bongo, Lydia had leaned in on the other side. "I sent Jakob my invite to the opening. Go, Jen. Don't miss him. And don't fuck it up." Then she'd slammed the door and thrown herself into Neil's arms.

Caning the Bongo back through Westhampton, Jen had allowed herself – because she was a ridiculous fool – to imagine in some rom-com way that she'd arrive and there he'd be, either in an *Attison's* apron helping out, already part of the furniture, or else standing waiting for her, spot-lit in the middle of the buzzing room. Only that wasn't the case; the room was empty, she didn't actually own a spotlight, and neither Alice nor Max had mentioned him being there.

He hadn't come.

Jen cursed herself for having fallen prey to the stupid, stupid rom-com ideas. Life was not like that. She didn't know how many times she had to say it.

And Lydia needn't worry about her fucking it up tonight. She'd done that weeks ago.

Jen was contemplating curling up on one of the banquet seats in the inspection pits, the walk home seeming more than she had energy to manage today. It was a warm night, she'd be fine. She had a pile of fleece IKEA blankets piled somewhere, for outdoor use – she could use some of them. The arch was deserted now, the hum of the fermentation tanks, dishwasher and fridges her only company. She also wanted to leave a safe period of time for Lydia to get home. A&E had released her quickly, according to her text, no stitches required. Jen couldn't handle listening to her and Neil going at it, as, knowing Lydia, they would be. Not tonight. It was only just gone midnight, but it felt like the wee hours. She'd give it another half hour to be safe.

The workshop was clear and ready for the morning. She'd mopped the floor and the glasses could be re-stacked before opening at noon. Jen moved towards the backyard, killing time now. Alice had said the yard had been very popular with the punters, but then it had been exactly the right kind of evening for it.

Jen flipped the switch by the door. Hundreds of tiny white fairy lights sprang to life across the walls. They were one of her few extravagances, but something about them had compelled her. She sat down in the on-end bathtub seat fixed to the arch wall. It gave her something to lean her head against too, in her bone-tired funk.

How was she going to fix this? She had the brewery of her dreams. The money they'd taken that evening had far surpassed her projections and boded well for the town embracing her concept. But she didn't have the one person she wanted to share the joy with. That wasn't even Lydia, though she would readily have convinced herself that it was before this evening. She'd learned plenty about her sister tonight, not least that she was right when she said she needed her freedom. Lydia would be alright. Understanding that now, Jen saw that, in time, she could be too.

But sitting in the dark, surrounded by the white lights Jen knew what was missing. To her left, Ninkasi seemed to agree with her, her expression rather lofty and judgmental. Jen suspected goddesses didn't make prats of themselves.

She could write to him she supposed. A text would be too casual, in light of her last actions. Letter then. Maybe. If she could dig up her inner nineteenth century. No. She wanted to see his face, read his expression, know whether she was on a loser. That ruled out phoning, but FaceTiming didn't feel right either – the pixels would get in the way.

She didn't know where he lived in the UK, and turning up at his work wasn't a plan. She wasn't sure *An Officer and a Gentleman* would work in reverse; sweeping him off his feet in the finance department didn't have the same emotional quality as a production line, and physically there were issues. She didn't really need the twinkling of the fairy lights to tell her what she already knew; she had to go to Copenhagen. She'd sit on his boat for a weekend and simply wait until he turned up, unless the police removed her for squatting first.

The last six weeks had taught her so many things – things she'd assumed she'd nailed already, simply by virtue of age and experience. Age clearly wasn't preventing her from making mistakes and clearly she had loads still to learn. She'd freaked out about Jakob's real identity, mainly through wounded pride at being blindsided and fear of it being Danny all over again. But he hadn't been like Danny; he'd given her his real number straight away when he'd texted it to Lydia, he'd told her his name at the start – it wasn't his fault she didn't know how to spell it. Essentially, she'd judged her man by another man's standards and that had been wrong. There was nothing fake about Jakob. He wasn't like the Kronegaard bottle, all icon and no substance. He'd had substance all the way, in fact he'd hidden the icon from her.

And on the job issue, perhaps – and Jen allowed this purely as a one-off event – *Lydia was right*; it was business and also none of her business. Other brewers could, she conceded, make their own decisions, and equally, she had to admit Jakob's intentions probably weren't some nefarious plan to infiltrate and subjugate the craft beer world. Her thinking hadn't been the straightest at the time. She'd been wrong to throw his Morfar at him, she was ashamed of that. He'd picked a path and clearly striven to succeed at it. Jen had no doubt Stefan Krone would have been proud of that too. Who was she to say it was no good? She was normally smarter than that, but then she wasn't always smart around him.

Perhaps she'd freaked at the sudden disparity between them. At face value, they were wildly unequal – he was a multi-millionaire for goodness sake – but he'd only ever treated her as his equal and he'd considered her a good match. Any problem with that was *her* issue, not his, and recent evidence would suggest her assessments could be flawed. She'd thought Robert considered her an equal, but that hadn't turned out to be true. She'd managed to get things properly backwards on both. *There* was a new lesson learnt.

And there was the lesson about the universe sending you opportunities to spot and exploit. That had proved true. Maybe that could be the case in love too? Wasn't that what Alice had been telling her? *No*, she wasn't falling for the rom-com idealism, don't be ridiculous, she was simply applying her business experience to her personal life and being open to opportunity, nothing more. And while she'd built the business angrily telling herself she didn't *need* him, Jen knew in her head she desperately *wanted* him.

In light of the mess she'd created and the aching regret she felt, garnished with the high emosh factor of the evening, it seemed justifiable to have a cry about it all now in the privacy of her own backyard.

Over her pathetic jagging sobs, Jen heard a scrabbling

sound from behind the boundary wall. Instinctively, she pulled her feet up in case it was rats. But it was too loud and bumbling for rats. Thank God. Jen listened for the sound of sniggering kids, but heard none. There was however a rumbling sound, which she suspected to be a wheelie bin being moved, and the thump of it hitting the wall. Then there was more scrabbling and a head appeared above the wall. Jen blinked a couple of times and tried to remember how many beers she'd had.

Jakob's gorgeous face, framed by his unkempt hair, was looking over her wall. At her.

He smiled. "Hello again." She nearly died.

"Hello again." She didn't know what to make of it, thinking perhaps, most likely, she was hallucinating.

"I tried the door, but it was locked and you didn't answer."

"Licencing laws. We're shut," she said dumbly. She made an effort to subtly smear her cheeks dry.

"My plane was delayed. I should have been here."

"That's OK, I wasn't here either." He quirked an eyebrow at that, but didn't question further, preferring instead to take a moment simply gazing at her as she sat, surrounded by fairy lights, in a bathtub, in the company of Ninkasi.

"I tried the house, but someone called Neil, who only wears pants, said you were probably here."

"If he was only in pants then I'm glad I'm here," she said, slowly beginning to come out of her disbelieving haze. But she thought she should check.

"Jakob, can you just confirm or deny you are in fact here and not a fantasy?"

He wiggled his eyebrows salaciously as that wolfish smile spread slowly across his face. "I am real and I'll happily be your fantasy." Jen crossed her legs.

Jakob cocked his head at her expectantly. "Can I maybe come in?"

"Oh, yes, of course," Jen sprang up and raced for her stepladder inside, which she promptly placed by the wall for him, then raced back in for some old hop bags to put over the broken glass Charlie had fixed at the top to deter thieves. The next couple of minutes were spent negotiating Jakob over the wall, grappling with each other to manhandle him across while keeping the glass from any major arteries. It only dawned on them halfway through that he could have gone back around and she could have let him in the door, but they both understood that would mean breaking eye contact and that wasn't an option at all. Instead, it was the perfect icebreaker, plus Jen had taken the time to secretly reacquaint herself with his aftershave.

Standing up, they were face to face, with little space between them. She wanted to snog his face off – right there right then – but realised there might be some necessary protocols to follow, given how things ended last time. The onus was on her; he was due an apology, and she was in a hurry.

"I'm sorry," she began and watched his face soften. Until then, she hadn't realised his cheery expression was tensed. He obviously wasn't any more assured about how this would go than she was. "I was an idiot. You were right – I was terrified of the way I felt about you, and so I grasped any excuse to damage it. What can I say? You have a unique capability of bringing out the inner prat in me." She gave him a wonky smile and a shrug. "I have missed you, Jakob. Every day. Not that I could admit it to myself, because of the prat thing again, but as you can see," she gestured to the space around her, which she'd totally created with his deck in mind, "some things come out anyway." He slid a hand around her waist, remaining silent as he sensed she wasn't done yet, but wanting the connection. "I thought I could pack you away, like I thought I could with the beer, and we saw how that turned out. But I thought about you constantly. I was totally rubbish at forgetting you. So I focused on this, building this, because firstly I needed something to do if I never found you again and also because you're part of the foundations of it all. I would never have had the guts to do it, if I hadn't had your support. This became, I think, my monument to meeting you."

He moved to say something, but she placed her fingers gently on his mouth. He wrapped the other hand around her too, and she was grateful for it. It gave her all the bravery she needed to go on, letting go of the safety ropes, grasping this opportunity with both hands.

"Someone, much wiser than me, once said you can't pack away a passion – not if it's a real one. And I've come to see that's true. Twice. Passions fester in you, nagging you, unable to dissipate until you recognise they are part of what make you tick right." She swallowed. "That's how I feel about you, Jakob."

He threw his head back and laughed. Deep and from

the belly. It wasn't quite the response she'd expected to her declaration of her passion for him. "You feel I am festering? Like an old wound?" Oh. She saw.

"Well," she said with a small smile, "maybe. It definitely aches." She laid a hand flat on her heart. "Here." His eyes dropped to her heart. She preferred to think it wasn't to her chest. "You make me tick right, Jakob."

He kissed her then, presumably to stop her talking and to show her her feelings were reciprocated and that her pratting was long forgotten. That's what she imagined, as she slid her own arms around him, heady in the reality of him being there. She wanted to sit with him and tell him everything about what they'd done to the place, and the beers she'd brewed and she wanted him to taste *Heartsong* and get his opinion, and discuss how to go forward with it. She wanted to share the whole experience with him. Just thinking about it made her heart swell almost to bursting, but then there was also the kissing, and that felt like an excellent use of time too.

"I was miserable, Jen," he said, pulling her to one of the cable spool tables, where they sat very close side by side, legs swinging, adjoining little fingers entwined. He ran the fingertips of his free hand through the hair at her temple, as if reassuring himself she was true. "My nieces called me a *sur ribs*, erm ... a sour redcurrant, it's a Danish saying," he translated with an eye roll, "and my sisters were worried about me, which is the worst. They can be overwhelmingly caring. And then you sent me the invite to the opening. I was so glad. First because you were still thinking of me, second because you'd realised your dream and third because you wanted me to see you'd done it."

There were times for honesty and Jen decided this wasn't one of them. She deemed Lydia's meddling as superfluous information in this case and didn't interrupt. Besides, as she now understood it, *everyone* needed a little help sometimes. "I've been following the progress on Instagram under a secret name," he said *"SurRibs* actually. Niece One set up the account and thinks she's hilarious." Jen had to agree. How nice that Jakob got to be teased too.

"I've been busy as well," he said.

"I saw. In the papers," Jen said immediately. While it was heartening that his sisters at least were talking to him, she was still worried about his leaving. "I didn't mean to cause trouble in your family. I shouldn't have said some of those things, I don't think I really meant you should actually leave Kronegaard."

He looked confused for a moment, then smiled. "I haven't left the company Jen, just my division. Don't tell the press – there's a big announcement planned – but I've convinced the board to make some structural changes."

"You have?" She didn't quite follow.

"I thought about some of the things you said. I can't change the fact Kronegaard buys other businesses sometimes Jen, but your point about us having our own craft and stories was something I understand. Like you said, we have the craft beers you tasted and we have an archive of old recipes, *plus* a team of brewers who have original ideas. So I'm heading up a new Development division, starting with a new range called Kronegaard Heritage and I'm establishing some brewing academies in different territories to bring in more staff, but also to introduce future generations to brewing."

He gave her a small shy smile and went on, "Believe it or not, you know me better than I know myself. You were right about my wanting a more creative role, Jen, I just hadn't wanted to acknowledge it, or displease my family. I've come a long way in the business side, which they recognised and like you said, they want me to be happy. I just needed to talk to them honestly about it and present them with a plan. This way I combine both and get to be creative in the brewing, the company and the industry."

"That's brilliant, Jakob," she said genuinely. Jakob looked the happiest she'd ever seen him.

"Your invite arrived on the first day in my new role. It was the best day in so long. I wanted to call you or text you, but I needed to see your face first. I had to see how you felt about me when you saw me again."

"I was surprised! You popped up behind a wall and I'd thought you were kids arsing about."

"Ah, but you didn't look angry and I was settling for basics."

They were silent for a moment, fully taking each other in.

"I wanted to see you too, Jakob. I needed to see you." Jen caressed his face, so, so glad it was back in her field of vision. He covered her hand with his and held her gaze with those eyes that made her smoulder.

"I'm sorry too. I should have told you about me. Much earlier. I'd become too ... guarded, and I should have seen straight away I didn't need to be, with you." He shook his head slightly, but then perked up. "But I am here to make up for it." He drew himself up and taking a deep breath, began. "My middle name is Bjørn; I'm born on leap day, so I'm much, much younger than you; my favourite colour is brown; I believe in unicorns – because my nieces make me; I'm sure parsnips are a crime against humanity; I am deeply in love with you; I believe all football players are wildly overpaid; I am an awful football player; I have been known to hum Justin Bieber songs when in the shower–"

"STOP!" Jen laughed, trying to cover his mouth with her hands, but he kept fending her off, throwing more ludicrous facts at her. "Don't tell me," she wailed. "I want to find out all of these things for myself." She leaned her forehead against his. "Except the love bit. You can tell me that bit over and over again." She didn't mention she'd already absorbed everything cyberspace had to offer about him. Her search history was full of his correctly-spelt name. She really had been truly awful at putting him out of her mind.

He smiled up at her. "I love you Jen Attison, brewster extraordinaire."

"And I love you right back, Jakob Bjørn Krone-Juul, brewing-baby and Belieber." Her Danish pronunciation might have been a bit off, but he didn't appear to mind.

"*Belieber* is pushing it," he said with a frown, but cast the thought aside and moved in for another kiss. She stopped him with a small prod to the shoulder.

"Brown? Your favourite colour is really brown?" Who did that?

Jakob nodded slowly, his eyes never leaving hers. "Beer is brown, your hair is brown, your eyes are brown, your gorgeous freckles are brown. What's not to love about brown?" Ah. That worked.

"Smooth, Krone-Juul," Jen said, impressed and made up the rest of the distance between their lips. "You make me very hoppy."

"Hoppy?" he asked, teasing. "Hops make beer bitter. I make you bitter?" He pulled his head back to check her face.

"No, you make me *better*," she smiled, adoring the dreamy blue cornflower eyes.

His lips were back to a millimetre from hers. "Ask you something, Jen?"

"Anything. I won't even reserve the right to lie."

"Be with me?"

She hoped Lydia had bought those earplugs. She definitely had this.

It's exactly four years since we started the blog, twenty-two countries down, one hundred and three cities seen, too many new sports and adventures to count. Scroll back to see, but the rock-climbing, white-water rafting, scuba diving, para-gliding and skiing were top highlights. And the laughter. So much laughter.

A daredevil shot with me for once. This is the

moment I proposed to Lydi, mid bungee-jump here in New Zealand, just before we got hurled back up in the air. #Aaawwwww #Aaaarrrrgghhh

Proposing was scarier than jumping. But she said YES!!!

That's my Gran's Art Nouveau ring I'm presenting her with while hanging upside down. Look at the shock on her face!

–Neil.

Footloose & Fancy Free Blog – Lydia Attison & Neil Finch.

Acknowledgements

It takes a village to raise a book. My 'village' for *Probably* looks like this and all have my deepest thanks plus big hugs and kisses coming their way;

My wonderful editor Charlotte Ledger, who had the capacity to love *Probably* at the saddest of times and whose insight and encouragement helped me find what it needed.

My ever-fabulous agent Federica Leonardis, who never batted an eyelid when I said I wanted to write about beer and loved *Probably* straight away. As always she pushed me to make it the best I could, because I am a lazy mare if I can get away with it and she is a guru of the Romance genre. You should now add Kiss Consultant to your credits, Federica.

The team at Harper Impulse, especially Catriona Beamish for making the actual thing happen and also Claire Fenby and Eloisa Clegg for the support. And Emily Ruston and Oksana Bakhovski for the edits. Plus the design team for the cover. You are all stars.

Suki Yamashita, my lovely critique partner, who reads my worst and cheers me to my best, who is generous with her time and her gifts. Big kisses to you.

My beta readers; Elizabeth Dunn, Gillian Evans and Charlotte Knappe for your constructive and supportive feedback. You rock, ladies!

Author Rosamund Lupton- Lydia paraphrases a writer in her anti-engagement rant. The correct lines are;

"Sex and laughter. The heart and lungs of a relationship." From *Sister by* Rosamund Lupton (Piatkus)

"... words are the spoken oxygen between us; the air a marriage breathes." From *Afterwards* by Rosamund Lupton (Piatkus)

These lines are what I write as wedding card messages, because I totally believe them and also because it's fun to write the word Sex in a wedding card when in-laws might read them. Yes, I know, I should grow up...

Stefan Ribeiro Maagaard Jensen for your Inco pad knowledge (For the record, Stefan's knowledge was professional, not personal. Just thought he'd want me to make that clear.)

Helen Moss-Black for medicalness. Any nonsense in that area is purely down to me not listening properly, as she is a Professional.

Nick Watson at Malt the Brewery, Prestwood, for answering the questions I threw at him while on the brewery tour (Every last Saturday of the month, folks!). Any mistakes are again mine, for not having asked the right questions. And to Jenny Watson for continuously filling our glasses.

All the women who have lost a leg (or more), particularly Sarah Dransfield whose appearance on *First Dates* was the spark for the character of Lydia, Leah Washington, Vicky Balch, Mama Cax, Kat Hawkins and Melina Nakos whose blogs, articles and social media I followed in my attempt make Lydia half the absolute queens they all are.

My Olds, Lisa & Bjørn Knappe, for stepping in when needed.

Anne-Dorthea Knappe, my niece, for checking my Danish spelling. *Tak* Dottie.

Ailsa Kent for name-gaming with me. Thank you, Jim.

Izzy Macmillan for WhatsApp games of Pin-the-comma-on-the-donkey.

The BookCamp lovelies of October '18, who saw me through the edit; Rosie Blake, Holly Martin, Cathy Bramley, Jo Quinn, Sarah Bennett, Cressida McLaughlin, Rachael Lucas, Isabelle Broom, Katy Colins, Hannah Richell and Basia Martin. Thanks for all the laughs, advice and sanity! And welcome to all the new babies!

All the good folks at *The Bestseller Experiment* and *Savvy Authors* who are a glorious fountain of support and publishing knowledge for a beginner like me.

My Pilates coven for the constant cheerleading and shameless promotion of my books to every single new person who joins the class. Thank you Sarah, Mel, Georgy and Gill.

Beth Lee Booth for Fridays and Fizz. Nuff said.

Clan Hughes, my very patient kids who put up with my distraction and my ever-patient and supportive better half Ian, who amongst many other things generously escorted me to breweries in the name of Research. Thank you my lovely Loves (Yeah... still just kisses for you to collect.)

And YOU my lovely lovely reader. There's no point me doing this if it wasn't for you. Thank you for picking *Probably* up. I'm so pleased you did. I really hope you enjoyed Jen's story. Now, it would really reeeeeally help me if you might leave me a review on Amazon. It doesn't have to be long, or 5 Stars (although those are my favourites, sorry, (not sorry)) and it's OK if you didn't buy this book. If you borrowed it from the library or were given it as a gift, you can still leave a review. And I would be very very grateful for it. Amazon gives us more attention the more reviews we have and then your fellow readers can find out about my books too. Big kisses to you if you do. Xx

If you'd like to see pictures of the things I've mentioned in Copenhagen, pop over to my Facebook page where I should have a little album of them (assuming I can get the tech to work), www.facebook.com/pernillehughesauthor or my pinterest boards which you'll find at www.pinterest.com/pernillehughes . You can also follow future pics on my Insta page www.instagram.com/pernillehughes , and I tweet all sorts of things on Twitter @pernillehughes. I also have a website now, and you are welcome anytime at www.pernille-hughes.com. If you'd like news popped straight to your inbox with news, may I invite you to sign up for the newsletter there and if it's news of deals then sign up to my Bookbub profile at www.bookbub.com/profile/pernille-hughes. Phew! I am all over the place now and becoming quite the media slut!

PS. If anyone is interested in crocheted tampons, I'll direct you to Etsy.com, which can offer you a range. I wasn't making it up!

HELP US SHARE THE LOVE!

If you love this wonderful book as much as we do then please share your reviews online.

Leaving reviews makes a huge difference and helps our books reach even more readers.

So get reviewing and sharing, we want to hear what you think!

Love, HarperImpulse x

Please leave your reviews online!

amazon.co.uk   kobo   goodreads   L♥vereading   iBooks

And on social!

f/HarperImpulse   ♥@harperimpulse
◎@HarperImpulse

LOVE BOOKS?

So do we! And we love nothing more than chatting about our books with you lovely readers.

If you'd like to find out about our latest titles, as well as exclusive competitions, author interviews, offers and lots more, join us on our Facebook page! Why not leave a note on our wall to tell us what you thought of this book or what you'd like to see us publish more of?

🅕/HarperImpulse

You can also tweet us 🐦@harperimpulse and see exclusively behind the scenes on our Instagram page www.instagram.com/harperimpulse

To be the first to know about upcoming books and events, sign up to our newsletter at: http://www.harperimpulseromance.com/